PRAISE FOʀ

IPSEITY

"A captivating tale of love, war, and deception that transports you into a little-known part of WWII . . . you can almost smell the ink of forgery. Pither skilfully weaves the complexities of love and war into a story you won't forget. He is a true storyteller: masterful, evocative, and original. Just when you think you know where it's going, there's another unexpected twist—one that will keep you up late into the night!"

—GEORGINA PETTY, journalist and author of *Top Dogs*.

"A wonderful dance in a beautiful hall of mirrors taking the reader through the decades of glamour and war, love and espionage."

—SARAH INGHAM, PhD, author of *The Military Covenant*

"Reading *Ipseity*, I was conscious of gaining unprecedented insights into the lives of my parents' and grandparents' generations—the world and the wars they grew up in and their everyday as well as existential concerns. The book is a joy—a deeply authentic story whose multiple layers and narrative strands draw together into a most satisfying conclusion. Deeply researched and deeply moving—a great book."

—STEVE LUNN, author of *The Price of Dormice*

"Love at first sight and the seductive secrecy of wartime undercover work, charged with shared passions for classical music. It's a rich, enthralling, and entertaining mix."

—MICHAEL CHANCE, artistic director, Grange Festival Opera

"... a journey of discovery on many levels. Set against the backdrop, the tensions, and the uncertainties of war, Charles Pither beautifully explores and captures the poignancy and fragility of love. Sad but uplifting."

—JONATHAN MORRISH, music journalist and
CEO of MorrishComms

"... a tale of love and loss, and the consequences, told with great skill. It revolves around the murky world of WW2 espionage of the Bletchley Park era, but of a much less well-known area. The narrator is a salty sea dog with his own stories, who now finds himself having to puzzle out a mystery of the past. Pither's laconic style is lightly spiced with brilliant descriptive passages, but it never loses pace and grips you to the end. Brilliant, a must read."

—COLIN FERGUSSON, FRCS retired orthopaedic surgeon

"With its layered narrative infused with themes of love, betrayal, and hidden truths, *Ipseity* is more than just a love story. It is a reflection on memory, identity, and the complexities of human relationships."

—LYN PETERS, reader

"A masterclass in marrying passion, reflection, courage and wartime intrigue. The most engaging, enthralling, heartwarming, slow-burn of a novel you could hope to read. The author's carefully crafted love of the characters is addictive—you will be enchanted, intrigued and chuckle aloud at the subtle twists and turns of this original and charming novel. The polished prose, brilliant characterisation, meticulous research, and ingenious plot of this debut novel is both astonishing and utterly rewarding."

—DAVID CRWYS-WILLIAMS, reader

To Dear Georgie & Marco
with fond memories
and endless regard.

IPSEITY

Charles Nti

Ipseity

by Charles Pither

Published by

K köehlerbooks™

3705 Shore Drive
Virginia Beach, VA 23455
800-435-4811
www.koehlerbooks.com

A NOVEL

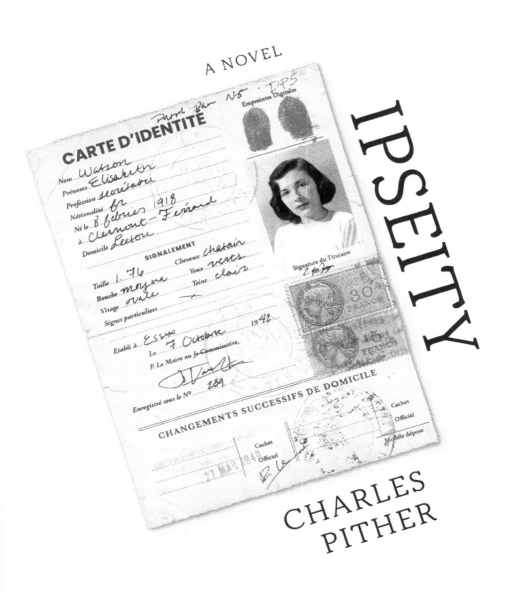

IPSEITY

CHARLES
PITHER

VIRGINIA BEACH
CAPE CHARLES

For my children, Claire, Kate, and Stephanie,
and the surety of their identities.

The only person you are destined to become
is the person you decide to be.
—Ralph Waldo Emerson

Forget the perfect offering.
There is a crack in everything;
That's how the light gets in.
—Leonard Cohen

CHAPTER 1

··

I had to end up near the sea.

From my terrace you can toss an olive stone straight into the ocean. On a fine morning the day is still and clear, the horizon a diamond line pencilling the boundary between ocean and sky, the air baked heavy with fennel and pine, the sea polished granite. But then the mistral arrives to chase eddies of dust round the terrace and flap the awning with its probing gusts, plucking the bay into dancing peaks of foam.

That's why I bought this apartment; because I can share the ocean's moody life, its changes of colour and mind, its seething anger and playful agitation, its growls and its sparkles.

That and the distance. From my eyrie I can watch the cape wake up in the clear light of the morning, glimpsing the humanity of the village without it intruding into my seclusion. I have been here too long; my routine is set. Some might consider it dull, but I see no reason to change. An Englishman abroad; insular, eccentric perhaps, set in his ways . . .

Until the letter arrived.

The postmark is dated June 24, 1992. Now dog-eared and worn, with a grease stain on the left-hand side, it sits in front of me as I do something I haven't done for many years—sit at my desk writing a story on my old Remington typewriter. But this isn't fiction.

CHAPTER 2

I t must have taken a week to arrive, but I cannot recall the exact date. The letter had been stuffed into the envelope the wrong way around so all I could see is "yours faithf . . ." through the wrinkled window.

Therese handed it to me with the simple words *"Une lettre."*

She usually calls out a muted, "Bonjour, Monsieur Pom," when she enters, as she heads for the kitchen to busy herself with goodness knows what. She is supposed to check the mailbox in the lobby on her way up, but I am not sure how often she bothers; it isn't a fruitful occupation. On this occasion she must have flipped open the anodised box to confirm its usual vacancy and found an actual letter. She appeared framed by the sliding glass patio doors, as yet unclad in the lemon-yellow polyester coat she wears when "at work" and stepped towards me waving the small white envelope.

I moved my chair back, and took the paper from her without a word, turning it over and over, like the nervous announcer of a competition winner. She stood back looking at me, her curiosity kindled. I took the last drag from my cigarette before stubbing it out into the yellow, stained Hotel Negresco ashtray.

The envelope was machine-franked "Smallwood and Lees, Solicitors, Dorchester." I knew nobody in Dorchester and could not think why I should receive a letter from a firm of lawyers. I wiped the marmalade off my knife on the edge of the plate, sliced it along under the flap and pulled out a single piece of headed paper.

```
Dear Sir:

Re: Lady Elizabeth Benville (née Elisabeth Antonia
Watson), deceased, of Knowle Stratton, Dorset.

We represent the Estate of Lady Knowle, who
died on 14 November last year. Peter Orwell
Mackay, formerly of Richmond Surrey and of the
yacht Undine, is a beneficiary in the will of
the above. We have had difficulty in locating
this person but believe you may be he.
     If this is the case, we would be pleased
to hear from you at your earliest convenience.

                         Yours faithfully,

                         Smallwood and Lees
```

I stared at the page for a minute before lowering it onto the table. My face must have betrayed my feelings because Therese approached with an anxious look and said, "Ca va?" She always spoke to me in French. I reply in English if it is simple or if I am cross and in French if neither.

She moved the three steps towards me to look at the letter over my shoulder.

"What is it? What has happened?"

She placed a hand on my arm. I put mine on hers in an act of intimacy which we had not shared in years.

"Someone has died."

"Who? Not your brother?"

She knew my brother to be my only living relative.

"No, not my brother." I thought of Ian and wondered what I

would have felt had the letter contained news of him. "Someone from long ago."

"A woman."

I turned back to look at Therese. Her tanned face, still pretty, although now lined by the Cote d'Azur sun and a habitual anxiety, wore a touching look of concern. I noticed her high cheekbones and pinched mouth and saw how grey she had become, not Lear grey but a dull civil-servant grey. I hadn't seen that before. Some strands floated free from her hair clip and looped across her forehead in wavering arcs.

"It was her . . ." Her voice tailed off. It was half question, half certainty.

I was surprised she had remembered. When had I ever mentioned her to Therese? Once? Twice perhaps, maybe ten years before, in a moment of unguarded candour shared after lovemaking. The price paid for pleasures of the flesh.

I was unable to say anything for a time. "She died last year. I didn't know. They have been trying to find me."

I placed the letter on the table, tucking it under the corner of the tray to prevent it being caught by the breeze. I got up and walked inside.

I entered my study and bent to the lowest shelves where the larger books lived. At the end of the middle shelf were seven identical, black-bound volumes with "Yachts Log" embossed in gold on the upper part of the spine. They were arranged in chronological order, the first labelled 1948–52, the last 1976–82. I pulled out the earliest volume and walked back onto the terrace.

After two minutes inside, the sun was dazzling. Therese was emptying the contents of the ashtray into a large earthenware ewer kept in the far corner. She looked at me while continuing to tap the ashtray against the side of the vase. I sat down, placed the book on the table, and reached for the Gitanes. I opened the volume, pulling out a cigarette and lighting it with my other hand. The stiff spine creaked as I flattened open the battered pages, some of which had become unbound and nestled untidily within the covers. Therese walked over to stand just behind me, curious to learn what I was going to share with her.

How many times had she cleaned and dusted around those volumes? Not that she would have made much of the brief entries typical of a yacht's log, besides which she found reading English difficult. Perhaps the occasional insert or picture might have provoked more interest, but I doubted that she would have looked in the small pouch at the back, which I now opened, removing a small black-and-white photograph, cracked and brown with age, enclosed within a folded piece of lined paper.

The picture showed a young woman wearing a swimsuit, sitting on the boom of a large yacht, the sail billowing behind her. The one-piece costume now looks impossibly dated, waisted and modest with the trunks cut horizontally like shorts and the bodice extending down in a frill around the waist. She is slender and pretty with a mane of hair, grey in the image but in life an auburn brown. She leans back against the canvas, not quite smiling. Her legs extend out in front of her towards the photographer. In her left hand she holds a reefing line for support. She looks like a child on a fairground swing, happy but perhaps worried and keen to get off.

I passed the picture back to Therese, who took it from me.

"I didn't know you had a picture of her."

"It's the only one."

"She was pretty . . . but distant. She wasn't happy, perhaps? The smile is false. No?"

I looked at the picture again. Could I muster a different scrutiny, find an alternative reality amongst the shadows and tones? Could I see uncertainty, or sadness? All I saw was what I had always seen: beauty and vitality. And then hurt. I couldn't reappraise, not now, not after all this time.

I took another drag from the cigarette and looked at the scattered white sails on the ocean—the same ocean, the same sails.

From here tiny triangles of white on a Dufy canvas, barely moving across the brilliant blue water, unimportant, insignificant; but down there, wind-stiffened canvas channelling the force of the breeze into movement and energy. It still tugs—the liberation of the mast—sanctuary in the eye of the wind.

I unfolded the paper in which the picture had been wrapped. It was a page torn from a small notebook. On it was written:

```
Dearest Pom,

I am so sorry. I should never have come.
I must go now. This is your life not mine.
There is no other way.

                                    Elisabeth
```

I stubbed out the cigarette and reached for Therese. Looking at the ocean I circled her waist and pulled her towards me so that my cheek rested on her belly. She put a hand on my head and gently stroked the few wispy strands of hair that still populated my scalp. I held her very tight.

"I am sorry," she said. And then, "You are hurting me."

I relaxed my grip but didn't let her go.

CHAPTER 3

....

London

Friday, July 30, 1948

E lisabeth stands in her bathroom rinsing her stockings in the stained basin. It is a cold and dank room with green glazed tiles up to a high dado and cream gloss paint above. The floor is a veined green lino, faded in the areas of wear but darkened around the walls and under the freestanding bath, where no amount of scrubbing relieves the impression of dirt and shabbiness. An Ascot gas water heater hangs on the middle of the wall, with a long spout that can be swung to either the bath or the basin. At best it produces a trickle of warm water designed to ensure that by the time the bath is full enough to cover your hips it is stone cold.

It is a horrible room.

It irks because it takes her back to the Spartan bathrooms at her school and the lack of privacy and vindictive comments of the prefects who "supervised" the younger girls while they prepared for bed. It is the room where daily she faces the unwelcome reminder that at twenty-six she should be living somewhere nicer. The rest of the day she is busy enough not to worry or think about it, but she has to steel herself for her twice-daily visits, especially in winter, where the circular vent set into the high window, rather than letting steam escape, seems to suck more cold air into the already freezing room.

She had tried to brighten it up by painting a window on one of the shorter walls, not trompe l'oeil exactly, because she hadn't aimed at realism, the panels of the windows being more like Matisse, with a Mediterranean azure sea splashed with daubs of white, fringed by a red ochre rocky shore and pastel houses before a pine-clad hillside. She had done it spontaneously one wet weekend, using poster paints that surprisingly adhered to the glossy tiles. Wendy was furious, being anxious about what the landlord would say and pointing to all sorts of possible problems with the paint flaking and fading, but Elisabeth assuaged her by showing her how easily the paint came off with a Brillo pad, and later she had even heard Wendy taking some of the credit for it when guests remarked on what fun it was.

But it didn't make the room any warmer or the bath water hotter.

She turns to hang her stockings onto the drying line that runs across the room when the doorbell rings. She stops still and listens. It must be a mistake. Nobody would call at this time of the evening; it is just before ten o'clock. She finishes arranging her hosiery, praying that the bell won't sound again.

Then it rings again.

She is wearing just a slip over her underwear. She curses as she enters her bedroom and pulls on her thick towelling dressing gown, which is long enough to disguise that she has bare legs.

Who could it possibly be at this time of the evening?

She unlatches the front door of the flat and descends the stairs. The dim unshaded bulb bathes the narrow hall in an unhealthy yellow glow.

Holding her dressing gown tight across her chest, she unlatches the door and opens it wide enough to see who is on the other side. She sees a tall man, bareheaded, with a mop of pale hair, worn, she thinks, improperly long. He is wearing a pale beige cotton coat almost to the ground, with leather edging around cuffs and lapels. He is thin with a lean face, eyes close-set, high cheeks, and a slender chiselled nose. She thinks he is nearer thirty than forty, but it is hard to see in the half-light. Her first impression in the crack of the door is that he is foreign—Scandinavian perhaps or, heaven forbid, German.

He wears an open expression, his face looking as a salesman might; not overly confident but not cautious either. He looks sufficiently benign for her to open the door wider. She can now see that the hair is thick and blond like a Labrador retriever. He carries a battered soft-leather Gladstone bag in his right hand.

He speaks first. "Oh, I was expecting Wendy. Is she in?"

"No, she has gone away for the weekend. She left this morning."

"Damn. I wrote a card, but perhaps she didn't get it."

Elisabeth stands silent, gatekeeper to her privacy, but with an itch of uncertainty. Her look betrays her confusion as he puts the bag down and offers his hand.

"I am terribly sorry for disturbing you so late. I am Henry Benville, an old friend of the Wilkinsons'; I was at Oxford with David and got to know Wendy then. I am flying to Austria tomorrow and was hoping for a bed for the night, but it's really no problem . . . I am sure I can find a hotel. There are always hotels near railway stations!" He smiles.

She notices the slight groove in his chin and creases in his thin face when he smiles. It is a welcome, open smile, generous and giving. If he is hiding something, he's very good at it.

Forgetting her earlier caution, she opens the door wider and stands aside.

Durham Cathedral. He picks up the card and hands it to Elisabeth. "I have been in the realm of St. Cuthbert for two days and didn't get away till late. I missed the early train and the next took an age, stopping at every backwater, halt, and hamlet between York and London."

Elisabeth looks at the card and scans the scratchy writing on the reverse. The characters are large and assertive, all askance, but she can make out little except for a flamboyant "Henry" at the bottom.

As he passes her the card, she notices the slender hand and elegant fingers, not someone used to manual labour, that's for sure. She is aware of two things: he seems harmless enough, wearing the inimitable stigmata of an English public school with effortless confidence and assertion, and that she is wearing only underwear under her dressing gown. She is confused about what to do. In her ear, she hears twenty years of her mother's voice iterating the threats and dangers of unknown men but finds it challenged by her own judgement. She looks at him and feels no threat.

"Well, you had better come in. Come on up. Would you like a drink or something?" She still can't bring herself to offer a bed for the night.

He looks relieved and grins, moving his head sideways in a manner that could be seen as deferential or obeisant in a religious setting, or simply a nod of thanks. The move that a maître d' might make, having shown you to your table.

"Thank you. How kind. I realise that it is a bit of an impertinence when a strange man arrives on your doorstep in the middle of the night."

She leads as they climb the stairs and enter the flat. She enters the sitting room; he follows behind, closing the door to the stairwell behind him.

It is a dull, tired room, papered in a patterned stripe of a faded puce. A dark gate-leg table is flanked by two oak dining chairs with backs of spiral spandrels and seats of leather, crackled and crazed in the corners as old leather tends to be. There is a sofa in grey corduroy, the armrests glazed and scuffed with wear; a small fireplace with a surround of cream tiles, above it a gilt overmantel mirror; and an upright piano. A wooden standard lamp wears a lopsided shade. The dark crimson curtains, bleached into vertical stripes by the sun and missing several hooks, are open, which Elisabeth rectifies as she ushers him into the room, having to tug the reluctant brass runners by standing on tiptoes.

"Have you been here before? I am sorry it's all a bit shabby, but it's very convenient and we have come to like it. I can't offer you much, I am afraid. What about a cup of tea? I don't have anything stronger."

"Gosh, don't worry about that. The truth is, I am terribly tired. I have been on the go for three days. Tea would be lovely."

She watches as he puts his bag down and moves to take off his coat. He wears high-waisted light-linen trousers with pleats over his hip bones adjacent to small pockets. He is not wearing a jacket. His white shirt is open-necked, without a tie, with a patterned waistcoat in a patchwork of dark crimson paisley. His brogues look like old friends, worn but clean and polished. The ensemble is extraordinary, and in the moment, she feels more secure. Surely this is not the clothing of a villain—a student theatre piece more like. A part of her is impressed. It may be avant garde, but so stylish, and it suits his build and demeanour.

She leaves to make the tea, entering the kitchen where she lights the gas and puts on the kettle. The gas pressure is feeble, and she knows she has time to return to the sitting room and make conversation, but the awkwardness of the situation causes her to remain. Instead, she goes into her bedroom and finds her slippers. Blue and too fluffy, but they will have to do. She glances at herself in the mirror of her dressing table and drags a brush through her tangle of hair. Normally she might have put on some makeup, but it's too late for that—and besides, it would seem strange to put it on now.

She returns to the kitchen, prepares a tray with teapot, cups and saucers, a sugar bowl, and a jug with milk, and reenters the room. She finds him looking at the mantel shelf examining a framed photograph of a smiling man in uniform. Suddenly she is reminded of somebody but can't think who. She puts the tray down on the table and starts to pour milk into the cups.

"Dad?"

"Yes. Captain Watson. Very proud of his commission in the Royal Engineers."

"Rightly so, I'm sure. Still proud?"

"Alas no, just his wife and daughters to bear any pride. I've never forgiven him."

"For what?" He pauses and looks across at her, seeming to be genuinely surprised. "Oh, I'm sorry how callous of me. What happened?"

"For leaving us too soon. Royal Engineer based in Hampshire, working on a project which we weren't allowed to know about. Doing dangerous things for four years without incident and then, while visiting an airfield in Bristol, blown up by a bomb in a daytime raid . . . So cruel."

"I am sorry." His face droops as if he knows about such sadness. He looks at the floor and shakes his head, as he might if he had known him or lost someone he loved. His gesture and its implication touch her strangely. The initial feelings of tiresomeness about his arrival are being replaced by fascination. She pours the tea and hands him a cup. He takes it and lowers himself into the sofa.

"Thank you." He looks at the piano. "Do you play?"

A look of anguish crosses his face, and he jumps up and puts his teacup on the mantel shelf.

"Christ. Ludwig, I am so sorry . . ." he dashes out of the room, flings open the door to the flat, and bounds down the stairs. She moves to the door confused, and peers down the stairwell. What now? She is totally at a loss, unable to make sense of this elegant but unusual man.

The front door opens and then slams shut. Seconds later he is reclimbing the stairs carrying a large but battered black cello case pasted with various travel labels.

He shakes his head, closing his eyes in disbelief.

"Thank god . . . How could I do that? Thankfully all the cello thieves in Victoria are tucked up in bed by now. He turns to look at the case, which he lowers carefully to the floor. "Ludwig, darling, how could I be so neglectful of you?"

He looks up smiling. "I left the case leaning against your railings. Perhaps I was distracted by the door being opened by a beautiful woman in her dressing gown! Ludwig, can I introduce . . . Lord, you haven't even told me your name. How embarrassing."

"Elisabeth."

"Ludwig meet Elisabeth. Elisabeth meet Ludwig. My friend, companion, confidant, occasional bedfellow—although not lover—and mouthpiece for my confusion, angst, and joy." He takes a deep bow.

Elisabeth smiles and then laughs. "Ludwig I am pleased to meet you, or at least the box you live in, and look forward to perhaps sometime hearing what you have to say." She speaks in a formal theatrical way with a dainty smile and addresses the box with a slight curtsy. She realises she is now trying to impress him. Where did that come from? "Does he take you everywhere he goes?"

He moves the cello into the corner, picks up his teacup, and flops down on the sofa, lying rather than sitting, diagonally. "Not everywhere, but we have visited many places. If I'm going anywhere for more than a week, then we travel together."

She perches on the arm of the armchair opposite. Suddenly it comes to her, the person he reminds her of, her godfather Craig Sandman, an architect friend of her father's. A man loved by all the family, flamboyant and funny, who would suddenly appear, often staying the night on the sofa, and then disappear. He was unmarried, which her young self could never understand, as he was totally charming. When she asked Daddy why he didn't have a wife, he chuckled and said he wasn't the type of man to get married. It was only much later when she had realised what that implied. That must be it; Henry must be queer.

"Do you do a lot of travelling?" she asks.

"Too much." He pauses, holding his teacup delicately while looking at the floor. His posture says there is more to tell. He looks up at her with a serious air. "I work for the foreign office, mostly to do with the resettlement of displaced persons. I am living in Austria now, still trying to trace families split up during the conflict. I have just been to a meeting in Durham with some Norwegians who came down from Orkney. Over the last two years I have not spent more than three months in England. The truth is, I am weary of misfortune; too many lives destroyed by the bloody war. Like your dad's." He looks up dolefully.

"And yours?"

"He was older. The war didn't get him, his heart did. But before it all started. I was sixteen. Old enough to remember him, but not to know him or to ask him all the questions I want to ask him now."

"What sort of questions?"

"Oh, I don't know. What he thought about things. What he did in his war. How to fish properly. Things that would have let me know him better, I suppose . . . Understand what made him tick. He was a complex man, and I know so little about him or what drove him."

"Do we ever know those things? Are they ever knowable?"

"Perhaps not." He says nothing for a moment, then, "Maybe I needed to know he loved me."

What an extraordinary thing to say! Elisabeth is wrong-footed by a man who she doesn't know talking about the love of a father. She glances at him and sees that wistful look again and can't face up to it, so she quickly turns away.

"Oh, we all need that," she answers glibly, rather than face the silence. "I am sure he did. Do you have reason to think he didn't?"

"No, not really. I missed him so much when he died. When I came to love him, he wasn't there!"

"It's easier that way, isn't it? I mean loving in absentia. No irritating reality to offset the feelings of warmth and tenderness."

"Yes, I suppose so, although he was never on my back. But he was away a lot. He wasn't irritating like my stepmother; she could win a medal for irritation! He was older and distant, but I respected him, and he was very kind. She was younger, didn't understand the English, and was left bereft and clueless when he died."

She is curious and wants to ask about his mother but doesn't want to pry. In the pause, it is he that breaks the thread.

"So how do you know Wendy?"

"We work together. She was very nice when I started the job and when her flatmate got married, she offered me the room. I had been living at home and was only too happy to get away."

"Remind me, is it a firm of solicitors?"

"Life assurance actually."

"Of course. So how are you finding living in London?"

"The flat can be depressing at times, but mostly I love it. It may not be Salzburg or Vienna, but it's fine. It's nice to be able to go to concerts and the theatre."

"Innsbruck. I see you are going to a Prom tomorrow." He points to a ticket on the mantel shelf. "What's on?"

"Malcolm Sargent with the BBC symphony orchestra doing various bits and pieces. But the highlight is Irene Kohler playing Rachmaninov's third piano concerto."

"How delectable. I am terribly jealous. I don't know the piece and would love to hear it. I love the second."

"Did you see *Brief Encounter*?"

"Of course—but it was good before that." He smiles, pausing to sip his tea. "And I will be alone in a stark *gasthaus* with a stein of lager and a schnitzel, with only Ludwig to talk to."

"But I had assumed Ludwig was deaf," she says with a grin. "Although, I accept that doesn't mean you can't talk to him."

He laughs. "Very good. He may turn a deaf ear, but I am a good talker, and he doesn't complain. Listening is different from just hearing."

"I hope the neighbours are understanding!"

"They don't have a clue! It is marvellous; the hotel is pure Pirandello. You have no idea of the cast of misfits, eccentrics, and ne'er-do-wells that inhabit Meraner Strasse. Talking to a cello would be considered a minor infringement or trivial misdemeanour compared with what the queer fish who share my world get up to."

She raises an eyebrow and glances at him with a look that suggests she has no idea what he is talking about, but he doesn't see it, as he is staring, distracted, at the floor.

He gets up to put his cup on the table. "So, you must be the pianist?"

"Not so much now. No one to badger me to practice. Too many distractions."

He moves over to the instrument and picks up the music on the ledge.

"Blimey, Bartok! Not exactly gentle chamber music."

"Now, be careful what you say about my hero Bela. He is a genius. Sometimes difficult, I agree, but he wrote lots of lovely piano work for beginners. I grew up on them." She pauses and looks at him. He is attentive, expectant, his eyebrows still slightly raised in surprise. He seems to be saying, *Tell me more.*

He sits back down on the sofa, flopping back into the cushions.

She continues. "When I was at school a Hungarian refugee joined the staff as a music teacher—it must have been 1936. She was a small, passionate woman, a fervent Nationalist who thought Hungarian music the be-all and end-all of all creative endeavour. Dear Mrs. Varga; I owe her a lot."

"A love of Bartok?"

"And Liszt and Kodaly, and those sprightly dance tunes. No, not just that. She was a lovely woman, and I was a bolshie teenager, and somehow, she channelled my anger and unhappiness into something fruitful."

"A piano?"

"Yes, a piano and making music with other people." Why is she saying these things to this stranger? She is surprised at the way she is discursive and open. She relaxes down into the armchair, its soggy cushions leaving her sprawled, mirroring his pose. She crosses her legs. Her slipper falls off the top leg.

"You will have to play for me, some Bartok perhaps. Dispel my irrational prejudices."

"Mmm, I am not so sure. I am out of practice and it's a bit out of tune. Last year I joined a choir and have been doing some singing. I love it."

"Perfect! I am sure there is a repertoire for cello and soprano."

Her mind jumps. Is this how he normally is or is he trying to chat her up? Perhaps he isn't a homo.

"Oh no, I am not sure about solos. I need to hide in the background. Mezzo actually."

Her dressing gown has fallen open a bit, and she sits forward, pulling it together. He doesn't seem to notice, and she is not sure whether to be disappointed or not, his gaze still abstractedly centred on the carpet, his legs crossed, the top bouncing slightly on the lower. It could be anxiety, or perhaps deep thoughts. She senses someone who thinks about things.

She tells him about her mother in Reigate, her sister and her small life working in a life assurance office. She talks of her friendship with Wendy, and yes, she had met David, and some of his Oxford friends. And then she realises that Henry has told her almost nothing about himself, but that does not seem to matter. He is good at leading the conversation without saying much about himself. It is something she has noticed with David and his friends—it must be Oxford—that makes her feel envious and inadequate, but not uncomfortable.

She gets up.

"Well, obviously you must stay. You can have Wendy's room. Would you like more tea? I am sorry I haven't got anything else. Are you hungry? I am sorry I didn't think to offer you anything to eat. I bet you are starving. I could manage a piece of toast?"

"No, I am fine. Thank you. The tea was perfect. I have to be at Northolt by ten in the morning for my flight."

"Northolt?"

"Yes, it's an RAF flight—they still ferry us around for official business."

"How will you get there?"

"Take a taxi I suppose."

"I can give you a lift in Evey. I have nothing better to do. Wendy and I have a week off work while they move the office. I am going home to see Mummy for a few days. I would have gone today were it not for the concert."

"How kind—but I wouldn't hear of putting you to any trouble.

I feel bad about arriving without warning and drinking your tea, let alone asking you to drive me to the airport."

"You are not asking, I am offering," she says with clarity and firmness.

He jumps up. "Right, Miss Watson. In that case, I will not carry out any further oral inspection on this particular gift horse! It is Miss Watson, I presume. There isn't a husband about to burst in on us and attack me with an axe?"

She laughs. "Well, there is, but he's in the pub and when he gets back, he won't be in a fit enough state to notice you or Ludwig. It will only take me a minute to change the bedsheets."

"Do you know, I am very happy on the sofa. Like lots of our generation, the war taught me to sleep anywhere."

"No, you stay there and read my mantelpiece while I change the bed."

She gets up and climbs the stairs to Wendy's room at the top of the house, grateful for a practical task to stop her thinking about her guest. It is a warm evening, so he won't need the eiderdown, which she rolls up and puts on the wardrobe. She makes the bed and turns on the bedside light, wanting to make the room welcoming and nice. She bundles up the dirty sheets and descends the stairs.

"There, all ready for you," she says as she reenters the sitting room. She looks up to see that he is slouched back on the sofa, head against the backrest with his eyes shut, fast asleep. She smiles. In his sleep he looks different. The fop of blond hair has fallen over his forehead, the blond eyebrows meeting above his nose. There is a flecking of stubble on his chin and cheeks, darker than the eyebrows. The face is relaxed and almost boyish in its innocence. The lips, now not speaking or smiling, are thin but well formed. In the open neck of his shirt she can see wisps of hair emerging and a line where the slightly darker skin of his face meets the pallor of his neck. As she looks, she worries that he will wake up and see her inspecting him, but she can't stop herself. A part of her would quite like to undo another button.

She is confused and embarrassed, although uncertain why. Is it prying? But it doesn't feel wrong. Why does she feel disarmed? He is flagrant and vulnerable but contained and without artifice. She is perplexed, partly by the uncertainty of having a man uninvited in her home and partly by the man he seems to be.

CHAPTER 4

Cap d'Ail, Var, France
July 1992

I remember where that picture was taken. We were just south of Toulon, heading for the Îles d'Hyères. The log tells me about that passage; south-westerly force four to five, a slight swell but calm, clear skies, warm sunshine. The course was 170 degrees, just keeping the land visible off the port bow. We were making eight knots on a broad reach. It was taken by a young American, Benson I think was his name. He hitched a lift from Toulon to Nice.

Undine, a water-sprite indeed, scudding through the surf, the bowsprit dipping into the spume like an oystercatcher, flicking plumes of spray onto the bleached sails, the polka dots of damp disappearing almost instantly in the hot breeze. At last, I had my girl, there, sitting on the boom, white from a London winter, but smiling and happy—or so I thought.

It was my grandfather who taught me to sail. In summer we would be dispatched to stay in his solid farmhouse in Arrochar overlooking the fickle waters of Loch Long. At the start it was fair weather sailing, skimming across the glassy loch on warm summer days in steady breezes, in *Misty*, a little gaff-rigged day boat by "McAlister of

Dumbarton," as was proudly cast in a small brass plaque in the cockpit. I was captivated and would await his pronouncement over breakfast as to whether the day was "set fair" and we would be going to take her out, squirming with silent anxiety, never daring to ask him directly.

"We'll no be going oot today, Billy Boy," he would say, (though why he called me that I never fathomed) knowing that the northerly blowing against the ebb tide would mean a choppy and nauseating beat back up the loch. But as I got older, the opposite held true, and he would deliberately take me out on miserable squally days of freezing rain, teeth gritted against the icy fret, handing over the tiller in a far bay of the sound, telling me, "Take her home, Billy Boy." He taught me to respect the weather but also to prepare for it. He was uncompromising when I had forgotten extra clothing, or my clothes were still damp from the soaking of the day before.

And then he let me do it alone, and I went aground and nearly capsized and got very wet and very frightened. I never wanted to do anything else but do it more and better and one day get myself a proper boat.

But then the war swept away the old routine, sailing for pleasure replaced by the rigours of the Arctic Ocean, and it was not until the end of 1946 that I was finally able to buy a boat of my own.

Grandfather had suffered a major stroke in the latter days of 1942, at a bad time for me and at a time when the conflict was at its most hopeless, and I hated his death. It angered me and conspired with the grim austerity to snuff out any possibility of joy or optimism in the dark days of 1943. But he left me £1133, and when we were finally released from the shackles of orders and uniforms, and I got my demob monies and a Moss Bros suit, there was no doubt in my mind as to my priority. Nothing that needed a suit; find a boat.

I found her, not in Hampshire or any of the sacred sailors' haunts, but in a yard on Eel Pie Island, near Twickenham. She was a seventy-foot ketch by Samuel White of Cowes completed in 1913, mahogany on cedar with oak ribs. She had been laid up for many years and was in a very dilapidated state, but she had lovely lines and a good pedigree. The craggy owner, only a little less neglected than his yacht, agreed to meet me in the White Swan, and after trading stories of the Corrie Vrecken over an emptying bottle of Old Pulteney, agreed to sell her to me for six hundred pounds. We hadn't mentioned her name in the discussions, but when I got to explore her properly, propped disconsolately and unloved at the back of the yard, overhung by the branches of overgrown ash and elder, there it was on the stern in a painted panel of curlicues and shadows: *Undine*.

But there was work to be done, a lot of work, and having nowhere else to stay, my priority was to get a part of the boat wind and watertight so that I had somewhere to sleep whilst scratching, scraping, sanding, and painting. Luckily Stone, the yard owner, took pity on me and found me a room in his mother's house in Richmond in exchange for some work in the yard. It was a grand white stucco house on Paradise Road, with a separate basement flat, which, although far from luxurious, provided better protection against the elements than the open hatches and portholes of *Undine*. Besides, I could never ask Elisabeth to stay the night on board *Undine*, who sat on the hard like a huge arachnid, propped on a cradle of pine posts, swathed in tarpaulins and accessed by a rickety ladder. The flat was at least weatherproof and provided a single bed, albeit luxurious it was not.

At best, I would telephone her in the middle of the week, and she would agree to drive down to Richmond on the Saturday, or even on very rare occurrences, Friday. At worst, she would find various excuses not to come and a pall of gloom would settle over me until the following week.

When she visited, we would meet in the White Cross or one of the pubs on the Green, and after a couple of pints, pick up fish and chips and head back to Paradise Road with the warm newspaper package squeezed between us. We would spread the paper on the skimpy table and pick at it with a pair of fine bone-handled fish forks. They were the only forks I had in the flat, orphans, we presumed, from an ornate fish service, the history of which we would invent in elaborate fantasies.

Such style!

"How is the job?" I asked.

"Largely tedium with moments of panic and suicidal contemplation." Her voice was a combination of resignation and sarcasm.

"Throw it in—I need a painter and cook. Together we will finish the good ship *Undine* much quicker than I can on my own, and then we can sail away for a year and a day." It was an old chestnut, and I knew it held little sway, but I kept on trying.

"Oh Pom, you know it's a ridiculous idea. You have no money— what would I live on? I need a proper job. I would be bored rigid in a week. Besides I hate the sea and abhor bouncing about in little boats." Now the honesty was tinged with rancour. I always hurt when she said, "little boats."

"You would get used to it. I know you would end up loving the life. Think of the freedom and all the wonderful places we could visit."

She didn't answer, probably fatigued from yet again revisiting the same hackneyed argument. But I wasn't listening. I was on my own journey, not hearing of alternate destinations, different modes of transport or the itineraries of others.

But then we would fall into the thin bed with its lumpy mattress, and it would all be fine. That bit was always fine. Like most aspects of her life, she was in charge, although you would never have guessed it from the beautiful, gentle exterior.

We would spend the day working on *Undine*. I still have this image of her slender self, inhabiting a voluminous pair of dungarees like a circus clown, with that brilliant mass of hair tied up with a piece of reefing line, a look of intense concentration on her face as she produced a perfect edge to the paintwork on the forward cabins. With Elisabeth it had to be perfect; there was no such thing as second best.

I was in love with her then. And always really.

And I thought she was still in love with me. Or rather I didn't think. I thought about *Undine* and about sea valves and water tanks and sails and stanchions and halyards and rigging and getting the engine refurbished and anti-fouling and a hundred other problems. I didn't think of her—except towards the end of the week and the phone call to try to persuade her to come down for the weekend.

But it became more difficult. As the summer drew on her diary filled with more enticing offers. True, she did sometimes ask me to take a day off and come up to London to a concert, the theatre, or to visit some friends for the weekend, but I was too focussed on getting my baby seaworthy to waste time with idle hedonism.

And if she did not agree to come, I would get madly jealous and put the phone down and pen a confused angst-laden note, which I would post in a fit of self-pity. She never deigned to pander to my paranoia by answering or even mentioning them when we next met.

"You know I couldn't bear it if you were seeing somebody else," I said in a moment of tenderness.

She said nothing and I said nothing more. Did I have no doubts about her, or did I push my doubts to one side and ignore them? There are times when we can choose to forget uncomfortable truths.

....

Piece by piece the good ship *Undine* returned to the grandeur of her former self, and by the end of 1947, with the hull repainted in a lustrous marine blue, she was ready to be lowered into the soupy waters of the Thames.

The plan was to sail her down to the Hamble, where we would undertake what I grandly called "sea trials" and then set off for the Mediterranean in the spring.

I had recruited Malcolm, a cousin from the Scottish side of the family, to crew. A steady lad, flighty but useful, hardened in the climes of the Hebrides, delighted to have an opportunity of sailing a passage to Gibraltar from where he would return home, and I would find local crew.

Undine sailed as well as I thought she would and cut a dash with her new sails and gleaming brightwork. I was happy and proud as we nosed her onto the Quay at Bucklers Hard amid a sea of complimentary locals.

The final send-off from Lymington involved a long lunch at the Ship Inn, after which Malcolm could barely clamber back on board. My parents had driven down to wish us well, mother thrusting two large fruit cakes into my hands as we left the pub. Elisabeth came as well, with a friend from work, driving down in Evey looking elegant and sophisticated amongst the salty smocks of the sailors. She had made covers for the cushions in the cockpit from old stripy curtains found in her grandmother's attic, which looked just the part, and I was genuine in my thanks and appreciation.

We said our farewells on the quayside; a peck on the cheek, a squeeze of the hand, and suddenly the lines were free and we were off.

"See you later in the summer," I shouted across the growing gap of inky harbour water, "Barcelona, Marseilles, Nice, you choose . . ."

She smiled and waved, blowing a kiss with one hand, trying to keep her hair in order with the other. I swung *Undine* around while Malcolm raised the jib. The sail whipped and then filled, I felt the tug on the hull, and we were away. I looked back at the ever-diminishing band of well-wishers as they receded into the quayside backdrop.

I had no doubts then. Not about Elisabeth nor about *Undine*. I was anxious about what Biscay would throw at us, but about the woman in my life I saw only certainty. Although I had no vision in my mind's eye, my confidence that we would be together did not require the nicety of detail. I had not had many girlfriends and had never been in love with anyone else, so why would I need to look beyond the woman who I found beautiful and entrancing?

I stayed at my desk for perhaps an hour leafing through the pages and recalling places and events before getting up and returning to the terrace. The sun was oppressive, and I took shelter under the canvas canopy. Already there was a haze coming off the rocks, with the townscape shimmering in the heat. I smoked a cigarette and then returned to my bedroom. I opened the wardrobe, selected a tie and put on my blazer. I called to Therese.

It was an old ritual. After she finished her "work" we would walk down the steps that wind through the pines to the Basse Corniche. The path is not steep, the brick-paved steps taking lazy curves through the hard-baked earth, studded with tamarisk and oleanders.

It is charming, pungent with those aromas of earth and pine that are so uniquely Mediterranean, and alive with the song of the cigale. As we amble down, she holds my arm, but we do not speak. When we reach the road, she detaches herself and gives me a peck on both cheeks before saying, "Au revoir," and going on her way.

I walk down to the yacht club where they know the table I prefer and indeed what I am going to eat. Roberto the steward, who insists that he is not French but Italian from what was Mentone, is nearly as old as I am and always panders to my routine. We have both seen the Riviera change too much.

CHAPTER 5

....

London

Friday, July 30, 1948

S he does not sleep well.

After she had found him asleep on the sofa, she was too discomfited to wake him and so went back into the kitchen, placed the linen in the laundry bag, and remade her entry speaking much louder and rattling the door handle. He opened his eyes wearing a look of confusion, and then jumped up embarrassed and apologetic, saying that he was mortified to have been so rude as to fall asleep. She smiled and brushed aside his concerns, genuinely finding the episode amusing rather than discourteous.

Refusing more tea or a milk drink, she showed him the bathroom, snatching away the underwear drying on the line above the bath, and then led him upstairs to his bedroom, holding open the door for him.

"I am afraid the bed isn't very long, and Wendy says it is rather lumpy."

"Of no concern; I can sleep anywhere, and as you have seen, often do," he said, stepping into the room and throwing his bag on the bed. "I am sure I will sleep like a baby."

He turned to face her as he closed the door, his hand on the door jamb, hers on the door frame. He looked her in the eye.

"Thank you," he said. "It was a lot to ask to let a strange man crash into your peace and security." He smiled. "I mean it."

She nodded imperceptibly as the door closed, squeezing his image through the narrowing crack.

"Goodnight."

Back in her room, she waited for him to use the bathroom, slipped out of her dressing gown into her nightdress, and flopped into bed an hour later than she had intended.

Lying in her narrow iron framed bed, her mind tumbles with conflicting thoughts and notions. *Who is he, this extraordinary man who parachuted into my house in the middle of the night with the hair, the avant-garde clothing, the cello! And then flopping onto the sofa and falling asleep!*

But he is a friend of Wendy and however hard she tries she can't find him threatening. The innocence of his visage when asleep and the childish embarrassment when he woke couldn't have been feigned. She smiles, being unable to think of a less threatening person. In any event, she can get rid of him in the morning and be left with an amusing anecdote to make the flighty girls in the office giggle.

So why is she confused? She thinks about the things he said and the easy chat they had enjoyed. How had he somehow given much away but remained enigmatic? A calm, thoughtful man wandering around Europe with a cello helping refugees, with all the credentials of Oxford and a public school (she assumed but didn't have reason to question) and yet he seemed placeless. He had that relaxed assuredness that she remembers from some of her senior officers in the war, a sort of unlearnable confidence and, yes, maybe even superiority—but his was tempered by a down-to-earth touch, a willingness to listen and not to judge.

Like many of her friends she had found it difficult to settle back into a routine when the war ended. Although it had been an awful five years, and of course everybody was relieved and grateful when at last the country could celebrate victory, it wasn't simply a question of returning to the old life. People of her age grew up during the conflict; before it they were children—there was no old life. The war had thrust them into places and situations that made demands of responsibility, application, and commitment that would never have happened in peacetime, and although she never spoke to anyone about what she did, in many ways she missed those days. The camaraderie, the focus, the sense of purpose, the unquestioning worth, and a less explicable recklessness, formed a potent mix, which while not quite addictive, had certainly caused symptoms of withdrawal when removed.

She lies on the bony horsehair mattress looking at the ceiling, wondering where Wendy is and how it would be different if she were here. She is probably staying with Sandy and socialising at the Golf Club, or maybe at a house party somewhere in Sussex. She is always at a party somewhere. The same old crowd, fun but predictable. She can't see Henry fitting in with that set, but then in a moment of insight she realises that if he was at one of those "do's," she would have been drawn to him in a way both compelling and dangerous.

Why? If he is peculiar and outlandish, wouldn't she have avoided him? Perhaps it was that element of enigma, the allure of the mysterious . . . Mysterious, that was it; enigmatic and mysterious. But she counters, also funny and playful. If she had talked to him, she would have found that he was easier to chat to than most of the men she had known for ages.

And the cello! She can't help but smile.

She had been out with a few men since Peter had left for France—nothing serious—and then in a moment of aberration she had decided to use up her slender holiday allowance and most of her savings, to make the disastrous trip to Marseilles, an episode that still brought on such an unwelcome sway of emotion that she tried her hardest never to think about it.

She wills a sleep that refuses to attend as bidden. Is there a woman in Henry's life, she wonders? What would she be like? Probably a clever girl from Oxford with real pearls and a private income.

No, perhaps not. Rather a Liberal feminist intellectual—maybe an artist or writer.

She knew she was not unattractive, and although when she stood in private in front of a mirror, or saw a photograph of herself, could always find a thousand faults, she accepted she could turn heads, albeit that she went out of her way not to. She could never find prettiness in her tight mouth and thought her face too fat and her jaw too angular and her chin just a little too prominent, but she did accept that her hair was special. Men adored it and women coveted it, an auburn mane the colour of a sunset reflected on sandstone, thick, long, and naturally wavy.

Now her mind is really racing, and she knows sleep won't come. In her restlessness she thinks she is too hot and throws back the blankets. The street is still and quiet, as is the house, with not a squeak from the room above. The window is open and the light cotton curtains don't meet in the middle and billow lazily in the occasional breeze. The glow of the streetlights throws a slant of light on the wall to the left of the door, which trembles as the curtain flap. At school if she couldn't sleep, she would count backwards from a hundred, but she can't get beyond ninety-five before her mind is off again.

She fears her life doesn't add up to much; a second-rate education, a tedious and uninspiring job, a head of hair and an all-right figure, a bit of common sense, a love of books, a talent on the piano, and the one thing she is proud of she can't tell anybody about. Not bait enticing enough to catch a fish as fascinating as Henry Benville.

But what if he does actually like me? Oh, how it might be to share his sadnesses and take away his restlessness, to have that smile just for me . . .

She finally falls into an exhausted sleep, and then dreams vividly.

She wakes startled, breathing fast, sweaty and clammy. She throws the bedclothes off and sits up. She calms her breathing and explores the memory of the dream, trying to assemble the fragments and recall the details. She remembers trees and a fire, with the wreckage of a plane, its wings buckled and broken, the crushed cabin ablaze. The location was vague, but it was as if a forest was burning, and she was trying to run away but also to get nearer. And then, in the midst of it, there was the cello case, and she called for Henry, but he was not there. She looked around for him and ran, shouting his name, but he never appeared. In the flames she saw what looked like a pylon or a tower. She was panicked because she feared he was on the wrong side of the flames and would get burned; there seemed to be no escape.

She recalls when she was twelve or thirteen seeing Errol Flynn in the *Charge of the Light Brigade* and spending the next twenty-four hours in a sweet daze openly declaring to her mother that she was in love and going to marry him. But that was then. This is now. She is supposed to be sensible and grown up now.

It is getting light, and she is too agitated to sleep. She looks at the alarm clock on the bedside cupboard; six-thirty. She gets up, puts on her dressing gown, and challenges the Ascot to provide water for a bath. She makes a cup of tea and then bathes, the teacup sitting on the tannic ring on the window ledge where she always places it. She washes her hair, which she rinses in the tepid flow from the water heater, drying it with a towel then running her fingers through it by the open window. She stands in front of the mirror on the chest of drawers, appalled at how drab she must have looked the previous evening. She brushes her hair into some form of submission, tying it back with one of the many ribbons that she keeps hanging on the side of the mirror. She rejects the scarlet—that would be too flagrant—choosing a dark peach which she knows matches a lipstick she keeps for special events. She mustn't overdo it. She finds a simple floral dress with a high waist and flat sandals with a strap around the ankle.

It is still only seven-thirty and there is no sign of life from Wendy's room. She goes into the kitchen and looks in the refrigerator. It is virtually empty, but that is largely because they were both going to be away for the week. There is a bowl of drippings, a nearly empty bottle of milk, a weary cabbage, and an open tin of sardines. She goes to the cupboard, where they both keep their ration books, and looks to see what's left. If she "borrows" Wendy's, she should be able to get some bacon and butter. Eggs may be more difficult, but Ginger, the wheezy, blue-lipped cockney who runs the greengrocer on the corner, is not immune to a smile and she is optimistic he will do her a favour. She slips out of the house and steps into a morning bright and welcoming. The Saturday street is deserted save for a milk float and a paperboy who runs a rolled-up paper along the iron railings, making a noise like a mute machine gun. The day is warm, almost languid, but her step is brisk and positive. She wears about her a vigour and purpose that she hasn't felt for two years.

CHAPTER 6

....

Cap d'Ail, Var, France

July 1992

I awoke early, after a night restless with loss and memories. I reread the letter as I finished my coffee on the terrace.

I'd had no contact with Elisabeth for all those years, now I learnt that she'd remembered me in her will. The implication of her remembering me in her death was that she had remembered me in her life. I had never forgotten her, but my never forgetting was not the same as her remembering. I had never been able to loosen the fetters that bound me to her thrall, but after half a lifetime of silence, why now?

Lady Knowle? I had no clue as to how she had acquired such a title. Had her husband been knighted? Had she married a baron?

I knew nothing about her later life.

I could not imagine the nature of the bequest. Was it a chattel or trinket she had wished me to have? We had nothing then, and besides, neither she nor I were sentimental. Surely it could not be money? My need for money or largesse had long passed, and my insular existence provided few enough opportunities to spend.

I could find no answers but was troubled by a gnawing curiosity.

I picked up the coffee cup and saucer, leaving the ashtray for Therese, and walked into the apartment. The change of air temperature was striking, as was the darkness after the glare of the Mediterranean morning. The log was still sitting on the desk. I picked it up and opened it at random.

It was a sailor's log with positions and tides, watches and courses, and details of ports and berthings, usually in pencil and mostly in my own scribbly hand. But interspersed within these dull technical details were photographs and entries in other hands where guests had written notes or comments, often amusing, or at least so they had seemed at the time. And then there were the occasional photographs. José, dwarfed by a bear of an American wearing a noisy Hawaiian shirt, holding a small tuna up to the camera, beaming with Hemingway pride at his magnificent catch.

Memories.

Memories safely contained in volumes bound in oiled cloth hidden in a shelf in a dark secluded room.

I took out the photograph again.

Forty years—no, more than that, nearer forty-five since that picture and our last moments together.

....

Undine raced across to Brest on a northwesterly track and then beat and bludgeoned her way through Biscay. By the time we made a welcome landfall at Coruna, Malcolm and I were weary and battered, but exhilarated. Then on down the Portuguese coast and finally into Cadiz, where suddenly the world felt different. It was hot, dry, and a mysterious essence of Africa oozed from the bleached stucco of the portside buildings. I felt a surge of liberation as we threw our lines ashore in the shadow of the Moorish cathedral and instantly found a welcome in the cheap fisherman's bars. Here was my first taste of the freedom I craved but had never been able to even glimpse, let alone capture, in postwar England.

I sent Elisabeth the first postcard from Cadiz, and then from everywhere else we stopped. The message was simple and always along the same lines: "Vacancy in main cabin. Warm body and deckhand needed." And then I would suggest she get on a train and meet me in the next port of call, communicating via Poste Restante.

We arrived in Gibraltar with Malcolm in a sombre mood, saddened by his need to return to Scotland and anxious about how he was going to get home. He had been a good crewman, competent but never cocky, affable but self-contained, and willing to take orders. I was going to miss him.

We moored in the harbour amidst the warships and merchantmen and headed for a bar. Within the hour we had sorted a return passage for him on a bulk carrier leaving for Rotherhithe the following day. We celebrated by sharing lobster and Vino Verde with the Maltese crew, who left the restaurant swaying and merry, intent on finding some girls in a "guest house" behind the synagogue. I tried to convince Malcolm that he should join them, but he hid behind his Scottish reticence and stumbled back with me to *Undine*.

With him gone I had to find crew. This wasn't easy, but after a week of fruitless enquiries, I was woken early by the cry of "Ola" and a knocking on the cabin roof.

José was a stocky Portuguese from the Azores who had served on British convoys during the war and as a result spoke passable English with a Liverpool accent. Of indeterminate age somewhere between thirty and fifty, unshaven and with fewer teeth than the Maker had intended. In the instant he presented with a mix of humour and casual irreverence, which I was drawn to. It was clear he was not going to be heeded by protocols or rules, but my question was whether he could sail. With assurances that he'd been sailing before he could walk, and the claim that amongst his other attributes he could cook "como Mama," I agreed to give him a three-month trial.

He stayed fourteen years.

At every port I checked the Poste Restante. I would query the whereabouts of the post office and make my way there through cities that captivated and thrilled me. But there was never any mail waiting for me.

Until Banyuls sur Mer.

It was a telegram.

"POM HAVE A WEEKS HOLIDAY STOP FREE AGENT STOP CAN COME WEEK JUNE 23 STOP REVERT WITH LOCATION STOP ELIS XX

I had no idea what the date was, but a calendar on the wall of the sleepy post office told me it was June 15. Marseilles was the obvious place. It would only take us a couple of days to sail there, but it was a big enough city to make Elisabeth's journey from London manageable, and if we got there early, she could communicate details of her arrival to us there.

I telegraphed her back.

UNDINE SMILING STOP WILL MEET MARSEILLES TRAINS STOP TELEGRAPH MARSEILLE WITH ARRIVAL TIME STOP POM KISSES

José knew something was up. I skipped down the quay to our mooring and dragged him to a bar to explain. His toothless grin said it all.

"So capitão tem uma namorada. Muito bonita! No worries, Capitano, I leave you plenty time alone!"

We dawdled along the uninteresting French west coast calling in St. Maries de la Mere before arriving in Marseilles on the twenty-first. The message in the Poste Restante confirmed Elisabeth's arrival on the twenty-fourth. There was little to do for four days but walk the town and try to escape the heat. José fished; I found a three-day-old English newspaper. We drank white wine and shared ribaldry with the other boats moored in the old port.

I was already on the platform well before the seven-o-clock train arrived, feisty as a tethered goat, scanning the crowds for that head of hair, watching the station clock tick the interminable minutes.

And then there she was, wearing a simple flowered dress with a beret perched somehow on the buoyant mane, carrying a small black case and looking, as they say, "like a million dollars." She smiled and kissed me, a light brush on the cheek. Was there coyness or uncertainty in her look? Did she seem subdued, a bit less excited than I had hoped she would be? I understood that she would be tired and weary after a long journey. It mattered not.

It was a warm evening, and she brightened up as we strolled through the terracotta streets alive with the voices and fragrances of the Mediterranean. Here was frying garlic, pungent tobacco, and the smell of drains. Tall buildings, shutters open to let the seedy apartments breathe, streets dirty with litter and low life. We ambled through the old town towards the port, trying to keep to the bigger roads with streetlights, watching the bustling folk pass us by, finding charm in the authenticity and the foreignness of it all.

A cheery fish restaurant beckoned, and we ate the freshest sardines grilled over pine wood. It was a stifling evening, leaden with the aromas of the cooking mingled with the portside tang of fish and fishing boats. The vin rouge brought a flush to her cheeks and flow to our conversation. She told me of her journey, and I tried to tell her of mine. She chatted of London life, how she had changed her job for something more challenging and was working for a life assurance company in Holborn. But it wasn't right. She was still restless and bored, straining at the leash of the limitations of her generation and class.

"The problem, Pom, is that it's all so dull; drab offices in grey, cold London doing repetitive, meaningless work. I know I am better than this. Am I allowed to say that I miss the days at Briggens? That excitement, the fear, the responsibility. I knew it was worthwhile. I worry sometimes . . . I mean, I feel guilty that a time that most people found terrible and awful I found exhilarating and compelling."

"I don't think you should worry about that. I have met various people who found meaningfulness in the intimacy and sense of purpose that the conflict thrust upon them. An uncle of Malcolm's spent three years as a POW and still speaks of it as the most exciting time of his life."

"But I can't talk to anybody about it. Never! That's what we signed, wasn't it, for the indefinite future? Such a long time . . . Too long!"

She was talking about signing the Official Secrets Act and our time making forged documents for the Special Operations Executive at Briggens House.

"I sometimes think I didn't exist during that time," she went on. "Have you ever thought how strange it is that we spent those years inventing people, giving them an identity, and all the while we were removing our own? We have become nonpeople, people whose brilliant war effort doesn't exist. Who am I? Am I me or that person who only I know existed? Well, you too, of course."

And then she smiled, with a compelling look of vulnerability in her beautiful eyes as she leant across and clasped my hand in both of hers. She squeezed it gently, turning it over and stroking the palm, looking down, and then looking up at me.

"You are the only person I can talk to about it. You know."

I nodded. "You are you. And it's wonderful to have you. Here. One day you will tell your grandchildren, and they won't believe a word of it!" I said, trying to lift the mood. We finished our dinner and strolled along the quay.

Undine was waiting for us, tactful José nowhere to be seen. For the first time I had made up a bed in the aft cabin with proper sheets and showed Elisabeth where to stow her luggage. I busied myself in the saloon, spying on her through the open door. She sat on the edge of the bed undoing the buttons of her dress then flopped backwards in her underwear, adjusted the pillow, closed her eyes, and in an instant was fast asleep.

The multicoloured harbour lights reflected off the rippling water and pranced across the cabin ceiling. Never had she looked more alluring, her long curves bathed in a muted lambency, that hair fanned over the pillow like a pre-Raphaelite painting. I slid off my shirt and trousers and lay next to her resting my hand on her hip. She was with me at last. My girl was where she belonged, next to me in a vibrant city on the Mediterranean Sea.

I wanted to visit the Calanques, those marvellous limestone fiords, then cut into the coast just east of Marseilles, and that was where we headed the following day. It was no surprise that José and Elisabeth found each other's company easy and settled into a flirty exchange of badinage. Sormiou exceeded all expectations. We swam in clear warm water, grilled fresh fish on the beach, and slept on deck. This was what I had always wanted and what I had dreamed about.

But something was different. I sensed it but refused to acknowledge it. There had been a time when Elisabeth and I had only needed each other, but now I felt she was looking past me, over my shoulder, trying to avoid being alone or leaving herself open to intimate moments. And the lovemaking wasn't the same either. She was reluctant, distant, and seemed distracted, playing along because she knew I was so expectant.

Here I am, aged seventy-three, the author of a couple of stuffy, serious books about naval warfare, none of which include a hint of sensuality or the pleasures of the flesh, now writing about my most intimate moments. Perhaps it is because I am not writing for a readership now. I write for myself now.

The weather, which had been wonderful, broke with a storm heralding an angry mistral. We beat into Toulon, where we hove up for three days. The conversation flagged. I could tell that Elisabeth had not managed to leave her restlessness behind, and sitting out a storm in Toulon was not helping.

The wind eased. In a bar we met a young American making his way to Italy by whatever means he could. Having an extra person on board made me more uncomfortable but seemed to please Elisabeth. We made Nice in an exhilarating evening sail that had José and me grinning but left Elisabeth looking green and clutching the side of the cockpit before retiring early to her berth.

We moored in the old port and Elisabeth recovered enough for us to walk along the Promenade des Anglais while the clouds dispersed, leaving one of those luminous poststorm evenings of diamond clarity and perfect stillness.

"Come on," I said, "let's have a drink in the Negresco; it's the best hotel on the Cote d'azure." I had to drag her up the flag-strewn steps and into the marbled hallway, sensing some reluctance. Was there a part of her not wanting to be there? Was it me or the grandeur of the hotel? I was wearing my grubby sailing clothes, but she had changed into a skirt and blouse and looked wonderful. I was the man everyone envied as we found a table on the terrace. It was me, the lucky guy with the beautiful woman on his arm. What has he got that we haven't? they were asking.

Well, it turns out I didn't have it either.

By the morning the weather had reverted to a fine day with a hint of a southerly. José was up early busy washing down the teak decks. I volunteered to go to find some breakfast and headed into the old town. I returned twenty minutes later to find José wearing a look of distress that I had never witnessed when at sea.

"She's gone."

"Where? When?"

"Ten, fifteen minutes. She found a taxi over there." He pointed towards the chateau.

And that was it.

I rushed to the station, but there was no sign. I ran through random streets, but where to look? I dashed hither and thither like a crazed animal, knowing that there was no logic in my searching but impelled to continue. Then I realised it was hopeless.

I found the note much later, after two hours in a seedy bar and the best part of a bottle of cognac. I stumbled on board and collapsed in the corner of the salon. Now it was José's turn to be anxious and flustered.

....

I reached down the side of the desk to the battered square box that resided there. It was wooden, covered in a shellacked fabric, patinated and abraded with the years. The word *Remington* was still legible on a transfer on the top surface. I placed it on the desk, sat down in my leather captain's chair, and opened the lid. The black enamel was still glossy, save in the corners where the dust had gathered. The cream keys with their bold letters stood up pert and correct, pledging accuracy and clarity. I took two sheets of headed paper from the top drawer of the desk, and a piece of carbon paper from the drawer beneath, which I inserted between them. I then fed the sheets into the roller. The machine still made a taught mechanical clicking as I wound the paper through the ratchet.

```
Dear Sir or Madam:

Thank you for your letter of the 24th ult.
regarding the Estate of Lady Knowle (née Watson).
     This is by way of confirming that I am Peter
Mackay, formerly of Paradise Road, Richmond.
I was indeed acquainted with Elisabeth Watson
(apparently latterly Lady Knowle) but have not
seen her for many years.
     I am saddened by her death, of which I knew
nothing. I was also unaware of her marriage or
indeed her title, which presumably relates to
her husband? Would I be right in assuming that
she was a widow at the time of her death?
     I look forward to hearing from you further
regarding the above matter.

                    Yours faithfully,

                    Peter Mackay
```

I pulled the paper through the machine, separated the copies and hand addressed the envelope, before replacing the lid of the typewriter and returning it to its place.

CHAPTER 7

....

London

Saturday, July 31, 1948

Her scheme to surprise him with breakfast does not go to plan. She enters the house, but while climbing the stairs is aware of music and finds him playing the cello. She enters quietly and steps towards the sitting room. He is sitting on one of the dining chairs facing into the room with the cello between his knees. He wears a long tan cotton robe with embroidery in black around the neck and down the centre of the front to mid-chest level. She has never seen anything like it except perhaps in a picture of a Bedouin in front of the great pyramid.

He leaps up with the same confused embarrassment that she had seen the night before when she woke him.

"Don't stop," she says. "It's lovely. I have never heard anything like it before. Who is it by?"

"But you are up and dressed! I thought you were still in bed. I was hoping to wake you with a gentle serenade, but you weren't here!"

"No, I've been buying you breakfast."

"Well in exchange I will play for you. Not singing for my supper, rather bowing for my breakfast. Here come, sit." He gets up and half pulls, half ushers her to the armchair. Then picks up the instrument again and resumes playing.

She is flustered, but obeisant, and then captivated. Simple harmonic progressions on the bottom strings hum from the rich warmth of the ruby shellac, and then leap to an almost vocal melodic line on the upper strings. It is jolly but courtly, albeit with a wry smile, with vaults and changes of rhythm, unexpected but exciting. It is a dance, a hymn, a paean. It is floral, charming, and sunny, with alternating passages of foot-tapping beat and less rhythmic melodic sections. He plays with his eyes shut, at times bowing his head and at other times lifting his chin and turning his head to one side. She is right, he plays well, with gusto when needed and sensitivity throughout. When the piece comes to an end and she starts to clap, he smiles and affects a bow.

"You play well. What is the piece?"

"It's called 'La Folia' by Marin Marais. He is my new hero. Forget Bartok! Don't you think it extraordinary? Really for the viola di gamba but I think it works on the cello."

"I love it. Thank you. Where did you find it?"

"Paris. I have some friends there who are mad about early French music, and they thought I would like it. Can you believe it—1701, before most of Bach."

"It was truly lovely; I am most touched. Now it is my turn to create a breakfast extraordinaire, no, of course, *petit dejeuner extraordinaire*, with real French coffee! And after that I am going to drive you to Northolt."

"Blimey. Where did you find proper coffee?"

"Ah well. We have our ways! Never underestimate a woman's ability to get what she wants." She smiles at him, raising her eyebrows, knowing she is being braver than her normal reticence might allow, but she doesn't care.

"You don't need to take me to Northolt. Really, they usually send a car, but I can get a taxi."

"No argument. You get dressed. I will start cooking."

He gently replaces the cello in its case and returns to his bedroom.

She starts frying bacon and lays the table. She grinds some coffee beans in a hand grinder that she clamps to the kitchen table and pours boiling water over the grounds in a tall enamel pot. She makes toast under the grill and finds a pot of her Nanny's plum jam at the back of the larder which, when skimmed of two patches of mould, she deems presentable. He emerges from the bathroom as the spread is coming together, freshly shaven, but dressed the same as the previous evening. He grins his way into the kitchen commenting on the delicious smells.

"I love the window picture in the bathroom. Did you do it by chance?"

"'Fraid so."

"I thought as much. Where is it supposed to be?"

"Make believe—the Mediterranean somewhere."

"Absolutely. Frejus. Antibes."

"Maybe. Perhaps the Calanques. I don't know it well. I have only been once. I still remember the blue. What a blue!"

"Yes, Klein, unalloyed Klein. It is extraordinary, isn't it? And that warmth. I love the heat. Clear waters, the smells . . . and the food . . ." He trails off looking out the window as if sad or reminiscing. "But you are doing everything. Can I help?"

"No, just sit down here and eat. How do you like your coffee?"

They sit and share the breakfast. He is impressed by the coffee and wolfs down the bacon and eggs. He asks her about her mother.

"Well," she says, "she still lives in the same house in Reigate as she has since she got married. She has never worked, still attends her weekly WI meetings, still makes jam. On the face of it she is fine, but I don't know, she seems to lack a purpose without the only man in her life who she ever loved. That's the problem with giving yourself to another—when they leave, you can end up stranded. At times she seems to be sleepwalking, just doing things because she's always done them rather than because they mean anything or have a purpose. I think she is still grieving for Daddy. She doesn't have much joy in her life . . ."

"Not even you?"

She smiles. "Oh, I'm not saying she doesn't love me, or my younger sister, but it's a sort of efficient measured love, not a gushing, demonstrative love. Poor Mummy, I think she just hates being on her own. I am going down to see her for a couple of days this week and she will profess to be pleased to see me and will have made a cake, and in the evening we will listen to the wireless and she will knit and I will read a book and after two days I will be bored to tears, and probably demonstrate my impatience in various little ways that she notices—although she pretends not to—and that leave me feeling cross with myself. Then I will make my excuses and come back here. And that will be that until the next time. It's just how it is."

"What about your sister? What does she do?"

"Married to a policeman in Tunbridge Wells, expecting a baby. She's lovely, kindly, and a good wife, but we were never close. I expect your family is much more exciting and interesting." She looks directly at him across the scrubbed pine table. Her eyes plead honesty with a sneak of whimsy.

He raises his eyebrows, shrugs, takes a sip of coffee, and matches her gaze but doesn't say anything. She doesn't find the silence awkward because her mind is dancing a hundred jigs and reels.

"Well?" she says.

He shrugs but doesn't say anything.

"Brothers or sisters?"

"No," he replies.

"What about your mother?"

"No."

"No?"

"Just me." He mocks a sad face, and then smiles. "I am sorry. I am not being evasive. I don't mind talking about it, but it's all rather complicated and long-winded. We would need a whole evening. But I do have a wicked stepmother who I mentioned, and various seedy aunts and uncles."

"How wicked?"

"Oh, pure Grimm."

"Where does she live?"

"In Dorset in the family home. She is only eighteen years older than I am. She is Austrian and still speaks a heavily accented English. When my father died, she should have gone back home but felt guilty about leaving me. God knows why, she was a pretty hopeless mother substitute. Then she had a ghastly time in the war, as the locals—who never understood that she was Austrian, not German—were sure she was a spy or harbouring agents or something equally nefarious. I am not sure whether that is the only reason she took to the bottle, but most days she's tipsy by noon."

"Oh dear. How often do you see her?"

"Not as often as I should. Isn't that what most parents say?"

"And stepparents?"

"It's only duty and guilt. There isn't much pleasure in it."

There is another silence.

"Would you like some more coffee? There is a little bit in the pot. Then we had better get cracking. By the way, where exactly is Northolt?"

"West London. Somewhere on the way to Bath, I think. Not exactly sure how to get there. Look, are you sure about this?"

"Absolutely."

"It's quite brave offering to take me somewhere that you don't know how to get to!"

"Evey never lets me down. She will find her own way."

"Evey?"

"She is a Morris 8. The number plate is EVE 131. She was Daddy's car, and since Mummy doesn't drive, I have her on semipermanent loan. I am not sure whether Mr. Morris designed his car with a cello in mind, but we will fit it in somehow."

He puts his things back in the Gladstone bag while she clears the table leaving the plates stacked on the wooden draining board to the side of the cracked Belfast sink. She puts on a cardigan and glances at herself in the mirror on her dressing table.

"Right, Miss Watson, ready as commanded. By the way, are you ever Liz or Lisa?" He stands in the hall with Ludwig in one hand and the bag in the other.

"I have an S not a Z. Not sure why. I think it was Daddy's choice, actually."

"So Greek rather than Latin. Nothing wrong with that. So, Lisa perhaps?"

"Permitted, but not Bet or Betty."

"Good Lord, No."

They leave the flat and walk round the corner into Warwick Square, where she introduces him to Evey.

"Shall we put the hood down? The day looks fair, and it will be easier to seat Ludwig," she asks.

"Yes, rather! How spiffing, a spot of open-air motoring will be terribly salutary." He grins theatrically.

They easily fit the cello and bag in the back seats.

"Now where do we go?"

"West for sure. Where is the sun? Do you have a compass? Or a sextant? What about a plane, we could follow that, but I can't see a plane? Look, there's a pigeon—will that do? It might be migrating west."

She grins largely to herself. Why does it not surprise her that this man, who flits across Europe doing important things, has no idea how to find his way to the airport?

"I think it's near Oxford," he chips in.

She feels he is trying to be helpful, perhaps concerned that his flippancy may be taken for ingratitude. "Oxford!"

"Well on the road to Oxford?"

"You said Bath!"

"Well, doesn't the road to Bath go to Oxford?"

"We are about to find out!"

They laugh.

She knows the way to the Great West Road, where they stop at a garage and ask the way. It turns out that they only need to take a minor detour to find the airfield. It takes all of Henry's power of persuasion and the fumbling for an identity card before the guard at the gate will let them in. Henry directs her to the main departure building, which is nothing more than a large Nissen hut, and she stops the car while he unloads Ludwig and his bag.

For the first time, she finds him awkward. He doesn't look her in the eye, holds out a hand for her to shake, and mumbles a thank you and how kind she'd been and then says more clearly, "Look, I would really like to repay you for doing this. Perhaps when I am next in London . . . Really it is awfully sweet of you. Perhaps we could go out for dinner or something . . ."

She looks at him with a mixture of tenderness, uncertainty, and disappointment. She has no clue as to what he is thinking. She shakes his hand, turns, and gets back in the car. He smiles, waves, and then turns to walk into the building.

....

She drives home in a muddle of thoughts and feelings, peppered with memories of the last twelve hours.

She lets herself into the flat to find congealed breakfast crockery still on the draining board. She piles the plates in the sink. Wendy isn't around and she has all day to do them. She flops on the sofa, aware of a pit in her stomach and a mix of heady exhilaration and unfathomable fear. She has never felt like this before.

Getting out of the flat would surely help, so she heads out for a walk. She sits in Warwick Square and watches a pair of squirrels playing in a plane tree. The question of *Will I ever see him again?* can only be answered in her mind by the imperative *I have to.*

But how? She has no address, no phone number, or any point of contact. Perhaps Wendy could get it from David. She feels a little easier, comforted by this possible safety net.

It's in his hands, those slender, elegant, unsullied, hands that finger the neck of a cello with a delicious sensitivity, that she wants to touch and hold and move over her own neck . . . The waiting will be impossible.

She is sure that distraction is the best approach and ambles towards Westminster Cathedral. She is not a believer and is wary of papism but can always be moved by the monumental. She recalls the obscure comfort she found in the cold stones of her parish church after her father died, and how calming it is to visit a country church or a great cathedral.

She stands in the shadow of the Byzantine frontage and admits to herself that she doesn't understand it. It doesn't touch her the way a soaring gothic column can or fine stained glass in a rose window. It lacks the tangible honesty of a worn fresco peering from beneath ancient lime wash. And then, instead of being distracted she finds she is wondering what Henry would say about it. What does he value? Perhaps he's a Catholic. Benville; sounds French. God, he could be! What she doesn't doubt is that he would know about architecture and that he would have an opinion, and that she would want to listen to that opinion. How annoying that she doesn't know more stuff. If only her school had been a proper school where you got taught things.

School was horrible. Awful. Her mother's parents hailed from Presteigne, where her grandfather had worked on the railways and her grandmother made jam, played the organ in the Methodist Chapel, and taught needlework at St. Catherine's. It was an undistinguished small girl's public school favoured by the scattered farming families of the Marches for its ability to drill manners and values into their earthy, stolid daughters, who, it was perceived, required better skills in the kitchen and on the back of a horse than in the library or lecture hall.

Nanny Mills, like other long-serving staff at the school, was offered half-price fees for offspring and grandchildren. Elisabeth's parents, with the promise of paying the remainder of the fees themselves, persuaded their daughter that it was much the best thing for her to attend. It was one of Elisabeth's longest standing gripes that they never reviewed the decision, even when it was only too clear that she was unhappy, descending into a tearful sulk three days before the beginning of term, all the while pleading with her mother not to send her back. But her parents remained unmoved, an issue which still provoked an element of resentment, especially in moments such as these when she regretted her feeble academic achievements.

Then Mrs. Varga took her under her wing. Sensing her unhappiness but seeing something worth nurturing in her musicality, with a mixture of central European stubbornness and persuasive empathy and kindness, she led the angry and unhappy teenager into the liberating world of music. Although the horrid parts didn't go away, there was now an escape available in the music room and in the cosy gas-fired sitting room of Mrs. Varga, who offered dogmatic commentary and grilled crumpets while playing her sacred gramophone collection.

She completed her schooling earning more respect and affection from the teachers than her peers, scraping through her school certificate, winning the Geraint Johnson music prize, and passing grade eight piano.

She had read a lot, that was a positive. She had whistled through little leather-bound editions of the classics in her grandmother's bedroom, devouring Austen, Dickens, Kipling, and Bronte but stalling on Galsworthy and Trollope. Then she moved to the downstairs bookcase and found that books could still be fun, if not classics. And now thought she was reasonably up to date with Steinbeck, Waugh, Greene, Shute, and Christie. But her history was very shaky, and she knew nothing about architecture or the classics.

What had Henry studied at Oxford? Probably Greats or ancient history or something terribly arcane. A cloud of gloom descends. The day is still bright, with fluffy clouds studding the blue sky, but she is immune to its cheer.

She walks on to the Army and Navy store, idly looking at dresses that she can't afford nor has the requisite coupons for. The windows are full of Dior and the "The New Look;" full skirts with tight waisted jackets, large belts, and coolie-style hats. *Not for me*, she thinks, better looser, less formal styles that suit her long limbs. She heads for the café and orders a cup of tea and a large piece of cake, which will suffice for lunch.

She returns home feeling flat and deflated. The frisson of the morning has vanished like the applause after a concert.

CHAPTER 8

....

Cap d'Ail, Var, France
July 1992

I knew there was little chance of a response to my letter for several weeks, but logic did not diminish my restlessness and impatience. Daily I checked the mailbox, but it remained as empty as a winter bird's nest. Normally this was nothing unusual, but now it was bewitched with expectation, casting a spell over my mornings. I was listless, irritable, and gloomy.

I couldn't sleep, nightly doing battle with intrusive thoughts and memories of times spent with Elisabeth. But they weren't simply dreams; I found myself in a place between sleep and wakefulness, where I had neither the pleasure of abandonment into the arms of Morpheus, nor the reassuring safety of wakefulness.

For the first few days the volume of *Undine*'s log remained on my desk, but when I realised that it was contributing to my restlessness and unease, I replaced it on the shelf. But it made no difference.

Therese detected something was amiss.

"Ca va? Tu sembles un peu distrait."

"I am not sleeping. I am not sure why."

"Tu es en deuil, je pense—C'est elle." It is grief—it is her.

Of course, I dismissed her idea. How could I be grieving for someone I hadn't seen for forty years? Besides, I wasn't sure I knew what grief was. But as the days passed, I had to admit that I was thinking of her nearly constantly, with a heaviness to my limbs and gloom in my heart. Perhaps this was what grief was like. It was loss. The loss of something I had never really had but now for certain would never have and it was painful. It was not like what I had experienced when my grandfather had died; that was a logical sadness, not this pervasive hopelessness.

Many of the memories were of our times in Hunsdon in the little cottage that Elisabeth shared with three other FANYs, or in the Crown or the White Hart where we spent so much time when off duty.

How strange that I cannot recall the first time I met this person who cast such a long shadow over my life. The truth is that I was in a terrible state, and dates for that period in the autumn of 1942 were a jumble then as now.

....

I celebrated my nineteenth birthday two months after war broke out. I was working in the family paper business, which, although I enjoyed it, had never inspired the passion that it had for my father and grandfather. Perhaps they had more commercial nous, which I knew I lacked, but also, I was too busy living a life. My weekends were occupied with partying and sailing, and I always found it a struggle to return to the firm on Monday morning, and I often failed to manage it. There was always a nautical excuse; the wrong tide or the wrong wind or a race that ended up miles from where we started. I felt no call from a vocation, certainly not in the selling of paper, and saw no reason to commit to a career.

Not that I didn't pull my weight; I believe and hope I did. I was a quick learner, had ideas, and could get on with people if need be. The year before, my father had sent me off to Europe to visit our suppliers. I had journeyed to Sweden to see the pulping mills and paper production on a scale unimaginable at home, using it as an excuse to spend a week sailing in the Baltic. I then headed south to Germany and Czechoslovakia, into Italy and then to France, spending a month or so in each country, visiting and learning from the great European paper makers. I returned knowing more about paper and a lot more about the world. I also realised that I couldn't live in the midst of continental Europe, not because of the terrifying politics of fascism, but because it was too far from the ocean. But as Europe edged towards conflict, it was clear that our business was going to need to change, at least in the short term, and what might have been my remit five years earlier, was now dominated by the awareness that I was going to have to join up.

At the outbreak of war recruitment was initially for those between twenty and forty and so I didn't have to decide immediately, but after Dunkirk the realisation that I was going to have to fight became inescapable. There was only one option: to go to sea.

After basic training I was allocated to a ship, the SS *Induna*, a seventeen-year-old coaster recently fitted with four-inch guns, scheduled for convoy duties in the North Atlantic. At the time, the prospect of joining the North Atlantic convoys did not concern me to the extent it should have done. I had sailed in the Western Isles, felt I was tough enough, and thought I knew about northern climes and bad weather. How naive was I.

The day before we left Glasgow, I got a message to say there was a man to see me on the quayside. At first, I didn't recognise the shrunken old fellow standing in a tan greatcoat wearing a flat tweed cap. It is strange how, when you unexpectedly meet a person you know, there is an instant before recognition that enables you to see them objectively. The frail old man was Grandfather. The strong, rugged, iron-willed man who had taught me so much had become a shrunken pensioner. He had travelled down specially to hand over a package wrapped in brown paper and tied with string. Inside were a pair of the fur lined leather boots worn by the Glasgow trawlermen. They were waterproofed with tallow, stitched with tough twine, and long enough to come above the calf. There were also two fine woollen vests with pairs of long underwear and two pairs of thick woollen socks, still oily from the natural lanolin of the Islay sheep.

He didn't say much, just stood looking at the unimpressive hull of the *Induna*, his hands deep in the pockets of his trench coat, the set of his jaw saying all that needed to be said.

"Nae much of a boot yer've found yer sel." And then a long pause. "But I've seen worse." Then he turned away from the inelegant tramp and not looking at me said, "Look after yersel, Billy Boy. Remember, any damned fool can be wet and cold. I want yer to promise me one thing . . ."

"I will do my best."

"Always sleep in yer clothes. Ne'er get undressed after a watch. Ye ne'er know when ye might have to be on deck in a jiffy, and there will ne'r be time to put on yer britches."

I laughed. "I will do it for you."

"I'm bein' serious, ye ken."

He paused, standing looking at the *Induna* and nodding slowly. And without looking at me, he turned and walked away.

It was the last time I ever saw him.

The Arctic convoys to Russia were all given consecutive numbers. The ships assembled in Loch Ewe became the ill-fated Convoy PQ13. Of the nineteen ships that left Loch Ewe, thirteen arrived in Murmansk.

In a perverse way I have reason to be grateful for PQ 13 because the experience ultimately became the basis for my book *Convoy North*, which, with the rights to the modestly successful film, allowed me to live a comfortable life in retirement, but it nearly did me in.

By the time I got back to my parent's house, barely able to walk with frostbitten toes on my left foot, tremulous and panicky at the slightest sound and afraid of the dark, I was a wreck. My condition has been labelled as various things over the years: shell shock, trauma, stress. It matters not what it is called, but it left me in a hopeless state. I couldn't sleep, couldn't concentrate, was as jumpy as a rabbit, and would burst into tears without warning.

I still believe it was Elisabeth who rescued me. Others have said it was due to the natural recovery processes that occur in any event, but I know that it was her. How could she not have carved a special place in my soul?

....

And then on the Wednesday barely more than a week after my response, there was another letter from Lees and Smallwood.

Dear Mr. Mackay,

Thank you for your letter of 3 July received in this office on the 7th.

We are gratified for the confirmation that you are the Peter Mackay, named in the will of Lady Knowle.

The bequest specified is contained in a large envelope, and although we have not had sight of the contents, it would appear to be papers or documents of some description.

Normally in such circumstances we would strive to pass over the documents in person, so that proof of identity can be facilitated. However, we are aware that this may not be feasible given your expatriate status. Nevertheless, if you are returning to England in the near future this would be the preferred option.

Elisabeth gained her title from her late husband Henry Benville, Earl Knowle, who was killed in a tragic accident many years ago.

Perhaps a way forward would be for you to telephone this office and discuss the matter with our Mr. Steven Smallwood?

We trust to remain etc.

Yours sincerely,

Smallwood and Lees

CHAPTER 9

London

Saturday, July 31, 1948

S he has some washing to do which she has been putting off all week and fills the bucket she uses with water from the Ascot, topping it up from the kettle. She is up to her wrists in soap suds when the doorbell rings again.

In the moment she is almost paralysed by the reminiscence of the previous evening, all that she had been avoiding hits her with a fist of confusion. She dries her hands and makes her way to the door of the flat. She descends the stairs and opens the front door.

It is him.

He stands in his shirt with a bewildered look, holding his case in his left hand. Ludwig is on the ground to the side leaning against the railings with the coat draped over him.

"Technical problem with one of the engines. Too risky to fly and as there were only three people travelling, they cancelled the flight. Not another till next week. So, I thought if you could bear it, that I might accompany you to the Prom."

"I, I . . . Of course," she says, wondering whether her voice betrays the flood of relief, excitement, and joy that she feels.

They stand facing each other. He fixes her gaze, so different from the confusing separation five hours before.

"Actually, that's true but not the point. The point is that I think you are the most beautiful person I have ever met, I have fallen madly in love with you, and I want to spend the rest of my life with you."

She puts her hands up to her face and feels it reddening. In the instant, the ground is swept away from under her and the knot in her stomach explodes in a dazzle of disbelief, happiness, and fear. *This cannot be happening. This is make believe or fairy tale; this isn't real life.*

She is lost for words but then realises that there are no words for what she feels. She matches his gaze and inches towards him, moving her hands to hold the collar of his shirt.

She shakes her head slightly, her gaze locked to his.

"You knew, you knew . . . How did you know? I lay there last night daring to believe in this and now you are here." She pulls and pushes on the shirt slightly. "Oh, you wonderful, crazy man. How did you know?"

He puts down the bag and puts his hands on the top of her arms.

"Es muss sein, es muss sein," he whispers, "Of course I knew, I have never been so sure of anything."

They don't kiss immediately, rather they move closer and closer until their heads are side by side with her chin on his shoulder. They stay standing, holding each other for the first time, breathing the other's musk and feeling the warmth and textures of skin against skin. He moves his lips to hers and she moves her hands to his sides, holding him around the waist. They stand like this for a while immeasurable in chronological time, their lips gently exploring, probing, brushing, crushing. There is an electricity in her pelvis. She feels she is melting.

Then she says, "Henry, we are on the street! Perhaps we should go inside?"

"And you don't like being a woman of the street?"

"I would prefer to be a woman of the bedchamber." She is amazed by her brazen candour. How could she dare say such a thing? But it is simply honest; it is her body speaking.

They disentangle, but not completely. She keeps hold of his hand, grabs the bag in the other, and pulls him into the house. He picks up the cello and follows her upstairs. Still holding his hand, she drops the bag uncaringly inside the door and closes the door behind them with her foot. She pulls him into her bedroom, the momentary concern about how tidy it might be dispelled by the reluctance to break from their embrace. She pulls him towards her, tugging his shirt from out of his trousers so she can feel the skin of his torso. Their kisses become more urgent as he also pulls her towards him as they fall onto the bed.

She struggles to undo his trousers, pulls up her skirt and flicks her knickers across the room. A minute or two later he is done and lies collapsed, spent and powerless, his slowing breaths harsh in her ear. She walks her hands up his back and into his hair. It is soft and fine like a child's. He lifts his head and looks at her with an intensity and tenderness that she instinctively matches.

"I am sorry," he says, "that's what happens when you wait twenty years to make love to a woman you have only ever dreamt of."

"It's fine. The concert doesn't start for two hours." She says with a coy smile. They lie still, their breathing subsiding to the unnoticeable. She is aware of a cling of sweat between their flesh. She feels his withering cock slithering out of her and has a sudden pang of anxiety about contraception. "Move over, I need to go and have a wash." She pushes him off and pulls her dress down. "No lying on my bed with clothes on. Get undressed. I will be back in a mo."

"Yes ma'am!"

She goes to the bathroom and sees the bucket of unfinished laundry. She smiles; never in her life will washing be interrupted in quite the same way! She gets the douche out of the cupboard, dusty with disuse. She finds it a demeaning and disgusting device, like some primitive medical contraption from a past century, but she knows she must make the effort. Afterward she dries herself and takes off her dress and bra, reentering the room confident in her nakedness.

He is lying on the bed covered by a sheet up to his umbilicus with his arms behind his head.

"Wow! Have I told you yet that you are very beautiful?"

"No, but you can. You know all women love to be flattered." She gets into bed beside him, lying on her side facing him, resting her hand on his chest. She idly twirls her fingers through the blond hairs.

"It wouldn't be flattery. I can't understand why someone so lovely doesn't have a boyfriend . . . although that is rather a presumption. I haven't actually asked, but you are not exactly behaving as if you have a boyfriend!"

"I don't, not this week. They are hard to find—good ones, that is. Best to wait until they come knocking on your door late at night."

There is a moment of silence.

"I want you to know I don't usually behave like this," she says. "You have done something terrible to me, infected me with some brazen germ of shamelessness. Do you have this effect on all women? I bet you do."

"Oh, if only you knew. I am completely hopeless. I set my standards too high, always finding reasons in my head why it won't work, and thinking the best way out is not to get tangled up in the first place."

He moves down the bed and slides his arm under her neck. They kiss again.

"Do you speak German?" she asks.

"Why do you ask?"

"Something you said downstairs. What was it?"

"Es muss sein."

"So, you do?"

"Ja, ich spreche Deutsch. Jetzt möchte ich dich wieder zu ficken"

"So, the answer is yes. What does the rest of it mean?"

He grins. "It's rude."

"Tell me."

"It means I am sure the concert will be terribly good."

"Rubbish! It doesn't mean that. Besides that's not rude."

He just grins.

"I can do rude too . . ." She moves her hand under the sheet and slides it down to his groin. She kisses him with more urgency. She breaks for a second and looks at him "as rude as this?"

"Ruder."

She slides her thigh right across him, and then her pelvis so she is straddling him. Now it is her turn, rocking slowly, grinding against him, her eyes shut, a look of intense concentration on her face, until it all changes and she rushes towards her climax then collapses onto him, spent and panting, with nothing between them but a fine film of moisture. She is unsure if the pulse pounding in her temple is hers or his.

"I can die now," he says.

She lifts her head "Die? That's an awful thing to say. What do you mean?"

"I mean that I always knew that somewhere in the world there was a beautiful woman with whom I would share a moment like this. Now I've found her." He pulls her towards him, stroking her back, the passion giving way to tenderness.

"You had jolly well better not die. Not yet anyway."

"Well, if you are going to make a habit of this you might need to call in to a barber's shop and get some johnnies."

She eases off him, peeling their skins apart like slices of ham, aware of the melange of their musky scents. "Would you like a bath? I'm afraid the hot water is rather dire."

She runs the bath, and they take turns to sit in the lukewarm water, dancing around each other as they dry and dress in the dismal bathroom. He is in and out in a few seconds. The touching is now replaced by looking. He is shyer than she, being swift to wrap himself in a towel, whereas she has always been easy with her nakedness next to her lovers. His skin is pale as pastry, his body long and lean, not well-muscled but broad across the shoulders and buttocks, and covered on chest, arms and legs with an almost golden blonde fur. Not a lion, perhaps a gazelle—no, not that either—something more cerebral, but she can't quite think what—the aesthete not the athlete.

She had suggested they walk to the Albert Hall but by the time they finally leave, it's half past six and they are in a hurry, so they jump on a 52 bus. The evening is clear but cool and she needs her cardigan. He has produced a crumpled green corduroy jacket from the Gladstone.

They climb to the upper deck and sit holding hands observing the city preparing for a Saturday night out. The sun is low and a golden light flickers through the overhanging branches of the plane trees on Buckingham Palace Road. The streets are busy with people stepping out with a few shillings in their pockets: men with women on their arms; pairs of girls tripping, laughing, stocking seams evident below skirts creeping up to their knees; older couples slower and stately. Suddenly she is one of them. For so long she had to look at lovers with envy, but in a trice that has changed. How different the world seems from the flustered fears of the morning. She still has uncertainty, with no idea of what the future holds, but it doesn't matter. Something fundamental has moved, there is something about the man next to her that has dispelled the fear. She knows so little about him but nothing that has happened in the last two hours has diminished the captivation and excitement that she felt the previous evening. On the contrary, she finds she gets aroused just thinking of their lovemaking.

They cannot quite see over the wall into the palace. He suggests they could call in for cocktails.

"They're not there," she says. "Balmoral, I believe."

"Oh, well how about the Duke of Wellington? We could call in there." He nods to Apsley House. You know the address is said to be number one, London. Not a bad address. Don't you think it is just brilliant? I love the proportions."

"You do know about architecture. I thought you would."

"Why?"

"It is just that this morning I was struggling with Westminster Cathedral and thought you might be able to explain it!"

He guffaws, "Explain it? Not likely. I don't dislike it though. I don't really know anything about architecture except what I like.

Such as John Nash," and he nods to Apsley house.

"Did he design it? There you are you see; you do know about it. I know nothing about anything very much. I don't even know anything about you." She pauses. "Except your name."

"Well actually you don't really know that." He puts on a mischievous face, "Well, you do, but because my father was also Henry, when I was little I was called by my second name, Chivers." He looks at her blank face. "Yes, I know. It's an old family name—nothing to do with the jam—but then when I was at school and university, I was called Sandy and most of my friends call me that."

"So, what shall I call you?"

He smiles at her. "Whatever you like, but not Chivers. And there is another thing about my name, but I'll tell you that later."

"Don't be so secretive."

"Look, I have a proposal for you. I've said my family is rather complicated. You have a few days off, and I have a week till my flight departs. Would you like to come to my family home for a couple of days and I can explain all about it . . . and you can decide whether you want to still have anything to do with me?"

"Why would I not? Is there something awful? Are there skeletons in the cupboard? One of your names isn't Bluebeard, is it?"

He laughs. "Ah Bartok again! No, I haven't got that one. I have got an Arbuthnot though."

"I knew you were posh when you first walked into the flat. You are, aren't you? Posh, I mean. I am not at all posh, Henry. Will that make a difference? Could you love someone unposh?"

"Of course, why on earth would that make a difference? What do you think about my idea?"

"I was going to go and see Mummy."

"You can still see her. How about we drive down tomorrow?"

"We?"

"All right, you drive. I will navigate." They look at each other and laugh.

"Don't tell me it is near Bath?"

"No, it's near Dorchester."

"And do you know how to get there?"

"Absolutely! At least when we get close."

They arrive at the Albert Hall and join the cheery throng milling around the building. They meet June as planned by the statue of Prince Albert at the rear, and Henry takes the two tickets and heads to the ticket office to try to get a third. Elisabeth had introduced him as a friend of Wendy's brother.

As soon as he is out of sight June looks at her friend.

"Who is he? He is gorgeous! He's not just a friend of Wendy's brother, is he? You're soft on him, old girl, aren't you? I can tell. You have that look about you."

Elisabeth feels her face redden. "I only met him last night but admit that I am rather smitten—I'm still in a bit of a daze. I think he's totally charming."

"And handsome."

"And very handsome."

Henry returns with three tickets together in the stalls and they file in to find their seats. He sits between the two women. As always Elisabeth is awed yet comforted by the plush red velvet and gold leaf, which makes her feel special and privileged. She loves the crisp formality of the black suits and white collars and waistcoats of the orchestra, the sheen of the woodwind and the shiny brass of the instruments. There is an air of joyful expectancy, in the chat and bustle of the promenaders and the tuning of the orchestra.

Irene Kohler enters wearing a long dark-blue dress of satin. She is tiny, with a thin face featuring a long nose above a tense, unsmiling mouth.

"She looks terrified," she whispers in his ear.

"Of Sargent or Rachmaninov?"

They file out for the interval and June offers to buy drinks. She returns with a Worthington and two pink gins.

"Well, what did the pianist think?" Henry asks Elisabeth.

"I loved it. Magnificent; such bravura. I really don't know how she manages those leaps. It's terribly difficult, even for a person with large hands."

"That wasn't a tear I saw during the Mozart, was it, Henry?" June asks wryly.

"Oh god, I prayed no one noticed. I am hopeless. Even an echo of an aria and I am in floods. Opera lachrymosa It's a well-recognised medical condition, you know, and I've got it badly."

"So is opera your thing?" June asks.

"Totally and completely. The trouble is getting to see it. It is, though, one of the advantages of spending time in Austria."

They chat on. Henry explains a bit more about the work he does, mostly talking to June. Elisabeth feels comfortable because she gleans more about him without having to ask him directly or let on that she knows so little about him.

They file back into the hall for the second half. Strauss, Handel, and then Rimsky-Korsakov. They leave the hall awash with the flamenco rhythms of the "Rhapsody Espagnole."

Henry declares that he is starving and suggests they might get a sandwich in the Queens Arms. June has to rush away, so the two of them hurry across Queens Gate and enter the pub. The only food they have is a pork pie and one scotch egg. Henry insists on asking for a plate and a sharp knife from the kitchen. He turns the egg around and around on the plate.

"What are you doing?" she asks.

"Planning where to make the incision. The question is how to locate exactly where the egg is within the sausage meat," he says with concentration and seriousness which, for a moment, takes her aback.

"And why would it matter where it is?" She plays the pantomime response.

"To divide it perfectly, the ideal incision should bisect it perfectly, silly."

"Is that really important?"

"Of course, it is; if I divide it unequally then I will be forced to give you the bigger bit and then I will feel peeved . . . Do you know how to spot where the egg is?"

"In all honesty, I can't say I do."

"Bother, neither do I." He holds the egg up to the light. I think it could be over this side."

"Oh, for goodness' sake, give me the egg." She grabs his hand and returns the egg to the plate. Picking up the knife she swiftly divides it in two and then into quarters.

"Now you have the biggest and smallest and I will have the middle ones. Does that work." She grins a silly grin, wobbling her head.

"You are a genius. I suspected it all along; now I have official confirmation."

She divides the pie, which is solid and tastes of little, and they sip their beers.

What a dream he is! the way he played with the egg with such fascination. Adorable. That look of focus and concentration on his face as he posed himself the question. Same with his cello playing, an intellectual curiosity, with an almost childlike joy in posing the question largely independent of the ultimate answer. How different this is from the oft awkward moments with other suitors whose attempts to please had been punctuated by heavy silences and left me knowing nothing very much about them, except that they were trying to impress. This man wouldn't know how to try to impress anyone, and by its very absence is achieving it.

They are almost the last to leave the pub, finally heeding the landlord's weary exhortations that it was "well past time."

It's a bit late for a bus," he says, "but we could walk."

"Yes, let's walk. It's a lovely evening. It's so nice not having to go to work tomorrow, I can't tell you."

And so, they stroll through the empty London streets just idly ambling but not touching, the route random and indirect. They look at buildings and trees and imagine the lives of the few souls they espy. The drunk slouched in a doorway, the lad with a flat cap hurrying purposefully to an assignation that they conclude is not quite legal, the painted face of the slender woman stepping away from a taxi in clacking stilettos. They come across a bombed-out building, cleared but not rebuilt and look at the fireplace hanging three storeys up with wallpaper still intact and a mirror still hanging above the mantel.

"Someone lived there," he says, pointing to the shattered room. "Someone would have slept in that room, got out of bed, and looked at themselves in that mirror. Someone's dad or daughter, a poet or a plumber. Someone's lover. Such a waste. It's terrible, isn't it? But we walk past it every day. Do you think we have become inured to loss? I do wonder about myself sometimes."

"Tell me about your war Henry. Where were you? What did you do? Did you lose pals?"

"I keep quiet about it mostly. I didn't do any proper fighting and find that difficult when my chums were driving tanks in Normandy. Intelligence, flitting about here and there. I was useful because I could speak German. But then because of what I did I never really got demobbed, just carried on doing it, only a bit different."

She doesn't know what to make of what he says and so doesn't respond. It seems as if he might be ashamed of what he didn't do, and she doesn't want to push on a sore spot. They walk on, silent and introspective.

But the sombre moment doesn't last. They come to a row of shops with window displays to ogle and covet and talk of clothes and fashions. She feels alive and excited. She is comfortable in her skin and happy, not because she knows what the morrow will bring, but because she knows whatever it is it will be different from yesterday and fascinating, stimulating, and fun.

CHAPTER 10

....

Cap d'Ail, Var, France
July 1992

I had decided to return to England and visit Mr. Smallwood. I won't say "return home," because it was not my home, and I had not set foot in England for more than twenty years. Looking back on the decision, I accept it was a strange one to make; I had hardly been anywhere of note for ten years and will not take an aeroplane, but I had been so ruffled by the news of Elisabeth's death and the maudlin mood my ruminations had provoked that I felt I needed to do something to jolt me out of my pit of despond. Rather than sit and wait for an envelope, I would visit the old country and explore Elisabeth's world— from which I had been absent for so long. I would meet Mr. Smallwood in person and learn about her later life. I convinced myself it would be more fruitful than simply receiving an envelope in the post.

I told Therese of my plans the next morning. Her expression said without words what she thought of the idea. The French can tell more in a shrug and a gesture than many English in a mumbled paragraph.

"Mais comment allez-vous voyager? Pas dans un avion?"

"No, I will drive."

"Mais c'est longue. C'est très longue." Her anxious look I knew to be heartfelt.

After she had done her busying and cleaning, instead of making our usual walk down the oleander path, we descended to the basement garage where I keep the Bristol. As always, she started on the button. I dropped Therese in town and took the car to Farouk, the Algerian mechanic who had looked after her for the past twenty years. He beamed when we rumbled into his backstreet garage, littered with the broken remnants of the rubbish that constitutes the modern French car. He spoke a mixture of idiomatic French and English, spat between thick lips.

"Ah la belle Breestol! The best of Breetish. Ma voiture favorite."

I explained that I wanted the car checked over, as I was planning to drive it to England. He was surprised but assured me that he would have it ready for me later in the day and would drop it off at my apartment. I walked down to the Corniche, picking up a newspaper en route and headed for the Club. While at the newsstand, I bought a postcard and a stamp and penned a note to my brother informing him of my impending visit and suggesting we meet.

My plan was to leave the following morning, breaking the journey with an overnight stay in Rheims or thereabouts.

....

I was given six weeks medical leave and signed off B3 until review by the Naval Board. I spent the time in the garden room of the anodyne suburban setting of my parent's home in Epping, that being where you move when you make money in the East End. Their new house, built five years previously in the thirties housing boom, was the model of middle-class aspiration, set back from the road with half-timbered gables and a decent sized garden, and almost identical to every other house in the road.

I found it very difficult to walk because of my feet. All the toes on my left foot were black; on the right they were still red and swollen. I have no idea whether the treatment of frostbite has changed, but in those days the accepted approach was to delay doing anything for as long as possible in the hope that the body will claw back some of the dead tissue. And sure enough, as the weeks passed the area of black slough decreased on all the smaller toes, with only the tip of the big toe needing amputation. But for several weeks I couldn't walk or even wear shoes because of the tenderness and swelling.

My hands were not good either. Although not frost bitten, they had been affected by the extreme cold in a manner, I was informed, akin to trench foot. I sat in my parent's home bored and restless, unable to sleep because of the harpies and sirens who seemed hell-bent on preventing even a moment of rest. It was a strange and cruel torture. I was a Tantalus not crazed by thirst but by tiredness. When I would finally fall into an exhausted torpor the screaming was there instantly, dragging me back to an unwelcome wakefulness in a welter of sweat and panic.

And then, two days after my twenty-first birthday, there was a knock on the door, which was opened by my mother. I heard a male voice address her by name and say that he hoped he was expected. Two men were ushered into my room, where I was sitting in front of open French windows with my bad leg up on a low stool. They were both wearing dark suits with ties, the shorter held a thin mac over his arm, the other a slim leather briefcase.

"Lieutenant Mackay? Major Avison, liaison officer intelligence service. Did your father inform you of our visit?"

"No, he didn't."

"No matter. We did telephone, though, yesterday to his office. He told us where to find you. This is Mr. Howe." The taller of the men turned to introduce his colleague, a thickset man in his thirties with heavy-rimmed glasses perched on a beaky nose over prominent lips. He leant forward to shake hands.

"Ellic Howe. You used to supply us with paper when I worked for Simpson Shand. You may remember the company?"

"In Hertford?"

"That's the one."

"Mr. Howe is a specialist printer," the taller man spoke. "How are you getting on?" he said, nodding at my beleaguered limb.

"Good. Yes, very good, thank you." What masters we are of the understatement.

"You still look a little shaky."

He must have noticed the tremulous urgency with which I sucked the last gasp of my cigarette before grinding it into the nearly full ashtray.

I suggested they sit, waving at the cane furniture, the pinnacle of my mother's aesthetic sensibility.

"How is the paper business?"

"You would have to ask Father. I haven't been much involved lately, but judging by his demeanour and his mood, the quotas and paper rationing are taking their toll."

"How did the Russians treat you?"

They had obviously done some homework.

"Being nice to foreigners doesn't come easily to them, but they can do the right thing when they have a vested interest. They looked after us as well as could be expected, but the hospital was pretty Spartan."

"No Florence Nightingale?"

"Not that I saw."

They talked about the convoys and the Arctic, and the progress of the war. Then they steered the conversation to my work before the war and the paper industry. The polite conversation became more inquisitorial. The tall man led the questioning; how long had I spent in Germany? Could I speak German? Did I still have contacts there? How was my French? Had I sided with Mr. Chamberlain in 1938? How had I found the Navy? Who were my close friends?

I answered them all without an inkling of the suspicion that, in retrospect, should have been obvious.

"Will you be going back to sea?"

"I suppose that depends on whether I get back to A1 status. Not for a time at any rate."

Then the tall man opened his briefcase and produced a single sheet of paper, which he passed over to me. It was in a foolscap page printed in German with the stylised SS insignia prominent at the head.

There was a moment of silence while they let me examine the document. I realised I was supposed to speak.

"I can't translate it," I said, "but I get the gist; it's a propaganda leaflet perhaps for distribution on the streets?"

"I was more interested in the paper," the smaller man spoke.

I looked at it in more detail, rubbing it between my fingers, and then holding it up to the light. It had a typical Germanic watermark of gothic *Fraktur* stylised script. I had seen similar watermarks in the various mills I had visited in Germany before the war.

"It's a high-quality watermarked plaid rag paper, nothing special. Made in one of a dozen mills on the Ruhr. The watermark is the only unique feature."

He reached into his bag and produced another piece of paper. It was a German ten-mark banknote.

I looked up at them both, turning from one to the other and saw a more intense scrutiny in their focused gaze. They were serious and expectant. I knew I was being tested but was unsure as to what the test involved.

I examined the banknote, folded it, scratched the edge, and then pulled it tight from end to end. I held it up to the light, the eagle watermark was clearly visible. The printing and graphic images were precise but in a monotone. If it was a forgery, it was a very good one.

"Specialist banknote papers are made by only a few producers. It is a much tougher paper and will use a higher proportion of rag or root fibre. In this country all banknotes are made by the de la Rue company. They are an international company, sourcing their pulp and indeed paper, from various countries. This paper could only have been made by three or four manufacturers in Europe. The printing is top quality, the engraving explicit and fine. Whatever is special about this, it would pass muster in anything but the most expert examination."

I looked up. The smaller man, Ellic's, face was now more relaxed, not smiling but with a look of contentment or satisfaction. Avison remained inscrutable, but once again opened his briefcase.

This time he produced a small, folded document, which he passed across to me. It was of four-pages, clearly German, and in the middle of the front was written *Kennkarte*, "identity card." It was covered in dark-green book cloth with a light brown tint plate in the centre spread. Ellic smiled and said with a look of irony, "We are having trouble sourcing this material."

Suddenly things became much clearer.

There was another pause.

I looked at the card more closely. The book-binder's cloth was unusual, and of a weave not used in England. But I'd had dealings with the Winterbottom company in Manchester and was confident that they could match it. I could give Avison their address and be done with it, but even in the unusual situation I found myself in, some commercial sense prevailed.

"This is not difficult to reproduce. I can source the materials for you," I said mustering as much conviction as I could.

"Excellent," Avison said. "We may need other papers in addition."

"I would be happy to help in any way I can."

"Good. Well, the first thing is for you to get well enough for you to be able to come down to the country to talk about how we might be able to work together."

They swiftly gathered up their papers and left me to my principal occupation, which was watching the sparrows play happy families in the shrubbery and chain-smoking Senior Service cigarettes.

A week later a car arrived and drove me to Woburn Abbey, where I found myself being grilled by two pokerfaced officers who instilled the need for absolute secrecy and then got me to sign the Official Secrets Act, mentioning casually that breaches would be treasonous for which the punishment was the death sentence.

The second part of the meeting was with Sefton Delmer, an intense man, focussed and in a hurry. I could tell that I was to be a very small cog in the machinery of his organisation, and I suspected, and indeed was proved to be correct, that I would never meet him again.

"We are needing to produce more and more counterfeit documents," he said in a quiet but measured voice from behind a cluttered desk. He fixed me in an unwavering and disarming gaze. "We have assembled a very skilled team, but sourcing the correct paper is proving a challenge. It's the water marks. I won't need to emphasise how crucial it is that the documents that accompany our agents are spot on. We are thinking that we will have to produce our own paper and need an expert in the field."

The proposal was that I would be transferred from the Royal Navy Volunteer Reserve to the SOE, given the notional rank of sergeant, and would be attached to section XIV working out of Briggens, a country house in Essex. My role was to advise on paper not only for identity cards used by agents working in France and elsewhere, but also in the production of political pamphlets and propaganda. I nodded and mumbled something vaguely positive about it being a privilege to assist the war effort.

It was another three weeks before I made my first visit to Section XIV, making the trip by train to the little station at Royden, showing my letters and papers to the sentry manning the barrier outside the old gatehouse, and struggling up the long drive. I was getting more adept at managing my walking stick with a soft tennis shoe on my right foot but still a slipper on the left, but after ten minutes walking with the house still not in sight, I had to rest. Luckily a truck pulled up and took me the last few hundred yards.

I stiffly clambered out of the high vehicle onto the crunchy gravel and made my way to the grand porticoed door. I was instructed to wait in a chair in the hall, dominated by a superb oak staircase turning up to a galleried landing. Five minutes later I was warmly welcomed by Morton Bisset, the officer in charge, and half an hour after that, while being introduced to staff in the basement, first set eyes on Elisabeth Watson.

CHAPTER 11

....

London

Sunday, August 1, 1948

T hey wake each other up soon after seven with light flooding into the room through the gap in the curtains. There is a chill, and she gets up to close the window. The sky is brooding and grey.

"What would you like for breakfast?" she asks, wrapping herself in her dressing gown. "How about a boiled egg? We may as well eat them before Wendy gets back."

"Perfect, and some more of that delicious coffee, if you have it."

She busies herself in the kitchen and then hears the cello. He is once again wearing the long jellaba, of which she saw no evidence in the night, and sees him sitting erect, leaning into the instrument with the same intense look on his face. This time she recognises the music as one of Bach's solo cello suites. She listens and then moves over to stand behind his chair, places her hands on his shoulders and slides her hands downwards over his clavicles.

He finishes the piece.

"Bravo. How did you know I love that piece so much?"

"Because it's miraculous, beautiful, and perfectly formed—like you."

"Oh yes, and to think that up to now I have believed what you say." She smiles and kisses him on the cheek.

She clears up the breakfast things and dresses. She has no idea what to wear but settles on a cotton skirt with a blouse and cardigan.

She must call her mother. She has been putting it off because she doesn't know what to say and doesn't want to have a long conversation. She knows Mummy will be disappointed that she isn't going to stay as planned, and she will find it difficult to explain the change of plan in a long conversation. In a short one it will be completely impossible.

She plucks up courage and dials the number. She opts for obfuscation and compromise; she has had this wonderful invitation to spend a couple of days in the country with some new friends, one of whom she has "rather fallen for," but will come towards the end of the week instead.

She can hear the disappointment in her mother's matter-of-fact voice, but the enticement of postponement suffices, and they finish the conversation warmly.

"Phew," she sighs, "that's a weight lifted."

Well done," he says, "but perhaps I had better call Mrs. B and tell her to expect us for lunch."

"Mrs. B?"

"The housekeeper."

"The housekeeper? Doesn't she have a proper name?"

"Mrs. Bagley."

"Not a Christian name?"

"I'm sure she does, but I am not sure what it is. Edith or Edna or some such."

"Henry, that's awful!"

"Is it? Oh lord, I hope not. It's just that she has always been Mrs. B—ever since I was a boy. She is as old as Methuselah. Once you start out as Mrs. B you end up always being Mrs. B."

He gathers up his things while she scans her wardrobe for some clothes to take. It is such a meagre collection of outfits, on the face of it the choice should be easy, but she has little idea about what sort of house she is going to. A part of her wants to impress, but that is going to be difficult. Will it be formal? Who will be there? If there is a housekeeper, is there other staff?

Many of the clothes have been made by her or her mother. She had learnt to sew at school, where needlework (taught by her grandmother), like domestic science, was considered at least as weighty as French or geometry. She enjoyed dressmaking and was good enough. Mummy would often give her a length of material, not always what she would have chosen herself, and patterns would be passed around between her friends of styles they liked. There was even a fine old Singer sewing machine somewhere in a cupboard. It was a beautiful machine of black enamel and gold curlicues which lived in a curved wooden box so heavy you could hardly lift it, but it worked well enough.

She finalises her selection, choosing what she considers the most flattering of her slender collection and gets her wash-things from the bathroom. She can't bear to take the douche; Henry will have to sort something. She smiles at the thought that Henry seems so unconcerned about contraception. It's so him to be unconcerned by detail, almost as if there is no connection between making love and having babies!

She zips up the soft bag and is ready. They lock the flat and set off to find Evey.

"I am not sure it's a day for open-topped motoring. I think we should keep the hood up. What do you think?"

"I agree. Wind in your hair is one thing; rain is less appealing."

They squeeze the two bags and Ludwig into the back seat and clamber in.

"Now where are we going?"

"Knowle Stratton."

"So near to Dorchester, you said last night."

"Indeed, four miles."

"And how do we get there?"

"The train goes to Basingstoke, Andover, Salisbury—that sort of way."

"Very precise Mr. Benville. We need to get some petrol, and luckily, I have some coupons. Perhaps we can look at a map at a garage and then plan a route."

They find themselves on the A303 busying along as fast as Evey will allow. The day is gloomy with low clouds but although rain threatens, it holds off and it is not cold.

"Right," she says once they are free from the urban sprawl. "Now I want to know about the man who is dragging me away from London to his mysterious lair in the country."

"I know I have been a bit enigmatic, but I don't find it easy to talk about me and my family."

"Try me."

"All right, the family are French, the name Benville probably an abstraction from bon ville or perhaps bien ville. There are various villages in Northern France with names like Bienvilliers or similar. Anyway, Jean de Benville was one of the Conqueror's henchmen who fought with him at Hastings and, like most of his cronies, was subsequently rewarded with lands—in his case, a few acres in Dorsetshire."

"A few acres?"

"Well quite a few. About three thousand at the time of the rebuilding of the house in 1367. The property continued in pretty much in the same family, waxing and waning in their fortunes and rebuilding or adding to the house at various times. Then my great-grandfather became MP for Dorchester in 1834 was given a peerage for his troubles, so my father became the third Earl Knowle."

He pauses and turns to put his hand on her shoulder. She remains looking ahead, with a barely perceptible nod.

"So that means, when he died, that you inherited the title?"

"That's correct. So, my proper title is the fourth Earl Knowle of Knowle Stratton. But I try to avoid using it, as you will have gathered. I have never taken my seat in the House of Lords.

"Blimey. Well, I guess Evey should feel privileged that you have taken up her seat!"

"Having a title doesn't make you feel any different, and I go out of my way not to abuse the privilege. But it does have advantages. I am a fortunate man and very lucky. I have always been lucky. There were two or three times during the war when I was very lucky. And meeting you is the biggest piece of luck of all."

"I don't believe it. A real lord? I have never met a lord, let alone did what we did last night with one. I knew you were posh, though. I spotted it on the bus."

"On the bus? Was I posh on the bus?"

"You didn't behave posh in the sense of being priggish or toffee-nosed, just I realised that you knew things that posh people know."

"I try not to be too posh. War is a great leveller. I am sure you found this. When you have seen the misery and suffering that man can do to his fellow man, you come to realise that poshness and titles guarantee nothing. You don't mind, do you?"

"Mind? I don't know what I think. I don't think I can mind. I know I am falling in love with you, and I don't have any control of that. What would I do if I mind?"

"Perhaps have nothing more to do with me."

"Mmm, I suppose that is an option. I'll certainly bear that in mind, Your Lordship; I can always turn around and go to see Mummy as planned."

He puts his hand on her knee and turns to look at her, suddenly more serious, and opens his mouth to speak but doesn't say anything.

She glances at him. "Don't worry; you'll get your lift to Dorsetshire. Why did you think I would mind?"

"It's a bit like being famous. You want people to treat you normally, as they would anybody else."

She laughs. "Henry, you are not like anybody else! I don't know much about you, but I know that."

"I want to show you Knowle so you can see my world, see if I can persuade you to share it with me." He pauses and reaches across to touch her arm. "You know I am being serious, don't you?"

She glances across at him and sees a worried, almost pleading anxiety in his pose, coiled as he is in the diminutive space of the Morris.

She smiles again, trying to keep concentrating on her driving. "I know you're being serious Henry, but don't be so serious about it!" She squeezes his hand.

She is grateful to be driving. She is forced to focus on her driving and can't touch him.

....

They reach Dorchester soon after midday and he is now able to direct her and does so with enthusiastic gestures and confidence. She knows he is making a point but says nothing. It continues to be rainy, with heavy low clouds. The wiper on the Morris make little difference to the visibility, transforming the spots of rain into an opaque sheen, and Elisabeth slows, occasionally poking her head out of the open side to get a clearer view of the road. But Henry seems happy enough, animated by their impending arrival. They are now on small country roads with high hedges but happily little traffic.

"Damn," he says. "I had so hoped you would see the house in sunshine. But no worry, maybe it will be brighter tomorrow. Turn left here."

They had been driving along one side of a gentle valley, with woods on the right of the road and a hedge and water meadows on the other. She imagines she can see a river meandering through the valley floor. They turn over the fields towards the stream, which they cross on a narrow humpback bridge with stone parapets. He directs her through a pair of stone gateposts hung with wrought iron gates. They are modest in size but capped with gabled coping stones and, at the front, a coat of arms carved into a stone panel.

"Welcome to Knowle," he says, "my humble abode!"

The drive is tarmac flanked on each side by metal railings. To the right, parkland extends back towards the river they crossed earlier. To the left, the open grassland soon gives way to laurel hedging with a separate drive leading to various structures that she guesses are farm buildings. She continues to peer through the smudgy windscreen to catch a glimpse of the house, which comes into view as they round a left-hand corner. It is long and low and of a pale sandstone, with a taller gable at one end and the roof of the remainder at right angles with a series of small dormer windows cut into the roof, which is of a similar stone to the front. The taller gabled portion is of a different stone, square cut and dressed, whereas the other is more random, with rough surfaces, and looks older. The windows have stone mullions, with the larger ones on the gable protruding somewhat. She guesses that it is Jacobean or even Tudor. The drive opens out to a gravel circle with a stone portico over the front door, with flower beds full of hydrangeas on each side.

It is lovely; not grand in an imposing way, but classy without being overstated, soft, warm, lived in, and private. She stops the car parallel to the building and turns off the engine. She can now look out of the unwindowed side of the car. She just sits and tries to take it all in.

He speaks first. "Well?"

She sits, her hands still on the wheel, taking it all in, the beauty of the house, the perfect setting, the lofty heritage tempered with intimacy, the unassuming quality of the stonework and mullions, a space lived in and loved but subtly grand and imposing. And she can't speak. Instead, tears come, and she finds herself sobbing.

This cannot be for real. This cannot be happening to me. Whatever I have done to deserve this, it must be some mistake, It can never last.

Henry leans over to her. "Elisabeth whatever is the matter. Did I say something to upset you?"

She tries to pull herself together. "You don't have a hanky, do you? I am so sorry. I just find it all a bit overwhelming. You certainly know how to impress a girl."

"Is it that easy?"

"Not with this girl; it's very difficult. But you are doing pretty well so far. It is wonderful, Henry. I don't know what to say. What can I say that wouldn't be trite or cliched?"

She notices that the front door has opened, and a stout white-haired lady is now standing, sheltering from the drizzle under the portico. A fat black Labrador lumbers out, wagging its tail so vigorously that it seems to articulate in the middle of its back. It bounds towards the car. The woman is joined by a younger man, taller, with a full beard and balding head.

Henry flings open the door of Evey and leaps out, failing to shut the door as he greets the exuberant dog.

"Hello Biscuit, old thing. How are you, old fella?" He stands up and hurries the four steps to the porch and hugs the woman, who smiles and laughs, pretending to fight him off. He breaks away from the embrace, standing back to look at her, still holding her on the upper arm. He lets go and shakes the hand of the man vigorously.

Elisabeth gets out of the car more cautiously and hurries the few steps to join them in the shelter of the porch, followed enthusiastically by Biscuit.

"Mrs. B, Malcolm, I want you to meet Elisabeth Watson, who I have by good authority is one of the most wonderful people in the world." His theatrical demeanour matches the enthusiasm of his speech.

Elisabeth shakes them both by the hand, and they move through the massive almost-square oak front door into a wood-panelled hall dominated by a huge stone fireplace surround and an oak staircase that turns through two right angles to a balustraded landing. She smells old leather and dog with a hint of polish and damp. It is an old saddle in a quiet country church.

The hall is cluttered, in the way that such houses are, with the souvenirs and artefacts of a dozen generations. There is a huge ornate hat stand draped with all manner of headgear, dog-leads, and bridles with sticks and crooks at floor level. Then there is the elephant-foot umbrella stand stuffed with brollies of various colours. Either side of the fireplace are two enormous urns that look Chinese, and there are other pieces of porcelain on the mantel and in the window alcoves. A grandfather clock ticks quietly in a corner. On the wooden floor in front of the fireplace is a threadbare oriental rug. The head of a large dead animal with magnificent antlers peers from a side wall.

Mrs. B speaks. "'Tis such a pity about the rain, and it was so fine all week, I was saying to Malcolm yesterday 'I bet it won't hold off for you.' Anyway, not to fret, let's hope it will be better tomorrow. Now would you like lunch straightaway or would you like to put your things in your rooms and freshen up? I have only done cold because I wasn't sure when you would be getting here and what with the short notice and all . . ."

She is cut short by Henry. "Now don't worry about a thing, Mrs. B. If Malcolm can get the things out of the car, I would like to show Elisabeth around just a bit and perhaps have lunch in about half an hour?"

"Of course, Master Chivers, that will be fine," she says, turning to the stairs. She walks with an arthritic waddle, pulling herself up the first few steps. "My poor old knees. Not getting any younger Master Chivers."

Henry turns to follow her, ushering her up the steps in a caring way while turning to raise an eyebrow at Elisabeth, who follows closely behind. "I think you are looking wonderful, Mrs. B. Younger than ever."

"And I wasn't quite sure about the sleeping arrangements either . . ." she says in an attempt at an aside, but clearly audible to Elisabeth. "I thought Miss Elisabeth might like to go in the yellow room. It was your mother's favourite and looks out over the walled garden. I didn't want to put her in the back wing, as the rooms there haven't been aired, but I opened the windows in the yellow room, although Miss Elisabeth might find it a little too breezy." She pauses to catch her breath, having been left gasping by the exertion of climbing the stairs. "Oh, it is nice to have you here Master Chivers. I was only saying to Mrs. Crick the other day how we hadn't seen you for too long. How long would it be? Was it Easter? Don't say it was before that . . ."

Elisabeth climbs the stairs slowly, having to reduce her pace to match that of the breathless Mrs. Bagley, but it enables her to look at the hall and the landing. The walls of the stairs are painted in a light seawater green, not her favourite colour, but most of it is occluded by portraits of people and animals. Above the first rise is a magnificent full-size picture of a woman in an evening dress. It is modern and stylish, with the background seemingly unfinished, but she guesses that is an aspect of contemporary style that she doesn't know about. She surmises that it is Henry's mother and is daunted by her poise and beauty. Then there are several older portraits, some full figures, others just heads, either in hunting apparel or military uniform. She is charmed to find that in amongst the formality are two smaller portraits of dogs, a spaniel and a retriever, and a jolly trio of children. She looks for Henry, but save for the assumed mother, the pictures seem to be from a previous century.

She is shown into the yellow room and any worries about having a separate room from Henry are dispelled by its charm. The walls are covered in a yellow floral paper with silver and white lilies in an informal vertical-striped repeat. In the centre of the room is an enormous bed, twice as high as her own, with a massive mahogany headboard. She wonders how many mattresses it has and whether there is a pea somewhere. Is it a test? Where will Henry be? Perhaps under the mattress as well. She would certainly notice that!

Malcolm brings her bag into the room and Mrs. Bagley bustles across to close the window.

"Will Annelies be joining us for lunch?" Henry asks.

"I called her, but she didn't want to come at such short notice. She suggested you call in for tea."

"Capital idea. Jolly good."

Mrs. Bagley and Malcolm leave, and they are, for the first time, alone. He comes up behind her while she looks out over the formal garden to a meadow beyond. It has stopped raining but is still grey and gloomy. He puts his arms around her neck, draping them down over her breasts. She grabs his wrists and backs into his embrace.

"Isn't she a marvel? Bless her soul. I don't think she has got any older for as long as I've been alive. She was always ancient. Don't worry, darling. I am next door, and I have no intention of sleeping alone. Let me show you." He leads her back to the corridor and doglegs into an arched expansion of the passage with doors on either side. They enter what she imagines is called the principal bedroom. It is vast, being the full width of the gabled newer part of the house with the oriel window at one end. This bed is even bigger and higher than the bed in the yellow room. It is a four-poster, with heavy carved posts in dark wood with drapery hung from the top. The headboard is also ornately carved with figures and foliage; she can tell it is antique but has no idea how old.

"Come and say hello to Guillome de Benville's bed. Allegedly the site of conception of all the Earls since the battle of Hastings.

"What about the ones from the wrong side of the blankets?"

"Well, there have been a few of those, but as my father used to say, they were from a 'different conceptual framework.'"

"What, you mean the stables, or the maid's bedroom?"

"Yes, that sort of thing! But it's rather grand, isn't it? Probably the grandest thing we've got actually. It's also very comfy." He takes her by the hand and springs onto the bed, dragging her beside him."

"My god, I will get lost in it. In the dark I will need a map to find the edge."

He kisses her. And sighs. "It is good to be home. I love it here, Elisabeth. It is so important to me that you like it. I have waited a long time to bring anyone here who I want to share it with. I am a bit nervous, actually."

"You're nervous—what about me? Frankly terrified."

"All right, we can have a nonanxiety pact. I won't tremble if you won't."

She rolls on top of him and grins, putting on an affected voice. "Well, Master Chivers, I think it is all just frightful and I will be on my way presently, but if there is lunch on offer, I might have a bite before I go. Come on, let's eat, I am starving."

....

Lunch is cold mutton, baked potatoes, and salad with pickles and a lump of rustic cheddar cheese. Mrs. B has made a gooseberry fool with fruit from the garden.

The dining room is a dark room, with walls of bottle green hung with sporting prints and a magnificent portrait of a horse. The table is laid for two, but Henry insists that Malcolm and Mrs. Bagley join them. They sit but don't eat. Elisabeth devours the food and the conversation.

Henry is transformed from the man she met only two days before. Gone is the weariness and fatigue, the slightly anxious reserve, the bumbling distraction. Now he is animated and confident, assertive, and assured. He is a clan chief back lording over his turf. He appears tactful and deft in the way he talks to his staff, listening to what they have to say, but on a couple of occasions saying things like, "Well, I'm not sure about that," or "Let's talk about that more later."

It seems Malcolm is a general dogsbody, being gardener, odd job man, driver, and support for the ageing Mrs. Bagley. He is not her son, which Elisabeth had supposed, but a nephew. Further information she does not glean.

After lunch Henry insists on giving her a tour of the house and immediate area before their tea appointment at three-thirty. He drags her through a succession of rooms. First, a formal sitting room with upright French wooden-framed settees which don't look very comfortable, the whole room having a museum-like quality that she doesn't like. Henry assures her that they never use the room and takes her to a much more attractive, smaller sitting room, which he calls "the morning room," with saggy sofas in a faded chintz on either side of a more manageable fireplace. Then onward through a succession of other rooms: the library, the study, and then the music room. It butts out from the main house into the garden, with its own conical tiled roof. It is an unusual shape, like a hexagon but with three of the sides converted to a square, with long French windows on the three smaller sides opening onto terracing and then lawn. It is light and airy, with the square walls lined with shelves which contain piles of music and gramophone records. In the centre is a large grand piano. A table houses a gramophone with a tarnished brass horn. Various other instrument cases are piled in one corner.

He beams. "Isn't it wonderful! It's my favourite room in the house. From here we are going to launch our country house opera." He moves over to the piano, upon which are various piles of music. He thumbs through them before pulling one out. "Perfect. Schubert—it's the precursor to the quintet, the "Trout" for piano and cello. Here is your part." He places the music on the piano. I'll just go and get Ludwig."

"Oh, Henry don't make me play. I am terribly rusty. Please!"

"Don't worry. It's just a bit of fun. I haven't played it for ages. It is not a test." He dashes out the door.

She looks at the music without sitting down, vaguely recalling playing it at some time in the distant past but instantly remembering the main motif. He returns but she still hasn't sat down. He opens the cello case, finds a chair and music stand, and opens the music. He starts tuning Ludwig and then looks at the music. He looks up. "I think you start."

"I really don't want to do this."

"Don't be such a stick-in-the-mud." He looks up at her and, seeing her genuine look of discomfort, puts down the cello and gets up, taking her hands as he fixes her with his grey eyes.

"It is only me. I am not judging you. It is just us. We have to be able to share these things. I honestly don't care if you don't play a single correct note. She looks at his pleading but sympathetic eyes and knows that what he is doing to her nobody else has ever done before, and that he is right. Proper intimacy has to be above embarrassment and self-doubt. She turns and sits, plays a few notes, adjusts the seat, gets the feel of the pedals, and nods to him.

They get through twenty bars before she gets hopelessly tied up in a complex arpeggio and ends with a theatrical discordant clash and shuts the piano lid.

"There. Now, you were showing me round the house."

He looks taken aback, surprised, and disappointed, but then softens.

"Brava! Brava! You did so well. Wasn't it fun? More tomorrow, I think." He puts down the cello. "All right, onward. There is more to see. It has stopped raining, but it is going to be pretty wet under foot. Let's see if there are some boots that fit."

He opens the door of a large walk-in cupboard, smelling of damp and old dog and stuffed with every manner of footwear and they find a pair of riding boots that fit. They leave through a backdoor into a mews and stable area, all in the same sandstone and with large pine doors, their red paint needing renewing. This area backs onto some more agricultural buildings whose open doors reveal various pieces of old farm machinery, then onto a better maintained building, with windows on two floors and a door marked "Estate Office."

"This is the estate office, run very efficiently by Geoffrey Burney and his team. You will meet them tomorrow."

They move on away from the house along a continuation of the drive past a decrepit tennis court. Its net sags, tired and unused, the knotted mesh tearing away from the supporting wire in several places.

They approach a huge barn. Unlike the house, the roof is old pantiles, and the walls are stone up to about head height, with black painted feather-edge timber above. In the middle of the long frontage an eve projects with two huge timber doors.

Henry opens the metal hasp and heaves one of the doors open. It is dark inside, but some light comes in from the open door and various chinks and gaps in the roof. She has never seen as big a timber-framed building. It takes a few moments to adapt to the darkness but then she can make out the massive supporting oak posts, at least eighteen inches square, coursing aloft into the cobwebbed roof space. Nothing is completely straight, the rafters sagging under the weight of the roof and the purlins bowing with years and weather. Graceful trusses brace the angles between the uprights and the horizontal beams. The timbers are soft and worn, as if they grew in situ. The building is like a slumbering giant, unwelcoming to intruders, and initially she feels uncomfortable entering the sacred space in its guardianship. It is ancient and carries secrets that she isn't sure she is allowed to share. It is largely empty, although she can't see into the dark corners, but at one end an old carriage thick with dust leans on three wheels. She smells hay and animals in the heavy air.

"This is the tithe barn, and if you really want to know, it has one of the best king post roofs in Dorset, and it is where we are going to put on the operas. Don't you think it would be wonderful? Such an evocative space. The stage goes here." He dashes into the bay and turns to face her, spreading his arms wide and moving forward. "The orchestra here . . . we might have to rearrange the entrance a bit."

She can't imagine how this dark, smelly, slightly sinister building could ever be the home to opera, although she has never been to one. She listened to Figaro at school and knows some of the Mozart arias, as well as the Bizet orchestral piece from Carmen, but this old agrarian building? Opera? When she thinks of opera she thinks of Vienna and pearl-wearing women in long dresses and men in evening dress.

"I don't know. I have never been to the opera. Not quite what I imagined. What are the acoustics like?"

He moves to the end where he anticipates the stage would be and starts to sing. "O sole mio . . ."

"Mmm not sure about that. Might be the acoustics; might be the voice."

"All right, you sing then."

"But I don't know any opera."

"Anything will do."

They change places and she starts. "Early one morning, just as the sun was rising—"

"Magnificent, next week La Scala."

"Henry Benville, has anybody told you that you are a bit loopy?" She walks up to him and stands directly in front of him, leaning forward to kiss him.

"Often, but I take no notice of those voices; it's part of the condition. The voices that I listen to are mine and nobody else's."

"So not mine then?"

"You are not nobody."

She smiles. "You know I am falling in love with you."

"Promise? Thank you, Elisabeth. It's what I want more than anything in the world."

"More than tithe barn opera?"

"Not sure about that."

"You pig. You will be—I will make you."

They leave the barn and continue to explore the gardens and grounds, Henry taking Elisabeth to his childhood hiding places: the overgrown walled garden, the secret summer house, and a collapsing icehouse. She tries to take it all in but cannot imagine ever being a part of such a landscape. It isn't allowed; it is too grand, too indulgent. It is not her place in the world. But then another voice asks could it be for real—just possibly?

"It is time for tea. We had better go and see Anneliese."

"She is your stepmother, is that correct?"

"Yes. She lives in the dower house at the rear gate. It is only about five minutes' walk, but we can drive if you like."

"No, I'm happy walking. Do we have to dress up?"

"Lord no. Anneliese may not have even got dressed."

They amble along the continuation of the drive, one side a hedge with woodland beyond, the other estate railings with meadows down to the meandering river. She finds his hand, different from the walk in London on the way home from the Prom. Now no one is watching;

there are no rules.

The dower house is of Victorian brick, with gables and elaborate soffits and ornate ridge tiles and hips. It is adjacent to a second gate that opens onto a lane surrounded by a simple garden, tended but unloved. Henry goes to the backdoor, which he pushes open.

"Hallo! Ich bin es." There is no reply, but a dog starts yapping.

He walks in with Elisabeth following, leading her through a primitive kitchen, cluttered and shambolic, through a hall and then pushing at a closed door, the other side of which a dog is barking and scratching. As he opens the door a small pug squeezes through, yapping even more vociferously. It growls and snarls, hideous and terrifying. It only has one eye, which bulges unhealthily from the folds of its compressed face. She recoils and holds Henry's arm as it dances around them, barking and snapping.

A voice from inside the room calls, "Tristan, ruhig, kommen sie hierher."

Henry opens the door gingerly, and they move into a small sitting room, followed by the still-barking dog. Anneliese is sitting in a high armchair by an electric fire, the elements of which glow red. The room is stifling and airless with all the windows closed. She has a fat, pasty face, heavily made up with a dusting of pink powder. She wears no lipstick, so her lips look pale in contrast to her cheeks. The hair is white, tainted with yellow and piled up on her head like a cottage loaf. Next to her chair there is a cigarette in an amber holder smouldering in an overfull ashtray on a small occasional table, which is cluttered with dirty glasses, a tortoiseshell cigarette case, and a decanter containing amber liquid. She is wearing a cotton quilted garment that could be a housecoat or a dressing gown. From beneath it emerges white calves descending into puffy, featureless ankles. On her feet are blue velvet slippers.

"Tristan halt. Hor auf! Hallo, Hallo, Vilcomen." She doesn't get up, beckoning with her arm.

Henry moves across the room towards her and, taking her pudgy hand, pecks her on the cheek.

"Leelee, can I introduce you to Elisabeth Watson, a friend of mine from London."

Elisabeth moves forward to shake hands. Anneliese looks her up and down. She pauses before speaking, the judgement process obvious and painful.

"You have nice hair. Mine was like that once but blonder. Now pfff." She waves her hand. "Now all gone . . . So, you take the trouble to come to see me, ya? Take a moment from the city party life to see the country cousin, eh. Shall we have tea, ya?" The German accent is very pronounced. "Or a sherry. Or perhaps a gin? Vot time is it, Henry, is it drinks time? Sit. Sit." She waves her arm vaguely across the cluttered room.

"Tea will be just fine, thank you," Henry says. "So, Leelee how are you? Are you getting out a bit?"

"Terrible, terrible. And this weather doesn't help. I haven't been out for three days. Sit, sit."

Elisabeth takes the only chair not covered by clothing or detritus, an upright wooden dining chair with an upholstered seat, on which she perches awkwardly. The pug ceases its barking and moves to Anneliese's feet. She stretches out an arm and scoops the creature onto her lap.

She glances around the room. It is not that small but seems so because it is so full of furniture, none of which matches in style or decoration. All the surfaces are covered with a random collection of bric-a-brac, ornaments, folded clothing, magazines, boxes, and chaotic clutter. On a sideboard is a silver salver containing bottles of spirits and other cordials that she can't recognise. On the walls are various pictures that she can only describe as tacky, sentimental landscapes in garish colours, and semiabstract figurative works. More than one of them hangs at an angle, something that always annoys her. The room is horrid, claustrophobic, and oppressive. How could anyone live like this?

"Shall I make the tea?" Henry volunteers.

"Ya bitte. Danke."

"Elisabeth can tell you all about her exciting life in London," he says, getting up and heading back to the kitchen.

She panics. How cruel and mean of Henry to leave her alone. She racks her brain to find something to say. Anneliese sits opposite stroking the dog, studying her in a manner both judgemental and condescending and then tilts her head back and takes a drag from the cigarette in its elaborate holder.

Her appearance is shocking; she looks old and ill. Could she have a medical condition, or does she not look after herself? Probably the latter. Henry said she was only eighteen years older than he is. She doesn't know how old Henry is, but she would guess early thirties. How can this broken woman still be only in her forties? She looks again at the room. Is there something she can complement her on? She notices a display case containing some dolls with porcelain faces. They are probably the nicest thing in the room.

"I love your dolls; do you collect them?" She gets up to look at them more closely.

"Nein. Not now."

"Where are they from?"

"Ach. Here and there." She takes a puff of her cigarette and then stubs it out in the chrome-plated free-standing ashtray on the other side of her chair. She pushes the black button in its centre which spins the base, and the butt disappears into the container beneath.

Elisabeth returns to her chair. The silence hangs like a leaden blanket.

Anneliese reaches to the small table next to her chair and takes another cigarette from the tortoiseshell case. She loads it into the holder with yellowed fingers. She doesn't offer one to Elisabeth but fixes her intently and peers at her, moving her head forward and screwing up her eyes.

"So, you are Henry's latest fancy girl. Where did he pick you up?"

Elisabeth reels, shocked and startled. Her normal reaction would be to give as good as she gets, but she doesn't want to upset Henry. But then again, he shouldn't have left her with this unkind woman. Now she is cross with him as well.

"I picked him up, actually, on the street, where I pick up most of my men."

"Ya, good answer. Ven is your birthday?"

"August."

"Vot day?"

"The twenty-sixth."

"Ah Virgo. Mmm. So, perfectionist, fussy too. You will be hard to please, but there are worse. Not good for a bogenschutz.

"I am sorry, I don't understand."

"The archer. Sagittarius."

"I am afraid I don't know anything about astrology."

"No, zat doesn't surprise me." Anneliese turns away, pulling on her cigarette as she looks blankly through the grubby panes of the French windows." The pug remains on her lap, its audible breathing punctuated by snorts and grunts. Occasionally its tongue snakes out to lick her hand.

Elisabeth shivers and turns away, unable to watch the unseemly pas de deux. She is now more content to ride the silence. She decides not to try any more, wanting only to distance herself from her discomfit, willing Henry to return. The kettle whistles and then quietens. Surely, he can't be long now.

"Do you listen to the wireless?" Elisabeth says, struggling for a bland commonality.

"Ya a little."

"Music?"

"Sometimes."

"I like the new third programme. Have you heard it? What sort of music do you like? Austrian music?"

Finally, Anneliese's mask-like mien creases with the semblance of a smile. "Ah the waltzes. Strauss. I love all the Strauss': the Younger, the Older. Ach how ve used to dance . . ." Her voice tails off.

At last Henry reappears with a tray with a tarnished silver teapot, milk jug, and cups. There is no surface to put it on. Elisabeth jumps up but is unclear how to help. With Anneliese's direction, she moves a box and some folded clothes from a Pembroke table making just enough room to slide the tray onto it.

"Now, who is going to pour?" Henry says.

"One person only," Anneliese replies. "Otherwise you will have babies."

Henry chuckles. "Is that right, Leelee? We don't want that now, do we? Perhaps I had better do it."

He clatters as he arranges the cups in their saucers, hindered by the lack of space, and awkwardly balances the tea strainer on the cups. Elisabeth is sure something will tip over.

"No milk for you, Leelee, that's right, isn't it?" He moves across to hand her a cup.

"No cake," Anneliese says. Elisabeth is unsure whether it is a statement or a question.

Henry brings another chair across the room from under a dining table and sits. The silence still hangs heavy over the room.

"So, has Elisabeth been telling you all about herself?" Henry manages a smile, but Elisabeth can see that even his resilient bonhomie is strained by the bizarre set-piece they are a part of.

"No. But I learned she is a Virgo. I guessed it. Not so good with a Sagittarian, ya."

"There's an exception to every rule," Henry says. "Do you follow astrology, Elisabeth?"

"I've never paid it much attention. My Nan always reads the horoscope in magazines and the local paper. It gives her comfort and an explanation for life's troubles, I think."

They sip their tea.

"Now, are you getting out enough Leelee? You know it doesn't do you any good sitting here alone. Have you been to town lately?"

"What is there for me to do? No opera or decent music." She spits out the word *opera* in three syllables.

"I thought we might go in tomorrow. Why don't you come? We might have lunch at the Casterbridge or the Kings Arms. You would like that wouldn't you?"

"Maybe I think about it. Perhaps if the weather improves."

Henry chats on about local things, often speaking in German and then correcting himself, reverting to English when he glances at Elisabeth.

They finish their tea and Anneliese declines more. Elisabeth prays that Henry will think it is time to leave.

"All right, Leelee. Well, we must be getting on. It's nice to see you. Have a think about tomorrow. I will phone in the morning to see if you are feeling up to it. Pass auf dich auf mein schatz."

Elisabeth says her goodbye and now safe and able to see the pity of the situation, warmly squeezes Anneliese's hand, which remains on the arm of her chair.

They escape to the overcast skies of rural Dorset.

"Phew," she says.

"I am sorry. It's terrible, isn't it? Pathetic really. I didn't want to tell you too much before."

"So sad. She's like an old lady. I was jolly cross you left me with her, couldn't think of a single thing to say, and she was jolly rude. But my anger is dissipated by the pathos."

"I am sorry. I couldn't really ask you to make the tea, and she wasn't going to do it."

"Forgiven, but you have to tell me the full story."

CHAPTER 12

Cap d'Ail, Var, France
July 1992

The next morning, I was up earlier than usual and packed a few items of clothing in a valise. I put in the volume of *Undine*'s logbook for 1948 but could think of nothing else of relevance that I might need to take.

As I was preparing to leave, Therese appeared earlier than usual. She had been to the boulangerie and made me a sandwich of *jambon cru* and tomato.

She has been good to me, Therese, probably better than I deserve. She doesn't have a husband; he left many years before she started working for me, but she does have an ineffectual son, who although apparently employed in some role working night shifts at the hospital, is mostly to be seen hanging out with a group of layabouts in a bar on the promenade playing *babyfut.*

I have only been to her apartment on two or three occasions, just to drop her off or pick her up. It is a grimy three-storey prewar apartment block off the Corniche, with a tiny balcony overlooking a jumble of buildings down towards the beach. The entrance is unappealing, with terrazzo flooring and stark grey walls without a hint of decoration or embellishment.

Her concern was touching as she saw me into the car and waved goodbye. We are so set into a routine that I sensed she was genuinely perturbed by my departure.

I reached Paris by late afternoon, fatigued by the volume of traffic, to which I was unaccustomed, and the concentration needed to fend-off the camions. I wanted to avoid Paris itself and the terrors of the périphérique, so reverted to the routes nationales and found a hotel in Beauvais, pleased that I had broken the back of the journey.

Of course, I thought about her.

....

The days after Elisabeth's departure were horrible, but as with grief, in the immediacy of her leaving, at first, I couldn't accept that she had gone. What is the term? Denial I believe. More disbelief, in my experience. I kept finding excuses for her behaviour, putting on her the blame and convincing myself that she would come to her senses and realise that she had made a huge error and that her future really lay with me on board *Undine*. I still expected a message saying that she had made a terrible mistake and would rejoin the boat in Monte Carlo.

Jose was much more realistic and circumspect.

"No good for you, that lady, Pom. She not made for boats."

I walked into the Hotel Negresco and asked for a piece of paper and an envelope. As I expected, the concierge handed over a sheet of headed notepaper without a murmur. I sat in the lobby and penned a letter to Elisabeth. I cannot remember exactly what I wrote, but I know I said I still loved her and something along the lines of "When you look at your options, I am sure you will realise that we can have a wonderful life together here." The concierge gave me a stamp, refusing to accept any money, and even offered to put the letter in the hotel post.

I realised that she had gone home and was unhappy, but I never thought for one second that I would never see her again. I just went on thinking the same about her as I had before, loving her with a blind, blinkered passion that ignored her part of the partnership. I assumed that we would see each other again, maybe not that year, but sometime, and then it would all be fine, and we would end up together.

Bloody fool.

....

We reverted to an all-male boat. I was the captain, and we went where I wanted. We ate simple food and enjoyed exhilarating night sails and evenings in portside bars. Gradually, through word of mouth and friends of friends, it became known that the boat was available for charter and skippering *Undine* was my life for the next twenty years. We went everywhere. The Mediterranean was wonderful then. The coast of Italy: Elba, Ventotene, and the spectacular Capri. The Aeolian islands, the Adriatic, the Cote d'Azure, then into the Ionian. You can see a lot in twenty years.

In many ways these were joyful days: freedom, a fine boat, Mediterranean weather and cuisine, life on the ocean. It was marvellous; but for me there was always one thing missing.

The first winter I spent in Taormina in Sicily, and strangely, that's where I wrote my book.

Byron Lieberman was a New Yorker and wasn't reticent about broadcasting the fact. He was a writer, or so he insisted on telling his audience, working on a memoir. Before the war he had been a journalist and, if caught before midday or in the early hours of his imbibition, was lucid and persuasive, but with a view of the world that had been irretrievably damaged by the war and the evils of power. He was a cynic, an anarchist, a pacifist, and a practising Catholic.

It was he who suggested I start writing, even buying me a ruled child's exercise book and a pack of pencils with rubber erasers on the end, which he insisted was the only way to work. It started with long dark evenings telling stories of our wartime experiences in the relative warmth of the Club or in one of the neighbouring bars.

"But I have never written anything," I protested. "I was useless at English at school; I can't string two words together."

"Bullshit! Goddam it, you can tell a story, can't you? I've heard you make good telling the truth. Think how easy it is when you make it up."

"But what would I write about?"

"Write what you know. Jeez you went through enough in the North Atlantic. Write about that."

So, I started writing some stories in pencil in an exercise book in a chilly cabin in a boatyard in Sicily. One night, after a bottle of Sicilian vino rosso, I was persuaded to read to Byron and a congregation, including several confused local fishermen, a tale of the frozen Arctic. Afterwards I was stunned to find that, those who spoke English at least, were appreciative and moved by my simple, unembellished account. Byron leant me his Remington typewriter, and with his encouragement and editing, the pages were shaped into a manuscript that became *Convoy North*.

By the end of 1951 my manuscript was as good as it was ever going to be, and I returned to Blighty in December. And in that strange week between Christmas and the new year, I met Charlie Wilkerson for lunch at the Royal Ocean Racing Club. He was the only publisher I knew and was frank in his scepticism about my volume but agreed to get it read by one of his commissioning editors.

I suppose we were both surprised when we met for a second lunch two weeks later at his venue (the Royal Yacht Club in Knightsbridge) when he confirmed that, although it needed some work, they liked the story and would publish. He suggested an editor who would tidy up my clunky prose, and we would aim for publication later that year.

Convoy North appeared in the spring of 1952. It sold well and then out of the blue, there was talk of a film, and rights were sold for what I thought was an unbelievable amount of money. I didn't really need much to live on in those days, but friends insisted I do something vaguely sensible, so I bought the apartment on Cap d'Ail.

Later there was a second book which sold modestly on the back of the first, but they didn't publish the third. Within ten years I was a literary has-been. I was never a proper writer, just a sailor who had some gruelling experiences and jotted them down in pencil in an exercise book. I had said everything I had to say.

....

I arrived in Portsmouth in the early evening of the sixteenth of July and headed for Lymington, from where we had set out all those years ago. Although it was high season, I was sure I would find a room somewhere and indeed that proved to be the case, with the Ship Inn being very happy to look after me and provide an evening meal. Already I was glad I had come.

CHAPTER 13

....

Henry and Elisabeth stroll back to the big house after taking tea with Leelee. Henry is talking as he loosely holds her hand, swinging her arm idly.

"My mother had a very difficult time with her pregnancies. She had at least two miscarriages before she had me, and I gather that she had to spend most of her pregnancy with me in bed. Afterward it was the same story; she desperately wanted another child but had two more miscarriages. The doctors said it wasn't a good idea to have another baby, but she was very determined. She became pregnant again when I was three and half and was told that it was crucial that she stay in bed. She became sicker and sicker with eclampsia. Of course, I don't remember any of this, but the time came when her local doctors feared that unless they delivered the baby she would die. An eminent obstetrician was sent for from London, who opined that the only course of action was an immediate Caesarean section. The problem was she was only seven months into the pregnancy. She was rushed into Dorchester hospital and underwent surgery. She did make it through the op but died three days later. My brother survived just a few hours.

"How simply awful Henry. Can you remember her?"

"I have just the haziest recall of her in the yellow room, on that lovely bed, surrounded by pillows and being allowed to have high tea with her, sitting up next to her with my own little tray. The trouble with memories from such an early age is that you are not sure if you are remembering the event or remembering the story of the event."

"Is that her portrait on the stairs?"

"Yes, it is, by de Laszlo. Do you like it?"

"She was very beautiful."

"De Laszlo was very good at making people look beautiful, that's why he was so popular—but I think she was. I will show you some photographs."

They have been ambling along the drive back to the main house. He has his hands in his pockets, distant, distracted. She tucks her hand in the crook of his arm.

"I do remember the terror and disbelief at being told by my father that she was not coming back from the hospital. In my rational four-year-old mind I just could not see a logical reason why she would not come back. Death was too big and too final a construct to comprehend. If it was about waiting, I thought I could wait. What was the problem? Never—that doesn't mean much to a four-year-old. When was the day that I finally realised she wasn't going to come home? I can't remember."

"How did your father cope?"

"How that generation coped I suppose. What I got was a mantra of being *tough* and *strong*, exhortations about being a man, pulling through together, keeping the show on the road, and that nonsense. It was a charade, but it was how he dealt with it. I suspect that he was devastated. I do recall one night being troubled by a nightmare and walking along the corridor to his room and hearing a strange noise. I pushed open his door and he was kneeling by the bed sobbing. Like most small boys I had never seen my father weep and found it terrifying, as if the world was going to end."

"Was he religious?"

"Not especially. I don't think he believed in God."

"But desperate people do pray, don't they? When they have no other recourse."

"Yes, I suppose that's right. Until things get even worse, and they reject God because he didn't listen . . . By all accounts they had a good marriage. In some situations, childlessness can drive couples apart, but I think with them her difficulties pulled them together. I think she was a very loving person. Her sister, my aunt, was very good to me. Still is actually! I had a governess while Mama was ill, and she stayed until I was packed off to school."

"So how did he meet Anneliese?"

"That's the Austrian side of the family. My grandfather's sister married into a big Austrian family called Kriegstein. We're talking 1860s or thereabouts. The result was that my grandfather used to spend holidays in St. Georgen, which is quite near Salzburg, and the families became quite close. My father spent lots of long holidays there as a boy, playing with the numerous cousins, who all descended on a crazy country estate on the banks of Lake Obersee. After Mama died Father thought it would be better for me to spend holidays with the Kriegsteins rather than mooching around here on my own. ."

"And you learnt to speak German."

"Ya! But it was more than that. I never felt like an only child. In the summers, there were maybe six other boys and eight girls, and I became one of them. We did all the things children and teenagers did, but in a privileged Austrian family rather than a privileged English one. I had a Germanic childhood; their food, their language, their social manners and priorities, their clothing."

"Mmm leather shorts?"

"Yes, somewhere in the cupboard!"

"And then your dad met Anneliese?"

"No, he had known her before. She wasn't quite one of our gang, as she was that bit older, but I can remember her from my earliest trips to Schloss Migberg. She had been engaged to a nice younger son of an Austrian count who then died of typhoid. She was terribly affected, retreated into herself, and then, as far as other suitors were concerned, ended up on the shelf.

"Who fell for who?"

"I think Anneliese had always liked my father but saw him as an uncle. Then Father noticed this sad twenty-eight-year-old, and one thing led to another, and suddenly they were engaged. She was very pretty, mind."

"Yes, strangely I could see that. Even in the miserable state she is in now, you can glimpse a beauty in the features."

"With his attention, her affection for him as a kindly English family friend transmuted into a love of sorts. I think she saw him as her best chance, albeit that he already had a son. I was twelve when they got married. Until then nothing changed. I still spent a lot of time in Austria and was happy with Father when we were alone here at Knowle. I started to do boys things with him like shooting and fishing. I had learnt to ride in Austria but was given my own pony and started to hunt. We were very close and contented. Mrs. B looked after us and I, at least, didn't miss a mother figure in the house."

They reach the house, and he opens the front door. "I am sorry I have been doing all the talking. I told you it was long and complicated. Do you want to talk about something else?"

"No, it's important I know about these things. I suppose most grand old families are a bit complicated. Skeletons in the cupboard and all that."

"Not so much of the grand! I don't think it is only old families that are complicated. Shall we go into the morning room?"

"But isn't there an afternoon room?" she says smiling.

"Ha ha. Funnily enough we use the morning room much more in the afternoon. It's much nicer than the sitting room."

They reenter the house, leaving their boots at the door. Henry guides her to the morning room, where she flops down on the sofa. Biscuit barges through the door and makes his presence felt, nosing up to her and demanding a pat. She leans forward, her skirt riding up her thigh.

"Have I told you that you have fabulous legs?"

She tries to look demure and wriggles to pull the skirt down.

"How about more tea? Shall we have another cuppa? I'll go and see what I can rustle up."

Elisabeth thumbs through the pile of magazines on the low table. There is *The Field* and *Country Life,* both from the previous year, and a couple of older copies of *Picture Post* and *Punch*. Biscuit tries to join her on the sofa, putting his front paws on the cushion beside her.

"Now Biscuit, I am not sure that is allowed," she says, pushing him away.

Henry returns, at which point Biscuit immediately desists and curls up in front of the fender.

"On its way. Mrs. B has made a cake! She is a wonder." He sits down on the opposite sofa.

"You were going to finish the story."

"You have seen the pitiful end to the story. Father brings his new bride to rural Dorset. She speaks minimal English. She fits into life here like a pig in a synagogue and all Father's friends think of her as a bit of fluff and don't even try to take her seriously. I am a sulky teenager resentful of having to share my father's attention with someone I thought of as an older sister, and then four years later he drops down dead while stalking in Scotland."

"Why didn't she go back home?"

"Well of course that's what she should have done, but she felt she had a duty as his widow. She was chatelaine to the house, and I think she wanted to step up to the plate, but she was only thirty-five and it was a world totally alien to her. She really didn't have a clue, and then there was me. She wanted to be a mother to me, largely out of duty, although we had always had a kindly sisterly relationship, but I was at Winchester and for the first time started making proper friends and didn't need her or respect her in a maternal role. Although we did go back to Schloss Migberg after Father's death, she didn't fit in there either. Then the Nazis started their mischief and after the Anschlus in 1938, it was impossible to go back. I went off to Oxford and was sucked into a life of hedonism and frippery. We can be cruel and self-centred at that age. And then the war proper came, and she was completely alone, vilified as being a Hun, which was cruel, unnecessary, and damaging. Ignorance is such a damnable thing . . ."

He pauses. Elisabeth catches the break in his voice and sees the sadness that washes across his face. It was that same look that had struck her so the first evening, something deep felt and truly from the heart. She doesn't say anything but gets up and sits next to him, putting a hand on his knee.

He looks up at the ceiling. "Ach zo. Nien matter. The sorrowful thing is that she was so talented and lovely. I understand why Father fell for her. It's a bit like Marie Antoinette or some such. A young wife out of her depth in a foreign country. She was a very good painter, sang, played the flute."

"Are those pictures on the wall hers?"

"Yes, but they are awful. Somewhere there are some very competent watercolours. Her angst emerged in her art. I just don't know how to help her now."

"Why Leelee?"

"She was always Leelee. I think it was a younger brother who couldn't manage the three syllables of Anneliese."

There is a crescendo of rattling from outside of the door, which opens with Mrs. B pushing a tea trolley.

They both get up.

"Here you are, Miss Elisabeth. I made a cake 'specially. It's a sponge with homemade jam. I hope that's orright," she says, turning back through the door.

"I am sure it will be delicious. Thank you, Mrs. B."

Henry reaches to the lower layer of the trolley to extract the cake and places it on a side table. "I will cut the cake. I have a special technique for cutting cakes."

"I could have guessed. Like scotch eggs?" she asks.

"Not dissimilar." He puts on his now-familiar lecturing voice.

"The thing is, most people try to cut cake equally, but in my great experience of cakes people tend to want different-sized portions. Therefore, the answer is a Fibonacci sequence; it's a mathematical progression where each piece gets a bit bigger. Let me show you." He picks up the knife and cuts a small slice, then one a bit larger, then one a bit larger still. He leaves a third of the cake uncut. "It's not quite accurate, but it will do." He looks up proudly.

"And which piece is yours?"

"Guess," he says, grinning.

"Henry, you are not going to have half the cake!"

"Of course not. Not in company."

She laughs. How quickly he jumps from the emotional trough of his stepmother's plight to a nutty theory about cutting cakes. She looks at his long lean body and the fop of blond hair, and realises she is hungry to kiss him again and touch him properly, but also knows that she loves the way his brain works, and that this is new for her, to be expectant and thrilled by what someone says and to want them naked as well. It is as delicious as the cake.

They finish their tea.

"Have you shown me all of the house?" she asks demurely.

He raises his eyebrows, seeming unclear about the question, but doesn't respond.

"I just wondered whether there were some interesting prints or artefacts in some of the bedrooms that you haven't shown me." There is a glint in her eye. She gets up smiling, grabs his arm, and pulls him off the sofa.

"Ah yes, indeed," he says. "I think there possibly are. Some important family jewels only rarely seen . . ."

"Let me guess . . . I think I know where I might find them!"

She pulls him close and kisses him, reaching down to the front of his trousers.

He drags her with a new-found urgency out of the room and up the stairs.

"Careful of the creaky step," he says. "It's number thirteen. Unlucky for some."

"What about along here? I am sure there must be something special to see in here." She twists the handle of a door off a corridor.

"Not much in there—only trunks and old pictures, but there might be something of interest in here."

And two minutes later they are naked on a 17th century Lit Bateaux, creasing the ancient French counterpane with their writhing bodies.

CHAPTER 14

Although very different from the town that I had left forty-five years before, Lymington was still recognisably a sailor's town, and the charm of the harbour side and high street were preserved. I slept well, finding the mewing of the seagulls as charming and natural as others might the noisy screaming of a school playground. Seagulls don't recognise national boundaries; I could easily have been in Taormina.

After a decent breakfast, at which I allowed myself the indulgence of bacon and eggs, I rang the offices of Smallwood and Lees. Alas, I was informed that Mr. Smallwood was not going to be in the office that day but could see me on the morrow. Mildly annoyed, I arranged an appointment at eleven-thirty and looked forward to a day exploring Lymington.

I found the high street more commercial than I had remembered, populated with shops selling trinkets and fripperies, and things I couldn't imagine anyone ever needing. I walked through the town, and then on to the marina, thinking I would luncheon at the yacht club.

Most of the boats in the marina were modern fibreglass vessels— ugly, albeit spacious and efficient. There were too many motor cruisers— vulgar, ostentatious, and charmless. There were three older wooden vessels and one lovely boat: *Berenice*, a fine ketch with a beautiful line not unlike *Undine*, that I had encountered in the Mediterranean. Then, tucked away in a corner looking very unloved, crouching under a tarpaulin, was a little Norfolk day boat by Hunter of Ludham.

And that took me back to a weekend spent with Elisabeth on the Norfolk Broads in 1941.

....

Briggens was the home of Lord and Lady Aldenham, a substantial nineteenth century country house of pale sandstone, set in fifty acres of parkland on the borders of Hertfordshire and Essex. It had been requisitioned early in the war as a training school for the Polish army in exile, with the recruits housed in Nissen huts erected in the grounds. At first, they had been very much left to their own devices, but their work had necessitated the production of counterfeit documents, and the ever-resourceful Poles had installed basic printing presses and photographic equipment in the basement. They soon commenced the production of a range of papers and passes necessary for their rudimentary espionage. They recruited from amongst their ranks men whose past dalliances, in pursuits not entirely lawful, were of great relevance to deeds nefarious. Happily for them, their habits and police records mattered not in the context of a global conflict and an army in exile.

I learnt all this from Morton Bisset as he sat me in his office on the ground floor of the building, overlooking what had been formal gardens, but were now given over to prefab huts, a sports and exercise area with assault course, and other paraphernalia of military training. A woman wearing the uniform of the First Aid Nursing Yeomanry bought us tea, who he thanked with a warm smile.

"You have some FANYs seconded then?" I said, with possibly too much enthusiasm.

"Couldn't do without them. Terrific women—to the man," he said with a guffaw.

He was a congenial man, with an endearing but asymmetric smile which gave the impression that he viewed everything with a sense of irony. He had undertaken an apprenticeship with Waterlows printers, one of the biggest and most respected companies in the country and knew all there was to know about every type of printing. He never appeared to be under pressure, even clearly when he was, always tackling the issues that arose with humour and tact. I came to respect him greatly. He somehow managed to keep the brilliant but disparate nonmilitary staff focussed and functioning despite their artistic temperaments and the lack of a normal military rank and hierarchy. He later described it as trying to train peacocks.

"So, Mackay, the rules are simple: secrecy is paramount. Nobody outside of this building must know what we do. That means no chat in the pub or on a train, none. Do I make myself clear? Within these four walls we work as a team. You will be answerable to me and to your section leader Major Roberts. Your role will, I appreciate, involve a lot of toing-and-froing, and will require deception and imagination when it comes to explaining to providers why we need what we do. The volumes will be small, though, so hopefully they can be slipped through your most trusted contacts. Invoices for this work should be brought directly to me and will be paid monthly. Now the other thing to mention is that I do understand that you are not yet fully fit. You still seem quite shaky. How are your hands?"

"Improving, but still numb and clumsy."

"Good. I am glad they are on the mend. It would be extremely helpful if you could start work, even on limited hours, while your fitness improves. Where are you living?"

"Still at my parent's home in Epping; it's not that far."

"How is the travel?"

"Train, with a walk either end."

"Not ideal, given I see you still need a stick. We have several staff billeted in Hunsdon. It should be possible to find you a room there if you need it. I will talk to Sergeant Percival about it, he is IC billeting.

Now, if you are ready, let's go and have a look at what we do. I will introduce you to Charles Roberts and the rest of the team."

He led me down a corridor off which was an alcove with a manned security desk and a large sign saying Passes Must Be Shown, behind which stairs curved downward. The soldier got up at our approach but didn't salute.

"Morning Wilson, this is Peter Mackay. He is with me for today. We will get him a pass later."

"Right sir."

We walked down a turning staircase to the basement, entering a long, arched corridor running the length of the building. Off this passage were a range of rooms of various sizes, some at the rear quite large and lit by windows in wells cut into the ground, others smaller with no natural light. I was led past various rooms occupied by large pieces of equipment, some of which I recognised, others I didn't. There were printing presses of various shapes and sizes and photographic equipment. Some of the rooms were occupied by men, mostly not in uniform, but some wearing khaki work coats.

I was seeing for the first time the engine room of what Ellic Howe called "the Black Game," the unassuming, eclectic posse of artists, printers, photographers, lithographers, linguists, and editors (about to be joined by a sailor who knew a little bit about paper), who had become the war government's officially sanctioned forgers. Forgers of incomparable skill and imagination, whose talents, commitment, and attention to detail produced all the important counterfeit documents and propaganda for the remainder of the war, saving hundreds of lives in the process. And here it was, under the perfect cover of a sleepy English country house, a bunch of non-English speaking squaddies doing calisthenics in the garden, while in the basement a brilliant and secret unit produced impeccable forgeries and nobody knew about it, then or now.

Morton knocked on the open door of an office labelled Captain Charles Roberts. The occupant sat at a desk which was almost bare save for a few papers and accoutrements arranged in perfect symmetry and all at right angles. Similarly, the shelves and walls were tidy and perfectly ordered, with not a volume or folder out of place.

"Charles, this is Peter Mackay." He stood by the door ushering me in.

"Welcome Peter, come on in." He held out his hand. "Charles Roberts." He was a neat, clean-shaven man with tortoise shell glasses and a baby-like complexion wearing an immaculate uniform, with trousers pressed to razor sharp creases, lapping over highly polished shoes.

Morton continued, "Righty-ho, I will leave you two to it."

"Tell me how you know about paper?" he said, indicating a chair while settling himself back behind his desk.

I explained the family business and my travels in Europe before the war.

"Very interesting and obviously of great value to what we are up to here. The biggest problem we are having is sourcing paper with the correct watermarks. I understand you can help?"

Watermarks are made by affixing a thin wire outline of the lettering or emblem of the mark onto the mesh "laid" of the mould on which the paper is made. Imagine a large square sieve—the deckle—the size of the piece of paper to be produced. This is dipped into the vat containing the pulped fibre. The water drains off leaving a thin layer of the fibres that, when dried, will become the sheet of paper. If a wire shape is fixed to the top of the sieve the pulp will be thinner in this area and this will remain when the paper is dried so that when held up to the light the design is visible. In machine-made papers the wire is attached to rollers, producing the same effect on a continuous roll of paper.

The problem with watermarks is that you cannot add them to paper after it has been made. To produce paper with the correct watermark involves recreating the wire frame and producing new paper to match. Although it is possible to make small volumes of handmade paper with a copied watermark, the paper is very obviously handmade and very different from the machine-made papers used by governments and organisations for official documents, which use a dandy roll to produce a continuous roll of watermarked paper. Producing forged watermarked paper cannot be done without the resources of a substantial paper mill. Happily for me, I had a very good relationship with Spicers, a very old firm making all sorts of paper, my father being on very good terms with Lancelot Spicer. I was sure that I could rely on their help at a time of such great need.

"I hope so, but I do need to see exactly what the challenge is," I said.

"Excellent, good show. Well of course we will need to discuss individual projects in more detail, but why don't we have a look around first?"

He led me along the passage, off which were several arched rooms of various sizes. The largest room contained several printing presses of different types, including both older letter presses and more recent litho machines. This section was largely run by a Polish team, led by Josef Hartman. He was a troubled man, morose and introspective, who spoke minimal English and was at pains not to learn any. His anger about what was happening to his country and the terrible things done to his family were forever simmering just below the surface of his sombre countenance.

If a foil was needed to the serious Hartman, it was the two key men on his team, Antoni Pospieszalski and Jerze Maczierski, known as "Pospi" and "Mac." They seemed to function as one body, always together whether at work or socialising, a sort of Laurel and Hardy, but with an understated and admirable competence. Irreverent, mercurial, often late or absent, and at serious risk if vodka was within reach, but once focussed on a task, they would work all night if need be, and the results were brilliant. Unlike their chief, they loved speaking very bad, heavily accented English and were always on the lookout for new words which I suspected they thought would be useful in pursuit of their dubious activities once the war was over. It was they who produced counterfeit five-pound notes at the Christmas party substituting the head of the king with that of Brigadier Gubbins, our commanding officer. Late in the evening they released bags of the notes from the balcony, which fluttered down like confetti onto the dinner tables. The notes were perfect in every other detail and were scooped up and strewn in joyful irreverent make believe as kids might play with autumn leaves.

Then there was the photographic department, with dark rooms containing a variety of specialist cameras and developing equipment under the charge of Vincent Whittaker, a quiet, mousey man who up until 1941 had been a staff photographer for the *Daily Sketch*. Most of the work took place in a large room brightly lit by a row of pendant lights. This was the creative hub where documents were put together and authenticated, which involved various techniques to make the documents look old and as dog-eared as would be the real thing.

Next door was an airless burrow of a room with a sign on the door that said THE CONFABULATORIUM OF IPSEITY. Within was an older man, bald but with electric grey tufts of hair above his ears. He wore thin gold-rimmed glasses and had to be a boffin. Roberts introduced him as Maurice Shilton.

"Maurice was professor of linguistics at Durham before we coaxed him down here. He hasn't quite come to terms with it yet."

I peered into the gloomy space, every wall of which was lined with bookshelves, every surface covered in papers and pamphlets. Maurice got up and, without making eye contact, reached to shake my hand but said nothing, a trait that I learned would change little over the years. It seemed to me that it was ironic that a man who knew so much about words in so many languages used them so infrequently.

"What does this mean?" I said pointing to the sign on the door.

"Well, 'confabulatorium' is a neologism but could be a Latin word meaning 'the place where fables are made'—con, 'together,' ipseity meaning 'identity.' In other words, the identity factory. It is what we do . . ." He didn't smile while speaking, remaining aloof as he stood holding an open volume in his bookish hands, with a faraway look in his eye. I nodded as he turned away. Roberts ushered me onward.

Next was Dennis Collins, a creative genius who had studied graphic art before the war and was a brilliant draughtsman, artist, cartoonist, and as I learnt later, musician. Pinned above his desk were various cartoons and sketches, landscape drawings, and numerous other papers. Roberts leant across to one piece of card on which was a small black square about a quarter of an inch across. He handed it to me.

"What do you make of that?"

I looked at it and could see that the black was not completely solid but could make nothing of it.

"Now have a look with this." He handed me a powerful magnifying glass. Now I could see that it was a block of miniscule writing, so small as to be completely invisible to the naked eye. I read "Our father which art in Heaven . . ." It was the complete Lord's prayer.

"Incredible isn't it," Roberts said. "That's the kind of talent we have here. Dennis can copy anything in the minutest detail." Dennis looked uncomfortable in the face of the compliments.

"How ever do you do it?" I asked. "What sort of pen do you use?"

"We have experimented with all sorts, but I find the best is a single hair. The ink is crucial, as is a good lens, and the paper is critical; but I suppose you would know about that." He smiled before continuing. "The best thing for forging typing is a very sharp, hard pencil."

"You can reproduce typing with a pencil?"

"Oh yes, not for a whole page of course—we have German Continental and Torpedo typewriters for that—with typical fonts and touches like the SS symbol, but on an identity card or travel permit when you can't fit it through the rollers it's the best thing. Elisabeth has become our expert in type work."

He moved towards a central table at which three people were working. Two were women. One of them was round in the face, with perfect cupid's bow lips and dark curly hair, who was introduced as Patricia. The other was leaning over the table, intently focussed on a small document in front of her, peering through a device the like of which I had never seen before: a large magnifying glass on short legs, which rested on her chest, held there by a string around her neck. In front of her on the desk were an array of pens, pencil rubbers, and rulers which spilled out of a white fabric pencil case on which was crudely embroidered a donkey.

But the dominant feature was a mass of auburn hair tied back with a blue ribbon. At the mention of her name, she looked up, removed the magnifier, and stood up. She was wearing the uniform of a FANY and was tall, willowy, and very pretty.

Was it love at first sight?

I have often thought about that, especially in the sad moments of rumination and introspection after I'd realised that I had lost her, but I think the answer is no. The circumstances in those wartime years were so peculiar, with the focus on bigger challenges and with so much at stake that my thoughts were far from love—and besides, it was my first day in a new job and I was still very shaken up from my experiences on PQ13. That is not to say that there wasn't a lot of loving and romance going on during those years; it is well-known that the situations people found themselves in during the war were a powerful aphrodisiac, and yes lots of people slept with each other, and indeed found love, of some form, but was I felled with one glance?

No.

Was she the one girl I would have picked out across a crowded dance floor and asked for a whirl? Certainly, yes.

Did I come to love her? Undeniably. But at the time I was nervous, miserable, and distracted. I am sure I was suffering from shell shock or whatever it is called nowadays, and those who have been in similar situations will affirm how the condition prevents you from thinking about anything very much except the unwanted terrors that stalk and haunt you.

Now it sounds like I am making excuses—I don't need to make excuses. She was the only woman I ever really loved and the moment it started is not important.

The tour continued. Small rooms of specialist equipment were manned totally by men (except for the two FANYs) who possessed an extraordinary range of skills. There was David Wilson, who had worked for seventeen years as a banknote engraver with the De La Rue company. Across from his office was the home of Arthur Gatward, a dour man who had been seconded from the Metropolitan Police with special knowledge of handwriting.

We emerged from the basement into the panelled hall, off which was a rec room with a large billiard table.

"Now," said Roberts in his businesslike manner which I was to get to know so well. "I think you might be surprised by what we have here." He led me across the lawn to one of the Nissen huts.

We entered and were welcomed by two more Polish men working in the heat in nothing more than trousers and vests. Behind the litho presses were various paper-making tanks with a large vat and stacks of moulds and deckles. In the corner was a substantial press and benches with wires and soldering equipment. It was very much a small paper-making unit.

"We were very lucky to have been able to purchase the whole unit from Eynsford Mills in Kent. Do you know them?"

"Yes, certainly."

"In that case you might even have met Bill Martin," Morton said as he moved towards an older hunched figure wearing a brown work coat. "Bill worked at Eynsford for thirty years until he retired. But we seem to have unretired him haven't we, Bill?"

The man said nothing but turned towards me and nodded without smiling.

Morton continued, "Bill was their senior technician. I am told there is nothing he can't do when it comes to making moulds and all the paraphernalia that you will know about."

I nodded to him, respecting his reticence, which in those times was often related to a class issue of us and them. He knew I was a toff, and he was a worker, and at his age (I later learnt that he was in his late sixties) that was not going to change.

In fact, we ended up working next to each other for more than two years. He didn't come in every day, cycling very slowly from Stanstead Abbots on his ancient bicycle. The reticence and shyness persisted but his skill and knowledge were exceptional.

"Well over to you Peter. We will have a briefing tomorrow when I will give you a better idea of our challenges. Just one more thing: you don't play cricket, do you?"

"Sorry, wasn't very good even when my feet worked properly," I said, nodding to my slippered feet.

"Ah of course. Sorry," he said, turning away with a look of disappointment and resignation.

My first task was to help supply authentic French envelopes. Most of the communications, and indeed the documents we made, came in and out of France. The traffic was both ways, and a crucial role of many of the agents dropped into France was to return with stolen identity cards, birth certificates, permits, food coupons, and the like. One fear we constantly lived with was that the documents we produced had been superseded by a new version.

The message we got down the chain of command was that some documents sent from France were never arriving, presumably being intercepted on the suspicion of the censor, or other security checks in place. It was thought that incorrect envelopes might be arousing suspicion, it being difficult to find the right tinted textured manilla, which was not used in this country.

I was sure that an old contact of my father who ran a shady business from a railway arch in Blackfriars could help and arranged to meet him.

It went well.

I was given the services of Pamela, a FANY driver, and following an early start, arrived at his scruffy premises midmorning. Eric Short was fatter and looked even less well than when I had last seen him. He wore a grimy vest over his vast belly. After enquiring about the well-being of my father and a long diatribe on the impossibility of making a living in wartime London, he asked what I wanted.

"French letters," I said, hoping that humour could obscure any more questionable motive. I explained what I needed. He grunted and led me into the gloomy interior of his premises, where among mountains of boxes piled seemingly randomly against the damp walls were rolls of papers of various sizes, types, and colours. Sure enough, in the depth of the troglodytic archways he inhabited, we found a role of a suitable paper, not perfect but good enough. I gave him a model of the envelope I wanted, and he assured me that in the absence of any "proper work" he would have them ready by the end of the week. We agreed on a price, and I promised cash on collection.

I wasn't sure how I was going to manage this, but when I approached Morton later, he reassured me that it was no problem. "Working the way we do, lots of our suppliers only work for cash. Just let me know what you need, and I will arrange it."

The envelopes were a success, Morton and James were delighted with the finished item and the prompt delivery, but I had found the week strenuous and the travel difficult.

I approached Sergeant Percival to see if I could take up the offer of accommodation in Hunsdon. The following day I arrived with a small bag of clothes and after work waited as instructed for a lift to my new lodgings. It was Pamela who swung by in the official Ford. She knew the address, which was around the corner from her own digs. On the main drive from the house, we passed Elisabeth walking home. Pamela stopped.

"Hi Lisa, care for a lift? Hop in. I am dropping Peter here at his new digs in Drury Lane. Have you met?"

"Thank you, Pam," she said, clambering into the back. "Well, not properly." She turned and smiled, "Welcome to the make-believe world of Briggens."

I turned around. "Thank you. Is my bag in the way? Just shove it up."

"Are you moving to Hunsdon? It's nice isn't it, Pam. It is quiet, but the pub is jolly and there is usually a crowd in there. We go quite often, don't we."

"You speak for yourself!" Pam teased.

"You were there on Saturday, and on Sunday if I recall," Elisabeth retorted.

"But that was a weekend. Besides you had to be there to know I was."

Elisabeth laughed. "Touché."

"I think it would do me good," I said. "When will you next be going?" It had been a long time since I had met a girl for a drink and even longer since it had been them doing the asking.

"It is traditional to welcome a new resident. What about tonight?" Elisabeth said.

"Any excuse," Pam said. "You just made that up!"

We all laughed and agreed to meet at seven.

The village was comprised of a row of gabled houses, some old and half timbered, other more modern and mostly painted white, strung between two pubs and a church. It was sleepy and unassuming. The RAF had an airfield between Briggens and the village which kept the pubs and local shops busy. Elisabeth was dropped by a small row of cottages before the triangle, while I was taken further down a lane bearing a No Through Road sign. My billet was with an elderly couple living in a small Georgian house in Drury Lane. My fellow lodger, Jonathan Parker, who I was yet to meet, turned out to be a quiet, doleful, and antisocial man, who when not working spent his time going for long walks and birdwatching.

I unpacked my few possessions, learnt of the house rules from the frail owners, and watched the clock until I thought it decent to head to the Crown.

It was a traditional English village pub, probably unchanged for two hundred years, with a saloon bar on one side of the entrance, a public bar on the other, and a small hatch for off-sales in between. I entered the saloon bar, ordered a pint of mild, and sat in a corner.

There was nobody else in the room, but I could hear voices from the public bar. Elisabeth arrived ten minutes later. She was wearing a dark blue skirt and a close-fitting jumper. Gone was the ribbon, her mass of hair falling loosely to her shoulders. I was very taken. She smiled as she made her way over towards me. I got up.

"What will you have?"

"A half of shandy please," she said.

I ordered it from the scrawny landlady.

"I wasn't sure which bar you usually used," I said.

"This one normally. The Poles and a lot of the RAF ground crew go next door."

I asked her how she had been recruited to Briggens.

"I knew about the FANYs from school and wondered what I should do for the war effort. Many of my friends were signing up to become Wrens, but that didn't appeal. An auntie convinced me the FANYs would be worthwhile, and I applied. The next thing I knew, I was being called for an interview in London."

"I gather the interviews could be quite tough."

"You've obviously met other FANYs! Yes, it was terrifying. The redoubtable Marion Gamwell—her reputation goes before her."

She told me of the six weeks training at Overthorpe Hall, near Banbury, and then being posted to Briggens. I was careful not to ask her anything about her current work or how she had learnt the skills to do what she was doing.

I would learn later, when we were walking out and could talk intimately, that she had just fallen into it. She didn't have any special skills and, like most of the FANY's, was sent to Briggens to help out, make tea, drive, and be a general dogsbody. She had done art at school but had not considered that a career. She started off by being given simple jobs upstairs but then when they came under more and more pressure with the increasing volume of work, she and Pauline Brockie were moved downstairs to help. At first it was easy tasks: cutting paper, working on ageing documents, which sometimes involved carrying them around for a week in her handbag. Gradually her responsibilities increased, and she found that the perfectionist side of her nature was well-suited to the tasks, which entailed hours of detailed work, often using a magnifying glass, meticulously finishing documents, and, not infrequently, when it was finished, having to start all over again because it wasn't right.

While we were still in the pub, though, she asked what had happened to my leg and my hands.

I told her about my love of sailing and how, when war broke out, it didn't take much to persuade me that going to sea was my best option and how I had volunteered for the RNVR.

"I was assigned to a dirty old freighter, and we joined a north Atlantic convoy."

"In a dirty old freighter?"

"Well, that's what she seemed to me. She had been fitted with some guns and we had been trained to fire them. Lots of practice off the Welsh coast trying to hit targets on old barges. We went to Iceland, which wasn't too bad, but then had to go to Russia, beyond the Arctic Circle. God, it was cold. So cold you can't imagine."

"What happened?"

"Three days out we were attacked by a couple of planes, but they didn't do any damage, and just when we thought we were in the clear, we were torpedoed, still three days from Murmansk. It was in the gloom of dusk. Suddenly somebody shouted and those of us on deck could see the torpedo coming towards us. It was very strange to watch and be completely powerless to do anything. I am told that often these moments are recalled in slow-motion, and that's how it seemed, just watching the wake inching towards the boat. Me and two others stood frozen, paralysed for what seemed an age but must have only been a matter of a minute or so. We had no idea where it had come from. There was no sign of a U boat . . . There was nothing we could do . . . I can still see the wake carving through the water towards us and then the whole ship rocked and heaved and the rear burst into a mass of flames and smoke. And then the sea was aflame, and the crew were trying to lower boats and we managed it, but others didn't and there were faces in the water waving arms and screaming as the flaming oil spread towards them . . ."

It was the first time I had ever tried to talk about what happened, but it did not go well. As I was telling the story my hands started shaking and I found it more and more difficult to speak. It was both terrifying and very embarrassing. I became more and more tremulous and panicky. And then I couldn't carry on.

I was mortified, embarrassed and ashamed, but could do nothing about it.

Elisabeth looked concerned and realised, before I did, what was happening. Holding my shaking hand, she stood up and led me outside. The act of moving was helpful and once in the open air I was able to calm down a little, but really didn't know what to say. One moment I was enjoying chatting to a cracking-looking girl and the next I was shaking and weeping like a baby.

"Has this happened before?" she asked, still holding my hand, with genuine concern in her voice.

"No," I said, turning my head from side to side and still gulping for air, "Well, yes . . . at night . . . I don't sleep," I blurted out.

"Have you talked about it with anyone?"

I shook my head.

"Well perhaps you should."

"Difficult, since I behave so badly."

"Peter, you are not behaving badly. It sounds like you went through something pretty awful. It's nothing to be ashamed of."

"You are very sweet. Thank you." I calmed down a bit and the tremors subsided. "How about we have another drink and change the subject."

"Good idea." She smiled. "My round."

We talked about ordinary things: her family and her friends. Life at Hunsdon and how, although she often worked long hours on a deadline, the companionship was very special, and they had a good time with trips to the pub or a dance. She played the piano and sometimes they went to the White Hart and had a singsong. There was also an amateur dramatic group which she helped with the music.

"Have you met Dennis?"

"I think so. Though I have been introduced to so many people, I haven't got everyone's name sorted yet."

"He is a very good musician, as well as being a brilliant artist. He organises us all. It's quite a little orchestra. Do you play?"

"No, I'm not very musical, I'm afraid. My family wasn't very cultured. Sailing was my thing, although I'm not even sure about that now."

I told her about my grandfather and how he had taught me to sail and my love of boats and my travels before the war and coming back to work for the firm.

We finished our drinks and got up to leave.

"I really do apologise for making such an ass of myself," I said.

"You are being an ass for thinking that," she said much more sternly. "I enjoyed listening, and besides, my view is that you have got to get it out of your system. Let's find a time when we can talk some more. I am a good listener."

She squeezed my hand and smiled. "Next time," she said, letting go, then turned and walked back towards her digs.

I turned the opposite way and walked back to mine, but I felt easier. I wasn't sure whether Elisabeth's warmth and friendship was just for me or whether it was her normal caring self, and that her concern was unrelated to whether she liked me. In retrospect, it was a bit of both.

CHAPTER 15

·······································

Dorset

Sunday, August 1, 1948

They lounge in a dozy torpor for a few minutes before Henry bounces off the bed and starts putting his clothes on. Elisabeth asks if she could have a bath and change before dinner.

Henry shows her to an antique bathroom next to the Yellow Room with an enormous freestanding cast-iron bath. She turns on the tap and is rewarded by a torrent of steaming brown water. She runs the tap for a minute, and it largely clears, filling the tub in no time with weak tea. It is too hot to get in and she must add cold. She opens a mirrored cabinet on the expectation of finding something to put in the water and sure enough finds a jar of Bronnley Lily of the Valley bath salts which looks as if it has not been touched for decades. She tips up the jar, but the contents do not move as the crystals are welded together in a solid lump. She prods it with her finger, but it remains unmoved. Then after gingerly tapping the jar on the side of the tub, a large lump falls into the water. Swirling it with her hand, the air fills with a sweet floral fragrance. She steps in and sinks into the oily soak, luxuriating in the pleasure of being properly submerged in scalding water. How she has missed proper baths. She lies staring aimlessly at the ceiling. It is painted a gloss white, although in places it is not very white nor very glossy, but the light from the window reflects off the sheen and she can make out the green of the lawn, and even the ripples of the bath water if she moves. She swirls the water with her toes, seeing how the reflection in the ceiling changes.

She hasn't seen a bath like this since school. Then it was once a week when Sidney the ancient gardener and groundsman was persuaded to stoke up the boiler to provide a full tank of water, and her dormitory took turns in the cubicled bathroom. Then it was in and out in four minutes, measured by the assistant matron; now she enjoys languishing, floating in the steamy water, too much going on in her mind to focus on any one thing.

There is a knock at the door. She is suddenly aware that the water is nearly cold.

"Have you drowned or are you still alive?" Henry says from the other side.

She chuckles at his modesty and proper manners. "Yes, fine. I will be out in a minute." She steps out into a huge towel, worn and scratchy but comforting, the roughness against her skin stimulating after the cool water. She dries herself, and wrapping the towel around her, tiptoes to her room to dress.

Dinner is a casserole, with vegetables from the garden and a plum pie. It is good hearty food and far too much for the two of them. Henry does not eat much. That's why he's so thin, Elisabeth muses, too distracted to eat. Mrs. Bagley bustles in to clear the plates and ensure that all was to their liking. Elisabeth cannot imagine what it would be like to have someone to cook for you. For one thing, she would be round as a barrel; for another what would you do with all the time? She just can't imagine being summoned for a meal. She thinks of Mummy, with her uninspired repertoire of meat and two veg with Bisto gravy. *What would she do if she wasn't fussing in the kitchen overcooking cabbage?*

"I must say it is nice to have you home, Master Chivers, nice to have the house lived in again. I hope everything is to your liking, Miss Elisabeth."

They both smile and acknowledge her sentiments and talk of the morrow. Sunday is normally her day off and Henry insists that she take Monday off instead. He has some meetings in Dorchester and suggests they drive there in the morning and have lunch in town. Elisabeth could have a wander around the town, then perhaps go for a walk in the afternoon.

It all sounds perfect.

She has a momentary pause for guilt about her mother, but it passes. Mrs. Bagley retires to her room at the service end of the house, and they get up from the table and walk back through the hall.

The sun has set but the sky is touched with a rouge glow which enters the tall window over the landing, casting a tawny tint on the wall. The house is totally quiet except for the creak of the ancient floorboards as they amble through the dusty shadows. It is timeless; even the ticking of the clock seems lazy and languorous. She just stands looking at it all, breathing in the enduring scents and absorbing the patina of the past. She can see the way the oak banister has been polished by the hands of generations and how the treads of the stairs are worn smooth by the footfall of years. How can such a random assemblage of furniture and accoutrements from every age and style be so harmonious and somehow unified? There is nothing contrived, nothing new or designed to impress, just valued things that somehow sit together to make an ensemble. You couldn't plan it; it has grown, like some slow-growing organism, one generation adding accidentally to the efforts of the previous.

Henry comes up behind her. God, you smell delicious." He puts his arms around her. "Penny for them?"

"I was just thinking what a perfect room this is. You couldn't do it if you tried but it just works somehow. It is you, Henry, and all you stand for."

"I am not sure I stand for it. Perhaps it stands for me. But it is lovely isn't it. The problem is one can't really change anything."

"Not the big things, no, but maybe some little things, bit by bit."

She looks up, worried that there is an insistence in her tone which she could have better disguised. But he doesn't seem to notice and stands staring distractedly at the portraits.

"Sometimes I think we should be brave and modernise here and there. We have to be careful not to be too stuffy. After all, some of the things that we love about ancient buildings are the brave additions which were groundbreaking and outrageous when they were first done."

"I suppose so, but if it works . . . It might be different if you had six children or something."

"Mmm that might change things a little!" He smiles and turns to her with a raised eyebrow. "Now what would you like to do now?"

"Presumably you are thinking of playing a few duets, or reading each other passages of Homer?"

"Not exactly. A duet sounds good though."

She leads him towards the foot of the stairs.

"But it's only eight thirty!"

"Eight thirty? My that's late . . . how have we waited so long?"

In his bedroom she pulls the curtains and then they undress each other. They stand facing each other kissing. He is taller than she, but she swings his turgid cock between her legs, pressing her pubis against him. They stand rocking, kissing deeply but then he backs away so he can touch her properly, his fingers churning her soft folds.

"God, you're so wet!"

"It's what you do to me, Henry."

She pulls him back to the bed. He breaks off.

"Just a moment. I think I have something in my dressing table."

She clambers onto the bed while he rummages in a drawer, emerging with a packet of condoms. She lies back pulling him into her. This time their separate urgencies collide and within two minutes their bodies are still, their ardour collapsed and spent.

And then after a while they talk, still with limbs entangled, lying naked, uncovered until their drying sweat necessitates pulling a sheet over their cooling torsos. She wants to know everything about him, now, instantly.

"Henry . . . If I ask you a personal question, will you tell me the truth?"

"Try me."

"Do you have a lover or mistress in Innsbruck?"

"Nope."

"You must have surely? Some little Fräulein who tidies your room and then smiles invitingly."

"No."

"Promise?"

"Promise. Cubs honour."

"I don't believe you. I bet you weren't a Cub anyway."

"Does that matter? Is it only Cubs who can claim Cubs' honour?"

"I don't know. I wasn't one either."

"Girl guide?"

"Nope. Guide's honour."

"Ah, but a girl's honour is different from a boy's. How does that verse go? 'She offered her honour; he honoured her offer, and all night long he was on her and off her!'"

She giggles. "Very funny, and also topical." She leans across to kiss him. "No, but seriously, you must have had the odd dalliance."

"Ah, that's different. And yes, some of them were very odd, but nobody I cared for or loved. Satisfied?"

"Yes."

"Convinced?"

"Promise. FANY's honour."

"Were you a FANY?"

"I certainly was."

"Do they have an honour? Most of the ones I met didn't seem to!"

She punches him softly. "Now, now. Don't be rude. FANY's did wonderful things during the war. Still do actually. I still have my uniform and badge somewhere in Mummy's attic. And I'm very proud of it too."

"I bet you looked great in it."

"Oh god, don't tell me you're one of those odd fellows who gets turned on by women in uniform."

"No darling, it's what was in it that I was thinking about, not the grey serge."

"Did you just call me 'darling'?"

"Crikey did I? I have never called anybody darling before. Not even my favourite Labrador."

"I should hope not—the Labrador I mean—I don't think I have ever been called darling before, except by Daddy and Mr. Featherstone, who taught singing at school and called everybody darling and was as queer as a coot."

"But the truth is I have never wanted to call anybody darling before. Do you mind?"

"No, darling, not for a moment."

"We are in trouble here, aren't we?"

"I am afraid we are in big trouble."

"I fear it could be fatal."

"There you go again!" She punches him lightly on the chest. "Don't say that. What's the opposite of fatal?"

"Vital"

"Yes, that's it, vital. We are vital, Henry. You and me. Vital."

They lie still for a few minutes, barely stirring, just the minutest movements of their chests as they breathe. Then he asks her about her other boyfriends.

"Men always want to know about women's past lovers. I often wonder why it seems so important, especially for you, Henry; you're a man of the present. You don't seem stuck in the past."

"It's because we are jealous creatures. It's the caveman in us. We want possession of our woman, sole right of access, and we are terrified that there may be competition."

"So, what you want to hear is that either there weren't any, or that they were hopeless lovers?"

"That sort of thing . . . Well?"

"It matters for women, too, you know. We don't want to be too far down the list."

"One thousand and three, in Spain perhaps"

"One thousand and three? Gosh!" she says in an uncertain tone. "What's that about?"

"It's from Don Giovanni; don't you remember? Leporello lists his master's conquests; in Germany six hundred and forty and in Spain one thousand and three."

"And in Dorset?"

"Just the one. One is enough."

She is silent.

"Have I upset you?"

"No, it's the same as on the bus. I don't know these things, Henry. I should know more about opera and architecture and things."

"Hey less about the 'should.' It isn't important what you know; it's who you are that matters to me. And besides, forget one thousand and four. Four is nearer the mark."

"Only four?"

"Ish." In the half-light she can see he is smiling.

"I don't believe you for a moment."

"What about you? You have very carefully avoided answering my question. Diversionary tactics I suspect. A flanking manoeuvre to outwit the advance."

"A few. Not too many, and I remember all their names. There are none that I am ashamed of." A shudder of panic stops her in her tracks. Should she mention Peter? She suddenly realises that it was only a month before that she was in France with him. So much has changed—but she can be vague—that will work. "I suppose Peter was the most significant."

"When was that?"

"We met during the war. He was needy and nice enough. He had had a very bad time on an Atlantic convoy, and I felt the need to look after him. He was a kind man, and we shared a lot, but when the war was over, I realised we had nothing much in common. He was a passionate sailor and in truth was in love with the sea. That was his real mistress."

"So, what happened?"

"It dragged on. He had bought a boat that he restored and sailed it to the Mediterranean. He pleaded with me to come and see him, which I finally did, but it was a disaster. I left him and the boat in Nice and made my way home." She pauses, idly twirling her finger through the hair on his chest.

"Glenda. St. Hilda's, 1937. First love. Poetry, punting, tentative lovemaking. Dreamy times among the spires, commitment to love each other forever, passionate love letters during the holidays. Typical Oxford narrative."

"Were you at St. Hilda's?"

"No, St. Hilda's is women only. I was at New College."

"Is that modern?"

"Not exactly modern. William of Wykeham, 1397."

"Argh, once again I put my foot in it . . ."

He doesn't say anything.

"What happened?" she continues.

"After a couple of terms, I found she was doing the same with two of my friends. I was heartbroken."

"Poor you."

"It's a terrible thing to be slighted in love. It really does hurt in your heart."

"Werther ''mit the dagger in his brost.'"

"Exactly. You see, you do know things."

And they lie and talk. They talk about their childhoods and their families and about friends and places they have been. But mostly they just talk about nothing, joking about what the other said, or about the response. She finds that she can say the first thing that comes to mind without worrying what he will think. She can speak her mind in all its random routes and diversions.

At some stage she notices it has got dark, and finally at a time unknown, starts to feel sleepy and dozes off in the feathery folds of Guillome's great bed, with Henry's leg across hers.

CHAPTER 16

Cap d'Ail, Var France
July 1992

Over the summer of 1942 my life had changed dramatically. Initially I was facing the challenge of the Arctic in winter on a converted freighter. Then I was sitting convalescing in my parent's suburban home in Epping, and now I was working for the SOE in a secret forgery unit. But if this wasn't enough to challenge my fragile physiognomy, I was captivated and enthralled by a beautiful woman, and that, as I learnt, was an all-consuming occupation.

After that first meeting in the pub, I walked home feeling embarrassed and unsure as to whether I would stand a chance of any greater intimacy.

I gradually integrated into the team at Briggens and physically became stronger. My foot improved and there came a day when I could wear a soft sailing shoe on my left foot, albeit that I still couldn't walk very far. I returned to the Crown a couple of times. There were faces I recognised, chat was easy, and it was all very congenial, but no Elisabeth. When she did appear about ten days later, she came straight up to me and, looking me in the eyes, asked how I was in a very genuine and heartfelt manner. I was touched and completely bowled over by her appearance. That first meeting she had appeared pretty, with a good head of amber hair, but now she was stunning. The hair was fresh and tied with a ribbon. She wore a bit of lipstick with that open smile. I was smitten.

We didn't have much of a chance to talk but at the end of the evening it was her who suggested doing something at the weekend, perhaps going for a walk.

"I don't think I could manage that," I said, nodding to my foot.

"Oh, I am sorry, I forgot. How insensitive of me. Well, something else then. The pictures? We usually go into Bishops Stortford; the Regent is quite nice, but the Phoenix is a bit of a fleapit."

"That would be wizard!"

We agreed to meet on the Saturday and took the bus into Bishops Stortford. We left in plenty of time and found a little café where we had beans on toast and then went to watch a matinee of the *Three Musketeers* with Lana Turner and Gene Kelly. It was all good swashbuckling stuff and just what we needed. The conversation was easy and fun, and she laughed at some of my jokes. I talked a lot about sailing as a boy in Scotland, and although the only boat Elisabeth had been on was a cross-Channel ferry, she seemed interested. I promised to take her out in a dinghy sometime.

She told me about her family and her dad, who was an engineer working on a secret project in Southampton, her schooling in Hereford, and her home in Reigate. We got the bus back home before it was dark, but by this time my foot was quite sore and so we parted at the bus stop.

"Thank you for a nice day," she said, standing facing me and looking me in the eye. "How are you? Are you sleeping any better?"

"Not much."

"I am sure talking is good Peter. You can talk to me, you know that. I am a good listener. Let's find a quiet time." She squeezed my hand, fixed me with a look of sincerity and trust, turned and walked away, and then turned back, smiled, and waved.

I felt anxious and inadequate and was not sure about talking—even to her. What I really wanted to do was to kiss her.

But later that week, she came to find me in the early evening, knocking on the door of the annex where Jonathan and I lived.

"Come on, it's a lovely evening and we are going for a little walk. I know you can't go very far, but there is a nice walk behind the church. If you are good, I might buy you a pint after."

I was so delighted that I would have crawled down a gravel road had she suggested it.

We walked through the village and into the churchyard, calm and warm on a late summer evening. Strangely, for once there wasn't even the sound of an aircraft wheeling overhead. The grass had been mown in a narrow path around the church and the smell of cut grass lingered in the air. We found a bench framed by two ancient yew trees and sat down.

"You haven't told me how you got home from Russia."

"Oh, we were packed onto a merchantman on a return convoy in April. Anything to get away from the hospital in Murmansk.

"Was it that bad?"

"I suppose they were trying to do their best with not very much. But it was very Spartan, and of course nobody spoke any English, so communication was dire."

"How many of there were you?"

"Forty-one abandoned ship—in two lifeboats. We started off with eighteen in ours, but by the time we were picked up by the Russian minesweeper three days later there was only twelve. It was minus twenty degrees, and we were all soaked by spray. The first night a bottle of whisky was passed around. We all had a sip, but some of the men wanted more and swigged it back. In the morning, three of them were dead. Just sitting where they were in the boat frozen stiff."

Elisabeth was looking down at the grass, but I felt her hand reach across for mine. She didn't say anything.

"My grandfather, the one I told you about who taught me to sail, used to work the trawlers out of Peterhouse. Before we sailed, he'd given me some special trawlermen's boots and clothing. The last thing he said to me was to promise to always sleep fully clothed. And I did, although it was at times very tiresome. Some of the men in the lifeboat only had a flimsy shirt under their coats, because they had undressed to kip and didn't have time to properly dress when the siren sounded, but I had proper long-johns and thick oily Shetland wool socks, and Grandfather's boots. When we got to Murmansk most of the men had severe frostbite and lost at least one foot. One guy lost both hands. The really bad news was that in the hospital someone stole my wonderful boots. But I guess I won't need them now." I smiled and she returned the glance with a look of caring concern.

I was doing well. I had managed to tell Elisabeth more than I had told anyone else and had even made a joke, although I had avoided the terrifying parts. By involving Grandfather, and not dwelling on the parts that I knew would lead to trouble, I avoided the scene I had made during our earlier meeting.

It is peculiar that even now, sixty years later, I would rather not write about these events. How is it that a few minutes of hell can, like some fearsome parasite, bury a terror in your mind which stays there forever? It lies there dormant and quiescent, undetectable until disturbed, mostly behaving itself, but when provoked by a careless nudge, it will rear into a spectre of undiminished horror. Nowadays I can joke about spending three days in a freezing lifeboat; but that wasn't the terror. The terror was seeing Jimmy Bowens and Alfie Clarke screaming in the water as they were engulfed by burning fuel oil. And I could do nothing about it except watch.

There, I have written it—and still the tears come.

Elisabeth sat next to me; her legs neatly crossed under her uniform. Then she said, "It's hard to imagine freezing in an open boat sitting here in the warm. I hate the cold. I just couldn't have done it, Peter. I would have had the whisky—the whole bottle I suspect, if the others would have let me. I would have wanted the easy way out. I think you are very brave. What about your friends, were they all right?"

That did me in completely, and I gave a sort of heave and pulled her towards me and put my head on her shoulder, trying not to sob. She put her arms around me and then I wasn't sobbing but breathing in her clean fresh warmth and putting a hand on that brilliant head of hair.

A moment later we were kissing properly. As I recall, we never made it to the pub that evening, and by the end of the month it was generally acknowledged that we were "stepping out."

Elisabeth was a very competent pianist and had been roped in by Dennis and Fred to play the piano in the Drama Club review they were putting on. This meant that she was rehearsing most evenings, and it was difficult to find time to be together, but there were special nights when she would find her way back to Drury Lane and creep into my narrow bed.

We didn't sleep much, only partly due to my fears. We would make love and chat, and then I found I could rest properly with the security and safety of a warm body beside me. And then it was up again early, with a walk or cycle back to Briggens and the breezy round of greetings to the crew as we assembled in the basement.

There was a forgiving collusion amongst the staff. There must have been times when we appeared bleary-eyed and sleepy those mornings—not just Elisabeth and me, but many of the others too. It has been spoken and written about a great deal; the abandonment and disinhibition of the war, resulting in an impetuous sexual liberation. There is no doubt that there was a change in behaviour, which then reverted at the end of hostilities to an apologetic embarrassment. Not that we were promiscuous; on the contrary, I was a one-woman man, but there was an acceptance and lack of judgement about such behaviours that represented a substantial change from the prewar mores.

I wanted to get her into a boat and introduce her to the joys of sailing and surmised that the Norfolk Broads would be a good starting point. Gentle inland waterways, nothing too frightening, pretty places to visit and near enough to get there and back in a weekend.

It wasn't until the spring of 1943 that we managed to pull it together. We agreed on a date in May and put in requests not to be rostered over the weekend. We took the train to Reedham and picked up a perfectly nice twenty-two-footer with a small cabin, ideal for the two of us. It wasn't really sailing—at least not as I see it—but we ate fresh crab sandwiches at a waterside pub and then shared pork pies by candlelight in the tiny cabin before bedding down to the sploshing of the wavelets on the hull. For a first outing on water, I thought it went well.

We got back late on the Sunday and walked into Hunsdon from the station, stopping outside Elisabeth's digs. Pam, her roommate, appeared at the door looking tense and anxious. The fear in her voice said all there was to say.

"Darling, you must ring your mother. Something has happened to your father. Roberts was trying to find you yesterday. He came over again this morning."

Elisabeth's blameless face creased with worry. In those wartime days a message suggesting bad news often did mean truly terrible news. We hurried to the phone box on the green. I waited outside while she went in and dialled her mother.

I couldn't bear to look and so paced around in the gloaming.

She emerged two minutes later sobbing almost hysterically, broken, barely able to stand. I bent to her, clutching her suddenly frail form as she shook and heaved.

"What is it? What has happened?"

"Daddy, not Daddy . . ." I couldn't think what had happened. Her father was an engineer working on a classified project in Hampshire. He wouldn't have been at risk, even in the difficult times we lived in.

She could still not speak, just sobbing and shaking her head. "No, no, no. It can't be . . . there must be a mistake. Not him—not Daddy."

He had been visiting a factory near Guildford when the air-raid sirens sounded. The group he was with rushed to an Anderson shelter on the site, but it received a direct hit, killing four. Had they stayed where they were, they would have survived.

Elisabeth was given leave to comfort her mother and attend

the funeral, and now it was her that needed the comfort. She was demolished by the news. I offered to accompany her to the funeral, but she declined, so I stayed behind and thought of her, comforting her only in my thoughts.

We forget nowadays how war changed the way ordinary people coped with loss and grief. Not that Elisabeth was ordinary; she was extraordinary in every way, but within three days she was back at work. She just appeared midmorning, walked to her place at the table clutching a bundle of papers, sat down, and got to work. The crew nodded to her and there was a moment of awkward quiet and then business as normal. Most of the men found a quiet moment to comfort her and offer condolences, and there were times when I noticed she wore the red eyes of tearfulness, but she just swung back into the routine. That was how it was then; somehow, we just coped and carried on.

"What could I do at home?" she told me that evening, as I held her, for once in a nonsexual way, "I just thought of you all here and the work that needed to be done. Mummy was wrapped in her own grief but there seemed no way for me to help. Although she hasn't a clue what I do, she knew I was better off here than there."

That was how we coped—the routine of work, humour, beer, and the physical distraction of lying next to warm flesh.

A month later my grandfather died. A heart attack while pulling his dinghy up the beach. He was found the next morning with the painter still clasped in his fist. Now it was my turn to grieve and to make the slow rail journey to Arrochar. In fact, Glasgow, because I was met at the station by my father, who had arrived the day before and had scrounged some petrol to drive to meet me.

It was a sombre affair. The dour granite of Scotland lends itself well to sombre, especially overshadowed by grey skies and a fret off the loch. There can't have been more than a dozen attendees: those left behind by the war—the old and infirm—and a few family members, cousins, and nieces who knew him from his pre-London life.

The journey home was even worse. The war was not going well. The Nazis were at the gates of Stalingrad, Rommel was storming across North Africa, the Eagle had been sunk in the Mediterranean, and the Americans were struggling in the Far East. Elisabeth was mourning the loss of her father and had lost some of her joie de vivre, and as I fought off an overwhelming helplessness, I once again noticed pains in my feet.

Now it was my turn to receive the curt condolences of the staff.

"Sorry to hear of your news, old boy. Tough one, that."

Or, "Bad luck, old thing. Chin up, what."

And that was it. Back into the routine. But it brought me closer than ever to Elisabeth. I had never lost a person who meant something important to me. (It is with regret that I must admit I never did again until the news of Elisabeth's death.) Now I had a parallel experience that removed her tendency to intimate that I didn't understand what she was feeling. We clutched each other in the storm, a battered and windswept haven perhaps, but nevertheless a secure place in the maelstrom.

CHAPTER 17

··

Dorset

Monday, August 2, 1948

E lisabeth finally sleeps, and then wakes to a split second of confusion as to where she is. Then the realisation and memories of the day before flood back. The heavy brocade curtains are almost fully closed, and the room remains dark, but she can see that she is alone in the huge bed. There is no clock, and she has no idea of the time.

She slides out of bed still naked and crosses to the bigger of the two windows, pulling the curtains apart. The morning is brighter than the day before, blue sky between streaky clouds, with the lawn slatted by slants of shadow from a row of poplar trees. Where the sun has not penetrated, the dew remains, leaving the grass a banner of green stripes. Swallows swoop and dive, tweeting as they scythe the air with perfect arabesques.

She worries it must be late, but there is no way of telling. She hasn't brought a dressing gown and is fearful that there may be people downstairs and dares not venture out of the room improperly clad. She finds Henry's dressing gown hanging on the door and steps into its scratchy comfort. It smells of him. Why is it that men have their own unique smell, while women don't seem to? Perhaps because they mask it with perfume and cologne. She buries her head in the time-worn woollen collar and inhales. It is too complex to characterise exactly: spicy, musky with a hint of shaving soap, perhaps, tobacco, old cupboards, and leather.

For a moment she recalls Daddy's smell. He never wore cologne or aftershave, but his clothes were tinged with the lingering tang of Balkan Sobranie, the pipe tobacco he smoked. When he came home from work, he smelled just slightly of factory, oils and tar, and chemicals. She still gets a lump in her throat if she goes into a garage or workshop.

The dressing gown is far too big, but she wraps it around herself, ties the cord in a bow, and pads barefooted onto the landing and down the stairs.

The landing and hall feel different in the brightness of the morning. Last night it was comforting, warm, enclosing, mellow. Now it is fresh and vigorous, positive and workmanlike. She climbs softly down the stairs forgetting the squeaky board which announces her descent to Biscuit, who gets up stiffly from a rug in front of the fireplace and wags his way towards her, his smiling eyes conveying a welcoming "good morning."

"Hello Biscuit. Where is your master? Go find him."

She has no idea where Henry might be but tries the morning room and dining room, which are both empty. She calls his name and is rewarded by a response from the corridor leading to the music room. He walks towards its source and meets Henry bounding towards her dressed in baggy white flannels with an open shirt.

"My darling person, you are awake. Isn't it a simply delectable morning?" He sweeps her into his arms and kisses her. "Nice dressing gown; it suits your green eyes."

"You are all dressed up! You look as if you are going to Wimbledon or Henley. Have you been up long?"

"Ages and ages. I am making breakfast. I thought we would have it in the music room. Come, Brahms for breakfast."

"Brahms?" She enters the music room to find he has thrown open the French windows, which open onto a narrow stone terrace and then the lawn as it rolls away to a pergola and then a lower-level lawn beyond. The grass is still damp with dew. It is fresh and airy, bordering on the chilly. She tightens the dressing gown, her bare feet exploring the rough wooden floorboards.

"Yes, I thought so, but it could be Bach if you prefer."

"Or Beethoven, I suppose. Or Bruckner."

"Lord no, not Bruckner, not at breakfast. All that brass and blaring horns. Very indigestible." He moves towards the gramophone and the pile of 78s next to it. "What's it to be, Hungarian dances? How about the first piano concerto?" He sorts through and picks one out, winds the gramophone, and places the record on the turntable. He lifts the needle into place and the room is filled with the swell of orchestral music.

He has prepared two chairs in front of a butler's tray on a stand, upon which is a teapot, crockery, and various jugs and jars.

"Now, I have done some toast and boiled the kettle. I just need to make the tea. I couldn't find any coffee, I'm afraid. Country life is so much more impoverished than the sophistication of Victoria! What would you like? I suspect I can find an egg, if you want. It's all a bit of a bore, Mrs. B being off, but she will be back tomorrow."

"Toast is fine. Is there some marmalade?"

"Ohne zweifle! There is always Mrs. B's marmalade!"

"Shouldn't I go and get dressed?"

"No, you look perfect like you are. Unless of course you want to take it off?"

"I don't think so Henry."

The record finishes and he gets up to turn it over. She sits on one of the chairs and takes a piece of slightly burnt toast. He joins her on the other chair and pours tea from a large stoneware teapot, which Elisabeth finds totally incongruous to the genteel setting.

"Who is it?" she asks.

"Guess."

She ponders for a minute, "Fischer, Furtwangler, and the Ph-Ph-Philharmonia."

"Ha! I love it. No. Try again."

"How about Krysler, Klemperer, and K-K . . . No, can't do another K."

"Do you give up?"

She ponders a minute. "No. I've got a good one; Backhaus, Bolt, and the BBC."

"Blooming brilliant, but . . . wrong! It is Horowitz."

"How habsolutely heavenly. Like this marmalade."

"It is, isn't it? When Father was alive, he used to give it up for Lent, about the only concession he made to his fallen-Catholic-faith mind. He said it was the one thing that he valued enough for it to be a hardship. Mrs. B used to get frightfully peeved, mind."

"Didn't he have any other vices?"

"No, not really. But it's just as well the shooting and fishing seasons weren't in Lent. It would have been different then."

They sit informally at the tray-table eating toast.

"What are we going to do today, Henry? I suppose I should get dressed. That would be a start."

"How tiresome, but if you insist. So how about we go into town about eleven? I am afraid I have to make some visits this afternoon and do some estate work. Will you be all right? There is also dinner to think about, with Mrs. B off duty."

"Of course I will be all right. I spend a lot of time on my own, Henry; I do know how to look after myself, and I will cook dinner for you."

"Topping! We can do some shopping in town. Are you happy to drive or shall we get Malcolm to take us in the Sunbeam?"

"Whatever is most convenient. I am happy to take Evey. Will Anneliese come?"

"I doubt it, but I will give her a ring."

The record finishes

"Right, what's next."

"It's all a bit noisy for this time of the morning, Henry. What about something gentler. How about Chopin?"

"But that's a C."

"Yes, and C comes after B, stupid."

"Oh, all right, but not a nocturne. It really is too early for that."

"A prelude, sweetness, a prelude to us!"

They finish breakfast as Chopin's gentle sonorities come to a scratchy end. Henry gets up and tidies the tray before setting off back to the kitchen.

"I thought I might have another bath, Henry. Is that all right? It is such a luxury soaking in that massive tub."

"Of course. I will do all the domestic chores and housework while you soak your beautiful self and preen and pamper!"

"Now you make me feel a real heel."

"Good, then I can look forward to a spectacular guilt-driven meal tonight. I will be in the library doing dull things."

She reaches up to kiss him, no more than a peck on his cheek. He can do nothing as both hands hold the tray. She ruffles his wiry hair, following him out of the room and returns upstairs.

She quickly runs a bath, being less indulgent than the night before, and only filling it half full. There is something wasteful about too deep a bath which grates with her innate frugality, but she tips more of the lily of the valley salts into the rusty swirl.

She returns to the Yellow Room and looks at her suitcase and the meagre selection of clothing. It isn't the wardrobe of a country lady, but neither is it the wardrobe of a woman about town, in fact it's barely a wardrobe at all, rather a worn and tawdry collection of old clothes, most of which she has made herself. The two skirts suddenly seem dull and weary, the dress lack-lustre and dated, the underwear cheap and unappealing.

She shuts the wardrobe and notices a collection of shells on the window ledge. They are beautiful, perfect spiral symmetries of creams and pink, some almost translucent, others flamboyant miracles of swirls and curlicues, better carved by nature than any craftsman's hands. But they are dusty, as is the window ledge, and the paint is peeling around the cobwebbed metal-framed windows. In fact, when she looks closer, the whole room is seedy and neglected. The yellow curtains have been faded by the sun where they hang facing the light.

It is sad, unloved, a reliquary. Shells in a shell; the empty shell of a person long departed. Not vital or lived in, rather unkempt and faded, a weary keepsake unloved and stale. It makes her think of her mother in her small, uninspired suburban tidiness. Washed net curtains and scrubbed floor tiles. That won't do either. She will do it differently and surely better, but she has never dared think about it. Could she countenance that she could make this hers? It's too terrifying.

On a whim, she decides that she will wash the shells and dust the shelf. She collects them up in the dressing gown and takes them into the bathroom. She kneels by the brackish water, surfaced with a sheen of bath oil, and lovingly rinses the pearly cases, laying them to dry on a towel. There is a cleaning cloth behind the basin which she takes with her back into the bedroom and dusts the window board and cleans around the window, rearranging the shells, their beauty and sheen restored in the morning sun. She is surprised at herself. What made her do it? Is she adding her votive offering to the memory of Henry's mother, or making her mark on the fabric of this tumbledown palace? But the swell of confusion sits with her and troubles her. Too many questions with no answers.

She returns to the bathroom still enveloped in Henry's dressing gown, unable to assuage the feeling of inadequacy and worry. The bubble of last night and the musical al fresco breakfast has burst. She steps into the bath's warm perfume but remains troubled and insecure.

What am I doing here? How have I ended up in this extraordinary house alone with this man? It has all gone so fast. What is a plain suburban girl working in an insurance office doing pretending to be the lady of the manor? How have I, in the blink of an eye, ended up enmeshed with a lord of the realm in a stately pile? It is unreal, unbelievable, and troubling. It will go wrong; I know I will trip up and make a fool of myself, reveal my ignorance or won't get the etiquette right. I won't have the right clothes or the right manners. Then he will see through the mirage and see me for what I really am—a fraud.

A wave of sadness swallows her within the lily fragrant water, which distracts her, but her mood doesn't lift, and she finds the pall of insecurity transfers to guilt about her mother. She should have gone to see her. This self-indulgence doesn't come easily. She lies concerned that the unease she feels implies her feelings for Henry have changed. Is this the end of love? Is it love or lust or infatuation? She notices that the water is tepid and clambers out to the small comforts of the bristly towel. She quickly dresses, finding nothing in her worn suitcase to feel good about. Her sombre mood shadows her steps down the venerable oak stairs.

She finds Henry in the library, a dark room with deep recessed windows shaded by an overgrown creeper. Bookcases line three walls with additional volumes and papers piled against the walls. He sits at a large desk in the middle of the room, equally piled with papers and documents.

He looks up as she enters.

"Hello, my love, are you all sweet-smelling and fragrant?"

She can't disguise her anxiety and makes a muted effort at a smile, but he picks up on it immediately.

He gets up "What is it, sweetheart? You look as if you've just seen the Grey Lady."

She frowns quizzically. "The Grey Lady?"

"One of our residents from the fifteenth century, sometimes seen and heard wandering around the west wing. What is the matter? You look decidedly gloomy."

"Oh, I don't know Henry I . . . I . . ." She looks up at him. "What am I doing here? I am just a middle-class girl from Reigate. I don't belong here. I don't fit. I am not grand or sophisticated. Your world is so different from mine." Her voice tails off and she looks at the floor, biting her lip to stop its trembling.

He gets up and puts his arms around her shoulders, pulling her towards him and enfolding her in his arms. Then, holding her by the shoulders, he pushes her away so he can look at her. He fixes her gaze.

"No, no, no." His tone is neither conciliatory nor comforting, rather forceful and certain. "Do you find me grand? I don't feel grand. The war did for grand. This is about you and me, not about an archaic system of heritance to which we feel we must conform. What matters are values and beliefs. My father was the most egalitarian person I have ever met. He may have had a title, but he never talked down to anyone. That's why all the estate workers loved him so. I have tried to live up to his standards, Elisabeth. I am not trying to impose anything on you; when you come here, you are you, and you bring your values and principles. I will always respect them. We have to make something together that works for us both. I know that all the things I want to do with my life will be better with you there as well. It is actually terribly simple; I love you."

She can't move or say anything. *He is like opium, this man. Being next to him, hearing him and inhaling his warmth removes all reality. All my doubts dissolve and melt. How naive to have worried. The power of having this man telling me he loves me is the most crucial emotion I have ever experienced.*

She calms and instead feels the rise of a fulminant exuberance, bundled with a physical lurch that twists her insides. She puts her hands to his cheeks and moves her lips to his to kiss him. She says something that she has never said to a man.

"I love you."

They stand enmeshed in a silent, immobile tableau.

"Oh, Henry, I am powerless beside you. I am totally useless. You do something terrible to me, terrible but wonderful. I love you. I love you. I love you." And as they stand there holding each other, she would be very happy if he decided to make love to her there and then on the threadbare old kilim, brought back from Afghanistan by the second baron.

They break off the embrace.

"So," she says smiling, "kiss it better. It never worked as a kid, but it does now. I will behave myself."

He smiles a conciliatory smile more like a teacher or a parent than a lover. "That's not right either; please don't behave yourself."

She pulls away with a businesslike air. "And what is His Lordship working on so avidly?"

"This and that. Mostly tiresome estate business: bills, correspondence from an aggrieved tenant about the well water at Lower Thorpe farm, a letter from the ministry about pig health. Fascinating stuff."

"What is this?" she says, moving towards a model of a building made of match sticks resting on a shelf of various ornaments and memorabilia.

"Ah the Knowle Opera House—my version of Bayreuth. I made it when I was about thirteen. I must have been terribly gawky and peculiar. I was in love with Wagner and thought that if he could build his own opera house, so could I. I drew a design and then made a model of it from match sticks."

"But I thought you were going to use the barn?"

"Yes, absolutely. I've got a bit more sensible in the intervening period."

"Really, more sensible? But then I didn't know you then, so I can't judge. So where would you have put it?"

"I had that all worked out. In fact, I had everything worked out. Teenagers with an idée fixe can be very obsessional. It sits in the field just below the barn on the water meadow. The design is a bit of Benville, but mostly Wagner, with chunks of Palladio and Soane."

"And you made it in matches? However long did it take?"

"I don't know. I can't remember now. Somewhere I have a book of drawings. I can remember that it was to seat six hundred and forty people, the same size as the House of Commons. You see even then I wanted it to be for the common man, not lords and ladies. I am really not that posh, Elisabeth."

"Saint Henry, patron saint of the great unposhed. I will remember that," she says, turning to him and placing a hand on his arm. "You are completely, totally bonkers, Henry. What you need is a sensible woman to look after you."

"As usual you are right. I was thinking that I might just have found one."

....

They leave the house at noon. The day is bright and warm, a few harmless clouds tumbling across an azure sky, so they put Evie's hood down. They set off for Dorchester, through lanes narrowed by banks of willow herb and cow parsley. At times Henry has to duck inside the car as they brush the verdant herbage. The car fills with pollen and petals, which Henry bats away with laughter and exaggerated gestures.

"Stop it. You are doing it on purpose," he says.

"Not at all. Road safety. The highway code and all that." Saying which, she again drives too close to the hedge towards a clump of hogweed, causing him to duck behind the windscreen.

They have been driving for ten minutes and are just entering the town when Evey slows and comes to halt. Elisabeth wears a puzzled expression and turns to Henry, who looks equally quizzical.

"Mmm, what's all this about, old girl," she says, pressing the starter button. The engine turns over but does not fire. "She never does this. Always behaves herself impeccably, especially when transporting important people."

She tries the starter again and then again. On the third attempt the engine catches and runs as before. She blips the throttle.

"Seems all right now. Mystery. Perhaps the Dorset air."

"Ley lines," he says. "Some pagan force disagreeing with the internal combustion engine."

They drive into the centre of town and park. Henry announces that he "could eat a horse" and they enter the Kings Arms, where a

sombre maître d' offers them a table in the stuffy dining room. It is
dark and airless, with blood-crimson wallpaper hung with sporting
prints, even in summer still requiring the feeble amber light bulbs
to be switched on. She is disappointed. It seems colder than outside
and much darker. She would rather be having a picnic in a field.

But she feels different. It is fine when they are together. It is when
she is left alone with her fears and inadequacies that her mood can
get sabotaged. Now she feels empowered and liberated.

She leans across and whispers, "It's a bit dismal Henry; is it
Dorchester's best?"

He looks around, up to the smoke-stained ceiling with its plaster
combed into lazy, yellowed waves and down at the stained and
threadbare floral carpet. There are a few other diners, all older, sitting
across from each other in silence, one eye on the brilliant couple that
have just walked in, the other on the bread roll and butter daisies.
They are tweedy, staid, steady, conservative. The waiter returns with
a folded menu in leather of dark plum, ragged and greasy.

"My god, perhaps you are right." There is a quizzical look on his
face as he scans the room. A sort of dawning realisation. "Spot on. It
is grim. I have been coming here all my life and have never noticed
how stuffy and tawdry it is. Perhaps it always was. Father and I used
to come here for lunch after Mama died, and then it seemed like a
treat. Of course, they knew who he was and made a fuss of me. But
it now seems very prewar. I am sorry."

"It doesn't matter. I hope you didn't mind me saying something."
She leans across to squeeze his hand, but then returns it to her lap.
It is not the place for visible intimacy.

"Not at all. God no. On the contrary. I need you to point out
these things. A new gaze on old mores. Leave London and turn into
a country bumpkin, anchored in routines of shuffling insignificance."

"Rubbish, Henry. There is no one less bumpkin-like on the
planet."

They eat an indifferent meal of brown Windsor soup followed by grey, overcooked lamb. She can't wait to escape, relieved when they finally step outside again and inhale the fresh summer air of the high street. He has to make a visit and do some other tasks, but she assures him that she will be fine for a couple of hours. He gives her a ten-shilling note to buy some food for dinner and the Knowle ration book.

She strolls down Cornhill looking into the shops, all tidy and bright, along the street. She stops to look through the ration tokens and wonders what she can cook, but it is difficult to think of food after the stodgy meal they have just eaten. Then she passes a fishmonger selling shellfish from a cart. There are prawns and cockles and a couple of crabs but also some trout, which look fresh and tasty. She knows she can cook that nicely; simple is best, fried in a pan in butter and a squeeze of lemon, if she can find one. Even better, with a smile and pleading look, the chipper 'monger doesn't want any coupons. She finds a friendly greengrocer who has nice new potatoes, fresh peas, a lemon, and a punnet of strawberries. Pleased with her purchases, she walks back to the car, where she puts the brown paper bags and wonders whether she can find a little surprise with the six and threepence that she has left from the ten-bob note.

She enjoys the shopping and strolling through the town. The bright sun helps to imbue the streets with charm and bonhomie, but it's not just that: now she feels wonderful, genuinely happy and positive. She feels strong, pretty, and desirable. She feels wanted in a way that she never has before, and how that feels is good. Very good.

Chocolate! That's it. Someone in this town will have chocolate and the way she feels they won't be able to resist selling it to her even if she only has one coupon!

....

Although she isn't a great cook and in truth finds it a bit tiresome, she is good enough at the basics and dons one of Mrs. B's aprons, opening various cupboards and drawers to locate what she needs. It takes some time to get the hang of the Aga, which she has never used before, but finally works out which is the hotter plate and the cooler oven. She hulls the peas, trims the strawberries, and makes a simple chocolate sauce, melting the precious confection in a bain-marie, adding a dab of precious butter, honey, and cream.

He is easy to please, rapturously proclaiming her skills in cooking the trout to perfection, and eating a huge number of potatoes, but saving his most obscure and indulgent adjectives for the strawberries and chocolate sauce.

"Stop it," she tells him, "It is not a pinnacle of refulgent gastronomy, it's a chocolate sauce. What is refulgent anyway?"

"Brightly shining, my love—like you—brightly shining."

After the meal, she clears away the crockery and insists on washing up, despite his protestations that Mrs. B will do it in the morning. He, realising he's beaten, picks up a tea towel and dries up for her in a dreamy way, standing rubbing a single plate for several minutes while talking earnestly about playing his cello in a ruined chapel in Antwerp.

Afterward he drags her to the music room, insisting that there will be some music they can play together, diving into a tall cupboard containing sheet music.

"No Bartok?" she asks.

"Mmm, don't think so. Afraid not."

"Kodaly, Schoenberg, Smetana, Martinů? Dvořák?"

"Dvořák, of course." He moves to another cupboard.

He finds a cello sonata and hands her the piano part. "What do you think? Manageable?"

She scans the first few pages. "Well, attemptable."

She moves to the piano and adjusts the stool, opening the lid one notch and plays a few notes. He picks up Ludwig, settles himself in front of the music on a stand leaning precariously to the side, and nods to her.

And they play, stutteringly and cautiously, concentrating on just playing the notes, but what emerges is music. They are making music together.

She has to concentrate very hard, aware of her own mistakes more than his, but she finds it enveloping. She had forgotten how completely engrossing it can feel to be lost in the rapture of notes. But this is different. At school her passion was fired by adolescent angst, loneliness, and a desire to oppress those who she saw as her oppressors. She pounded out the tonal cadences of Bartok alone because it enabled an escape from a world she hated, and the music expressed her discord, and her rejection of convention. It was essentially and necessarily solitary. Now she was playing music with another person with no angst or grievance. She had to play a duet with understanding, sympathy, love—condescension, even. It was even more difficult than the notes on the page.

They get to the second movement, the scherzo. Both struggle and agree to move on to the third, marked andante. She plays a series of sustained chords while he dances arpeggios before reverting to the central theme. They struggle to the final bars, the music more conclusive than the playing.

They both clap and smile.

"How about something a little less taxing," she says.

"I know just the thing—a touch of Vivaldi," and he gets up to rummage through the cupboard.

They play on, engrossed and focussed, with a growing confidence which hints at competitiveness. Eventually he gets up and comes to stand behind her, putting his hands on her shoulders. She closes the piano in an act of finality and stifles a yawn.

"Does that mean it's time for bed?" he asks.

"Yes, please. I thought you would never ask." She turns to him. "Thank you for making me do that. I need to be pushed, but I loved it. It reminds me of what fun it is to make music. Sorry for all the bishes."

"I didn't notice them. I was concentrating too hard on my bit. Can we do some more please? Soon. Lots more." He leans forward and pecks her forehead. "Are you happy to go on up? I better let Biscuit out and lock up."

She gets undressed in the Yellow Room. It is not completely dark, but she turns on the light and pulls the frayed curtains across the wooden mullions, shutting out the indigo sky. The bulb is dim, and the room looks less attractive in the gloom. She slips into her cotton nightie and meets Henry on the landing outside his room.

She isn't sure which side of the bed to get into, but suspects it doesn't matter much, it is so vast, sides matter less.

"I didn't tell you—I washed your mother's shells."

"I beg your pardon?"

"I washed her shells, the ones on the window ledge. At least I assume they were hers."

"Yes, they were. What a strange thing to do. I mean why would you do that?"

"I don't know, quite. It just seemed that they were looking unloved. If they are a memory to her, they should be cherished. It was all terribly dusty. The curtains are very ravelled, and it all needs a coat of paint."

He is silent, clambering into bed beside her but not immediately embracing her.

"I am sorry," she says. "Have I said the wrong thing?"

He reaches across to touch her and finds an arm and then a hand. "No, not at all. It just seems as if you are speaking a language that I understand but can't speak. I would never have noticed it—I don't see these things. You're right of course. Things here just are because they have always been. I am stuck, a behemoth wailing in the mire, or a beetle trapped in resin to be preserved forever in amber. I need you, Elisabeth. I need you to bring light into this fading twilight."

"Oh piffle. You talk a lot of complete nonsense. You are none of those things. You just need a good woman," she says, and emboldened by her bravura, she reaches across to him, slides her leg over his pelvis, and lies astraddle him, kissing him on the lips.

CHAPTER 18

....

I have been writing for a few weeks now and have enjoyed the routine. I write in the morning, outside if not blowing a mistral. I have around me the Briggens papers, and I have taken the one picture of Elisabeth out of the log and placed it on my desk. I can see the menu for our 1943 Briggens Christmas Dinner—can you believe it was very nearly fifty years ago? Then there is the picture of Robert Benville in amongst the pile. They make me think.

I had never analysed my time at Briggens in much detail; I never had reason to. But now I find myself raking through memories and finding things surfacing that I have either forgotten or buried. Were there things about my time with Elisabeth that I had missed? I know it is said that no two people's memories of distant events tally properly, and I did not have anyone to check with, but had I glossed over things, colouring them with my chosen sheen?

The major focus of our life in those years was the work. It was all-consuming and, at times, draining, albeit the wartime resilience and fortitude carried us through periods of crisis and sadness that at other times might have been overwhelming.

Elisabeth's best friend was a chirpy girl called Janet Lewis. I remember her as ebullient and irrepressible, happiest in the pub after a couple of gins. She was the antithesis of Elisabeth's more measured introversion, but as is often the case, the opposites seemed to attract. But outward jollity was tinged by tragedy and was the reason why she had given up her job in Liberty selling frocks to train as a FANY. Her fiancé, an airman, had been shot down over Belgium and then was confirmed as having been mortally wounded in the event. Janet and Elisabeth were often to be found nattering in a huddle in the saloon bar of the Crown when I finished work late.

"Ah, here he is, the dashing Pom," Janet would say. "Do you ever get tiddly, Pom?" It was a hackneyed and not very funny joke that she seemed to find amusing. Elisabeth would say nothing.

I would order a round and join them, but it was always Janet who made the conversation when we were in a group. She would chat and prattle and loved to gossip. Who said what to whom type of stuff. Janet didn't work downstairs, rather did the work much more typical of a FANY: driving, making tea, and being a general dogsbody, and so got to hear lots of office chat, albeit we could only talk of the human aspects, with not a hint of the work that filled our day.

On the way home I asked Elisabeth if she was all right.

"You seemed very quiet tonight," I said.

"Well, you and Janet hardly let me get a word in," she said with an edge.

"It was her who was doing all the chatting," I said. "I mostly nodded and listened."

"But you were joking too. It seems to me that you are always very jolly when she is around."

"She is that kind of girl. I am not sure you can be serious with our Janet."

But perhaps there was a hint of something else. Did she see a different me, or did she wish for something that Janet had?

Later Janet became close to one of the Poles, a passionate poet called Alexi. He cut a romantic figure with his long black hair and dark skin. His English was not good but that didn't seem to matter much for either of them when they were alone, and when he came to the pub, he mostly listened to Janet. He would sit, gazing at her with Labrador eyes.

"Janet seems smitten," I said to Elisabeth after they had allowed their dalliance to become public.

"Have you seen the way he looks at her?" she replied. "It's lovely. So touching. He adores her. You never look at me like that."

I didn't respond. I didn't know what to say. But in truth, I didn't really think about it—just got on with the work and life. Neither had I thought about it since, but now found I was picking apart all sorts of aspects of our togetherness to understand her better.

By 1944 Elisabeth and I had been going out for two years. Why had we not got married? Why had I not proposed to her? After all, those were the mores of the time: meet a girl, fall in love, get married. The answer was that although I loved her and wasn't looking elsewhere, (nor since, sadly) I was looking to the future, and making plans seemed to be on hold until the war had ended. There was something else, which I have hinted at: in truth Elisabeth was in charge. I always felt beholden to her feelings and motivations, and she never behaved as if she wanted to settle down. Or at least with me.

Sometime later that summer Janet appeared one evening very subdued and sombre. Elisabeth immediately picked up on her uncharacteristic gloominess, quizzing her about what the trouble was.

"Alexi has gone," she said.

"Gone where?"

"I don't know—on a mission somewhere. Poland, I suppose. He left me a note, but it didn't say much, just that he would see me after."

The weeks after were tense, the shadow of the absent Pole darkening our days and evenings. At first it was of no concern that there was silence; it was what was expected. But as the weeks went by and there was no news, I could see it was eating into Janet's jollity. The chatter dried up and her usual ebullience was crushed by the weight of her worst nightmares. But we wouldn't hear the news even if there was any. We were a cog in the machinery of war and espionage, totally distanced from operational matters.

He never came back. Not that we heard anything definitive, he just never reappeared, and all we had was silence. The mission that he had been sent on was so secret that only a handful of people would have known what and where he was sent to do. If it was a secret that he had gone, how could we expect to hear news of his progress? Their liaison was, although not secret, certainly not acknowledged by the Polish commander, and if he knew anything he kept it to himself.

Poor Janet. Losing two men to the war. After the loss of Alexi, she was never quite the same. The charming vitality and ebullience drained out of her. I wonder what happened to her. Like everyone at Briggens, save for Elisabeth, I never saw her after the war. No annual reunion. No members club. No newsletter. Nothing.

CHAPTER 19

I t is she who wakes first. The curtains were not properly drawn closed and light streams into the room. Henry seems fast asleep in a tumble of bedlinen, so she subtly slides off the edge of the bed and walks to the window. The day is perfect, still and warm with a cloudless sky, the kind of flawless summer day that etches childhood with gilded memories. A blackbird chortles its way into the hedge behind the lawn. She pulls on her nightie and leaves the sleeping Henry to find a cup of tea. She hasn't a dressing gown of her own, so she slips a cardigan over the nightgown, which will make her decent enough should she meet Mrs. B but has no idea what time it is or when she starts work.

The front door is open, with no sign of Biscuit. She steps out through the great oak portal but sees nobody and returns inside to head for the kitchen. Mrs. B and Malcolm are sitting by the mellow scrubbed-pine table with a large teapot between them. All three are startled. Malcolm gets up, as would have Mrs. B in the years before her knees became so troublesome, and hops from foot to foot, unused to having an unfamiliar woman intruding into his domestic purlieu.

Elisabeth smiles and calms the awkwardness by offering a bright good morning to them both. "What a perfect day. Makes you feel good to be alive."

"Good morning, Miss Elisabeth. I hope you slept well. Is the

Yellow Room orright for you? I hope you like it. It can be a bit cold in winter with those draughty windows, but not too bad at this time of year. I was only saying to Malcolm how nice it is to have the room used again. Not often we see Master Chivers. Not often enough . . ."

Elisabeth realises that Mrs. B wouldn't have been upstairs and seen that the bed in the Yellow Room had not been slept in. She butts into Mrs. B's diatribe and asks if there is a cuppa in the pot. She stands slightly self-consciously with her arms around her torso, thankful that she did at least put the cardigan on.

"Of course, dear. Malcolm, can you pass me a cup and saucer please. No sign of Master Chivers yet, then?"

"Apparently not." She is not sure if appearances need to be kept up, but glad that she can maintain a facade of ignorance on his whereabouts.

"He often sleeps in a bit when he first comes 'ome. He does work so hard, such important work he does, too. I don't know. Trying to find 'omes for all those poor refugees. I think he's done his bit, more than his bit, in fact. But it is nice to have you here, Miss Elisabeth. I hope everything is to your liking and you managed yesterday. Do you have a big 'ouse?"

"No, I live in a pokey little flat in London. My mother lives in Reigate."

"That's Surrey, isn't it? Very nice, I'm sure."

Elisabeth is handed a cup of strong, tepid tea, which she sips, doing her best to hide that it is not to her liking

Malcolm takes a last swig from his plain stoneware mug, and muttering that he must be getting on, backs out the side door.

"So, what are plans for the day, Miss Elisabeth? Will you be wanting lunch? Master Chivers mentioned you might be taking a picnic. I can do you some nice sandwiches. Such a lovely day for a walk and a picnic."

"I am not sure what Henry is planning, but a picnic sounds wonderful. Don't go to too much trouble, Mrs. B, please. Something simple and easy."

"No trouble, dear, no trouble at all. It's a pleasure to have you both here. I spend too much time with nobody to look after—save for Malcolm of course, but he's family." She looks to Elisabeth for confirmation that she understands the distinction.

"Is Malcolm your son?"

"No dear, I don't have no children. Malcolm is my sister's boy. I had a husband, mind, but no babies came our way. More's the pity. But still I had Master Chivers for a lot of the time and Malcolm's like my own, really." Her face wears the look of rueful acceptance, but not without pride.

"How long have you been here?"

"I first come with my Bert just soon after we were married. Can you believe I shared a birthday with Lady Sybil—that would be Master Chivers mother—but she was a few years older than me. Of course, we didn't realise for quite a time, about the birthday I mean. I was twenty-eight when Henry was born, and I'd been here a good few years then. My Bert did the vegetable garden, and I was cook—"

"Morning, morning, morning." Henry marches into the room wearing his dressing gown, pyjama legs visible above velvet slippers. He strides up the chair where Elisabeth is perched and puts his hands on her shoulders, stooping to kiss her on the crown. She places a hand on his. "Is Mrs. B filling you in on all the local gossip?"

"Oh yes. And what a rogue you are and how badly you treat your women."

"Have you been outside? It is simply the most perfect day. I think we should go for a walk and take a picnic. Can you knock us up a little something, Mrs. B? I want to take Elisabeth to the Old Church and show her the priory. I thought we would do the river walk. How does that sound?" He addresses the last remark to them both.

Elisabeth turns her head to rub their clutching hands on her face. "Sounds like the best thing in the world."

"Now what would you like in your sandwiches? I have a nice bit of boiled 'am, or there is some Double Gloucester, and a tomato or some pickle."

"Perfect. Why don't you make us a selection? Now what about breakfast? I am starving. You don't have a duck egg do you, Mrs. B?"

....

They set off for the walk at noon. He carries a small wicker picnic hamper; she a rug. Biscuit dances excitedly around them, running ahead and then rushing back for reassurance that he is not alone. Elisabeth wears a simple cotton dress, a floral pattern of pinks and greens on cream. She is not sure it goes with the tennis shoes she found the day before in the labyrinthine cupboard off the cloakroom but doesn't feel it matters on a country walk. She finds a simple straw hat on the hall hat stand. Henry is in his baggy cream flannels, a pair of old brogues, and a tatty formal shirt without a collar. He doesn't wear a hat, his exuberant hair tousled and unbrushed. Elisabeth thinks he looks marvellous. *There is something about the long limbs, the fine features, and the foppish hair that perfectly suits the loose clothing.* He is louche but forgiven. She tells him he looks like a poet heading for the Spanish Civil War.

He laughs loudly. "So, I took her to the river, believing she was a maiden, but she already had a husband . . ."

She looks puzzled.

"Lorca," he says. "How apposite."

"Lorca? And who exactly is Lorca?"

"Lorca was the Spanish poet of the Civil War."

"Ah. So did he write that? It's pretty trite. What happens next?"

"No idea. Perhaps it is better in Spanish."

"Henry, you are extraordinary, how do you know these things?"

"Just happened to share rooms at Oxford with a fanatical communist who left college to go to fight Franco. He was passionate about Lorca and used to pin poems on the wall, along with quotes from Engles."

"All right, that's a reasonable excuse. But not too much cleverness or else I'll get to feeling like a complete nincompoop again."

They walk down the drive and across the lane, finding a footpath bounded by tall banks of cow parsley and wildflowers. The path is so narrow that they can't walk side by side, Elisabeth happy to follow his languid steps. He doesn't seem to be walking, rather wafting through the sway. Biscuit is the pathfinder, out of sight ahead. She lets her hands and bare arms drift through the verdure, catching petals and seeds between her fingers. Her mind is idle but completely at ease. The sun shines, she is warm, there are pretty things all around her, and her heart skips.

The path reaches the river, which in places is so narrow you could almost jump across it but then slows and widens, not perceptibly moving. Willow and ash overhang the black water, the surface flecked by pollen, leaves, and insects. Every now and again the surface is broken by a fish rising, sending circular ripples bankwards. Now they can amble side by side through the water meadow, the soft grasses brushing their ankles. They hold hands loosely, oft just linked by a finger.

They talk of the countryside, he of summers spent in Austria as a boy and winters hunting and shooting through this same landscape. Following the beagles, cold short days out with a gun, with red-faced beaters and craggy farmers from neighbouring estates. She tells him of holidays in Hereford with her grandparents, walks collecting wildflowers, and being taught their names by Grandpa.

"I am hopeless on flowers—I seemed to be in Austria for the summers. I can tell a golden plover from a snipe, but I can't tell a burdock from a dandelion."

"I bet you can. I will test you . . . This one you must know . . ."

"Well, it's not a foxglove, and it's not a tulip."

"A tulip!" she guffaws. "Meadowsweet."

"What about this one?"

"Ermm . . . not sure. The pink ones all look the same.

"Campion." She smiles complacently and tickles him under the chin in a mock taunt.

"Look, I think this is unfair. You see, you do know things, lots of things. Do you feel better now?"

"Yes, I do, actually. There is more to life than dead Spanish poets."

"Lots more." He grabs the hand holding the flower and twists it behind her, pulling her close for a kiss. She matches, or perhaps even exceeds, his hunger for the embrace.

They walk on. *This is bliss. Just perfect bliss. The most perfect day of my life.* She is suffused with a daze of wonderment; every sense seems heightened and intense. The leaves are fresher and greener, the cerulean sky is bluer, the air hotter and heavier. She feels as if she has taken a mind-altering drug that is allowing her to see things that she has never noticed before, to feel things in a way that she has never previously. She has not allowed this before, this complete transfer of her will to something over which she has no control. There have always been conditions, caveats, reservations—brakes and controls to keep her on a route and direction of travel, commanded by some unknown person or deity. Her world has been governed by a lexicon of rights and wrongs somehow installed in her psyche, a sort of inbuilt Baedeker's guide to how she should feel and how she should respond. But it has gone, pulled from under her feet like a bunch of willow herb. She is no longer scared; now it is enthralling, thrilling, somehow dangerous and secure at the same time. She feels so heady and wonderful she skips along the path.

"I was thinking about what you said last night about Mother's shells and the Yellow Room." He breaks into the dream.

"Oh Henry, I am sorry. I know you found it upsetting. Let's leave it. We don't have to go back there."

"No, I want to. I realise you have a point; the room has become a shrine and untouchable; it has become a monument to itself. I really don't remember Mother well enough for it to be a memorial to her. Rather, I think of the room as representing what she valued, and thus it has become sacred."

She pauses before answering, thinking about what he has said.

"There is nothing wrong with that; I think that's fine. Henry, I don't want to change anything—I just point out what I notice. As far as I am concerned, boys need their mothers. I can't bear to think of you as a five-year-old with no mum, and I can completely understand why your father wanted to keep the room as it was."

"That's not the point. That's not what I am trying to say. I need a new view on things. How easy is it to become stuck, to think in a groove, to just go on doing the same old things? I love this house, but it cannot be sacred. It needs a new broom. On Friday, when I first set eyes on you, I wanted you. By god, I wanted you. Now, three days later, I realise I need you as well! What are you doing to me, Miss Watson?"

"Rather the same as you are doing to me, I suspect. But I am not going to be a mother substitute." She squeezes his hand.

"Heaven forfend. It's strange, isn't it, that we all find the loss of a parent traumatic, especially at a young age, but half the world who have mothers don't talk to them or find them insufferable. I don't think I need a mother—I need a woman."

"And perhaps, although I hate to acknowledge it, perhaps I need a man. Well, one man anyway." And she tugs at his arm.

They walk on through the baked air, disturbing crickets and butterflies as their feet kick through the unmown grass. Clouds of tiny flies soundlessly orbit invisible planets. A chiffchaff chugs through its repetitive song sheet. Sometimes the river can be heard contentedly gurgling or a pigeon coos or the panting Biscuit joins them in a frenzy of slobber, but mostly they walk through silence.

"When are we going to have our picnic?" she asks. "I am getting hungry."

"Nearly there. There is a favourite place we always came to when we were children, where the river curves and has cut into the bank. It is really very special; we often bathe there."

"Well, it's certainly hot enough. I am sweltering."

The river bends into a glade of trees and takes a sharp turn, cutting into the bank, which is a yard above the water and pocked with burrows and holes. The grass above is shorter than they have been walking through, almost as if it has been mown, rolling down a gentle slope along the bank to a shingle beach. One of the willows on the opposite bank leans precipitously over the water, an old rope dangling from a branch over the water. It is secluded but not enclosed, the grass in full sun.

"This is it. What do you think?"

"It's perfect, just totally gorgeous." She spreads the rug out and sits down. Biscuit stands on the bank above the water nosing the air.

"Is this where you bathe?"

"Yes, the water is surprisingly deep on the bend. You can jump in and not touch the bottom. When we were kids, we would try to leap onto the rope and swing across." He opens the hamper and extracts a bottle of cordial and two glasses.

Elisabeth looks at him with a smile, provocative and challenging. "Well?"

"Well, what?"

"Last one in's a sissy!" She stands up, pulls her dress off over her head, undoes her bra and steps out of her knickers, and turns, tripping naked across the soft verge towards the sandy beach.

"Oh no. Elisabeth, you are outrageous. Not so fast." He stands and quickly undresses, flinging off his shirt and trousers, but hesitates over his underpants before removing them too. He runs to the higher bank and leaps into the air before crashing into the sluggish flow, submerging and then surfacing again as he splashes towards her.

"Who's the sissy, then?"

She wades in towards the pool where he is now swimming, the water only up to her knees, before suddenly missing her footing as she steps into the deeper water, which immerses her. She screeches with the chill.

"It's freezing!"

"Rubbish. Most temperate. It's good for you, good for the circulation."

"My circ—" She splutters, catching her breath. "—ulay...shun...is fine . . . thank you."

Biscuit, who had been whining on the bank, moves down to the little beach, where he too paddles in and swims towards the two who tread water opposite each other.

"Isn't river water so marvellous to swim in? No chlorine, no salt. I love it. So wet. Much wetter than the sea." He speaks assertively.

"Wetter than ordinary water?"

"Oh, by far. Feel it between your toes, infinitely wet, those molecules of H_2O clinging to the pellicle."

"I think you will find that is mud, Henry."

"Are you able to stand? Mmm. So can I."

They stand up, the water up to their chest. She puts her arms around his neck and kisses him. He returns the kiss with growing commitment. They take a couple of steps into shallower water, although still waist deep. Biscuit takes exception to their intimacy and turns to the shore and starts to bark. Elisabeth reaches under the water to find his hardening cock, her breasts pressed against his chest.

He breaks from the embrace momentarily to admonish Biscuit in a hushed tone. "Stop it, Biscuit. Shush. Quiet." The dog looks up guiltily and paces from side to side in the shallows but continues to whimper.

She continues to kiss him, pulling him into the shallower water by his growing cock, until it emerges, when she bends forward and takes it into her mouth. He stands immobile, his hands on the back of her head, his eyes shut. Biscuit resumes his barking. He opens his eyes. "Bloody dog, stop it Biscuit."

She stops what she is doing to laugh. "Seems like he doesn't approve!"

There is more barking, but of a different tone.

"Oh Christ, there is another dog!" he mutters sotto voce.

She looks around to see a collie further down the bank, feet anchored on the grass barking wolf-like at the sky. Biscuit redirects his attention to the newcomer. Elisabeth and Henry stumble up the bank to reclaim their clothes, she giggling irreverently, he looking more embarrassed and concerned.

"Whose dog is it?" she asks.

"No idea. He's got his timing to a trick though!" He is also now smiling as he struggles into his baggy white underpants. She dives into her dress, which clings to her wet back, so she sits and wriggles it down over her torso. She bundles the underwear into the picnic basket. The dogs stop their barking and approach each other, dancing in playful aggression.

"Can you see anyone?" she asks in a whisper.

"No. It looks like a farm dog, but they normally come with an owner in tow. Coitus interruptus canis; that's a first!"

"Not exactly coitus," she proffers.

They finally manage to regain a semblance of composure, Elisabeth retrieving her underwear from the basket. Nobody appears. Henry calls Biscuit, who emerges from the undergrowth with no sign of the collie.

"Now, where were we . . ." he says. "What about lunch?"

"I had already started mine," she says coquettishly.

"You are incorrigible. Here, have a sandwich. I think there is ham or cheese and homemade pickle."

They eat their picnic and laze together on the rug.

Her desire for him smoulders, an instinctive urge, both fearsome and delicious, tugging her to him. But they are coy now, and she must content herself with lying at his side as he lies on his back, her leg over his, her pubis nuzzling his thigh. The sun is warm on her back and exposed limbs. Biscuit is now slumped in the shade, head on paws, not asleep, rather keeping them on probation after their previous misdemeanours, with expectantly raised eyebrows in the manner that Labradors do so well.

Henry's shirt is unbuttoned, and she strokes the fine golden hair on his chest.

"Can there be anything in the world better than this?" she says. "Lying here, being in love, just you and me. Will we remember this always, do you think? It can't get any better." She tails off. "Oh god, does that mean it could get worse—fade into ordinariness?"

"Never. It will never fade. I will always love you and we will always remember this moment."

"I believe that, Henry. Let's make it true." She twists around to kiss him.

They lounge in silence for minutes, then Henry says, "Now, my darling person, you had better put your knickers on because we are going back via the ruins of the priory and the Benville chapel."

"Oh, cripes best behaviour then. The dress code includes knickers, does it?"

"Afraid so. Just for a time anyway."

They leave the river, crossing the water meadow and a further field and following a track which then joins a small, tarmacked lane. They go through a stone-pillared entrance flanked by iron railings. The chapel comes into view, set behind a low stone wall capped with weathered sandstone. She sees one wall of a ruined ecclesiastical-type building abutting onto the chapel, which has two large gothic windows at one end but then the roof height drops, the far end being of rubble stone and flint. A stone path winds towards an arched doorway. There are scattered yew trees and clumps of hazel and dogrose. It feels sleepy, unnoticed but incongruous.

Henry starts explaining, striding forward in his animated way. "It is a bit of a curiosity—part Saxon church, aggrandised in the fourteenth century by the addition of an Early English chancel, which became part of the priory church. When the institution was dissolved in the sixteenth century the chapel was salvaged, with repair work over many years, and became the private chapel for the house."

"Oooh goody, am I going to get the full guided tour?" She can't avoid a hint of sarcasm.

He looks abashed, and she regrets her tone. "No, please Henry, carry on. I want to hear about it. I want to know everything."

"I am sorry. Was I being too didactic?"

"No, enthusiastic. You were just being you, and I love it and you."

He holds her, fixing her gaze. "Thank you. Thank you more than I can ever say. But there is something else I do want to say inside." He pushes at the great oak door, which creaks on its old iron hinges. It is cool inside, dark compared to the brilliance of afternoon, with a musty smell of damp cellars. Biscuit barges in and immediately lies on the cool stone floor. The space is closed, reticent, sacred, as if undisturbed for centuries. She feels she is intruding and shivers because she does not need serene and sacred on this particular afternoon.

He takes her hand and guides her to the memorials, pointing out the monument to Jean de Benville, with his reposeful plaster effigy and his pint-sized wife, with the loving greyhound at their feet. He looks calm, childlike almost; a caring man of purpose, she feels, not a warrior. Some male traits obviously breed true.

"She gave him thirteen children, nine of which survived to adulthood. Not bad, eh? Apparently, she was a loving, devoted wife, who insisted on educating the daughters as well as the sons."

She nods in silence and moves on to look at the other plaques and reliefs to the succession of Benvilles. Henry points out the plaque to his great-grandfather, engraved brass in curlicued gothic almost unreadable in its elaboration, and then the charming, simple stone memorial to his parents, tasteful sandstone with the lettering in a beautiful italic script and the words *in hoc salus perpetuum*

"What does it mean?" she asks, close to his side, linking her arm through his.

"Oh, something like 'in safety forever.'"

They stand next to each other quietly for a minute, her eyes scanning the statuary and plaques.

"And I suppose one day you will be here somewhere too?"

They stand, shoulders touching silently, linked by an eternity of tumbled thoughts and feelings. He says nothing for an age and then:

"And you with me, here in safety forever. I wanted to bring you here. For me this is a sacred place. The ghosts that sleep here are happy ghosts. They are a part of me, and I am of them. This is as near as I get to religiosity."

He speaks without looking at her, quietly and seriously. But then he turns to her and places his hands on the upper part of her arms. "There is another reason why I wanted to bring you here—I want to marry you here. Shall I get down on bended knee, isn't that what I am supposed to do? Elisabeth, will you marry me?"

She looks into his eyes and sees such pleading and need that even if she had doubts, she would have found it impossible to say no.

"Yes Henry. There is nothing in the world I want more."

"How about tomorrow?"

"Tomorrow!" She could have guessed that the sublime moment of solemnity was to be punctured by something outrageous.

"Well, Thursday then. There is no point in wasting time. If we do it now, you can come back with me to Austria."

"But Henry, I have a job and am supposed to give at least three weeks' notice, and what about the flat and everything?"

"Hadn't thought of that—but what would happen if you just don't turn up? There's not a lot they can do. I am good at problem solving. We can get around these little things."

He is grinning, his voice enthusiastic and positive, while she looks worried and troubled.

"But where would we live? What would I do while you are at work? Besides, I don't speak German."

"It will be fine. I can extricate myself from work within a couple of months. The truth is that I can't bear to be apart from you. Going back to Innsbruck on my own would be purgatory. We can marry here and then have a big party later when we come home. I have it all planned."

"But I don't."

"You know what the war taught me more than anything? Carpe diem. You never know what is around the corner. We can make this work, my darling. We will go straight to see Bill Jackson and ask him to marry us. He is the chaplain and lives in a tied cottage in the village and doesn't have to do much for his stipend. He is a marvellous man—chaplain to the Hampshire regiment at Gallipoli, then taught me Greek at Winchester. When he retired, we found him a role here as honorary chaplain to the priory."

"But, but . . . I have to talk to Mummy and Claire. Don't we need to put it in the paper? I have nothing to wear, and I don't know, Henry, I . . . I . . . am supposed to be back at work on Monday; I can't just not turn up. Can't I come to Austria as your mistress?"

For a moment he looks disconsolate, as if his persuasion hasn't been enough, but then she sees the small boy in him again and cannot bear to burst the balloon of his expectation, and now it is she who softens.

"All right, Henry Benville, if you can fix it. I remain unsure whether even you can arrange a marriage in two days." She smiles coyly, a smile that concedes without conviction.

"Well, what about trying? I want you to have exactly the wedding you want, with all our friends and families, the king if you like, but that needn't stop us just doing it now. We don't even have to tell them, if you don't want!"

A look of uncertainty hangs on her face. "It's not that I don't want it, Henry. It's just I need some time to get used to the idea and what it all means. It is one thing knowing I have fallen head over heels in love with you; it is another working out quite what that means. But if we can arrange it, then yes of course. Let's try. The last three days have been such a whirlwind of excitement and adventure, I suppose there is no reason not to add marriage into the mix as well!"

They stand and hold each other, embracing now not with passion but with other things: endearment, perhaps, contemplation, security, permanence.

They arrive at the house, with Henry flinging open the front door and calling for Mrs. B as he marches into the kitchen.

"Mrs. B, I have some important news to impart . . . where are you?"

They find her sitting in an ancient pine carver by the open window in the kitchen, knitting in her hands.

"Mrs. B, Elisabeth has agreed to marry me. Isn't that the most exciting news in the world!"

"Oh my!" She puts the knitting down onto her lap. "Oh my," she repeats. "Well, I never did." Her hands come up to her mouth, her eyes have a watery vacancy that focuses nowhere. And then the mouth tightens, her eyes fill with tears, and she sobs big sobs, looking down at the knitting, her head moving from side to side. "I never thought I'd see the day."

They both move towards her. Henry speaks first, reaching out to her and crouching to lay his hand on hers.

"Mrs. B! Whatever is the matter? Aren't you pleased? Oh dear. Oh, dear me. I thought you would be pleased."

Elisabeth doesn't know where to put herself, standing beside Henry but not knowing Mrs. B well enough to gauge the climate of her distress.

Finally, Mrs. B speaks. "Oh Master Chivers, I never thought . . . I never thought I'd see the day. Well, I never did, what a thing. Master Chivers is going to be wed. I knew it, I swear, I knew it when I first saw Miss Elisabeth. I knew she was the one." She dabs her eyes and smiles, broadly gripping Henry's hand and reaching out for Elisabeth's. Pulling them tight towards her as if she herself was joining together what no man can put asunder.

Henry takes back control. "I am so pleased, Mrs. B. For a terrible moment I thought you didn't approve. Now we must celebrate, but first I need to tell Anneleise. Where is Malcolm? Let me see if I can find a bottle." He opens a panelled door off the kitchen which Elisabeth hadn't noticed before and descends into a cellar, emerging a few seconds later with a very dusty bottle of champagne.

"Dom Perignon '34. Hope it's all right. Haven't had much call for champers for a few years. Better order some supplies, eh what! Let's put it in the fridge while I go and find Geoffrey and Anneliese. Will you be all right here with Mrs. B, darling?" He doesn't wait for a reply before striding out, leaving the two of them alone.

Elisabeth turns a chair and sits to face Mrs. B, flopping down with obvious exhaustion.

"Are you all right, dear?" Mrs. B asks. "You suddenly look tired. You are happy, aren't you?"

"It's just all a bit of a whirl, Mrs. B. I haven't really had time to catch my thoughts. What I'd really like is a cup of tea."

"Of course, my dear. You just sit there, and I'll put the kettle on."

"What a lot changes in a few hours—here we were sitting together this morning with me still finding my place with Henry and now I am going to be his wife. The truth is, I can't believe it. I haven't even told Mummy or Nanny yet, or my sister. I keep wondering what Daddy would think, but I know he would respect Henry and ultimately be happy with what I wanted."

"I'll tell you what, Miss Elisabeth, he's the best. I've never heard him say a bad word about nobody. All the village love him, as they did his father. But in my life, I've never seen him like this with anyone. You've caught him proper, I'd say."

"Oh, but I didn't set out to catch him, Mrs. B. He just arrived on my doorstep with that crazy cello, wearing a pantomime costume! I wasn't caught—I fell. I just fell. In fact, I'm still falling." She smiles, looking nowhere in particular. "And without a parachute."

Henry returns subdued and perhaps crestfallen. He enters the kitchen with Malcolm behind him, who, looking uncomfortable, slips off his working shoes and pads across the floor in stockinged feet.

"I am sorry, but Anneliese won't be joining us. She says she has a headache but sent warm felicitations to you on your engagement." Henry smiles, saying the latter part of the sentence in an exaggerated formal manner.

Geoffrey appears a moment later, beaming with genuine excitement and offering his hand along with effusive congratulations.

Henry opens the refrigerator to retrieve the champagne and asks Mrs. B to find some glasses. She bustles off to the dining room to retrieve the best crystal, which she then proceeds to polish vigorously with a tea towel before placing them on a silver salver. Finally, Henry is allowed to open the bottle to a muted pop.

"Oh lord, I hope it hasn't gone over."

The others look on expectantly as Henry fills five glasses.

"To us."

They lift their glasses, each according to their own. Henry, confident, boisterous and assured; Mrs. B, cautious, unsure that she should be part of the celebration; Malcolm, embarrassed, never having tasted champagne before, wishing he was somewhere else; Geoffrey smiling, quietly rocking onto his tiptoes, ever the executive; and Elisabeth, with eyes only for Henry but suddenly troubled. A wave of uncertainty washes over her. She feels her anchors slip from under her. What is she doing here with these strange, muted celebrants? She is assailed by images of her girlfriends and the London pals who she sees regularly. Why aren't they here to celebrate her engagement? Why is she only sharing the immeasurable man who she loves with the cook and the gardener? It hits her hard enough for Henry to notice and leaves her fumbling for an excuse.

"Sorry Henry, I was just thinking of Daddy."

He consoles her and she recovers, helped by her noticing Malcolm's obvious dislike of the champagne, which he touches to his lips but barely sips.

Geoffrey is much more enthusiastic, raising his glass to the newly engaged couple and quaffing a slurp.

"Would you rather have something else, Malcolm?" Elisabeth says, rescuing him. A minute later they are all joking that his engagement party will be a cheap affair, with pints of cider all round. Mrs. B finds him a bottle of beer in the scullery, barely touching her own glass of champagne, muttering about not getting tipsy with supper to make.

The bottle is still half full when the party breaks up—Elisabeth to telephone her mother, granny, and sister; Henry to change for dinner; Malcolm heading out to the Waggon and Horses; Geoffrey back to the office; and Mrs. B to prepare dinner.

She calls her mother, building gently to the announcement that she is engaged to be married. She starts by saying she met this wonderful man "some time ago," but doesn't mention his lineage and doesn't let on that they hope to marry the next day.

Her mother is matter-of-fact in her manner, leaving Elisabeth almost disappointed that she wasn't either more shocked or more obviously delighted. But then that is her way, never prepared to voice an opinion on anything much since she lost her man. Elisabeth ends the conversation with the promise that she and Henry will come for lunch on Friday, come what may.

Then she phones Claire and ends up in floods of tears because Claire starts to cry and asks a hundred questions about Henry that Elisabeth finds she loves answering because, for the first time, she can tell someone close to her about him. Even so, Elisabeth is a bit economical with the detail, keeping the title out of the picture. She puts the phone down feeling elated. It is one of the few times in their lives they behave in the soppy, filial way that sisters do so well.

She feels calmer as she heads upstairs to find Henry. The maudlin moment has passed, and she is now more relaxed about her family; she knows there is more to be said but can see a way forward. The details and explanations can come later once they have got used to the idea.

As she heads up the stairs, she meets Henry coming down.

"Darling person," he says, "there is something else we must do before dinner. Come with me." He reaches for her arm and turns her back to descend the stairs, dragging her towards the study.

"Where are you taking me, you wicked man? What mischievous plans are you now cooking up?"

"Wait and see. Now, where are they?" He lets go of her hand to open a desk drawer, fumbling through papers, pens, pencils, and other clutter. "Must be in this one." He opens a second drawer and emerges with a key. He walks across the room to a cupboard, which he opens on a latch revealing a large safe. He inserts the key and opens the door, stooping to view the various shelves before extricating a velvet jewellery box. He turns, presenting it to Elisabeth, holding it open towards her.

"A ring. We need a ring. Mother's jewels. I have a feeling we might find something in here. If you don't like any of them, then we can always use a curtain ring."

"But Henry, they were your mother's. I can't . . . They are beautiful. So many lovely things . . . Wondrous things." She slowly and carefully lifts out various pieces—earrings, a brooch, a gold stranded necklace—letting them tumble through her fingers. "They are beautiful, so beautiful."

"I think the rings are here." He pulls the box's sides apart, which open on struts to reveal a second layer. "Let's take them over to the window."

They sit on a wide, low sill with the box between them as she continues to delve into the box's glittering contents.

"I could never have any of these, Henry. They are your mother's."

"Au contraire, they have been waiting for you. They must see the light of day. What is the use of them being locked in the safe? Look, how about this one? Is that an emerald?"

"No Henry, it's an amethyst."

"Oh whatever, it's jolly pretty. Now this is definitely a ruby, yes?"

"Ten out of ten."

She pulls out a simple diamond set in a cluster of aquamarine, elegant but not ostentatious, and dares to try it on. It is too small, but she fits it on her little finger, extending her arm and moving the hand from side to side.

"Beautiful, stunning even. You have lovely hands."

He finds a simple gold rope necklace which he places round her neck, reaching behind her to do up the clasp, moving close enough for her to be reminded of his scent. He smells musky, of masculine sweat and a hint of something animal, but mostly it's just him—delicious, evocative him. She kisses his neck.

She doesn't choose the aquamarine, rather a single diamond in a nest of tiny emeralds. It is also too small, but he assures her that they will be able to get that sorted in town. He insists that she keep the gold necklace, which sits well on her slender neck.

CHAPTER 20

....

Dorchester

July1992

I found the premises of Smallwood and Lees without any difficulty and parked the Bristol in a car park nearby.

Mr. Smallwood was indeed a little man, or to be kinder, small statured. He was, at a guess, in his early fifties, neat, wearing a nondescript grey suit and sober tie. He had glasses with a black bar across the top but no frame underneath, giving him an owl-like appearance. He was smiling and affable as he introduced himself, seeming to walk on tiptoes, taking tiny steps like a ballet dancer, pitching forward in an obeisant manner as he herded me into his office.

The room was decorated in a nondescript style, designed, I assumed, to sit comfortably with all the vagaries of the human condition with which solicitors must deal: death, divorce, crime, injustice. I noticed on the table a large brown manila envelope. Adjacent to it was a pile of other papers and a pen.

He welcomed me and said how grateful he was that I had taken the trouble to visit in person. The table was large and round and sitting opposite him would have been inappropriately formal. I chose a chair adjacent to his pile of papers.

"I have to ask how you knew Elisabeth."

"We met a very long time ago. Actually, it was during the war."

"Really. Whereabouts?"

"We worked together in Essex."

"At Briggens?"

I was taken aback. Never had anyone I had ever met known about Briggens.

"Yes. I am surprised you know that name; not many people have ever heard of it."

"I knew nothing about it until about three years ago. It was when her illness came back. She did an interview for our local paper, at her behest I think, and thrilled a cub reporter by revealing the work that was done there. It was something of a scoop for the *Dorchester Echo*. How interesting. It must have been fascinating work."

I was drawn to his gentle but precise way of speaking. His voice seemed to care.

"I am surprised she was willing to talk about it, let alone give an interview."

"That is why I know about it. She came to see me and explained a bit about the work at Briggens and whether she would be at risk of prosecution under the Official Secrets Act. I think she knew that with a progressive illness she wasn't going to live forever and wanted to tell someone."

"Progressive illness? I am afraid I know nothing about her recent life."

"I do apologise for making assumptions. She first had breast cancer about twelve years ago, but after treatment it went into remission, and she had another good ten years. Unfortunately, she suffered a recurrence, as is often the way, that did not respond to treatment."

"What very bad luck."

"It was, as you say, very bad luck. I looked into where she would stand talking about Briggens and concluded that there was very little risk. After the publication of *The Ultra Secret* in 1974, and with more and more Bletchley Park staff coming forward to tell their stories, secrecy was no longer an issue. My advice to her was to consider that she was now free of any constraints imposed by signing the Act forty years previously. Public curiosity is rightly a bigger driver than keeping a lid on these secrets after all these years."

"I didn't know that. I live a quiet life in France."

"Cap d'ail, I believe. Charming. I am sure it must have its dispensations." He smiled, sitting with his elbows on the table, tapping his outspread fingers together.

"Yes, although the Riviera has changed a lot. Sadly."

"I can imagine."

He paused for a minute. I could see he would be good reading a will: attentive, serious, precise, deferential but firm.

"If it is not too an impertinent question, can I ask when you last saw her?"

"Nineteen forty-eight."

He looked surprised. "Nineteen forty-eight! I had imagined it would have been more recently than that."

"No. I have had no contact since. That's why it is so surprising that she remembered me in her will."

"Well, of course people do make odd bequests, and it is not for us to do anything but execute their wishes. I think my father first helped her with her will about twenty years ago. When he retired, I took over her file and she revised it several times since. I would like to think I was close to Elisabeth. This firm, and my father in particular, have been handling the Knowle estate for many years—long before Elisabeth first arrived here. A small firm like ours in this sort of town becomes very closely involved with our clients. Everybody knows everybody else and thinks they know what they are up to. We often met socially. For many years I played squash with Philip."

"Philip?"

"Philip Wood—her partner, if that's the right term."

"So, she remarried?"

"No, she didn't. I am sure Philip would have liked to, but they lived together for more than twenty years."

So, there had been two other men in her life. Why did that small piece of information hurt me?

"Well, as I was saying, although I had seen the will on numerous occasions and must have noted the bequest, I had not realised that we didn't have a proper address."

"When did she leave the envelope?"

"Well, that I can't tell you exactly. It would probably have been when my father finalised the first will. As I say, it must be more than twenty years ago now."

"And you have no idea about what it contains?"

"None whatsoever. One might venture a guess that it is something to do with your time together during the war."

"Yes, that's what I was thinking."

"How long are you staying in England?"

"I am not sure. I haven't booked a return ferry."

"I see. You drove?"

"Yes. I find flying odious."

"Quite." He smiled again. Facial tact. "Are you staying locally?"

"No, I am staying in Lymington; one of my old sailing haunts."

"Not too far then." He fumbled with the papers on his desk. "I do just need you to sign a form to say that you have received the items specified in the bequest. I am sure you understand." He produced a document on headed paper and passed it across to me, proffering a ballpoint.

"Naturally." I reached into my pocket for my Parker pen.

"Ah a proper pen—how satisfactory—I can put my biro away then! If you would just like to read it through and sign here . . . and a copy for you . . . Thank you so much. I must say it has been a pleasure to meet you, Mr. Mackay, and I hope all will be revealed when you explore the contents."

He got up and, as he shook my hand, made an obsequious bowing gesture like an entertainer at a children's party. Perhaps he was better in small doses.

"Of course, if there is any way we can be of further assistance, my firm would be delighted to help." He tripped his balletic patter to the door and ushered me out.

"Thank you," I said. "I may be in touch," and walked back into the thin autumn sunshine.

I couldn't decide whether to open the envelope there and then or return to my hotel. I chose the latter.

But I made a wrong turn and ended up in Salisbury in a traffic jam at some temporary traffic lights. The envelope sat on the passenger seat, begging to be opened. I was like a kid at Christmas and couldn't wait, so while stationary opened the envelope and pulled out a bundle of papers. There on the top was a printed card that I immediately identified as a French ID card that we must have made. It was a poignant moment. It was not complete, but the name written by hand (Elisabeth's I suppose) was Corinne. She must have secreted it into her bag, strictly against the rules and would have been severely punished if discovered.

So, we had been right, the bequest was nothing more or less than mementos of Briggens, or at least that's what I thought at the time.

....

Producing these identity cards for agents being dropped behind lines was just one of the challenges we faced at Briggens. Sourcing the right paper was often the biggest problem. I had built relationships with Barcham Green papermakers in Kent, who had the capacity to make machine-made paper to our specification. The only problem was that because of the set-up process and to avoid suspicion the minimum order was two tons. We might have only needed to make a few dozen identity cards the size of a driving licence and yet we had to order two enormous rolls of paper, so large that it took a crane to lift them off the delivery lorry.

We did experiment with dry pressing watermarks onto finished paper with some success, but although the result was passable, it was not up to the scrutiny of Charles Roberts or Morton Bisset.

I talked to Bill Martin about whether we could make small batches of paper on site with the right watermark. Bill had made all the wire watermarks at Eynsford, and he showed me how he could produce the wire frames required, sitting at a bench with coils of different size brass wire and a soldering iron. Like most of the tasks performed at Briggens, it was exacting work and sometimes the pattern needed adjustment before it was right. But the problem was the paper. We all think that paper is simply wood pulp, but that is a huge simplification, as specialist papers have various added fibres that provide strength or texture, and we couldn't source the raw materials even if we knew what they were.

An alternative approach was to start with a paper that felt and looked right and turn it back into pulp. We found it simple to soak the paper and mash it up, but doing this by hand we couldn't produce a fine enough pulp. The need was for a mechanical device that had sharp rotating blades. Nowadays you can buy a kitchen liquidiser that does the same sort of thing but then they weren't available. Soon we had the Poles on the case, and, sure enough, using a large aluminium mixing bowl from the kitchen and a motorcycle engine attached to blades from a sugar beet mangle we were able to make a device capable of mashing all sorts of paper into a fine enough pulp. It was a terrifying machine which I insisted remained outside in a simple lean-to shelter and could only be operated by a bullet-headed Pole with no neck called Vlad.

We experimented with various papers and materials and could usually produce the texture we needed. However, one particular paper, if I remember correctly, for Dutch travel carnets, was difficult to recreate due to its thinness and strength. Our first few attempts failed. We could get the paper of the right thickness and texture, but it just wasn't strong enough.

"Gampi, that's what we need," Bill said.

Gampi is a Japanese tree root that has been used in that country to make paper for a thousand years. I had never used the material, which is of legendary toughness even when wet.

"I have an idea," he said with an uncharacteristic smile and headed out of the shed. He returned three minutes later with two rolls of lavatory paper. In those days toilet roll was not the soft absorbent tissue it is now but a shiny, thin paper most unsuited to the task for which it was intended but containing a high proportion of Gampi or similar. Into the mix it went, and after a few trials and a light-hearted request to Roberts for an order of an extra gross of rolls, we achieved what was needed.

Then, with the right deckle and a huge press, we could get close to what we needed. But it was never straightforward.

I remember on one occasion Dennis storming into the hut with a very uncharacteristic scowl. He was usually such a mild-mannered man. "The bloody size. There is no size."

I didn't quite understand what he was on about but walked over to his bench.

We had been working on Norwegian papers for the brave fishermen who ploughed between the Shetland Isles and coast of Norway in what later became known as the Shetland Bus. He thrust the identity card at me.

"Look at the ink," he demanded.

I could see that the ink he had applied to the paper we had worked so hard to produce had spread as it might when writing on blotting paper. All commercial paper must be "sized," which involves covering the surface with a substance such as starch which prevents the ink from spreading between the fibres. In commercially made papers this is done as part of the process; what we had to do was apply a size by brush or spray to the finished sheets. Too much and the ink did not adhere (as when trying to write with a fountain pen on a glossy picture), too little and it was like writing on tissue paper.

We must have forgotten to size the paper.

Bill said nothing—as usual—just took the work away to his desk and started from scratch all over again.

Sometimes we just needed the paper to look old and it was much better if it was truly old, rather than aged in Elisabeth's handbag. We were always on the lookout for suitable sources.

One evening I was just heading home when Charlie Roberts asked me if I played billiards. There was a fine table in the library, which I had only ever spied when walking past the door. I accepted and joined him while he set up the table. Most of the internal walls of the room were shelved, containing His Lordship's collection of large leather-bound tomes. In between shots I examined some of the volumes. Sure enough, in many of them, at the back after the printing ceased, there were several completely blank pages.

I still wonder if, after the war, Baron Aldenham ever noticed that many of his fine books had evidence that pages had been removed from inside the rear cover. Bill and I were the culprits, using the excuse of a game of billiards, which he couldn't play. We told no one else. The fewer who knew the better. We reasoned that if we could have asked His Lordship whether he would mind us using a blank page of a book nobody had looked at since the flood to make an authentic-looking letter to go into the handbag of an agent being parachuted into Normandy, the answer would surely have been yes.

Another challenge was the bias binding where the documents were hinged. I couldn't source the material in London but that gave me the perfect excuse to make a trip to the Winterbottom company in Manchester, where I wished to cultivate a reliable contact.

Within a couple of weeks, we had a very convincing *carte d'identité* available, but this was not all that was needed; the agents needed a life, a background, a family. Mostly they were women and they needed to have in their bag, or satchel, all the things that an ordinary girl would have; clothing coupons, an old railway ticket, a love letter, makeup, a set of keys, an address book, ration vouchers, perhaps a card with a prayer on it—often revered in Catholic countries—or a trivial keepsake, and that was where the FANYs, and Elisabeth in particular, were so brilliant.

Remember that we had photographs of the agent, the date and

place of their birth, along with the names of their parents and the like because these had to be inserted into the documents. The difficult part was not knowing who they really were. We were creating an alias, but who were they really? Just as one can make up an imagined history for a person opposite you in a railway carriage, so we created a life for the girl with the gaunt face, or the man with the neat moustache. We turned them into people and gave them a life without ever meeting them. Perhaps it was insulting and impertinent, but it was also vital. The photographs were taken at the Baker Street headquarters of the SOE and would be sent by motorcycle to us. The whole team would assemble in the briefing room to be told about the task, Captain Roberts addressing us in his tight, precise manner, frequently stroking his dainty moustache.

"What we have here is a twenty-seven-year-old Josette Norville from Nantes. Her parents are Cecile and Jean Paul. She has one sister, who is the mother of a child and still lives in Nantes. Her brother is missing in action. She works as the representative of a chemical company. She has an erstwhile boyfriend working in the docks in St. Nazaire."

He passes round a photograph, a not-quite full face which shows a pretty, dark-haired girl looking slightly uneasy and serious, with a crucifix on a thin chain around her neck above a lace-trimmed blouse. She looks unremarkable—the girl next door. She could have been Jane Smith or Mirabelle de Courcy Houanbeck or even Elisabeth Watson. We were never to know.

I looked across to Elisabeth as the photo reached her. I knew what she would be thinking. This "girl next door" isn't just that or anything like that, she is an incredibly brave woman, probably brought up in France and certainly speaking perfect French, who is prepared to be dropped by parachute in the middle of the night into a field in Normandy with a gun and radio set and live a life of hide-and-seek, in constant fear of capture, interrogation, torture, and death. She will link with the local resistance and send crucial messages home about troop strength and movement, defences, command structures, and the like. She will live from hand to mouth, often sleeping on a couch or even in a barn. She will try not to draw attention to herself but nevertheless obtain worthwhile information. She will walk a tightrope between security and keeping a low profile, with the risk of not gleaning any useful information on the one hand, and overly brazen and intrusive behaviour which would draw attention to herself on the other—all the while trying to avoid arousing suspicion amongst her neighbours, who could well be informants.

But she was also our child, we created her ipseity. We parented her, nurtured her, and every man and woman of us willed her to be safe and evade detection. We did everything in our power to make sure our contribution would not let her down.

Reg Smith asked if the boyfriend had a name.

"Not yet, Reg. Over to you."

"What about a pet?" asked Elisabeth.

"I don't think so, not living in the city. What were you thinking?"

"Perhaps a picture of a dog?"

"What about a picture of her sister's little boy?" said Dennis.

"That's a better idea."

"And a letter from the boyfriend perhaps?" Arthur chipped in.

"Or a card. How about a saucy postcard?" Willie said.

"Have we got anything suitable, George?" said Roberts.

"I'll see what I can find," mumbled George.

"Can you get your French ladies working on a letter, Peter?"

"Yes, but I will need a different address and some suitable paper."

"Can you manage to find something?" said Roberts.

I smiled, "I have the perfect source."

"Glad to hear it."

"What about the parents—a photo or a gift," said Pauline.

"Or perhaps just a novel she is reading, or a book of poetry," Bruce suggested.

"Possible. Probably better to source that locally, I would think.

Now anything else?" He looked around the room with an assertive air. "All right then, let's get to work. Deadline on this one is 1100 hours on Friday."

The French have a very characteristic style of handwriting, which was even more pronounced in the first half of the century. We often needed envelopes, either to be posted or, as in this case, to be part of a memento, or part of a person's identity. Rather than try to get forgers to copy the style, which it transpired was difficult, I had the idea of getting French women to write them for us. I put the problem to Morton Bisset, who passed the request up the chain of command.

Sure enough, by means that remain unclear, a cohort of senior French ladies were found who were happy to write addresses on envelopes. I never met the women who did this work, but I imagine with some pleasure elderly French mesdames doing their bit for the Resistance by writing letters to imaginary people in the characteristic hand taught to them *en primaire*.

A week later we would once again be around the table for a final assemblage of items. Here was the *carte d'identité*, scuffed, worn, and tattered. Here was a birth certificate on watermarked paper, creased and partly faded, where it may have been left on a shelf or in a drawer. Here was a letter from the chemical company confirming her position and need to travel to visit suppliers, a postcard from Phillipe (the boyfriend) with a French stamp and circular post mark clearly reading St. Nazaire and a date (hand drawn by Dennis), a photo of a smiling boy with "Luc Francoise" written on the back and a date of birth in blue ink, a powder compact engraved with a *NB* and the date of her confirmation (which of course we invented), an old train ticket, and some food coupons. A sepia picture of her dead brother was mounted in an oval window on a tasteful card, hand painted with lilies and roses and with *en mèmoire* and two lines from a poem by Baudelaire that Arnold had sourced printed on the front.

And after the final nod of approval from Roberts, that was how we sent her off. That was exactly how it felt; *us* sending *her* off. As we left the room, Pauline, a church-going Catholic, would cross herself, lean across the table, and say, "Godspeed, my child." It was always a sombre moment, usually ending in silence as the crew filed out to their desks to resume the other tasks on their list.

The importance of what we were doing was not lost on any of us, nor the bravery of the agents, but most of us left our involvement behind when we walked out of the security gate at the end of the drive and headed for the Crown. Perhaps that is why we headed for the Crown. Not so for Elisabeth, who found it much more difficult to leave the work behind.

I couldn't sleep because of terrifying images of sailors in the Arctic flailing and screaming in flaming fuel oil. She couldn't sleep because she worried about what was happening to young women parachuting into enemy-occupied France. What about the agents, did they sleep? When they woke up, who were they? How long did you have to pretend to be somebody else before you forgot who you really were?

Perhaps that was why we found each other, because in our mutual insecurities we found a place of safety and constancy. She clung to me because I was stoic, steady, and put on a brave face. I sought her out because of her grace, charm, and beauty and because she seemed to care. That's what we all needed in those times: a little island of safety and constancy. And that's what she gave me.

But with time it became apparent that it was genuinely upsetting, for the women especially, not to know what happened to the agents. We would expend so much time and put so much emotional energy into trying to get everything so right, and then—nothing. No word, no news, no information, just another job the next week. Another brave person flying into a terrifying unknown. It was agonising not to know what happened. As if the last reel of the film had gone missing.

We didn't socialise much with Major Perkins, the unit's superior officer, but at the Christmas party at the end of 1943 I found myself chatting to him at the bar and explained the problem to him.

"Would it be possible to arrange just a bit of feedback about what happens to our agents? I can't see it would be a security risk; all we would need to know was that they had got home safely or some such. Anything, just . . . something."

"Mmm, I am not sure, Mackay. It doesn't really work like that. As you know, we have a job to do and are completely cut off from the operations side. I am not even sure who I could ask."

"But the crew get so involved with these people, they feel they know them. They admire them terribly and know the risks they take. Just a word is all we need."

"Well, no harm in asking, I suppose. I will mention it to Gubbins."

And two months later, after a briefing session about a new mission, Charles Roberts announced: "Now, I know some of you have been asking after your protégées and I am happy to be able to pass on news to you that Josette returned home and is having tea with her mother in Basingstoke."

There was silence amongst the sea of bemused faces. He said it again with a smile on his face, "Josette has returned home safely."

And then we understood what he meant, and everyone started to clap and even the most unmoved and stoic amongst us joined in the celebration, Arnold taking his pipe out of his mouth for a rare moment and muttering, "Oh, bravo. Bravo" and banging the table, spilling ash and soot over the whole affair. But that little piece of news was all we needed and was a real fillip to our morale.

We also got other feedback. We heard that a Polish agent had been stopped at a border and his documents scrutinised by a Nazi patrol and handed back without comment, the holder being allowed on his way. This was what we needed to hear—that our long evenings and attention to detail passed muster under scrutiny.

Early in 1944 we had to produce the documents for a new agent whose false name was Corinne Leroy. At the briefing two things were apparent: the first was that she was very pretty, the second that she was only twenty-two.

It affected Elisabeth greatly.

"She is only twenty-two," she said, "younger than me. What guts must you need to do what she is about to do? She is five foot three; she is tiny. Parachuting out of a plane at night into a field with a bag of false documents and a gun. I could never do that."

Although, I suspected she probably could, had the circumstances been different.

Two months later Charles Roberts came in wearing a more relaxed visage than usual, his oiled black hair neatly parted and pasted to his cranium. He sat down.

"Before I start, we have news of Corinne which I know Elisabeth will want to hear: she was picked up two weeks ago having completed a successful mission and is safe and sound with her family."

Once again spontaneous applause broke out. Elisabeth's relaxed grin was a joy to see. I caught her eye and winked, returning her smile.

But on this occasion, that wasn't the end of it. Only a few weeks later a new brief came in; this time the agent's alias was Mme Villeret. Roberts gave the usual summary before passing around the photograph.

"It's her—it's Corinne," Elisabeth blurted out.

We all had a second look. The photograph was different, but she was right, this was the same young, thin-faced woman, with dark hair and a coy smile.

She was going back for more.

We never heard any more of Corinne, which I knew troubled Elisabeth. Whenever she had the chance, she would ask Roberts or Bisset if there was any news, to which the reply was always negative. Alas, we knew that in this situation no news was bad news.

I don't know if Elisabeth ever saw the film *Carve Her Name with Pride*, but I cannot imagine she didn't. It came out in 1958 with Virginia McKenna playing Corinne. I rarely went to the pictures, living the life I did, but there was an English cinema in Monte Carlo that I occasionally visited. But when I heard a friend talking about the film, I realised I had to see it. It tells the story of Corinne—in reality, Violette Szabo—and what happened on that second trip with her capture, transfer to Ravensbruck concentration camp, torture, and cruel execution. I know how I felt when I saw it, and if an unemotional old seadog like me was reduced to tears, I don't know how Elisabeth would have coped. At the time, we all still felt bound by the Official Secrets Act and couldn't even admit to the little roles we'd played in the story.

What we now know is that she wasn't the only one to die. Of the forty female agents sent into France twelve died. Andree Borell, Vera Leigh, Diana Rowden, and Sonia Olschanezky were murdered by injection of phenol, an agonising, terrible death. Yolande Beekman, Madelaine Damerment, Elaine Plewman, Denise Block, Yvonne Rudellat, and Lilian Rolfe were shot. Cecily Lefort also died in Ravensbruck.

Someone has to remember them. I know their names by heart; it is my thing. I will be their torchbearers. They deserve it.

As do the men, of course. How many other identity cards and documents did we produce during those extraordinary years? How many brave men were sent into enemy territory carrying in their wallet crucial documents that made them who they were, lovingly made in Essex?

I have no idea. But neither does anyone else because the records were all destroyed, and we all went back to our other lives and didn't say a word to anyone for forty years.

....

At the end, as with Bletchley Park, the instructions were to destroy all traces of our activity, and that's what we did. Machinery was moved out and sold or scrapped, records were burnt in massive bonfires, other furniture and fixtures were taken away in a series of Ministry trucks, and the staff was forbidden to remove any mementos. I cannot have been the only one who felt the irony as we handed in our identity cards.

We shook hands at the gates and went our own ways. I continued to see Elisabeth, but I never met any of the others again.

That part of our lives just disappeared. Every single page and piece of paper, photograph, plate, print, and document had been destroyed or removed—along with the camaraderie, laughter, commitment, and sense of purpose. The concerts and parties, the nights in the pub, the friendship and companionship all ended. Turned off like the last lightbulb, extinguished at the flick of a switch. We turned our backs on the cloistered coterie of Briggens and marched into the new life that peacetime threw at us. But not only that, with the last turn of the key on the padlocked gates our identities vanished too. Those four years became invisible, as if they never existed. The Confabulatorium of Ipseity was closed—forever.

We left our lodgings in Hunsdon to a round of fond farewells to landlords and landladies with promises to keep in touch, relief and liberation tinged with regret and an awareness that something monumental and important was coming to an end. I went back to Epping, Elisabeth to Reigate. I bought my boat, and she got a dull job in the city.

I have told you the rest of the story.

CHAPTER 21

S he wakes with a nagging worry that she may have been prattling the previous evening. At breakfast she apologises, owning up to flopping into bed while he let Biscuit out and locked up, intending to welcome him into the huge bed with an ardour befitting their engagement, only to find it was morning, the bed was empty, and she has a sour taste in her mouth from the wine and champagne.

Henry, in contrast, is brimming with energy, itching to get out of the house to see William Jackson. However, he then disappears, and it is Elisabeth who gets anxious when the kitchen clock strikes ten and he is still absent. Mrs. B suggests she looks for him in the estate office, where she finds him busy with Geoffrey discussing the troublesome water supply. They finally set off at half past ten.

They approach a small stone cottage set behind a neat garden, the front door barely accessible behind a rambling white rose and the blooms shedding cascades of browning petals as they push past.

The door is opened by a small man of considerable age wearing a white shirt open at the neck with red braces holding up trousers now too large for his shrunken frame. He is mostly bald with wisps grey hair above his ears. Half-moon glasses perch askance on his beaky nose.

"Henry! How very good to see you."

"And you William, Salvete! I have someone very important I want you to meet. Can I introduce Elisabeth Watson?" He stands aside, ushering Elisabeth across the threshold. Even she must stoop to avoid the rampant rosebush.

"What a delightful surprise. Come in come in."

"As of yesterday, Elisabeth and I are betrothed," Henry says as they are led in through a book-laden sitting room and into the garden, where a table is set under a pear tree. They are offered tea or lemonade, and both choose the latter. They catch up with pleasantries before Henry reveals the purpose of his visit and his request that William marry them.

William's response is one of genuine delight at the engagement and the prospect of a forthcoming wedding. Elisabeth notices the warmth of their conversation and exchanges, humour mixed with respect and unaffected interest which transcends the fifty-year age difference.

William launches into what she suspects is a long-practised diatribe reserved for engaged couples seeking his services. He enquires as to whether she is a Catholic but is not visibly affected by the negative answer. He talks of the wonderful potential of marriage, its many purposes, and the reality of the commitment required.

Henry butts in. "The thing is, William, I am supposed to be back in Austria this week and really cannot delay my return on Saturday. Can you marry us this week? Friday perhaps?"

Elisabeth studies William's features and sees the humorous responses of this sprightly man make way to a more serious look.

"Oh, dear. I see why you want to hurry, but I think that will be difficult. Very difficult . . ."

He looks upwards as if to assemble his thoughts and then launches into a spiel about protocol and the need for the banns to be read and permission from the diocese, as the chapel is not a parish church, and how it really would be impossible to get everything organised in time.

Henry sits, silent and deflated. William clasps his hands together *in apologia*. Elisabeth does not know what to think. A part of her is relieved, another part sad. The biggest emotion is empathy for Henry, who looks crestfallen and deflated.

"If you are really set on it, you might be able to find a register office who would marry you at short notice. I would have doubts that Dorchester would be able to oblige, but somewhere in London possibly. They are more familiar with the impetuous and those in a hurry." The corner of his mouth smiles as he turns to look at Elisabeth and Henry in turn, peering to look over his gold-rimmed spectacles.

"Capital idea. How might we explore that possibility?"

"I am sure there will be a list of offices in the public library, but the person who would surely help is Percy Smallwood. Why not ask him? You know we can arrange a blessing in the chapel at any time."

William sits back in his chair and looks at Elisabeth, taking his glasses off and twirling them in his fingers, his elbow to his side but his hand away from his body. He looks more serious again, more like a vicar.

"Is this what you want, Elisabeth? Many young women dream of a glamorous white wedding with lots of bridesmaids, champagne, and tiaras. Is that you, dear?"

Elisabeth is taken aback and has to assemble her thoughts without being sure what they are.

"Well . . ." She pauses, giving herself time. "I have never dreamed of a formal wedding with ceremony and rigmarole. I am not that type of person. I value authenticity over formality, but then I have never met anyone like Henry, and have only had a few hours to think about it. I would love for you to marry us now but would also want a party." She turns to look at Henry, reaching across to touch him. "That would be all right wouldn't it, Henry, a party? Mummy would like that, and all my friends would feel a bit cheated if they didn't get a glass of fizz at some time."

"Oh god, I love parties. No, we absolutely have to have a huge bash," Henry interjects. "Sorry, William, I seem to have invoked the deity in an effort to convince my betrothed of my enthusiasm for the bacchanalian."

"We'll let it pass this time," William says amiably.

"No, I want more than that, darling," Henry continues. "I want a proper wedding and to fill the house with all our friends and to dance until dawn and behave badly on the tennis court and have a do that everyone will remember as the best day ever. But I don't want to go back to Innsbruck on my own. Now that I have you, I can't bear to let you go, not even for a day."

William puts his glasses back on and once again adopts his ecclesiastical manner. "It is, of course, traditional that the priest takes something of a role in advising couples about the commitments and undertakings of marriage; it is, after all, holy matrimony that you are contemplating. I can see why you feel the need for expediency, but also am somewhat saddened that I may not be the one to bind you together in the eyes of God in this honourable estate . . . but so be it. Try Percy!"

Henry perks up considerably. "Try Percy indeed! Come on, Elisabeth, let's find Percy."

Impelled by the potential resolution of the issue, they bid a hurried farewell and walk back through the verdant lanes to the big house.

"Who is Percy?" she asks.

"Percy Smallwood—friend and family solicitor. Rather a good cricketer and plays off a handicap of seven. All round *bon œuf.*"

"Don't tell me you were at school together."

"No, we weren't actually. He's a local boy. Went to Sherbourne, captained the XI, did law at Cambridge, just missed a blue and then joined the family firm of solicitors started by his uncle."

"So, Percy will sort it?" she says.

"If anyone can, Percy can."

....

They walk home Henry leading with long-legged strides. He dives into the study from whence she can hear him talking in animated fashion on the telephone, emerging half an hour later. He finds her in the music room thumbing through the records.

"Sorry, darling, got caught up with some other things."

She looks at him expectantly, "Well?"

"He is on the case. I am not sure if he's very optimistic but if anyone can sort it out it is Percy. What have you found?"

"All sorts of things, a lot of which I don't know," she says.

"Shall we make some music? Records or instruments?"

"Instruments, providing it's not too taxing. I'm very rusty, as you heard on Monday."

"The rust was divine."

He dives into the music cupboard.

"Here we are—Wolfgang or Antonio? Your choice," he says.

They settle for a piece for cello and piano by Vivaldi. He tunes the cello while she flicks through the first few pages. He sits straight-backed adjusting the music stand, the focus and intent evident on his face.

"Right."

"Right."

She starts tentatively but is more relaxed than the previous time and glosses over the errors, ignoring Mrs. Varga's insistence that she stop and repeat a phrase until it was right. It is not that difficult, but she is out of practice and has to concentrate very hard to get her fingers to do what her brain tells them. He, too, makes a few mistakes, acknowledging them with a smile and a nod of his head.

....

After lunch they walk for an hour, having been nudged out of the house by Biscuit's insistent chivvying. They return to find Mrs. B setting out tea in the morning room. The cake doesn't need slicing, as the bulk of it remains from Sunday. Elisabeth is pouring the tea when they hear a car on the gravel drive. Henry gets up to see who it is.

He reappears three minutes later with a dapper man wearing a grey suit and club tie. He is trim, with a full head of hair greying at the temples.

"Elisabeth, meet Percy Smallwood. This dear boy has come all the way from town to tell us what he has managed to arrange."

Elisabeth gets up and shakes his hand. "I was just pouring tea. Would you like a cup?"

"How kind. Yes please."

Henry strides towards the door, saying he will ask Mrs. B for another cup, an action that is clear as he shouts down the corridor to her before returning.

Percy stands plain-faced, with his hands clasped together as if about to be offered the sacrament. "Let me say, Miss Elisabeth, that I am delighted to be able to offer you the warmest felicitations on your engagement." But then he breaks into a heart-warming grin, as if the human emotions have finally overridden business protocol. "I am so excited for you both. This really is terrific news. All Henry's friends have been hoping he would find someone to share his life with, and from all that I have heard, he has picked a winner. Marvellous. Quite marvellous."

Mrs. B waddles in with a cup, saucer, and plate.

"Thank you, Mrs. B," says Henry. "Cake, Percy? It's one of Mrs. B's specials. Damn good too. I've saved you a very small piece. Now what's the news?"

"Well," Percy says, looking as if he is about to give a judgement in the Court of Appeal, "it isn't easy because of the seven-day rule."

"Otherwise known as a week," Henry pipes in.

Percy looks down at him, his air of seriousness undiminished. "Indeed, Henry, but the problem is that the registrar is required to have seven days' notice."

"Oh bugger," says Henry, looking momentarily nonplussed.

"But . . ." Now the smile creeps across Percy's open face, "How does Croydon Register Office at three pm on Friday sound? They had a cancellation and, after a lot of buttering up, the registrar has agreed to fit you in. It is against the protocols, you understand, as I was told no end of times, but if you have the right documentation there should be no just impediment."

"You are a genius, Percy. I knew you'd pull something out of the bag. Actually, it was William who suggested it."

"In truth, I am only taking part of the credit, as the leg work was done by my assistant. I was only required when it came to persuading the somewhat stubborn registrar, who kept muttering about the unacceptable breach of protocol. But I leant on him pretty heavily. Just so as you understand, you are not only a member of the House of Lords and an important diplomat working on a secret project whose successful conclusion is vital for national security, but also you report directly to the secretary of state, who has intimated that your departure could not be delayed under any circumstances."

"And why, exactly, would the terribly important person doing crucial things, need to get married in a hurry on a Friday afternoon?" Elisabeth asks sarcastically.

"Mmm. I think I was a little less convincing on that. Recalled at short notice, frightened of the dark, can't sleep alone, needs a wife to make soldiers for his soft-boiled breakfast egg. That sort of thing . . ."

"All true!" Henry exclaims. "All true. I knew it could be done. It is auspicious. Writ in the runes. I saw a flight of birds earlier. No need for Tiresius. What are your tea leaves saying, Elisabeth? No, bugger tea leaves! Let's have another bottle of champers."

Henry bounces out, leaving Percy and Elisabeth alone. He sits down adjacent to her and asks the typical questions one might expect about where she comes from and what she does but does it with a warmth that surprises her and even seems interested in the answers.

But her mind is elsewhere. Until Percy's arrival the dreamlike

Elysium of the past few days had not been anchored in the real world. The falling, the capture, the enchantment, the sexual bliss of his body on hers, even the dream of being permanently tied to him with the promise of a ring on her finger had been floating and unreal, detached from ties of work, parents, dates in diaries, places you had to be. But now it seemed as if it really was going to happen. The make believe is over, reality beckons. There will be just such an event—in two days' time. A huge part of her wants it more than anything else in the world, but another part is terrified. This love is all-consuming; it has taken over. Where is the logical, sensible person she had been for the previous twenty-six years?

If this is what I want, why do I feel this lurking fear?

She realises it's the impetuosity that's so alien—doing something without properly thinking it through. Normally she would be methodical in her analysis, weighing the pros and cons endlessly, sometimes, she would admit, until she would end up so confused, she had no idea of what she should do. And then there were her friends. Although she wasn't a chatterer, and found gossip tiresome, she had always liked sharing things that mattered with her small group of girlfriends, but this time not only had she not been able to ask their counsel, but they hadn't even met the man she was going to marry. She was on her own and it was terrifying.

She thinks of Daddy—it is him that sits on her shoulder and speaks in her ear as her moral guide—not her mother. *Why is that?* she wonders. Because her mother was a loyal follower, not a decision maker, who loved her man as a nun might love Jesus: with total conviction, unswerving devotion, obedience even, and with deference as to which path to take. This was why her mother's life had been so empty since the rock had been taken from under her. Elisabeth tried to be her own decision-maker, that was always what Daddy had told her she should strive for, but she still needed his approval. *What would he be telling me now? Would he say I should follow my heart?*

She had never talked to him about affairs of the heart, and she knew little of his courtship with her mother, so hadn't much to guide her. She did know he would want her to be happy and God knows she had been sensible in virtually every other of her life decisions.

"Follow your heart, dear," a voice says, but whose voice is it?

Percy brings her back to the real world.

"I have promised the registrar that I would send through the personal details tonight so he can have them in the morning. Elisabeth, if I can whisk you into the study for a second to get some gen, I can get everything ready to catch the six o'clock post."

"Oh dear," Henry says. "So you can't stay for a bite?"

"'Fraid not. Besides, I don't have a shore pass from Norma." He pauses for a moment, a slight smile creeping into the corner of his mouth, before raising his eyebrows slightly and saying, "See what you're letting yourself in for, Henry? You'll never be a free man again."

"Not sure I want to be, old boy, not sure I want to be," Henry replies.

CHAPTER 22

....

Dorchester

July 1992

I got back to the Ship Inn in time for dinner. I went to my room
to wash, changed my jacket for a blazer, and headed for the bar.
I ordered a pink gin, which had the young barmaid looking at me
blankly. I was able to see the bottle of Angostura tucked away on the
mirrored shelf behind the bar and pointed it out to her, then rescued
her from her confusion by suggesting that I add it myself. I found a
chair in a corner and examined the contents of the package properly.

There was the identity card, and several larger envelopes.
The largest single item was a school exercise book, handwritten
in Elisabeth's hand. There was then a small pocket diary for 1948
and three other envelopes. The first contained memorabilia from
Briggens. There were two programmes from entertainments: one a
concert, featuring Elisabeth and Dennis amongst others, the other
a performance of *The Importance of Being Earnest*. Then there were
two editions of *Snoop*, the quarterly section magazine containing
jokes, gossip, and snippets of interest. There was a copy of the menu
for the Christmas dinner of 1943 at Green Man. I had completely
forgotten about it and was immediately surprised at how well we had
eaten. Turkey, ham, sausages, and all the trimmings.

Then there was something I hadn't seen before, a page from the
Daily Mail but without a visible date. It was an article about Violette

Szabo. I can see why it must have caught Elisabeth's eye. Although not mentioning Briggens by name, it alluded to the work of Section XIV in the production of false documents provided for SOE agents dropped into France. My opinion was that it would have been from a time when she would have felt unable to acknowledge her work at the unit, and so would have perhaps secreted it away without probing questions of the reasons for her interest.

I opened the second, smaller brown manila envelope, which also contained wartime memorabilia. There were two ration books, one in the name of Elisabeth Watson and another for Audrey Peters, along with some clothing coupons. There was a thin paper programme from June of 1944 for a Myra Hess lunchtime concert at the National Gallery, and the service sheet from the funeral service for her father, dated May 1943. Then, in a separate envelope, there were two marriage certificates: one between Elisabeth Watson and Henry Chivers Arbuthnot Benville, marriage solemnised on Friday, the 6th of August 1948, at Croydon Register Office, and a second for Audrey Peters, from the parish of Addiscombe in Surrey, and Terence Brian Wilson, also married at Croydon on the same day.

The third envelope contained a colour photograph of a young man at what I assumed to be a degree ceremony. He was wearing an academic gown and holding a roll of paper tied with a ribbon and wore a smile of coy pride. He looked vaguely familiar but there was nothing written on the back or any other indication of who it might be.

I spent twenty minutes thumbing through the papers before putting them down on the table in front of me and finishing my gin. Some of it made sense; some of it did not. I could understand why she had wanted me to have the memorabilia from Briggens—after all, I would have been the only person still alive to whom she had been close who had shared those times, but it still seemed somewhat contrived to go to the trouble of making a specific bequest and depositing the items with the obeisant Smallwood. But the inclusion of the other items made no sense at all, especially the marriage certificates. I had no idea who Audrey Peters was, save that she had married at Croydon Register Office on the same day as Elisabeth.

I was hungry, so I scooped up my papers and wandered into the cheery restaurant, where I was shown to a table in a corner dimly lit by a wrought iron wall light with a scorched red shade perched askance on the conical bulb. I ordered soup and Dover sole and took another look at the diary and the exercise book.

The diary was typical of its time; in those days we all kept small pocket diaries, in which we put appointments and kept telephone numbers and scribbled notes. A week occupied a double open page, with Saturday and Sunday squashed into a smaller space at the bottom. It was scantily filled, as I would have expected. Her address was given as Flat 2, 27 Cambridge Street, London, SW1. I looked for the dates of the detailed entries in the diary. "Office move— Holiday," was scrawled across the whole week in pencil. "Mummy?" was written in smaller letters on the Monday. In the previous week "Prom with June" was entered for the Saturday night.

The first page of the exercise book was blank, but the second was headed Friday, July 30, 1948. The writing was largely in blue ink, but with additions in pencil and other colours that were clearly amendments and additions. Some pages were like a palimpsest, with scribblings in a different colour across the original wording. The book was not full, with headings for the eight days from Friday through to the following Saturday, with a variable amount of verbiage for each day. The remainder of the book was blank.

My soup arrived; thin and not very hot. I started to read the journal contained in the exercise book. It must be remembered that at the time I knew absolutely nothing of Elisabeth's life since that punishing departure in Nice. I had gleaned that she had been married, indeed to someone titled, but knew nothing of him nor her subsequent life. Now it appeared that I was looking at an account of her first meeting and passionate affair with the man who became her husband. Furthermore, the marriage certificate was for the sixth of

August, a week after they had met.

I was being given a view into the intimacies of their passionate encounter, and what would be fair to be described as a shotgun wedding. By any measure, this was extraordinary. The Elisabeth I knew—that stolid, reliable, considerate woman—had suddenly been swept up into a passionate affair and got married within a week. I felt as if I didn't know that person. Was the woman I thought I knew a facade? How could those years at Briggens have not been truthful? Who was the real Elisabeth Watson? The FANY I had met at Briggens or the impetuous, hot-blooded woman glimpsed from her diary. I felt confused, uncomfortable, and not a little hurt.

Although in no way salacious, the account was nevertheless still intimate. For example, it mentioned them both having a bath together the day after their first meeting, and on various occasions "bed."

As I read on, I found it more abhorrent. I did not need or want to read this material. Was she somehow trying to punish me after her death? For what? For her making such a cruel exit in Marseilles? It should be me punishing her. I could not see my relevance to her marital relationship and was still at a loss as to why she had wanted me to be privy to it. It was unlike her to be deliberately cruel, but that was my initial interpretation, as if she was trying to say the failure of our relationship was nothing to do with me, look here I am having a whirlwind relationship with someone I really loved. I had found the previous few weeks an unfamiliar emotionally laden time, a jolt out of the blinkered contentment of my cloistered existence. Now I added resentment to the sentiments of the week.

Mostly the entries were purely factual; where they went and what they did. The addendums appeared to be where she had recalled something additional which she had wanted to document. For instance, one breakfast they listened to music, but she later added a jokey conversation about guessing the conductor and orchestra.

On the Wednesday she first meets Smallwood senior, who as intimated by his son, had been looking after the family for two generations. He appears to have arranged the marriage at Croydon Register Office. And then it all ends; after a brief entry on Saturday morning, nothing more.

I was really none the wiser. I felt deflated, disappointed, a little upset; cheated even. I had struggled to imagine what it could have been that the bequest contained, although I had thought it more likely to be some memorabilia from our time together than a gift or token. Up until the time of the opening of the envelope I had found my reacquaintance with Elisabeth poignant and melancholic but not unpleasant. I had refound an intimacy which had reminded me of what it is like to be in love and had for some foolish inexplicable notion thought that her gift might have been an indication of an endearment on her part. A keepsake or memento, perhaps an explanation, for in truth, I still felt I needed one for her departure. But instead, I was left with a random collection of wartime ephemera, along with a personal diary of the meeting with her husband.

I sat and pondered what to do over bread-and-butter pudding and a glass of Madeira.

There were two options. Return home and forget about the whole episode. Go back to my stale, crusty, but comfortable routine on the Cape, to the unspoken tenderness of Therese, to the light and warmth, baked earth, and bougainvillea of my escapism. Or, learn some more about the life of my one great love and see if there was a better explanation for her action. I was still not convinced that the sole purpose of the bequest was to punish me; why would she want to do that?

So, what then?

The one person who might be able to throw light on the matter would be her partner, Philip Wood.

It wasn't a difficult decision. I knew that to return now would be to leave a job not half finished but half started. I would be forever asking myself questions about Knowle, Henry, and indeed this Philip character. Elisabeth was logical, often obsessive, and a perfectionist.

There was certainly more to this bundle than was apparent, and I would try to garner what it was.

The following morning, I would drive back to Dorchester, talk to Smallwood, and perhaps visit Philip Wood. I would go back to Knowle and try to touch the life, and perhaps the death, of Elisabeth Watson.

The night manager said he would explore hotel options in Dorchester and make a recommendation. I trudged the stained, paisley-carpeted corridor to my room and clambered into bed, feeling, more than usual, the weight of my age.

I lay restless and troubled in the sterile room, vainly seeking the refuge of sleep. The curtains billowed in through the open window, the seagulls mewed in a supporting act to music from a bar along the street.

How had I for so long seen my relationship with Elisabeth as a paragon of perfection? How had I come to think that she too had viewed our time together as a halcyon time of untainted bliss? Had I chosen to forget the times when it was less than joyful?

I have mentioned that Elisabeth was very involved with the musical productions organised by Dennis Collins. They called themselves the Hunsdon Players and met whenever they could to plan new productions and share ideas. Once a show was planned then the activity went into overdrive, with writing sessions, rehearsals, and all the other activities, such as making costumes and building a set. The productions were put on in one of the Nissen huts at Briggens, normally used as a gym by the Poles, with a crude stage erected at one end and hand-me-down green velvet curtains loaned by Lady Aldenham.

Elisabeth would always be dashing off to a rehearsal in the village hall, often straight after her shift, and I wouldn't see her at all that day. At other times we would agree to meet for a drink after the rehearsal, which they would try to finish before closing time. The cast would burst in, a bundle of noisy extroverts, eager for beer or gin and enthused by their thespian aspirations and another sort of camaraderie. I wasn't a part of it all but wasn't resentful—the stage wasn't for me, and it was so obviously something that Elisabeth valued. I was happy to see her happy.

But then there was Bryce Goodman.

God, I hadn't thought about him for a hundred years. Before the war he had been a photographer, mostly taking society pictures of debutantes and their pets. On the face of it he was charming, good looking, with chiselled Hollywood features and a flippant humour that quickly attracted strangers in a crowded bar. But he spoke through the side of his mouth, with a demeaning cynicism that soon left you wondering whether there was anything underpinning the avuncular smarm other than solipsistic self-interest. I never took to him; I only wish Elisabeth had felt the same way. He had a good tenor voice and could act in a pantomime style and so was snapped up for schmaltzy roles in the shows.

I can't remember the show they were doing—it might have been Gilbert and Sullivan or perhaps a cut-down Broadway show—but I noticed that they would often end up chatting after the rehearsals. Then he seemed to need more one-to-one time to get the song just right. I didn't notice to start with—I have never been a jealous man— and so accepted that the rehearsals were going on for longer and that she was coming back later than usual. Then one evening we had agreed to meet at the pub but when I arrived there was nobody there, so I walked across to the village hall. People were leaving and I nodded to Dennis that I would see him in the Crown. Bryce and Elisabeth were virtually the only two left and were sitting in the dim space, having a very intimate conversation. Was her hand on his? Smoke curled up from his cigarette, held in his girlish hand. Elisabeth took a drag from hers and exhaled, turning her head away. Cole Porter, Ella Fitzgerald, Gershwin, whoever—they were playing out the role in real life. It could have been a bar in Manhattan.

I turned and walked back to the pub, in my mind making excuses for her.

Later, in the dark of a room enclosed by blackout curtains, I challenged her, asking her where she had been and saying I had called into the hall, but seeing she was "busy" had left.

She leapt to the defensive. Of course there was nothing between them, I had got it all wrong. Bryce was a tender, lost soul who put on a bravura facade to cover his insecurities. He had a young daughter in Somerset whom he never saw. He masked his sadness and insecurity with cynicism and bravura.

I didn't know what to believe. Was he just a needy guy who Elisabeth was compelled to rescue or was there something more? Or both? I don't know what went on between them. Perhaps nothing?

I never saw them together after the show. They moved on I suppose. To me he was still that shallow chancer but what did that make her? Had she "moved on"—is that what she did? And I didn't?

CHAPTER 23

....

Dorset

Thursday August 5, 1948

They sit at the table chatting over the remnants of the meal.

"Henry," she says with a strange mix of formality and caution, "what do people wear for a wedding in a register office?"

"Something old, something new, something borrowed, something blue. Isn't that what it's supposed to be?" Then he pauses, looking thoughtful, "But I wonder what the origin of that aphorism is?"

He asks it to himself, in what Elisabeth realises is a very characteristic habit, a sort of intellectual pondering of things that most people would never question, mostly directed rhetorically, with no expectation of an answer or reply.

"I was thinking more about you," she says, mustering as much irony as she can in her look. "What will you be wearing?"

"A suit I suppose."

"Have you got a nice one?"

He looks at her, realisation captured in his smile. "I always thought so, but admittedly not very often."

"Let's have a look," she says, getting up, grabbing him by the hand, and leading him out of the room to the stairs.

She opens Henry's wardrobe, which unsurprisingly is full of a peculiar array of clothing, many of ethnic origin, many moth-eaten and most many years old. She finds two pairs of lederhosen which she holds up against him. One is huge which he claims must have been his father's. They laugh as kids might over a box of dressing-up clothes.

In amongst the collection, she finds a couple of suits, one a heavy tweed, best befitting a grouse moor, the other in grey wool, tidy but far from elegant.

He insisted that his better clothes were all in Austria, but she remains far from convinced that even they would ever be categorised as smart or elegant.

"I want my beau to be just that," she said. "You could look really good in a modern suit, nice wide lapels, double breasted, in a nice navy worsted."

"Well, we had better go shopping then."

CHAPTER 24

....

Dorset

July 1992

By midday the next day I was back in Dorchester checking into the Old Ship Inn. No bosun's chair involved in this Ship-to-Ship transfer! It was a quaint but uninspiring establishment, but the kindly landlady (Irene McMurray from Dundee, as she proudly told me), made every effort to address my needs and showed me to a room at the back of the building, where she assured me that it was quieter than facing the main road.

I put a call through to Smallwood, telling him briefly about the contents of the envelope, explaining that I was at a loss to understand why she had felt I should have the documents but perhaps he could spare me a few minutes to talk further. He agreed to fit me in later in the afternoon. I made my way to the cosy saloon bar, empty save for a pair of Texan tourists and contemplated a sandwich for lunch.

In the entrance lobby I had noticed a cardboard box of tourist brochures for local attractions, houses owned by the National Trust, and the like, but one had caught my eye: "Knowle House Opera," and I had pulled out a copy. I now looked at the folded leaflet. On the cover was a picture of an old country house. I am not an expert, but the appealing building looked Tudor or Jacobean, with Virginia creeper clambering over the sandstone. Overprinted on the front was "1993 season, *Marriage of Figaro, Rinaldo, Rigoletto*." Inside the brochure were some more pictures, including one of a slightly unusual building which formed the auditorium, along with images of musicians rehearsing and formally dressed guests picnicking on well-manicured lawns. It all looked very sophisticated and charming but not of great interest to me. I have never cared much about music, classical or otherwise. Perhaps it was another reason why Elisabeth rejected me, along with her lack of interest in sailing and the sea.

Mrs. McMurray saw me reading the brochure from the other side of the reception desk, peering over the top of a pair of reading glasses.

"Would you be thinking of going over to Knowle? It's very pretty down there."

"I am not much of an opera goer," I replied.

"Me neither. I've never been to a performance, but they say it's very nice. It has a very good reputation. We often have guests staying who come down here just for the opera. You know they have singers from all over the world." Her natural garrulousness, delivered in clipped Scottish tones, hinting, with a touching amazement that such travel was possible at all.

"I am afraid that opera is wasted on me, but I was thinking of visiting the house. I hear that Lady Knowle died last year, was she much to do with it?"

"Ooh aye, the top, bottom, and sides I'd say. She would occasionally come in for a meal with some of the singers or friends. Sometimes they were quite famous. She was ever-so sweet. Nice smile. She was always in the local paper doing this or that. A lovely woman for certain. Very well respected. They had a memorial service for her in St. George's not three months back."

I decided not to reveal more, and she bustled off to go about her business. I can't recall Elisabeth having a love of opera particularly, but then it was wartime and what opportunities would there have been to go to the opera? Classical music for sure, and of course her piano playing, but how did she end up being involved with an opera house in the middle of Dorset? I had yet more questions for Smallwood.

Two hours later I was once again strolling towards his offices. It had been a pleasant afternoon. I wandered around the town of Dorchester very much as a tourist might. I didn't feel it belonged to me as an Englishman, rather it was a place I recognised from a distant time past. I could observe and judge, but at a distance, knowledgeable in some ways but ignorant and detached in others. It was a bit like hearing people discussing a book that you had read or a film you had seen but had come away with a different understanding of. In some ways I felt better able to view middle England from my stance than had I been while living in it.

I walked into Smallwood's building and was ushered into his office by a receptionist. This time he seemed more relaxed and less formal.

"Welcome, Mr. Mackay. How nice to see you again." He stood up from behind his desk and walked towards me, extending a hand.

"Peter, please. Thank you for finding time to see me."

"I owe you an apology. I now realise that you wrote *Convoy North*. How stupid of me; I never put two and two together. You were on the Arctic Convoys?

"PQ 13."

"I am sure I am not alone in being of the view that to contemplate joining a convoy in a sea swarming with U-boats required a degree of bravery possessed by few; to do it in the frozen Arctic Ocean in winter . . . Unthinkable. I salute you, sir." And he stood upright and nodded his head. But it was done without pomp, and I accepted his genuine sentiment.

"It was a long time ago. We all do things in wartime that seem peculiar after."

I moved to sit at the table, placing the envelope on the functional wood veneer. He joined me as I spread the contents in front of us. Amongst the papers was the Knowle brochure that I had picked up in the hotel.

He reached for it. "Are you thinking of a visit to the opera while you are here? I doubt you would get tickets, mind; they sell out months in advance."

"I am not an opera goer. I found it in the hotel, and it was another thing I wanted to ask you about; I gather it is quite an event."

"Have you not heard of Knowle House?" He raised his eyebrows slightly but did not wait for a reply. "To a large extent they invented country house opera as we know it. The quality is superb, with world class singers and very lavish productions, but it is also very much a social event, firmly in the summer calendar alongside Wimbledon or Henley. You take a picnic and sit in the glorious grounds and sip champagne. Elisabeth was kind enough to give us a pair of tickets most seasons."

"And I gather Elisabeth had a lot to do with this?"

Again, he looked surprised at my comment. "Oh absolutely. It was all down to her. Of course, it was Henry's idea, but she made it happen. One of the obituaries called her the "Doyenne of English provincial opera." After his death it became her raison d'être."

"I had no idea. I remember her loving music, but I don't think she ever mentioned opera."

"Really? In my experience opera, like fine Burgundy, grows on you with age. That may have been true for Elisabeth, although I can't recall a time when she wasn't an enthusiast. It is a sad truth that Knowle House is mostly populated by the grey and the good." He smiled at his own joke. "Perhaps there weren't many opportunities for attending opera during the war." He leant towards the documents that were spread on the table.

"So, what have we here?" he said.

I sorted through the papers.

"As we surmised, some of the material relates to our time together at Briggens. This is a copy of *Snoop*, the Section XIV magazine that was published in-house, and this is a piece from the *Daily Mail Express* that must have caught her eye, telling the story of Violette Szabo. All perfectly explicable, albeit odd that she should have wanted me to have them after so long incommunicado. Then there is a diary and some writings of her meeting with Henry in July 1948."

He picked up the various documents with the courtesy and care I might have expected from him, examining them as might a museum curator a folio of Shakespeare.

"Then there is a copy of her marriage certificate and one for an Audrey Peters from Addiscombe, married the same day. Do you know of an Audrey Peters?"

"I don't think so, no. Addiscombe is not far from where she grew up. My guess would be that she could be an old school friend."

He looked at each of the various items carefully, not saying anything, maintaining the perfect reserve of his legal training throughout, never wishing to countenance uncertainty. He paid particular attention to the copies of *Snoop* and papers from Briggens.

"These are remarkable. The section produced its own magazine? Some of these drawings are terribly good."

"Yes. I can't remember how often it came out. Perhaps twice a year or quarterly. It was mostly the genius of Dennis Collins. It certainly is largely his artwork. But what was even more remarkable was that for security reasons the content couldn't even touch upon the work we were doing, so all the jokes and gossip had to be unrelated to our work."

"Well, surely these papers would be of historic interest. I suspect a museum or somewhere. Is there an archive of material from Briggens?"

"Not to my knowledge."

"Pity. Perhaps there should be, but I agree it is a bit mysterious why she should have included these personal papers. I am afraid I can throw little light on it."

"There is mention of your father in the handwritten material, at least I presume it's your father, Percy Smallwood."

"Really? Yes, that would be Father. Percival Thornton Smallwood. Percy to all and sundry. He was much more down-to-earth than the name suggests. That's why he called me Steven."

"It seems as if Elisabeth and Henry asked him to help arrange the marriage. He somehow managed to make a reservation for them the following day at Croydon Register Office."

"Good lord. That is remarkable, even for Father. He was an obstinate man; wouldn't take no for an answer."

"But would you be able to get married at a day's notice?"

"You would need a bit of give-and-take from the registrar. Normally they would want to see documents beforehand, and as I recall there should be a minimum of seven days notice." He paused for a second before continuing. "You know, we might well have some papers for this period. Father never threw anything away and, as the Knowle file is still active, it is quite likely that if there was any correspondence, it might still be on file."

"Or a fee note," I said, smiling.

"Indeed," he replied, a crease softening the mouth of his usually serious face, "or possibly a fee note."

"But that doesn't get us any further as to why she left me the papers."

"No, agreed. My only suggestion is that you talk to Philip Wood. I know he would be interested and might have some further insights. I can give you his phone number, if you like. In fact, I can do better than that; I will call him now."

He picked up the phone and waited for a response, then asked his secretary to call Philip.

"He still lives at Knowle in what they call the dower house. You can kill two birds with one stone: visit the Knowle Estate and meet Philip—" He cuts short the sentence by a response in the earpiece. He smiled as they exchanged pleasantries, before giving a brief explanation for the call, and asked if it would be possible to arrange a meeting. He took the handpiece away from his ear and looked back to me.

"How about tomorrow morning at eleven? Can you make your own way there?

"Surely."

"Excellent." He resumed his conversation down the phone, closing with "Don't worry. I will give him directions."

"All arranged; he will be expecting you. He suggests you meet in the foyer by the ticket office, which opens at ten," he says, looking at me to suggest that our time together has served its purpose.

"Just one more thing," I said, finding the third envelope and passing him the picture of the youth in his graduation outfit. "Do you know who this might be?"

"Oh yes," he replied warmly. "It is Robert, the fifth earl of Knowle, Elisabeth and Henry's son and heir. It is his graduation picture from the Royal College of Music."

Once again, I was taken aback, and it probably showed in my tone. "I didn't know she had had a child."

"Oh yes, very musical like his parents."

"So, did he take over the running of the estate?"

"No, he was not the slightest bit interested. He plays the French horn in a German radio orchestra. He has lived in Germany for nearly twenty years now. The trust does pay him a stipend though, which must make his salary go a bit further."

We said our goodbyes and I walked out of the offices, lit a cigarette, and ambled back through town towards the Ship. Perhaps there was a museum in town where I could while away an hour or so before it closed. Mrs. McMurray would be sure to give me lengthy advice on the matter.

When I approached the hotel, I noticed there was a piece of paper tucked under the wiper on the windscreen of the Bristol. It was a printed card from a Reg Harrison of Dorset Classic Automobiles. Handwritten was a message: "If you ever think of selling your fine car, we will pay a good price. Don't hesitate to get in touch. Reg."

....

Knowle House was very beautiful.

The setting was key: a valley with a river, still flowing in late summer, a gentle hill behind providing a sheltered dominion, then pale sandstone gables clad with Virginia creeper and a tidy swathe of manicured lawns, hedges, and gardens set behind estate fencing fringing the gravel drive. The impression was of class and order. If this had been home, Elisabeth had done well for herself. Better than a cabin on a creaking clinker-built yacht, albeit I hated to admit it.

Outside the main gates, two large signs told visitors they had arrived at KHO—Knowle House Opera—and further signage made it clear that you must park in the car park opposite the house. Offset some distance towards the river was an unusual building, which I took to be the opera house itself, thankfully not obscuring or interfering with the sight lines of the old house. Hardly Covent Garden, it was circular in shape, with a series of simple Romanesque brick arches around the circumference with considerable detailing and embellishment. It was not to my taste.

I parked the Bristol and followed signs to the ticket office, which was situated in a splendid old tithe barn away from the mansion. The building had little natural light, but the high beams were cleverly illuminated by spotlights hidden amongst the timbers. The floor was modern oak contributing a hint of polish to the aromas of coffee and cakes. At one end was a ticket counter with desks behind, and at the other a café. Across the alcove opposite the entrance was a partition in the centre of which was a very large portrait of Elisabeth.

It had to be her; the likeness was incontestable. Elisabeth in middle age as I had never known her; elegant, beautiful still, with a magnificent head of hair, now zinc white, and a look that I remembered, which I recalled she would wear when she knew she was right about something. It was a harsher look than I might have wished for in a portrait, but it spoke of competence, strength of will, and clarity of vision. She was wearing a bottle-green silk blouse with a high collar and a knotted gold necklace. On the lapel was a fine floral brooch. I hate to admit it, but I was moved with an unwelcome pang of regret. This was a woman who had achieved, who was somebody, was poised and sophisticated yet graceful and alluring, but who I had never known. A lump rose in my throat.

To the side of the portrait there was a glass case fronting a bronze bust of a youthful man reminding me a little of Peter O'Toole in Lawrence of Arabia. He looked to the horizon, high forehead, fine lips, long hair—clumsily executed I thought—trailing over his collar. In the case was a model made of matchsticks of a building obviously similar to the auditorium in the water meadow, and next to it a somewhat grubby linen pencil case with a donkey embroidered on it. Alongside were other artifacts, including what looked to be an Austrian passport. The sign informed me that this was Henry Benville, 4th Earl Knowle. Standing in the case was a cello case stuck with various travel labels, battered and scorched.

So, this had been the enemy—unseen but powerful and clearly dangerous. I didn't believe the likeness for a minute; the features were too fine, the chin too chiselled, the gaze overly assured.

"Mr. Mackay?"

I turned to see a pleasant-faced man proffering his hand. "Philip Wood."

"Peter, please." I took the hand. The handshake was positive but brief. Why do I still judge these things? Where is it writ that a handshake means anything other than a customary greeting? But whether valid or not, he passed muster; it was a strong grip, swiftly terminated. He was shorter than I had imagined; I suppose I had assumed that Elisabeth would choose a stronger, more charismatic type, more like the man in the glass case. Full head of brown hair, clean-shaven, an uplifted mouth offering warmth and approachability, white shirt open at the neck, casual trousers, and then some peculiar semisandal shoes of perforated leather.

"I see you are looking at Henry—he cuts a fine figure, doesn't he? I never met him but am assured it is a reasonable likeness. We were the also-rans, you could say."

I was struck by this comment, which implied more knowledge of my relationship with Elisabeth than I had presumed but was humorous and friendly. I smiled. He had subtly acknowledged so much in a trivial comment.

"Steven said that you were an old friend of Elisabeth's from wartime days and that she left you something in her will, have I got it right?"

"Spot on."

"Did you work with her at Briggens?"

"Yes, that's where we met."

"That's remarkable because these are Henry's forged identity papers. Elisabeth always assumed that they had been made at Briggens." He pointed into the case.

This was by any means extraordinary. Had Henry been an agent that had necessitated a forged identity?

"I do know your name because I recall watching the film of *Convoy North* on television and Elisabeth mentioned that she knew you. She then went and found her copy of the book and pointed out the dedication. I don't think she told me that you worked together at Briggens but then her whole disclosure of that part of her past was relatively recent. My guess is that she meant quite a lot to you at the time."

I had entirely forgotten the dedication. All that was printed was "For EW," but I recalled adding something to the copy I'd sent her.

"And, alas, for a long time after," I said.

"She had that effect on people."

"Did you know of her bequest?"

"Not at all. No idea; she never mentioned it. I thought we might have a cup of coffee?" He nodded towards the café.

"Thank you, that would be very pleasant."

The end of the barn made a sympathetic space. The ancient oak framing sat on low stone staddles, the huge, twisted beams, pale and worn, as old as forever, exuded a soft vernacular warmth, as if they didn't object to their new purpose. On the lime infill panels were hung large black-and-white photographs of singers, presumably performers at Knowle, although their names meant nothing to me.

A waitress moved towards us, acknowledged Philip with a smile and his Christian name, and took our orders.

"Do you enjoy opera, Peter?" he said as we sat.

"No, I'm afraid not. I have no interest, I am sad to say."

"Oh, what a pity. Rigoletto tonight. The cast is very good and the reviews excellent. Elisabeth would have been delighted with the quartet; she so loved the piece. Well, anything by Jo Green actually." He looked pensive for a second. "I probably could find a seat for you somewhere if you are interested."

"Not for me, thank you," I said.

I opened the envelope that I had placed on the table, extracting the contents.

"So, down to business," he said, forcing a smile.

"As Steven told you, Elisabeth left this bundle of papers to me in her will. Apparently, they were deposited there many years ago, although Steven couldn't say exactly when. Can you throw any light on that?"

"No, I am afraid not. She never discussed the details of her will. Of course, all the estate is tied up in trusts. She made various small bequests, and some of these she mentioned at odd times. She left my two daughters some jewellery. If Steven can't remember the date, it must have been a long time ago. It could even have been in Percy's time."

"I understand that she gave an interview to the local paper about her time at Briggens?"

"Yes, the *Dorchester Echo*. That must have been ten years ago or thereabouts. I can find out, as I have a copy of it somewhere."

"But the bequest would have predated that? It just seems a bit odd that when she came to talk about her experiences, she didn't present any of the keepsakes that she had retained from that time."

"I agree, but it wasn't an in-depth piece—more about the fascinating work done at Briggens and that some of it was done by young women." He paused. "And by someone as well-known as Elisabeth."

Our coffees arrived as I shuffled the pages towards him.

Philip took a pair of reading glasses from his top pocket and picked out the documents one by one, carefully studying them with reverence and interest. He dwelt on the menu for the Christmas dinner, remarking that rationing must have been off that week, and then looked at the copies of *Snoop*, commenting on Dennis' artwork. "This is fine graphic work. I suppose it isn't surprising that there were some very talented people on board."

"Correct. Although Dennis Collins was by any measure exceptional."

"Ah, hold on, that rings a bell. I am sure Elisabeth talked of him. He might even be mentioned in the piece in the paper. Didn't he become a cartoonist? Would that be right?"

"I have no idea. He was certainly a very fine musician. He and Elisabeth were the mainstays of the pantomimes."

He spent a few more minutes looking at the material before I chivvied him with the further papers.

"This is more confusing." I passed over the other bundle, giving a brief description. He thumbed through the handwritten pages reading odd passages, and then flicked through the diary."

And then there are these." I said handing over the marriage certificates. "Did Elisabeth know an Audrey Peters?"

"It doesn't ring any bells. I do have her old address book; I can check in there. Look, there is quite a lot here, Peter. What I would like to do is to borrow it and have a look tonight. How long are you staying? Perhaps we could meet again tomorrow. I would be happy to come into town if it suited you."

"That would be fine; I have little else to do. There is a lot about Elisabeth's life after we split up that I know nothing of and which I would be interested in hearing about. Why not come to dinner at the Old Ship tomorrow?"

We agreed to meet the following day, continuing to talk as we walked back to the exit.

"I was very taken with the portrait," I said. "Very much how I imagine she would have looked in middle years. Perhaps more severe than I would have wished for."

"It's a Wraith. The trustees commissioned it for her sixtieth birthday. It is beautiful, isn't it? She was very pleased actually; she didn't want it to be all smiles and mumsy. I think they got the balance right. I find it difficult coming in here now. Her presence is everywhere at Knowle, but in the barn, with her looking down at me . . ." His voice broke as he shook his head slightly.

We walked back to my car.

"I have to say, Knowle is very lovely. You are privileged to live here."

"Yes, I live in what we call the dower house, just a bit further up the drive. It suited us better than the big house. Elisabeth's mother moved there from Reigate after she had a minor stroke, and when she died, we tarted the place up a bit and moved in. We were happy there." And then he added; "I rattle around a bit now, though." I looked at him again and for the first time I saw a sad man. Whatever I had felt, his loss must have been much more acute than mine. I hadn't thought about that.

"Who lives in the big house?"

"There is a flat for the chief executive, but we usually have artists staying in the rooms. The whole estate is now in the hands of the trust. That is one of the reasons KHO is so unique: even international stars love performing here because it is like staying in a big family." And then he checked himself. "At least it was while Elisabeth was around. I am now considered Grace and Favour," and I saw his sadness return. *La douleur*, Therese would have diagnosed.

"Was your career in opera?"

He guffaws. "Good heavens, no. I am a psychotherapist. Before that I was a doctor. In fact, for a few years I was Elisabeth's GP."

My look must have betrayed my surprise.

"There is a lot to talk about Peter. Let's continue tomorrow eve. I will look out some stuff for you."

CHAPTER 25

Dorset

Thursday, August 5, 1948

The question at breakfast is where to go to find a nice dress. The choices are few. Mrs. B is brought into the discussion but is of little help, other than commenting that her friend Marjorie in the village had bought a nice blouse in Dunnings in Dorchester.

They discuss the options and decide it must be Bournemouth.

They agree to set off at ten, after Henry has talked to Geoffrey and made some phone calls. The day is clear, with a breeze from the west driving harmless clouds tumbling across the blue sky. It is still warm, but the heatwave has passed. Elisabeth takes Biscuit for a turn along the drive, the lawns still damp from dew, but fresh with the scent of grass and greenery. Blackbirds screech their warnings in the laurel hedge as they are disturbed by his nosing. She walks towards the dower house and wonders if she dares to call in on Anneliese. She hasn't seen her since Henry broke the news of the engagement and has no idea what she really thinks, but the thought of calling in terrifies her. Besides, she can't imagine that she is an early riser and the notion of disturbing her in a dressing gown bleary from sleep and sherry doesn't bear thinking about. She returns to the house and makes the decision that the day is fair enough to have the hood down on Evey, who is still parked incongruously in front of the magnificent Knowle gables.

She unscrews the catches on the windscreen and lifts the metal frame up, and then down, folding and tucking the creases in the canvas behind the rear seat. She turns on the ignition to check the petrol and then thinks she may as well start her up. The engine turns over but doesn't start. She tries again and a third time with the same result. Bother. This is not what Evie does; she has never not started. She assumes that this was the same problem that caused her to stop earlier in the week.

Elisabeth walks around the house to the garages and sheds to see if she can find Malcolm. She knows that it would be a waste of time asking Henry, who by his own admission is completely useless with things mechanical.

She calls for Malcolm, who emerges from one of the farm buildings wearing a long brown work coat. Together they walk back to the car, Malcolm silent and awkward in her company. He opens the bonnet and looks while she again tries the starter. He does something in the mysterious interstices of the engine that she can't see and then asks her to try again. The little engine bursts to life. He closes the bonnet, wiping his hands on his coat.

"What was the problem?" she asks, not sure if the answer will make any sense.

"The lead from the coil was loose," he says, more comfortable now he is on familiar ground. "I just pushed it back on tight. You should be orright now, miss."

Elisabeth has not the faintest idea what he is talking about. "Thank you, Malcolm. You are very clever and very kind." She gives him a big smile which makes him blush.

Henry is not ready on time, and then when he sees the open car, insists he needs a hat and a jacket which involves delving into the miraculous cupboard.

During the process she finds a Hermes silk scarf which is much more elegant than the cotton one she usually uses when driving. They get into Evie and set off, heading down the drive, the laurel hedges shaking their polished leaves with mild impatience. Henry fumbles through his pockets.

"Sorry, sorry, sorry. Cheque book. So sorry, darling, but I have forgotten my cheque book, which, given the proposed stratagem for the day, could be a deficit of considerable tactical consequence."

She backs Evie into the entrance to the stable block and turns around, speedily swinging the car on the gravel outside the front door. He leaps out and strides briskly back into the house.

Of course they would forget something. Probably not just the cheque book. Time will tell what else is missing. She will have to be careful on the morrow. Make sure they have all the papers. But it doesn't matter. In fact, it's rather funny and maybe makes it easier; how would it be if they were both obsessional?

He reappears and jumps into the car. "Right. All set. Pro secondo. Sorry, darling."

"It doesn't matter a jot. We have all day. I was just thinking . . ."

"What?"

"That you need a wife."

He turns to her, leans over to kiss her lightly on the cheek, and squeezes her thigh.

She is happy and excited by the day's prospects, finding a thrill in everything new that they do together.

"So, what is it about Dorset and puddles?" she asks jauntily as they pass a sign for Tolpuddle. "We've just been through Puddletown and now Tolpuddle and Affpuddle. Is it always raining, or don't they mend the roads?"

"Well, what about piddles? There are some of them too; Piddlehinton, for example."

"It could explain the puddles I suppose—the piddles I mean."

"Absolutely. A county of incontinents, the taken-short of Dorset.

Now they are both smiling. He has his hand resting on her thigh, the motoring hat at a jaunty angle, the ear-covers flapping in the airstream, an eccentric contrast to her elegant scarf. She drives confidently and fast.

They come across a crocodile of primary school children holding hands in pairs being led along the pavement by an elderly teacher, her long skirt almost to the ground, grey hair piled into a neat bun.

"Ah, children," he says.

"Yes, Henry, children." She steals a glance at him with a hint of a smile and finds he is looking at her.

"Possibly?"

"Certainly."

"Certainly-possibly or certainly-certainly."

"Definitely-certainly."

"Lots?"

"Some."

"You haven't told me about your school days," he says, "except for the remarkable Mrs. Valma."

"Nearly right. Varga. Boarding school in Hereford. I was sent there because my Nan was a teacher at the school and got half-price fees. I don't think we could have afforded it otherwise. I never liked it, though. In fact, I hated it. I would go into a brown study and sulk three days before term started and Mummy would take me to the Lyons Corner house for tea to try to assuage my sulky depression with a cream slice."

"Did it work?"

"No, not really. It was clear that they weren't going to change, so you stop voicing reasonable arguments and just sulk and retreat into yourself. I don't suppose it was that bad, but I didn't like it. I found it difficult to make friends with the other girls, who were loud and haughty. It was the piano and reading that kept me sane. Escape, I suppose."

"I cannot believe you found it difficult to make friends with people. You made friends with me pretty quickly, and I was a total stranger." His light-hearted tone hints at sarcasm.

She does not say anything for a moment. "You were different. You cast some magical spell over me with your mellifluous companion, Ludwig. Thankfully there was no one at school who did that."

"Mmm, I wouldn't have blamed them if they had tried. There weren't boys, were there?"

"God no. Never, nowhere near. Didn't know what one looked like till the war, and then, like buses, there were dozens of them."

"No masculine women teachers with deep voices and female companions?"

"Oh yes, several, but they weren't threatening or predatory—at least not towards me. Perhaps I wasn't their type."

"Too feminine."

"I doubt it. Not sure I was very feminine at the age of fourteen. Unhappy, anxious, lacking in confidence for certain. All the usual stuff. I was bullied a fair bit."

"Why would anyone bully you?"

She drives silently for a couple of minutes, the elation of the day washed away by the recall of the hurt and confusion of those days, before reminding herself where she is and shaking off the shadow of the rumination.

"I can't believe that you fitted in at school Henry," she says more assertively. "Surely you weren't conventional. Wasn't that a source of teasing?"

"I don't remember it as a problem. There were so many individuals and unusual people at school . . . we were all a bit peculiar. The thing I remember best about school was the smells. All the different houses had their distinct pong, and then there was the boiled cabbage smell and the Friday fish smell and the pipe tobacco smell of the tutors' rooms."

"Oh yes, I remember the smells, the basement, and mouldy fruit. Jeyes fluid . . . And bells. Everything controlled by the bell. I can still get a shiver if I hear the same type of bell chiming."

"Bournemouth twelve miles," Henry says, reading the large milestone at a road junction.

"Where do we go first?" she asks.

"Jeweller, then frock shop, then lunch."

"What about you? I thought you were going to get a new suit?" The disappointment shows in her voice.

"I had forgotten that. We could do it after lunch. Let's see how we get on."

She is not sure if he is prevaricating or just being his usual distracted self. She has never been shopping with a man before—at least not a man she cares about. What is strange is that she feels proprietorial about the mission; she has ideas about how she wants him to look. He has the features for sure, and the louche, baggy look that he prefers suits him, but is twenty years out of date. She wants to wish upon him the style of Clark Gable or Ronald Reagan. New shoes too, maybe even a haircut.

....

They drive into the town centre and immediately see the lavish frontage of Beales department store, but while finding somewhere to park they come across Bobbies, another large store in the square. The sky is brightening, and the town is bustling with people and traffic. She is surprised to find it so busy but then realises that it is a holiday destination, and it is August. They find somewhere to park near the sea front and walk back into the town centre. The pavements are crowded with trippers and holidaymakers of all ages. Girls in skirts above the knee laugh and window shop while licking ice-cream cones. Men in shorts and sandals in open-necked shirts and straw hats stroll, arms linked with matrons in short-sleeved floral dresses, shoulders reddened by too much sun. A sandwich-board man ambles past, advertising entertainment on the pier with little obvious enthusiasm. Outside a newsagent, a billboard carries news of a sailing gold medal at the London Olympics. She had forgotten that they were still going on. No news of the outside world had penetrated their bubble of intimacy.

They step through the curved frontage of Beales which advertises "art and Liberty fabrics," to be welcomed by a uniformed doorman with a fine waxed moustache who seems to sense the purpose of

their visit and directs them to ladies' fashions on the second floor.
They climb the stairs past mannequins adorned with the latest styles.
Once again Elisabeth finds herself gazing at the New Look fashions,
but her reserve remains; she doesn't find the look appealing. She
can't work out whether she is being staid and old-fashioned, or it
really is the aesthetic that is unappealing. They are approached by a
thin saleswoman who addresses them with a weary professionalism
and marches them briskly to a carpeted area with two full-length
mirrors and an armchair, while summoning a young assistant.

Elisabeth explains that she would like to look at some dresses
without specifying the reason. Marjorie the "manageress," as a badge
on her blue dress announces, asks if "sir" would like to sit and wait
or perhaps; "has some shopping of his own to do?" Elisabeth had
rather assumed that Henry would join with her in choosing the dress
but then realises that this isn't what would normally happen; the
wedding dress would never be seen by the groom until the church.
But this isn't normal, is it? Nothing is "normal" now. She wants
him to stay, tugging at his sleeve and pulling him towards the chair.
Henry sits with a bewildered look on his face and demurely obeys
the instructions to sit awhile.

Forty-five minutes later even the frosty distance of Marjorie has
diminished, and she enjoins in enthusiasm for the purchases, clutching
Elisabeth's hand in her nicotinic fingers and wishing her well as they
complete the transaction. The dress is the palest of yellow cotton with
a slight texture to it, with a pleated skirt and three-quarter sleeves. To
complete the outfit Marjorie had found a broad white patent leather
belt, and some yellow shoes with heels higher than Elisabeth was used
to. The young assistant is silenced by delight, tinged with envy as she
carefully wraps the items in yards of tissue and places them in a large
Beales bag. How lovely it had been to dress someone other than the
middle-aged women, who were the usual clientele. That beautiful hair,
so perfect with the lemon-yellow, and the strange tall man with the
long hair and kindly smile with eyes only for her. One day . . . maybe.

They leave with helpful advice about a small jeweller on Old Christchurch Road and head off to follow the precise directions from the sentry-like doorman.

He finds her hand as they cross the road. "Are you pleased?" he asks.

She stops him when they get to the pavement, reaches up, and kisses him.

"Delighted. Couldn't be happier. It's perfect."

"Traditionally it isn't something the chap gets involved with, is it? Choosing the wedding dress."

"Well, if we were to have another ceremony later in the chapel, I could still surprise you."

"Not sure it would be any prettier."

"Oh, I'm not so sure. Ivory silk with a long train."

"I was thinking about the contents."

"Those would be hidden behind a veil of tulle."

She squeezed his hand. She wonders if she looks as happy as she feels inside. Has there been a time over the last few days when she hasn't been smiling? But that's only what others can see. What they can't know is the brimming joy that she feels inside. All those romantic novels she read as a teenager suddenly don't seem so silly. It is not just her that is smiling—everyone is smiling—she is walking on air. The world is a joyful place. There is good in everything.

The jeweller is helpful, if taciturn. He is a shrunken caricature, a wizened old man with a beaky nose and a crumpled stoop, hung with a suit that might have once fitted, who moves slowly through the glass-topped cabinets of his dingy shop, fighting for his breath. Happily, his more able assistant can enlarge the engagement ring posthaste and promises to have it ready by early afternoon. They look at wedding rings and quickly find a slim band that Elisabeth feels befits her station. Nothing too grand or ostentatious, you understand, something a bit like the frail band still adorning her grandmother's bony hand, worn impossibly thin by fifty years of washing and cleaning. The ring is placed in a small satin-lined box which Henry slides into his jacket pocket.

They leave the shop with Henry suggesting lunch, but Elisabeth has other ideas.

"What about your new suit?"

"Is it really necessary?" he reposts. "How about we leave it till the proper wedding."

She doesn't say anything but espies a Gentleman's Outfitters on the opposite side of the road and, grabbing his hand, tugs him across and through the shop door before he really has any idea what is happening. But it is a dreary establishment, with a disinterested owner who does little to extol the virtues of his lacklustre selection. Elisabeth can see from Henry's uncharacteristically tight-lipped manner that he is not impressed and hastily thanks the owner for his time and ushers Henry out.

"Oh dear," she says, with an exaggerated look of hurt and disappointment. "Perhaps there is somewhere better." She glances at him, and then adds "After lunch."

He smiles. "Well, it was a jolly middling selection, I'd say."

"Totally pedestrian and mediocrely below average, I'd have to agree," she says, mocking him. "But I haven't given up. Let's have some lunch and see if a glass of Worthington improves the quality any."

They stroll down towards the sea through the pleasure gardens, Elisabeth tightly clutching her precious bags. The day is bright now, with occasional clouds casting cool shadows and an overly brisk breeze coming off the Channel, but it is not cold. The Bellevue Hotel beckons, and they find a bright table with views of the pier and the paraphernalia of a seaside town. Here are sunhats and donkey rides and ice-cream stands and deck chairs and striped windbreaks and a few kids braving the waves.

They eat simply, she a bowl of soup and he a dressed crab. She had noted the prices and worked out that she could just afford to buy the lunch. Paying her way was something that her father had drummed into her and during the war the equality of role and experience made it the norm, so she had hated that Henry was paying for everything. A simple lunch was but a gesture but made her feel a bit better. Besides, she wanted to buy him things. She had always preferred giving to receiving presents, although mostly all she could afford were things she had made herself.

She announced that she was going to pay, and of course, he protested, strangely she thought, for someone who seemed so removed from the grubby reality of money, but she prevailed, and he was genuinely pleased.

"Thank you, oh wondrous person, what a thoughtful gesture. I am not used to having people buy me things."

"Oh, come on Henry, it was only a cheap lunch. I would love to buy you more but that will have to wait." She wasn't sure what would be at the end of the wait. If she was going to give up her job what would happen then? Her mother had had a small allowance from her father paid into her account, but never really had any money of her own. That wouldn't do. Things had moved on. She would need to keep her own account, but how would she earn anything? Somehow the idea of getting a job alongside being Henry's wife didn't fit. She would have to have a conversation with him at some time but didn't look forward to it, not because he might object or take a stance, rather that he would be vague and agree to something nonspecific without doing anything about it.

"How about an ice cream at the end of the pier?" Henry says. "Let's be trippers for an hour; perhaps we can leave the bags here. Get some ozone into our lungs. 'I must go down to the sea again . . .'"

"'The lonely sea and the sky . . .'It won't be that lonely, by the look of it. Yes, let's," she says.

They descend further down to the promenade and join the other holidaymakers. There is the tang of the sea in the air and the breeze feels healthy and invigorating. Seagulls squawk and wheel above, children shout and cry. A man in a striped kiosk shouts, "Crabs and prawns, fresh prawns and shrimp."

"I do love prawns," Henry says. "I have to have a pint of prawns."

"But you've just had lunch. Ice cream for me."

"We don't need to eat them now; we can take them home for later. Don't you like them?" he says.

"I love them, but don't want to get covered in prawn juice, thank you very much."

She is still anxious to find a tailor's or gentleman's outfitter and keeps her eyes out for a suitable shop. They enter the jewellers to find the elderly owner is not in evidence and the younger man is more forthcoming, even if not managing charm. The ring is beautiful; he has cleaned it and the stones dazzle as she slides it onto her finger. She is almost overcome by this tangible mark of their union. Although their romance has progressed impossibly fast by most standards, the ring is one more stage of her becoming his, and at this moment there is not a flicker of doubt that it is what she wants most in the world.

As they leave the shop, with the attendant holding the door open for them, there is a long mirror and she smiles at the image of the tall man next to her, with a wedding ring in his Austrian jacket pocket and a pint of prawns wrapped in newspapers under his arm.

Although not Elisabeth's intention, they find themselves back at the car without having found a menswear shop. They stand next to the car as Henry makes to get in.

"What about your new suit?" Elisabeth says with genuine hurt.

"Oh lord." He looks crestfallen. "Is it really that important?" he says, raising his eyebrows.

"But I do want you to look your best Henry; your present wardrobe is hardly haute couture."

"But nobody will see—none of our friends are going to be there. I promise I will get a beautiful Italian suit before the proper wedding. And you can help choose it." He smiles pleadingly.

She swings the bags into the back of the open car and opens the front door, curling her skirt round her legs before swinging herself into the driver's seat. "Humph. You win Mr. Benville, but don't make a habit of it."

....

After dinner she asks him if he has a candle.

"A candle? Whatever for?"

"To light the bedroom. The bedside lights are awful."

"Well, I imagine there will be one somewhere. Where would Mrs. B keep them, do you think? Perhaps the scullery."

They search in vain through the jumbled contents of the scullery but then Henry remembers there is a copper candle holder on the dresser in the dining room. It has the short stub of a red candle. Matches are no easier to find, but finally she is climbing the magnificent oak staircase with its creaky thirteenth step through the shadowy landing and into the master bedroom. She lights the candle, placing it on Henry's dressing table, and turns off the lights. She dips into the bathroom and then undresses in the yellow room, pulling on a cotton slip before returning to the semidarkness of the bigger room.

She loves candlelight. The huge bed lies like an enormous square cake, the carvings on the headboard exaggerated by the flickering flame. She clambers between the cool of the coarse linen. She lies still in her slip but wants to feel the sensual brush of the linen on her skin and so sits up and pulls it over her head. She lies back, pulling the sheets up under her chin, her nipples tightening against the cool, rough material. She can see the reflection of the flame dancing in the mirror of the armoire, the corners of the room vanishing into shadows. This is a fairy tale, and she has become a princess. For the now there is nothing to diminish the wonder of her fantasy. The petty anxieties of the morning melt away. She has no tedious job, no sad isolated mother, no lonely evenings longing for laughter and stimulation. Nothing matters save for this bed, this flickering luminescence, this man. She can't believe how aroused she is. It is as much as she can do to not touch herself, instead she clenches her buttocks and presses her thighs together, arching her back. She aches with a delicious insatiate electricity.

At last, she hears him in the bathroom, and then he enters the room.

"Wow. The seraglio beckons. Such a simple idea, yet a man wouldn't have thought of it."

He slips out of his clothes, tossing them onto a chair. She eyes him coyly from under the sheet pulled up to her chin. He strides to the bed, his hardening cock swaying as he walks. He pulls back the covers, briskly exposing her completely. She doesn't move as he leans over and kisses her on the mouth. He tastes of toothpaste and him. His stubble is rough on her face. She responds eagerly. He breaks off.

"God, you are lovely. I just need to look at you."

After, they lie drenched and panting until he rolls off her, his shrunken cock scampering like a damp mouse across her thigh.

Their breathing subsides in parallel, for a moment in perfect synchrony, then out of phase, he in three-four time, she in six-eight. She rolls over and kisses him on the cheek, cupping his cock in her hand.

"What's it like to have one of these?" She gives it a squeeze.

"What do you mean?"

"Well, doesn't it get in the way—all this kit, these bits and bobs. Where do you put them when you walk about?"

He guffaws. "I don't know. I've ever thought about it. They just sit there, minding their own business."

"Not always just their own business."

"True, they do interfere with other people's business at times."

"Not other people, just one person."

"Just one person."

"But one person often."

"Hope so."

"Well, what about you? What's it like to have those squishy bits? If I had one, I would want to get it fucked all the time."

"And what makes you think we are any different!"

"But it is different, isn't it? Men are all outward—hard, thrusting, aggressive. Your little puss cat is soft, accommodating, passive, inwards."

"Puss cat?"

"Whatever; fanny, pussy, quim. Best not cunt."

"Occasionally cunt. Not fanny. For me anyway."

"Of course. Once a FANY never a fanny, I suppose."

"Quite."

"So, tell me about your FANYing. Where were you based?"

"In sunny Essex. Not very glamorous. I was stationed at a house called Briggens. It was the training centre for the Polish army in exile. Full to the brim with chunky Polish refugees learning how to become saboteurs and to blow up railway lines."

"How did you find them?"

"They were a marvellous lot—loyal, humorous, tough, and respectful of those trying to help them. Driven entirely by hatred of the Nazis and love of vodka."

"What did you do?"

"Oh, boring stuff, like most FANYs. Our roles were pretty menial: driving, filing, typing, occasionally skivvying. The stuff nobody else would do. Running around after people, being at their beck and call. But I loved it."

And that was it. That was all she told him. Her lips so conditioned to remain sealed that even in his arms she didn't tell him. And she would forever regret it.

"What about your war?" she asks. "You haven't given much away. 'Intelligence. Working here and there.' What does that mean? My guess is the Austrian connection was important and you speaking German."

"Yes, good guess. Can I show you something? I have never shown it to anybody before. I wasn't supposed to keep it." He gets up, naked, sliding off the side of the bed as if he was on a toboggan, and walks across the room to a large clothes press. He opens the upper part, which contains several drawers, and pulls out the top one. He lifts

out a small cardboard box. He brings it back to the bed and jumps
up to sit on its edge, but even his feet don't touch the floor.

He pulls out an envelope and opens it, removing two booklets.
One is a folded single sheet of paper; the other is a green cloth-covered
document that looks like a passport. He hands them to her. She turns
the green paper over in her hands; it is thumbed and worn. On the
cover is written REISEPASS, REPUBLIK OSTERRICH. She opens it. Inside
there is a picture of Henry looking much younger. The name is Pieter
Mueller, the address a road in St. Georgen. She flicks through it and
then picks up the other paper, opening it out. It is an Austrian birth
certificate for a Pieter Mueller born on the twelfth of July 1918.

For a moment she is frozen, unable to believe what she is
being shown. How can this be possible? She knows all about these
documents, more than he can possibly imagine and will ever know,
and in the instant it all swims before her eyes.

She sees the briefing meeting in the basement room at Briggens,
perhaps with wintry sunlight slanting in through the low window.
Captain Roberts defines the task of producing a forged Austrian
passport and accompanying birth certificate. He hands over to Charles
Hazell, who opens a folder and produces two original documents in
different names, an Austrian passport and a birth certificate.

"We are very happy with the passport, and reasonably confident
about the birth certificate. It is from 1907, but we don't think that
they have changed since."

They would be told the name and all the details of this Peter
Mueller, whom they were required to create, wondering as always who
he really was, where he was from, and how he had come to be needing
an Austrian passport. Then the real documents would be handed over
to Vincent Whittaker for photographing, and the negatives would be
worked on by hand, often for hours, to remove the information relating
to the original owner, to be retouched by Bill Byrne until they were
happy with the basic blank document. Meanwhile Ellic Howe would be
matching the fonts from his connections at the Monotype Corporation

and produce the right punches to press the matrices with the exact Fracktur lettering to enable the plates to be made up. Three days later Peter would waltz in, a big smile on his face, and produce several sheets of the correct watermarked paper that he and his contacts at Spicers had somehow made. And then the printing would begin, Jerze and Antoni standing over their clanking machines to provide the blanks that would be sent back to Roberts for approval. He would never be completely happy. The colour of the ink not a perfect match, the lettering too bold, the paper wrong. And he was right, of course. Then there would be a second, third, and sometimes a fourth attempt before he was finally satisfied. The blank copy would be finally fit to work on, requiring all the details to be added, either in long hand or one of our several German typewriters, with their special keys including the "SS" moniker. And then it would need the little postage stamp in the bottom, which would have been perfectly copied by Fred Giles on the correct philatelic paper. And it would need to be stamped with an official eagle, hand drawn by Dennis. And she herself might have worked on it, adding writing or aging the document by refolding it or leaving one side exposed to the sun or an ultraviolet light, or using very weak tea to yellow the paper. Tony Gatwood would be there to sign it, copying the original signature with uncanny skill. And there would be a panic at the end because of the deadline was nearing when it had to be presented to Major Egdell for final inspection, and sometimes it still wasn't deemed good enough, or there would be a simple spelling mistake in the German—an umlaut left off or a misplaced capital—and they would have to start again.

All these memories career through her mind and tears roll down her cheeks as she starts to sob. She puts the papers down beside her and flings her arms around Henry's neck and shakes and heaves uncontrollably.

"My love whatever is the matter? It's only a piece of paper." He tries to comfort her, wrapping his arms around her.

She continues to weep, but after a minute or two she can speak between the sobs.

"No, it's not. I know what you had to do and where you had to go to need these. I know what you went through. Some of you didn't come back, did they?"

He pauses momentarily. "No, some of us didn't come back." It's barely a whisper.

"And some of you were imprisoned, tortured—friends, pals, good men."

"Yes."

"Shot."

"Yes."

"But you came back . . . and this saved you." She is more animated and able to properly speak, tears still rolling down her cheek. "We saved you. We looked after you."

"Darling, I don't understand."

"This," she picks up the passport again, "this brought you home to me. This little piece of paper kept you safe. Kept you safe for me. We looked after you. And I never thought that I would be able to say that . . . You brave, brave man."

"No, not brave . . . just an ordinary man doing what he had to. I have told you I am lucky. I am sorry you are so upset. Perhaps I shouldn't have shown you."

"Oh no! You had to show me." And she kisses him.

He folds up the papers and replaces them in the envelope, then gets up, carefully puts them back in the box, and takes them back to the cupboard. He returns to the bed and they both get under the blankets.

She is calmer. "I am sorry I got so emotional. I don't know why they upset me so much. You don't mind, do you? Have I worried you?"

"Not at all. It is of no importance. Let's say no more about it." But his tone is unusually businesslike, almost as if he has become Pieter Muller. It's done, finished with. The case is closed. Now we move on.

But she does know why she was upset, of course she does, and she knows exactly what he means, even as a throwaway line. She will not say a word about it, and she is sorry for her outburst. She knows that very few people will know what she now knows, and she would never betray his trust. She knows that secrets need to be kept, and that after the war many people chose to put their remembrances and memories into a box and throw away the key. Perhaps that's the only way to deal with these things; to compartmentalise them, see them as being from a different life and never make a return visit.

She now has more to add to his list of attributes: war hero. What had he said, "just an ordinary man doing what he had to." She remembers the eulogy at her father's funeral read by one of his oldest friends, a brigadier in the tanks: "Ordinary men, doing exceptional things, during extraordinary times." But she knows the man lying next to her is not ordinary by any measure.

She can feel his still, warm body next to hers and moves across the great bed to touch him, turning on her side and resting her hand on his chest. He doesn't stir, the breathing slow and regular. She can't see him but feels she is watching over him as one might a small child. She snuggles into his naked form and moves her hand to his hair. *Ridiculous hair! Too long by far and too blond, and never, ever to be changed.*

But she is concerned about her outburst. What will he be thinking? Will he think that she is soppy and sentimental? She doesn't want that; she wants him to love her and feels she would do anything to secure that. She wants to tell him that she, too, has secrets, and that they will forever be safe. Perhaps one day he would share with her some of what he did when he needed a forged Austrian passport. But then why should he?

Would she ever tell him about her little role at Briggens?

The answer was no; she cannot think of an occasion when she would break her vow of silence.

Does it matter? Should she have told him? The thing she knows for sure is that all those marvellous people she worked with, whether ordinary or exceptional, would not have breathed a word.

But later, how many times did she wish she had.

CHAPTER 26

Dorset and London
July 1992

I had been putting off talking to my brother Graham since my arrival. We were not close and had lived in different worlds for forty years, but nevertheless I felt honour bound to see the old soak. His world was suburban Essex, the golf club and, in particular, the nineteenth hole.

He was four years younger than me and had avoided active duty, but after his national service, joined the family business started by my grandfather. This was at the time when I was restoring my boat and leaving him and Father to their own devices.

Graham had been a steady but unimaginative assistant to Father, taking over when he retired. Of course, the business had changed, with ultimately, the inevitable sale to a bigger corporation. Graham had done reasonably well in the deal and retired to the golf course and gin bottle.

I telephoned him from the hotel, his frosty wife reporting that he was watering the hanging baskets, but she would endeavour to locate him. He was a little more affable than she, taking some time to glean that I was in England.

"So, what could have been important enough to drag you back to Blighty? I thought you didn't like flying."

"I don't—I drove."

"Blimey, must have been important. Do you still have that old Bristol, or have you traded it in for something sensible?"

"I find it perfectly sensible, thank you. I thought we ought to meet; it has been too long."

"Some would say that, others not long enough." I was used to this sniping banter.

"Would you care to meet me in town for lunch tomorrow? I remember you always used to enjoy the RORC. We could meet there."

I had not been to the Royal Ocean Racing Club for years. It had been a favourite haunt way back, when I could guarantee to meet, if not a friend, then someone who had sailed on a boat I knew. I figured that I could catch the train and be back in time for my appointment with Philip.

The train from Dorchester was hardly speedy, but nevertheless I was able to walk through the doors of the Club just after twelve thirty.

Graham looked awful. He had put on a lot of weight and had a great purple nose and a lumbering bovine manner. He was grouchy and unpleasant in his greeting. Little changed with his first gin. I ordered a beer to see if they still served it in silver tankards. The answer was yes.

"What brings you back to the country you dislike so much? Was it a woman?"

I reminded him that I was seventy-three and had never been a womaniser.

"What about the maid in France—you still screwing her?"

"Trains for Dorchester leave Waterloo on the hour. I can catch the next one if I get a cab. I will be perfectly happy to leave now if you can't be civil."

He grunted. "You weren't prepared to come for your mother's funeral. I've never forgotten that." He took a slurp of his drink.

I asked after the family and tried to make conversation around the few mutual memories we shared. It was hard work, but he softened a little.

"You still haven't told me what you are doing here," he reiterated.

"Do you remember Elisabeth Watson, an old girlfriend from—"

He cut me off. "Of course I remember Elisabeth. Every man with blood in his veins would remember Elisabeth." I had forgotten that he must have got to know her quite well when I was restoring *Undine*.

"She died last year, not that I knew anything about it."

"So, I was right," he snorted, "it was a woman."

"She left me something in her will and I had to come and collect it."

"Blimey! What was it, a diamond tiara?"

"No. A bundle of papers. Some that relate to Briggens but others that don't make much sense. I picked them up from Dorset. I will head back there tonight and probably return to France later in the week. Did you know she married a lord and set up an opera company?"

"No idea. But you know she phoned me once, many years ago."

"Really? When?"

"Oh god, I don't know, must have been forty years ago. You were still on *Undine*. I don't think I was even married."

"What did she want?"

"She didn't say. Said she wanted to talk about something and arranged to visit but then never turned up. I can't remember any details, but she wasn't making a lot of sense. I remember it because I was a bit disappointed that she didn't turn up. Like many of your friends, I had a bit of a crush on her."

"How strange. I wonder what that was all about."

We resolved little over the next hour, him quaffing most of the house claret and devouring a guinea fowl with unappealing zeal. Within two hours I was back on the train to Dorchester.

CHAPTER 27

....

Dorset

Friday, August 6, 1948

This morning it is she who wakes first, restless and excited. She has no idea of what time it is but reaches for him among the shambles of bedclothes that range over the massive bed like the floor of a hotel laundry. She finds a shoulder and slides towards him, throwing a thigh across him.

"Are you awake, Henry?"

"No."

"I am too excited to sleep."

"Humph," he grunts.

She nuzzles up to him, but he remains lifeless and immobile. "You're no fun. I am going to get up." She moves away from him and swings herself down from the great height of Guillome's bed. She strolls into the bathroom where the curtains are open, and she can see a patch of sun on the lawn.

That bodes well.

The shadows are still long and there is a touch of dew on the grass, so it must be early. She turns on the hot water to run a bath and notes that it isn't as brown as before. All the bathing she's been doing must have washed the system through. While the water's running, she walks to the window and pulls off her nightie, standing naked stretching her arms up and arching her back, the low sill edge brushing against her hairs. It is nice to be naked; she enjoys the sensual feel of the absence of clothing. There are few opportunities for nakedness in Victoria; just a race to get covered as soon as possible in the freezing bathroom.

The sill is deep, the leaded panes a foot away so she can see a vague reflection of her bare self superimposed on the shapes and textures of the beds and hedges of the garden. Seldom does she look at a reflection of her naked self, and inevitably she is critical of her curves and form. Her waist is too thick and her hips too heavy. Is it good enough for him? A week ago, it didn't matter. Now suddenly it does; she wants to be what Henry wants. She needs him to want her, but more than that, she needs him to want her more than anyone else, and that matters in a way which it never has before.

She leans forward, the vague pressure on her pubis just enough to remind her of the excitement that he provokes in her. She has always enjoyed making love. In fact, there were times when she worried whether she liked it too much, inevitably linking it to some moral deficit or weakness and a subsequent storm of self-doubt and loathing.

Most of her sexual experiences were of trying to get the most out of the man's often too-brief efforts to reach his own climax, her arousal being left to her. What had emerged over the last few days was something different: a magnificent awakening triggered by his excitement and urgency. He wasn't doing anything special or different from her other lovers, but her response was somehow magnified. It was mysterious in that she had been left surprised by the reaction of her own body. Was it his insistent need, that focus solely on her, that was so erotic? His overwhelming exigency, his taut hardness, seemed to come from her just being her, not by anything she physically did to him.

She hates to admit it, but he has possessed her, leaving her submissive in a way that she has previously never imagined possible, and it provides heights of both vulnerability and power that are as terrifying as they are ecstatically joyful.

The bath! She snatches herself away and returns to reality,

stepping briskly into the steaming water.

Henry Bounds in, dressing gown and slippers to the fore, exuberant in a way that is unusual even for him.

"Good morning my sweetness—ah, I see you are taking your wedding day ablutions with the utmost gravity. How divine you look in your watery repose. A veritable water nymph, I should say. Do you need tea?"

"I would love a cup, if you are going down."

He never reappears, and not wanting to don her finery at this time of the morning, she puts on the borrowed dressing gown and heads for the kitchen. It is a bustle of activity. Mrs. B is standing by the Aga filling a large teapot with boiling water, Malcolm is sitting in his customary chair at the table cradling a teacup, wearing his habitual "I wish I was somewhere else" face. Henry is talking to Percy Smallwood while Geoffrey Burney hovers, grinning as usual in his waistcoated summer tweed.

Elisabeth feels embarrassed she is still in a dressing gown but takes comfort that it is like an overcoat, and nobody seems the slightest bit concerned.

"Darling, Percy popped in on his way to town to offer us luck. Look what he brought you."

He reaches to the table and picks up a neat posy of flowers. There are white roses with blue cornflowers and phlox bound with fronds of greenery and tied with a pink ribbon.

"Miriam thought you should have a posy even if you are diving off to the back of beyond," Percy says. "There is a card too." He hands both over with a beaming smile.

"Thank you, Percy. What a lovely thought. They are gorgeous. Are they from your garden? I think flowers work even in Croydon," Elisabeth says.

"Especially in Croydon," Henry adds.

"Where exactly is Croydon?" chips in Geoffrey, accepting a cup of tea from Mrs. B. "Can one toast good health with tea? To both of you the very best wishes for a long and productive union."

"Thank you, Geoffrey, but you will have time to do it properly in September. We will have the best and most glorious celebration here at Knowle. Elisabeth has it all planned," says Henry.

"Elisabeth has it all planned according to Henry's plans," Elisabeth says, sipping her tea with a coy smile.

"No," says Henry, "Mrs. B is in charge. We will do what she tells us to!"

"Of course," Geoffrey says, "it goes without saying."

Mrs. B suddenly looks embarrassed. "Well, I have meself a few ideas, and I don't mind sharing them, I must say. We must do things proper. It's only what Dorothy would have wanted for her boy," she says, nodding to herself.

"Well, I had better get on," says Percy. "Divorces and deaths wait for no man. Look you two, have a marvellous day. Where are you going afterwards? Have you booked somewhere special, Henry?"

Henry looks abashed. "Umm, not quite yet. It's on the to-do list."

"Settle for nothing less than Quaglinos or the Ritz, Elisabeth," Percy says as he backs out the kitchen door.

The kitchen returns to normal. Elisabeth sits, still in her dressing gown, and has a piece of toast. Her mother is expecting them at midday and, after discussion with Geoffrey, who knows about these things, it is agreed that the trip will take about three hours. They suddenly realise that they need to get a move on. Henry rushes to pack his things. Elisabeth follows, with assurances from Mrs. B that she will clear up the breakfast things.

It's half past nine before the whole *équipe* is assembled on the gravel outside the front door. They decide to leave the hood up, as it is still early, and it is a cool morning. Mrs. B is beside herself, clutching the ball of a screwed-up hanky, tears on her cheeks. Susan and Pat from the estate office are joined by Geoffrey and stand back a bit exchanging whispers, and then there is Biscuit pacing the ground, hoping that whatever is about to happen will include him. And then, just when they are ready to leave, a figure is seen waddling down the drive from the direction of the dower house. It is Anneliese, wearing a peculiar house coat and fur slippers. Henry gets out of the car followed by Elisabeth and walks towards her.

"So wirst du es wirklich tun?" she says without smiling.

"Of course we are going to do it, Leelee. This afternoon at the register office in Croydon."

"Vell, good for you. You know best."

"But we are going to have a big party and blessing in September here when I have liberated myself from my work commitments."

Anneliese turns to Elisabeth and deliberately looks her up and down. "You look very nice. She ist pretty, ya. I have a little gift for you." She holds out a small jewellery box, scuffed and obviously not new, and gives it to Elisabeth.

"Thank you, Anneliese. How kind." She takes the box and opens it. Inside is a brooch of filigree gold with emeralds and pendants of a yellowish stone that she doesn't recognise. It is a bit old-fashioned, and not what she would have chosen, but a generous gift.

"It's beautiful. Thank you."

"It was my mother's, but . . ." she waves her hand, "ven vould I vear it now?"

They stand for a moment, Henry and Elisabeth eager to get on the move but not sure how to end a rare moment of rapprochement.

Henry takes charge. "Leelee, it's a very thoughtful gift. Thank you, but we have to get going, as we are lunching with Elisabeth's mother in Reigate."

"Ach so. I haf no idea where is Reigate, but off you go." She turns and trudges back up the drive, her thin little legs pale beneath the floral housecoat which hangs like a lampshade above the incongruous, fluffy slippers.

Henry ushers Elisabeth back into the car and finally they set off.

"Well, I never expected that," he says.

"It was very touching; she didn't have to do it. Oh dear, there is so much hurt and sadness lurking under that battered exterior. Perhaps we could end up as friends," she says.

"Maybe. It would help if she could moderate her drinking a bit."

"Better she stops completely. Isn't that what you have to do?"

"You are probably right. But if we see the gift as a peace offering, it bodes well for her acceptance of a new mistress at Knowle."

"Mistress! Is that my role?"

"Amongst others."

The day is less kind, overcast and dull without the invigorating sunshine that they have enjoyed in the week, but Elisabeth is animated and doesn't really notice the weather.

"So, what exactly is the plan?" she asks. "Tomorrow you jump on a plane to Austria while I sit in Victoria—how do I get there? And when?"

"I do have a plan Elisabeth, I promise. Perhaps I haven't communicated it very well. I did make a few calls in the week trying to work things out, but it was a bit difficult doing it all on the telephone when I had so many distractions." He reaches over and squeezed her knee, turning to her long enough to see her risk a glance in his direction. "The big question is whether I could get you onto an official flight, but I think it unlikely. More likely would be a flight to Prague and then a train to Vienna, where I would meet you. Could you manage that?"

"Oh, I think so. I'm a big girl now, you know—tie my own laces and know my times-tables. I could possibly just manage. In fact, it would be rather exciting, especially if you are at the end of the journey."

"I thought we could stay a few days in Vienna, perhaps go to the opera."

"That would be wonderful! A sort of honeymoon."

And there are some great museums and galleries. As well as cake—they do good cake, the Viennese."

"Don't tell me they cut them into weird unequal slices."

"Possibly not. Everything is very uniform, precise, and equal in Vienna, unless you are poor."

They press on, chattering about Vienna and other places in

Austria that Henry loves, not aware of the time until they stop for petrol and Elisabeth notices the clock on the garage forecourt. She realises that they are running terribly late and will never get to Reigate by midday. A growing burden of worry tugs at her contentment. She really doesn't want to be late. She gives her mother so little of her time and all week has had to cope with a nagging feeling that she should have involved her more in her plans for the wedding.

Elisabeth says they should call, but telephone boxes are few and far between and her anxiety translates to a tense silence, the usual carefree, fun space between them replaced by something more sober and serious. Henry detects it and realises he needs to respond. They pass a roadside hotel, and he suggests they pull in and ask to use the phone. He offers to drive, which she accepts. Within ten minutes they are back on the road, with an estimated time of arrival of one o'clock. She is more relaxed, as Mummy seemed very unconcerned. She hadn't even put the potatoes on.

They finally arrive just after one, Elisabeth directing Henry into the gravel drive of the prewar house in its pleasant, unremarkable road, a testament to interwar aspiration and application. Now that he is with her, she is more aware of how tired and shabby the house and garden look. The lawn could do with mowing and the white rendered frontage is greying, with patches of green mould under the windows and around the garage doors. She is ashamed and hopes Henry won't notice. She then realises that he will, but his charm is that he won't judge. That is the thing about him: his astute eye would pick up the detail, but he wouldn't give a fig. That was what she loved about him. Well, one of the things.

The front door is locked by a Yale lock and, as she has no key, she rings the bell. You could walk into the front door of Knowle with all its treasures by turning the brass handle, but suburbia is different; although there is nothing worth stealing, the door is tightly secured. Elisabeth pulls down the hem of her dress and brushes out the creases as she stands under the tiled porch with Henry at her side.

The door opens and her mother is standing there, smaller than ever in her light-blue cardigan with the floral buttons, not quite smiling but not looking severe either, an almost quizzical look on her round powdered face. Unflappable, perhaps reserved, or maybe detached and distant. Elisabeth gives her a peck on the cheek and stands aside to introduce Henry, who shakes her hand with a gushing commentary about how delightful it is to meet her and how sorry he was that he couldn't ask her formally for her daughter's hand, most of which seems to go over her head as she ushers them into the narrow hall and closes the door behind. There is a stale smell of polish, cabbage, and something faintly antiseptic.

They are shown into the sitting room with metal-framed French windows which open onto a crazy-paving terrace and then a small lawn, before flower beds and a wooden fence. In the room, a three-piece suite in dark blue textured cotton is set around a low coffee table, upon which is a silver-plated salver with a decanter and three sherry glasses. Over the back of the sofa and chairs are small multicoloured crochet rugs.

Henry affirms how charming everything is, pointing to a competent marine watercolour over the mantelpiece which he examines closely, remarking on the light and shadow and then pointing to the crochet work.

"This must be your work, Mrs. Watson," he says, not waiting for or expecting an answer. "They are lovely. So, you are a secret crocheter, if there is such a word. What do you call someone who crochets, other than someone who crochets?"

"I think crocheter," Mummy says.

"You are really a knitter, aren't you Mummy? Always been a knitter since I can remember. You not only knitted us jerseys and hats and scarfs, but none of your friends could have a baby without a matinee jacket or pair of booties."

"Yes, I love my knitting, but crocheting is a good way of using up all the little bits of left-over wool."

"Well, they are most agreeable."

"Would you like a glass of sherry? I am afraid I don't have any champagne, but we should toast your marriage. Elisabeth, why don't you pour us all a glass?"

Mummy stands over the table while Elisabeth unstoppers the decanter, fills three glasses, and hands them round. "To you both," she says.

Elisabeth and Henry exchange glances. "To us, I suppose," says Elisabeth, immediately echoed by Henry.

"I have to say, this is all a bit of a surprise, Elisabeth. You kept very quiet that you were courting. When did you two meet?"

Henry steps in. "Today, Mrs. Watson, we celebrate an important anniversary—we have known each other exactly one week," he says and beams before taking a sip of sherry. "I know that may seem a bit rash by some measures, but I am unashamed in my admission that one glance of your daughter and I was smitten. They may talk of fallen women, but I was a fallen man. Still am, actually." He gives a chuckle.

"Do you like my dress, Mummy? You haven't said anything about it," Elisabeth says, doing a little twirl.

"It is very nice, dear. A lovely colour. It suits you."

"I think it is divine. Henry bought it for me in Bournemouth. We had such a lovely day shopping."

Elisabeth sits, chatting about the trip and the week at Knowle, bringing Henry into the conversation now and again to confirm that the weather really had been that wonderful, or the house was beautiful, or the chapel terribly old. Elisabeth is aware that she is not saying anything of importance, but chatting is better than sitting in silence waiting for Mummy to say something.

And for the most part Mummy seems to be listening, but she does not say much and then suggests they must be hungry, and she needs to do a few things to get the lunch ready. She sedately gets up to go to the kitchen. Elisabeth jumps up with the offer of help, leaving Henry on his own with an empty sherry glass, but not before stepping across to him and giving him a quick kiss. She squeezes his hand and shares a resigned smile. He returns the smile and reluctantly releases her hand.

"It's fine," he whispers. "Just fine."

Lunch is boiled ham with mashed potatoes and cabbage, followed by apple pie and custard. They sit in the spartan dining room at a tablecloth embroidered with edelweiss.

Henry picks up on the edelweiss, asking where the tablecloth came from.

"It was my mother's, but I don't know where she got it from."

And that allows Henry to talk about Austria and the wildflowers and the lakes and cities and opera and his work there and how lovely it is, taking over from where Elisabeth left off, filling in the otherwise empty space and uncomfortable silence with his knowledgeable charm.

Elisabeth relaxes. She sits opposite her beau, glowing. He has got it. He can do it too. Why did she need to worry about him being judgemental? He knows exactly how to perform for a mother-in-law. It was almost as if he had had one before.

And then she remembers Anneliese and the way he is with her. Of course he can do it, he has had years of practice at being tactful and nice and kind. At not being judgemental, at beguiling people with his patter and charm.

Henry talks about his work amongst the dispossessed of Europe. Elisabeth looks at him and then Mummy, who seems to be interested and listening. And in that moment, she just glimpses another future for this placid, kind but damaged person; she could come to Knowle, not to live necessarily, but to stay. She can see her sitting, chatting in the kitchen with Mrs. B and being drawn into the life of the big house and just maybe getting out her secateurs and cutting some flowers for the table or doing some baking. Would she come? Could she find some joy somewhere? A grandchild? No! That is too far, she can't think of that just now.

They finish eating but Elisabeth is getting worried about the time.

She doesn't wear a watch but catches Henry's eye and taps her wrist. He pulls up his cuff and checks his watch, mouthing to her that it's past two. Now they are both moved by the need to hurry. Elisabeth apologises for not being able to help with the washing up while stacking the pudding bowls and taking them through to the kitchen.

She suddenly remembers her birth certificate.

"I so nearly forgot. Mummy, I need my birth certificate for the register office. Do you know where it is?"

"I suppose it is in the drawer of your father's desk, along with the other important papers." They leave the room and head for a little study to the right of the front door. Henry follows at a distance and stands in the hall examining a pair of uninspired lithographs from a series entitled *English Cathedrals*.

The women emerge but with no paperwork.

"Perhaps it's in my dressing table." Elisabeth climbs the stairs while Mummy enters the kitchen and starts clattering pans and dishes. Henry looks at his watch again with a look of concern on his face.

Mummy reappears in her apron, wiping her wet hands on a tea towel, and calls up the stairs, "Elisabeth dear, I have thought of somewhere else it might be," and goes back into the study, to emerge a minute later with a buff envelope from which she pulls several folded papers. Henry moves towards her as she opens them one at a time.

"Here it is, got it," she calls up the stairs.

Elisabeth hurries down to join them.

"Thank god for that," she says as she takes the document, which she gives to Henry. "Righty-ho, how long will it take us to get to Croydon?"

"Not more than half an hour, I would say."

"It's quarter past, so we should be all right. Sorry, Mummy, but we have to rush. I will write to you from Austria," Elisabeth says as she gives her a peck on the cheek and opens the front door.

They jump into Evey and head out, waving at the dumpy, apron-clad figure standing framed in the doorway, her expression as blank and unreadable as when they first arrived.

CHAPTER 28

....

Dorset

July 1992

H e was on time, as I expected he would be. I was sitting in the dingy bar, cigarette between my fingers, nursing a gin and tonic that was mostly ice and water. He was wearing a tie and a Harris tweed jacket with the same aerated shoes as before and carried a small canvas bag. I stubbed out the Gitane, got up, and asked what he would like to drink.

"Just a half of bitter please, Peter."

I requested the pimply barman to put another measure of gin in my glass and we walked back to our seats. He placed the bag flat on the table and put his hands across the top, interlocking his fingers as if protecting the precious contents. But his look was more relaxed and affable than at our first meeting.

"How are you finding the Old Ship? I suspect you are more used to the Negresco."

He didn't look the type of person to know the Negresco. Although clearly broad-minded and worldly, I expected him to take his holidays on the Tweed. "It's fine for what it is. Mrs. McMurray looks after us like a mother hen. How do you know the Negresco?"

"Elisabeth and I stayed there for a night once when we were on our way to the Aix-en-Provence Opera Festival."

That simple comment bit me like a viper. All those years that I had longed to take that woman to a fine hotel. "To your liking?"

"Typical French grandeur, as I recall—a bit over-the-top."

"Certainly that. Not a criticism you would level at the Old Ship." I smiled my way out of my discomposure.

He opened the bag and pulled out my bundle of papers.

"Thank you for letting me see this material, Peter. I found it fascinating, but not all of it easy. As you say, the papers from Briggens are pretty straightforward, but once again I am struck by the extraordinary work that you did at Section XIV. It is surprising that there isn't wider knowledge about the unit. What was your role exactly?"

I told him about the family paper business and my trips to Europe before the war and how, inadvertently, I had become something of an expert on making paper and, in particular, continental paper.

"But what about your experience in the Navy?"

I told him a bit about PQ 13 and how Grandfather's advice about keeping my clothes on had probably saved my life; and certainly had saved my feet.

"Some of the crew were wearing nothing more than their underwear under their greatcoats when the ship was hit."

"And that experience was the basis for *Convoy North*?"

"That's right."

"When did you write it? Were you still with Elisabeth?"

"Oh no. I was waiting for her! Pining in cheap lodgings through a Sicilian winter."

Philip delved into the bag on the table and pulled out a book and other papers and documents. He picked up the book and passed it over to me. It was a hardback with the torn dust jacket still intact. I recognised the typical fifties artwork; a pastel stormy sea with a shadowy destroyer and *Convoy North* splayed diagonally across the brooding sky.

"This is Elisabeth's copy. I knew we had it somewhere. Have a look at the frontispiece."

I opened the book and found it. In print was the dedication

"For EW." Next to it, written in my hand was ". . . who replaced my nightmares with beauty and light. Always room for you here at my side. Ever waiting, Pom."

"Soppy," I said. "But true, alas."

"Were the nightmares about the convoy?" he asked.

"You sound like a doctor."

"I am a doctor! I don't mean to pry. I am very interested in the effects of trauma on people, especially wartime trauma."

"Is wartime trauma any different?"

"Yes, I think it is. In war servicemen, well generally men, end up in terrible situations, experience ghastly things, come close to death, see their buddies die, and other grim things, but they then return to a different world and somehow cope and adapt. I am interested in how people recovered from wartime trauma when they often don't from much less severe experiences in peacetime."

"Not always."

"Not always, exactly right. Although the effects of trauma were recognised in the latter stages of the first war . . ."

"Shell shock."

"Yes, shell shock, but huge numbers of men had symptoms they didn't tell anybody about, and those that did often got no treatment. Then there is the context of war, which is so different. Maybe the trauma can be better compartmentalised, can be seen to be separate and justifiable. I am sorry, I didn't come to talk about this. Do you mind talking about it?"

"I don't know. I say that because I have never talked about it—apart from with Elisabeth—she was the only person I ever talked to. Perhaps it would have been different if I'd had children, you know, dandling little Johnnie on your knee and answering the 'what did you do in the war, Daddy' question."

"This is the whole point. In my experience, huge numbers of servicemen who would have fulfilled modern diagnostic criteria for a post-traumatic disorder somehow just coped, hoping that by burying their problems they would go away. Sometimes it worked, other times it didn't."

"And then what? The service revolver never handed back?"

"Sometimes, or the gin bottle."

"Is it better to talk?"

"Probably on balance, but it's not a cure."

"Thinking about it, I found writing helpful."

"I can imagine that; you put a lot of emotion into the book."

"Do you think so? It never felt like that. I thought it was cold and factual."

He smiled. "I didn't see it like that. You were good at leaving the reader to do the work, but the emotion was there, lurking in the icy water like the U-boats."

"I will take that as a compliment."

"Do please," he said.

"Do you mind if I smoke? I know what you medics are like . . ."

"If you must." He smiled and took a sip of his beer, returning to the pile of papers, two of which he pushed towards me. "I have made you some photocopies of a few documents I thought you would be interested in. This is a copy of Elisabeth's obituary from the *Times*, this one is from the *Dorchester Echo*, and here is the piece in the *Echo* about her time at Briggens. There are also a couple of other magazine articles about her; this one is from *Country Life* and this one from the *Sunday Times Magazine*. The press loved her; you can just imagine 'woman tragically widowed builds husband's dream.' You know the kind of thing."

I took the papers from him, the topmost being from the *Times*. It was one column, with a picture at the top of Elisabeth, taken I would guess in her forties, or perhaps, knowing her handsome and youthful features, her fifties. The strap line read "Influential and Much-Loved Founder of Knowle House Opera." I skimmed a couple of lines, noticing the strap line: "The Doyenne of English Country House Opera."

The piece from the *Echo* was dated March 1986, but the Elisabeth in the picture looked different. She looked older, of course, but there was something else; it was the hair. It was much shorter and looked softer, less buoyant and alive. I turned the page towards Philip. "She looks different here," I said, "something had happened to her hair."

"Very observant. All her hair fell out after the chemotherapy. It grew back, but it was different, softer, and finer. Nearly white."

"Did she mind?"

"Terribly. It was the one thing that nobody could console her about. She took to wearing an old Hermes silk headscarf, which she wound round her head like a turban. It suited her fine features, but we all took a bit of time to get used to the change."

"Thank you for these," I said. "I shall look at them with interest."

"The Briggens stuff is self-explanatory, as you pointed out yesterday. I am sure it ought to be in a museum, in particular the French ID card. Have you thought of that?"

"Yes, Steven Smallwood also suggested that yesterday," I said. "My only question was whether anyone would be interested in it."

"Oh, I think so, what with the fiftieth anniversary of the end of the war coming up. You have no idea about the number of fanatics who love all war-related memorabilia."

"What about the other bits? Any idea why I should be the one to be singled out to receive them?"

"The short answer is no."

"And the long answer?"

"Probably no as well," he said, laughing. "But I found it very interesting, as it told me a few things I didn't know about Elisabeth and that fateful week, in particular the distressing dream she recounted in the exercise book."

"Yes, the dream. But why was the week fateful? Wonderful, more like."

But our conversation was interrupted by a grey woman with a silk scarf who tapped Philip on the arm and with a smile said, "Dr. Wood, how nice to see you."

Philip stood and, with the woman apologising for the intrusion, they chatted for a couple of minutes.

"I am so sorry," Philip said. "An old patient. They still stalk me."

"Once their doctor, always their doctor, eh?"

"Well, I don't mind too much actually. You get enmeshed in their lives and the interest, and, at times, affection doesn't leave when you retire. I am sorry, Peter, where were we? The dream?"

"She writes the dream in some detail, doesn't she? But it meant little to me when I read it. I've never paid much attention to that sort of nonsense."

"Yes, it's disconcerting isn't it; as rational beings, we seek answers. We reach for explanations but find there are none and so disbelieve."

"What exactly was Henry doing in Austria?"

"A good question, and I'm not sure anyone really knows. During the war he had been in intelligence, but what that really meant is anyone's guess, except that you and I would have called him a spy."

"Hence the documents in the display case."

"Exactly. After the war, like many similar agents, he continued in the same sort of work notionally employed by the Diplomatic Service, on the face of it repatriating refugees and displaced persons, while continuing to work closely with MI6. That is possibly unfair as he certainly did some of that and rather well, but he would have had other roles of a more clandestine nature. Elisabeth met a few people over the years who appeared at odd times claiming to have worked with him. They were a shady bunch, long macs and trilbies—you can guess the kind of thing—but all from the top drawer: Eton or Winchester and Cambridge, usually. They would appear out of the blue, shake her hand, and tell her how remarkable he had been and how much the country owed him, and then disappear. There were a couple of his wartime friends who stayed in touch and were very supportive of Elisabeth in those early days and onward. In fact, one of them, Francis Wilkinson, is still a trustee. I suppose it was helpful for her to meet people who knew him and could reaffirm his qualities, but equally it made the tragedy of his premature demise even more painful. Like Mozart or Mendelsohn, you are left wondering what great things he could have done later in his life, albeit he might have just wanted to settle down as squire and family man."

"But Elisabeth didn't do too badly in his stead."

"Absolutely; it was extraordinary, what she achieved." He reached across for the handwritten exercise book and opened it on the table. "This is very poignant, isn't it?"

"Indeed," I said.

"Mostly it's a catalogue of times and places with a few memories of shared jokes and moments. It is odd that there is no mention of the wedding itself; there is a bit about the lunch with her mother and then a gap until the evening when they listen to the radio."

"I, too, found that odd—well, surprising, at any rate."

"Agreed, but the moment when they are listening to the radio made sense. Do you recall; a piece of piano music for four hands is played on the wireless, which neither of them knows. Later in a different pen she writes 'Schubert Fantasia in F Minor.' That was always one of her favourite pieces, and I never knew why. Do you know it?"

"No, I don't."

"Oh, it's marvellous." He hums, 'der-der, der, der-der, der der-der um.' Elisabeth learnt it and used to play it with a pianist friend."

Suddenly he looked sad and rueful.

"But then it stops. Just the comment about driving to the airport on the Saturday and all the things they had done, along with Henry's confession about delaying his flight. How bittersweet was that? But odd that she didn't write more."

"I know. It's strange, isn't it? Perhaps she found it too difficult to write about that, or maybe she just never finished it."

"Unlike Elisabeth to not finish something she started," I said. "Like forming an opera company and building an opera house."

He smiled, nodding his head while looking distractedly out the window. "Like building an opera house . . . But the diary is more interesting; have you seen these entries for October?" he picked up the volume and thumbed through to the right page. "She visits various churches in Hereford. She was obviously staying with her grandmother, who lived nearby, but you see that on the ninth she visits St. Mary's in Kington, then a week later St. Andrews in Presteigne, All Saints in Kinsham on the twenty-third, and then St. Peters in Titley. There is one more entry that you might be interested in . . . Look at this," he said, leaning over and pointing to October fifth.

The entry stated "Mackay's, 237 Commercial Road."

"What would that be about? Any ideas?" he asked.

"That would be the family paper business in the East End. That is peculiar because I saw my brother for lunch and he mentioned she had arranged a visit, but not arrived, although he couldn't remember when. He couldn't recall much about it."

I thought it time we ate something. "Are you hungry?" I said. "Perhaps we should go into the dining room and order some food."

He drained his beer, and we moved into the dining room, which was a newer extension to the rear of the building, with higher ceilings and ridiculous Georgian coving and brass wall lights. The furniture was dark oak with the requisite maritime paraphernalia on the walls—reproduction ship prints and a box containing miniature sailor's knots. Mrs. McMurray appeared and steered us to a table in the corner, nodding to Philip, albeit I suspected she couldn't place where she had seen him before. We sat for a moment or two, studying the menus before ordering our meals. I suggested a bottle of Cotes du Rhone despite Philip's protestations that he was driving and wasn't much of a drinker in any case.

"Arghh musak," Philip said.

"Pardon?"

"Piped music. Elisabeth couldn't abide it. She used to say, 'Don't these people realise that someone spent days struggling to write this piece of music, and then talented and highly trained musicians play it beautifully in a recording studio, for which they are paid a pittance, and now nobody is even listening to it?'"

"I've never thought about it," I muttered.

"I am sorry. She is still here at times."

In that moment he looked punctured and bereft.

I nodded, not knowing what to say. How could I add my pathetic perspective that it was her absence, not her presence, that hurt?

"So how do you fit into the story?" I asked.

He chuckled. "I wondered when you would get around to asking that. My family came from the West Midlands, around Bromsgrove, if you know it."

"Were you from one of these huge medical families where even the dog is a doctor?"

"No, not at all—my father was a teacher. After qualifying, I joined a general practitioner training programme. I did an attachment to a practice in Dorchester and got on well with the partners. When they advertised a job, I got it. I moved down here with my new wife and thought it was wonderful."

"And that's how you met Elisabeth?"

"Yes, and no. You are going too fast, Peter. The practice had a branch surgery in Knowle village in the front room of the Lawns, a large Victorian house off the green, and that is, indeed, how I met Elisabeth, but she wasn't usually the patient. The patient was either Henry's stepmother, Anneliese, or her boy, Robert. Anneliese was only a few years older than Henry, was Austrian, and without breaching medical confidentiality, was a reclusive alcoholic. She was demanding, difficult, and rude."

"When was this?"

"They appointed me in 1960, so around about then. I visited Anneliese a few times in the dower house, and then one day I met Elisabeth in the drive. I had heard mention of her *en passant*—the beautiful young widow rattling around in an enormous house—"

"Hold on, you haven't told me how Henry died?"

"Apologies. He died in a plane crash."

"So, you fall for the poor lonely widow?"

He looked at me with a flash of hurt in his eyes. I wasn't sure if it was because I had touched the truth or offended him because I was way off the mark.

"I am sorry," I said. "I didn't mean to offend."

He smiled. "Well, you are probably right. I hadn't anticipated meeting such a beautiful person. I was completely bowled over."

"Love at first sight?"

He smiled. "That old chestnut . . . Yes, if you like to put it like that, although as a psychotherapist it is a bit of a blanket construct. She was eight years older than me, but I remember walking back to my car parked at the Lawns thinking, *Wow, what a woman.*" He paused for a moment, that melancholy look returning to his kindly face. "And I never stopped thinking that, actually."

"But you were happily married."

"Up to a point. Jennifer and I had married very young, when we were still students. She was studying comparative religions and was always intense and had firm beliefs about what was morally acceptable."

"Sex, you mean."

"You don't mince your words Peter, I am learning that," he said, somewhat accusingly.

"We were in love, it was a first for both of us, and before I knew what was happening, we were married, had two daughters, and I was a GP in Dorset. But she didn't take easily to motherhood, lost interest in our new house, and didn't engage in the local community. She became more and more obsessed with her religious convictions. She had been a regular churchgoer for years but decided that the Church of England was too lax in its outlook and converted to Catholicism. Then after a few years, even their devotions weren't enough, and she searched elsewhere for an even more devout platform. She went on a weekend retreat in Wales run by a strange sect calling themselves the

Second Church of the Evangelist, and we lost her; me and my girls. We lost her." Again, he looked distant and melancholic.

"I suppose the children were about eight and ten. She started off attending one weekend a month, but then she was gone for the entire week. I didn't stop loving her; she just found an exclusive love for someone else that left no room for me or the girls."

"God?"

"Yes, God."

"What did you do?"

"Eventually, she permanently left to join the Order, and that's where she remains even now; in a closed religious community near Lampeter."

"And you divorced her so you could shack up with Elisabeth." I immediately regretted the bitterness that crept into my tone.

"Oh no, we are still married. She wouldn't divorce me. 'What therefore God has joined together, let not man put asunder.'"

"How difficult. I hope I am not talking out of turn, but Steven thought that you had proposed to Elisabeth."

"I don't know where he got that from. No. I suppose I could have divorced Jennifer on grounds of desertion or some such, but it never arose. It was never an issue. Elisabeth didn't need a piece of paper, and neither did I. Besides, I was aware of what us marrying might imply for the inheritance of Knowle."

A pretty waitress appeared and stood holding two plates. "Who is for the steak and kidney?" I nodded as she slid the plate in front of me. "And the cod must be you, sir. I will bring the vegetable shortly."

I looked around the room at the cross section of ordinary folk enjoying a meal out. Next to us was a couple in their twenties, their animated discourse all smiles and laughter, the woman reaching for his hand as she prattled gaily. They would be making plans, plotting a future, dreaming dreams. And then in the opposite corner was a sedate couple, the man with a tie and waistcoat under his jacket and the woman with a brooch on her smart cotton jacket, her hair permed with a tint of blue. She held her knife like a pen while carefully loading her fork. Her sherry glass was empty, but he still had a frame of bitter in his pint jug. They didn't speak, but it was clear that she was all ears to the conversations around her. Their world was very different, a simple meal out once a month, or perhaps once a week, regular trade for Mrs. McMurray. Their viewpoint would be backward looking; reminiscences and memories, lives lived with contentment and blinkered achievement.

And at our table two lonely old men reminisced about the same woman. Our memories had been so different. My time with Elisabeth seemed a thousand years before. Did it mean anything other than as a notch carved in my heart? I had never had to cope with the quotidian drudgery of a long-term relationship. Was I the better for it or the worse? What had I put in its place?

The waitress reappeared with steaming boiled vegetables and the Cotes du Rhone. I splashed some into Philip's glass before he managed to lift the neck of the bottle out of the way and then filled my own.

"I am sorry if I sounded accusatory. It wasn't intended; please continue," I said, spearing the robust steak and kidney pudding with my knife; one of the few English dishes that I miss in the Var.

"Anneliese developed heart failure, and I always volunteered to do the visit and took to calling in on Elisabeth, on the face of it to update her about the patient. Anneliese was horrid to Elisabeth, but then she was horrid to most people. Elisabeth took no notice and still cared for her. We would sit in the kitchen, have a coffee and chat, a lot about music, but also about kids and parenting. It wasn't easy bringing up Robert by herself, and I was also in effect a single parent. We found we had a lot in common. She had been running summer concerts in the tithe barn for a couple of years and was planning her first opera. She was still unfamiliar with the operatic repertoire, and I offered to lend her some of my LPs, but I was still her doctor and saw her once or twice for minor complaints."

"So, you became lovers on the side?"

He looked disapproving again. "Not even. Elisabeth wasn't looking for a relationship. She was still driven by her desire to validate her position at Knowle by delivering Henry's vision for a country house opera company. At that time, I think she saw me as nothing more than a friend who also happened to be her doctor. But for me it was different. Naturally I was drawn to her looks, but I just loved being in the same room as her. I would leave with a smile on my face and a spring in my step—a sense of joy. And then I would tell myself to be sensible and find excuses for my feelings, with terrible recriminations and guilt that I had allowed myself to get emotionally entangled with another woman when I was still married."

"I am sorry. I didn't mean to offend."

He nodded as if to accept my apology, took a mouthful of his fish and then continued. "It all progressed very slowly. By this time Jennifer had left the marital home. Lots of people knew the truth about her. I was pitied by some, decried for unspecified misdemeanours by others, and perhaps seen as a potential catch by some single women. Finally, I realised I had to be with Elisabeth and to share my life with her, but I was her doctor.

"Did that matter?"

"Oh god, yes. The General Medical Council is very hot on that one. Gross professional misconduct. They strike you off the register at the sniff of an inappropriate relationship with a patient. Goodbye medical practice forever. It was a huge dilemma; pursue the woman I loved or continue in the job I loved."

"And you chose the woman?"

"I decided to change my career and retrain to be a psychotherapist. I resigned my partnership and signed up for a year's training at the Tavistock Clinic in London. Luckily for me, my kindly partners enabled me to do locum work while I did my training, so I could still pay the bills."

"Did Elisabeth know your plans?"

"Not at the time—although she would often joke about it later when we were an old couple. I was lucky to get a job as part of the counselling service at the University of Bath and started to see patients privately in Dorchester. Then there came a time when I could give up my medical licence."

"I researched the schedules for the opera houses in Italy and found that there was a performance of Verdi's *Un Ballo in Maschera* at the Teattro dell' Opera in Rome in September 1965. It was term time, so Robert was away at school. I turned up at Knowle as nervous as a kid in a talent contest, with the tickets in my pocket. I didn't want to startle her, as until then I honestly don't think she had seen me as a suitor, although it has to be said that there were plenty of other men obviously in that category. I had planned my speech but, in the end, didn't say any of it, just presenting her with the tickets and asking if she would come with me. She was thrilled and immediately said yes. And then I said something along the lines of "You realise I am not your doctor anymore," and looked at her and touched her hair. I think I then said something trite about caring a lot about her, but as I recall, she looked completely confused and flummoxed. We used to laugh about it after."

"But you went to Rome?"

"We went to Rome and had separate bedrooms, but it was a marvellous trip. Gradually things changed after that. She would ask my advice, share her problems with me, and soon started inviting me to Knowle. She met my kids. They didn't fight and got on well with Robert. We spent more and more time together, but we were having a non-relationship, relationship. It was ironic in a way: here was this therapist fixing everyone else's emotional problems but not sorting his own."

"Eat, you must eat," I said.

He took a few mouthfuls before continuing. "The problem was that she had this one idea of what a relationship was like, the blissful otherworldly week with Henry, the ecstatic madness and intensity of sexual love, and she knew that nothing else would match up, nor did she have any reason to explore to see whether this was the case.

The result was that any intimacy was not on the agenda."

"How did you win her over?"

"Time, mostly, I suppose, along with consistency and honesty. That and telling her how much she meant to me. I tried not to be her therapist, but it was difficult. I could see that she had compartmentalised her relationship with Henry as being the perfect package of emotional intensity and physical passion, and rightly knew she would never find anything to equal that, ignoring the fact that many ordinary people find love and joy in something more mundane and ordinary. What is it they say, 'Perfect is the enemy of good?'"

"She was still very keen to visit small European opera houses, and I helped her do the research. Elisabeth had not done much travel really—as you probably recall—and I thought Aix-en-Provence would be special. I organised the whole trip and made the reservations, only this time I booked a double room."

"The Hotel Negresco?"

"Yes, amongst others."

He smiled and looked across at me. He was a reticent man who had been surprisingly disclosive. I wasn't sure why. Perhaps it was an opportunity to talk about Elisabeth and because he knew he would never see me again, but I was grateful for his openness and felt that I, too, could be honest.

He continued. "I spent more and more time at Knowle. We did more travelling together, mostly visiting opera houses. My girls were grown up and at university, and they fully understood the situation with their mother and loved Elisabeth. After Anneliese died, we set up house together in the dower house."

"And they all lived happily ever after . . ."

He glanced up at me, finding seriousness in my flippant comment, holding a forkful of fish in the air. "Woah, we psychologists are very wary of happiness as a goal. Contentment we accept; happiness is like a heatwave—wonderful if one comes along but you can't rely on them nor seek them out."

"But you weren't unhappy."

"No. God no. I am over analysing. We were happy, very happy. We did some wonderful things together." He paused to take a mouthful of food.

"I am sorry," I said. "I have been asking too many questions."

He chewed for a second and then said, "What about you? I know you met Elisabeth at Briggens, but she never talked about you save for mention of the book when we watched the film."

"Why am I not surprised to hear that?"

He looked up at me more empathetically. "Are you bitter?"

"I have never talked about this, but you have been very frank and open, Philip. Yes, in a way I suppose I am. I felt we had something special. I was sailing my boat in the Mediterranean and begged her to come out and join me. The Riviera was wonderful in those days; totally undeveloped, marvellous unspoilt ports and villages, no tourists. It was heaven. She finally did come, but she only stayed four days and then jumped ship. She left the boat in Nice, leaving me a note, and disappeared. In fact, it was just before she met Henry. That was the last time I saw her."

"But from what you said, you kept a torch burning?"

"Yes. I couldn't understand why she didn't want to share the wonderful life I had. A beautiful wooden yacht, no crush of time, marvellous places to explore. The world was an open book. We had shared a lot. I loved her and I couldn't see why she didn't love me back."

He nodded silently and then said, "That must have been very painful for you."

"It was, and still is, especially this last month with all the memories being rekindled."

"I can understand that. Wasn't there someone else?"

"Nobody serious."

"I am sorry about that too. I know nothing about her feelings for you at the time, Peter, but I recall that she didn't like boats much. Perhaps that contributed to her decision. Maybe it wasn't you she was rejecting, more the maritime life. That doesn't appeal to everyone—it certainly wouldn't have suited me—I hate sailing!"

I thought about what he said. There was some truth in it. Elisabeth was a good sailor, but I am not sure she liked it that much. There was a couple of minutes of silence as we ate our meal. The pie was fine; not *haute cuisine* but I enjoy the tang of kidney.

"I have to ask; did she love you?" I said.

"I was right about the directness, Peter."

"I've never talked to a psychiatrist before. Does it imply something sinister to do with my mother?"

"Probably, but we will let it pass for now." He smiled. He wore an "I am a doctor, and I know best" face, but it was with levity, not conviction. "Not psychiatrist Peter, psychotherapist; there is a difference. There are many different forms of love, Peter. Did you love your father?"

"Some. I certainly loved my grandfather."

"And you would say you loved Elisabeth?"

"Surely."

"But let me ask you, was it the same kind of love?"

I pondered but said nothing.

"What about the love you might have for a pet, or a sibling? The mistake people make is to think that all love is the same, and that love is a feeling. It can be, of course, when we are 'in love' we are completely subsumed by joy and feelings, but that doesn't last. It always wears off in time. Sometimes in days. Being in love is a form of madness; sweet, divine, blissful madness—but still madness. Freud talks of the loss of ego boundaries; being subsumed into someone else is marvellous because we can abandon all our own concerns, troubles, and responsibilities. We cease to be constrained by our own limitations. We become supermen—for a time!

"I know Elisabeth loved me because she showed it daily. She was a very loving person. She chose to love me, and for that I was grateful every day of our time together . . . well not every day. We had our spats, naturally, but most days," he chuckled. "In fact, she wasn't that easy to live with. People on a mission often aren't. I always knew that the love she had for Henry was irreplaceable, I never expected that passion from her; their love had a time and a place, which is why it is fascinating to read her jottings about that week. The problem with the tragedy of a death such as his, when a passionate young relationship is suddenly cut short, is that it gets frozen in time, like a woolly mammoth in ice. Nothing can change. Although tragic, the memory for the survivor is of a blissful, perfect liaison, which in their mind they think would have gone on for eternity. The dream never gets sullied by the reality of who takes the bin out or how you squeeze the toothpaste tube.

"What happens in real life is that relationships move on. Even if they remain happy and loving, the passion and the fervour change, but this never happens when one party dies. I am not sure I did it very well. I suspect many others could have done it better. Someone more extroverted or more confident perhaps, but I managed it. I wooed Elisabeth by sneaking up on her, by allowing her to have a different sort of relationship without her realising she was having one. Eventually I got my girl."

I sat, pushing a potato around my plate, chasing a smear of gravy, and thought of the mild-mannered man sitting opposite me. He still had a youthful look on account of his full head of mousy hair and a floppy forelock which wouldn't have been out of place on a fifth-form schoolboy. But this was a man who was very easy to talk to, and similarly easy to listen to. I was drawn to him.

I saw his relationship with Elisabeth in a different light. He wasn't a threat in the masculine way that I had first perceived him. There was never this heroic Paris-Menelaus encounter or a pistols-at-dawn duel, rather he had been the support and rock that she needed. I was touched by how his gentle patience paid off and how crucial he had been to her success, just by being there for her, being in the backroom, being kind and supportive. Yes, damn it, being loving.

I continued to consume the Cotes du Rhone and, in fact, was surprised to see that the bottle was almost empty. I poured the remainder in my glass and swirled it before taking a mouthful. "Thank you for talking, Philip. So how did Elisabeth manage looking after Knowle on her own?"

"Well, she had marvellous support from Percy Smallwood and William Jackson, along with the staff at Knowle. Percy and his wife Miriam realised that she would have no idea about the responsibilities of running Knowle but equally it ran pretty well with Henry *in absentia*. Geoffrey Burney was a brilliant estate manager, and financially it was just about breaking even, but even so, was this what she really wanted— to become the widowed lady of the manor in her twenties?

"I talked to Percy about it once. When I met him, he had nearly retired and was getting on a bit, but he was a marvellous man. Typical old-school family solicitor: worldly, discreet, tactful, charming. He was a much-loved . . ." He tailed off.

"You were saying?"

"Sorry, yes. I asked him about how Elisabeth had coped during those early years. I gather that the most crucial person was the housekeeper Mrs. Bagley—she is referred to in the diary as Mrs. B. In fact, everyone called her Mrs. B. She had had a stillbirth and never had a child of her own and so doted on Henry. Then she had to cope with the death of her husband. They would sit in the kitchen for hours nattering. It meant Elisabeth was never alone in the big house."

"Did you meet Mrs. B?

"Yes, I did. She died a few years after I joined the practice. I knew Elisabeth quite well by that time, well enough to know she was badly affected. She is buried in the grounds of the chapel. Have you visited it yet?"

"No, perhaps I should," I said, thinking that there was little chance that I would subject myself to more pain and disconsolate introspection.

"Percy, and then Steven, were very forward-thinking and

persuaded her to set up a management company, which in effect took over the running of the estate. Most of the personnel were the same, but their titles changed a bit. Elisabeth became a director, and she owned all the shares but it no doubt made it easier for her. However, within a few years she was calling the shots, persuading them to spend money on converting the barn as a venue for concerts. She had friends, of course, and they would visit for weekends, and she insisted on meeting Henry's chums, who also came down. It would have been my advice, had I been her therapist, to try to keep busy, set goals, and keep in touch with her friends and support systems. Still pretty remarkable, though. I know that music helped."

"Did I tell you about the concerts and shows she did at Briggens?" I said.

"No, you didn't. I didn't know about that."

"There were several very talented musicians amongst the team. Elisabeth played the piano and teamed up with Dennis to organise a little orchestra. They did all sorts of things: Gilbert and Sullivan and the like. We loved it."

"One thing I must ask, Peter, is how you all managed to just walk away from that time. Years of intimacy with a small group of dedicated people, doing work of such import that nothing we do now gets even close, building bonds and friendships, enduring hardship, working under pressure . . . Soldiers and servicemen all have reunions and officers' associations and the like. You chaps had nothing; you couldn't even talk about what you did. How did you do that?"

"I suppose it was because secrecy was so drummed into us at the time. Did Elisabeth tell you the time when her reliability was actually tested?"

"I don't think so."

"She and some other recently recruited FANYs were having a drink in a pub somewhere when a man in a colonel's uniform came up and made conversation. He started to tell them about some other FANYs he'd met who were doing terribly exciting work in intelligence and then asked them if they did that sort of thing. The answer was automatic: 'Oh no, nothing as glamorous as that; we just make the tea, do a bit of driving, and are general dogsbodies. There's not much excitement in what we do, is there girls?' It was only later that they realised he was a plant, sent in to test their confidentiality. Apparently that sort of thing was common, but the point was that secrecy was ingrained; you didn't have to think about it, it was just how we were."

"But still, weren't you itching to tell people about what you did? I think I would."

"Perhaps more if I had remained in Blighty and been more in touch with popular culture. This trip has made me realise I have become rather isolated."

The waitress appeared and noisily collected the plates and dishes, asking if we wanted dessert, to which we both shook our heads with muttered regrets.

"It's what you chose, Peter. Don't be hard on yourself," he said.

A heavy silence fell across the table, a shadow of sadness and loss.

It was broken by Philip. "In spite of it all, she never became a victim. Well, that's not quite true: she was a victim of Henry. She was his Brunnhilde, destined by the gods to fall in love with him. I'm sorry, I forgot you are not an opera fan, are you? Well, it doesn't matter . . . I remember once when we were in Rome, I wanted to see the Bernini sculpture of St. Theresa. It is in a typically lavish Baroque church, not remarkable by Roman standards, and then there is this quite exquisite marble. Do you know the story?"

"Remind me."

"Well, the scene depicts St. Theresa being penetrated by the voice of God, although it looks as if she is rather enjoying it, but she is no doubt swept away by the moment. Elisabeth stood in front of the piece and was totally transfixed. When I finally dragged her away after several minutes, she had a tear on her cheek. 'That's what he did to me,' she said. 'That's how I felt in that moment on the doorstep.'"

Not for the first time that evening, I looked across at my dinner companion and felt something shared. We were both pensive, but this time it wasn't an individual inadequacy that I felt, rather a mutual sense of being second best. Disappointment tinged with regret. For me it had only happened the once, but I suspect there are others for whom there may have been multiple times when the slight of unrequited love has left them uncomprehending. I suppose I had never thought explicitly about our inability to influence another person's emotions. Those things that we kick against but can't change. We are the victim of our heart's choices and must live with the consequences. That was true for Philip and me as well as for Elisabeth, but perhaps she didn't have any choice? I have never believed in fate; luck yes, but not fate. Perhaps I had got it wrong.

It was him who spoke, sensing a natural pause in the flow of the evening. "So where are we Peter? I am not sure I have helped unravel the puzzle of why Elisabeth left you all these papers. My best hunch is that they were all together and she didn't take the trouble to go through them. It was certainly some time ago that she left them with Smallwoods, didn't Steven confirm that?"

"Yes, he did. He couldn't even recall when it was."

"So, what are you going to do now? Will you be heading back to France?"

"Yes, I suppose so; back to the old routine." I didn't say how little appeal the idea of returning to the Cape held for me. Although not overtly envious of an English rural existence—chocolate box bucolic held little appeal—for reasons that I couldn't fathom, I felt a restlessness and grumbling dissatisfaction at the thought of rejoining my azure life.

"Do you live alone?" Now he looked at me as a therapist, not as a friend or acquaintance, the probing eyes seeking my inner self.

"I do. I go to the yacht club most days for lunch; there are still a few of us left. The last of the Riviera Set. I keep busy."

"Good. I can imagine it could be lonely unless one had a good group of friends."

Yes, I thought, lonely. That's a good word.

CHAPTER 29

E lisabeth gets up and turns on the wireless. Within a minute the valves have warmed, and crackling emerges from the loose fabric behind the vertical veneered slats that hide the loudspeaker. She turns the Bakelite knob until scratchy piano music is heard. She carefully adjusts it further, finely turning the dial to obtain the clearest sound. She turns up the volume, until the playing fills the room, and returns to the sofa. They both listen. She doesn't know the piece but is captivated by the gentle lilt of the melodic line. Their focus is drawn to the music as they listen intently.

"What is it?" she asks.

"It is wonderful. There must be two pianos."

"Or four hands on the same piano."

The four hands dance and challenge each other, now with tenderness, now with bravado, and all the time the melodic line runs through, a poignant threnody, introspective and questioning but not morbid. And then as the piece progresses, the arguments become more complex and assertive, but suddenly we are back to the skipping melody with its searching sensitivity.

"Is it Chopin?" she says.

"Not sure. Perhaps Brahms?"

"No, too meditative and warm."

"Not necessarily," he says. "He can be sensitive and warm."

"Mmm, still not convinced," she says.

They listen in silence, the piece perfectly mirroring the space between them; four hands on one instrument; sharing, yet crucially individual; insistent yet perfectly paced. As the piece ends, she finds tears start to roll down her cheek. Once again music has said everything that couldn't be put into words. They sit forward, awaiting the announcement of what it was, but instead they get the Greenwich time signal and a starchy voice announcing that they are listening to the BBC from London, and then the national anthem plays signalling the end of the broadcasting day, and the crackles are replaced by a quiet hiss.

She can't bear the thought of him having to go back to Austria without her tomorrow, rather, today. They have been together every minute of every day for the last week. How quickly she has got used to having someone to laugh and joke with, someone in her bed, someone to be challenged by and learn from, someone to make music with. Someone to make love with. That's what it feels like; together they are making a love. A great love, something miraculous and magical.

"I love you," she says. "You have no idea how much I love you. I am going to fade away without you." She leans across him and buries her face in his shoulder.

"It won't be for long, my darling. Only a week or so."

"Too long. I won't last a day." She lifts her head and kisses him, a gentle drift of soft kisses on his neck and cheeks. He wraps his arms around her and pulls her more tightly into him, and then she is brushing her lips on his and he responds, and then that thing starts to happen and her leg slides over his lap and she is sitting astraddle him, and he can't do anything but pull her down onto him. She breaks away, stands up, lifts the beautiful yellow hem and slides her knickers down, kicking them off her stockinged toes. She reaches for his fly buttons, and he assists as she pulls open his trousers. She clambers back onto him reaching between her legs for his hard cock, sinking down, guiding him into her. Instinctively he moves, but she stills him.

"No, don't move. Just be still. Feel. This is what I want to remember while you are away."

Throughout the week they have become more abandoned in the fervour of their lovemaking, an exhausting and magnificent but often all-too-brief gallop to the finish, but she wants this to be different. Now she wants to savour the very moment of him inside her and around her, extract every morsel of sensation and pleasure. She wants to imprint this moment into her selfdom, a forever tattoo of carnal bliss. She kisses him again, gently and sensuously, trying to make it the only part of her that moves, but he can't help but thrust into her, pulling her onto him.

"Uh-uh. No," she barely whispers through pursed lips, lifting a bit to move away from him.

She sinks back down, and he is still for a moment, but she can feel him inside her and even the slightest movement enrages the animal that is her desire. She can't step aside from his probing urgency, and as he moves, the waves and flutterings in her pelvis grow unbidden and then her resolve fails completely and once again they are dashing to their shaking climaxes.

Then it is over. They are still and panting, glued together, as intimate as it is ever possible to be with another person. As her breathing subsides, she tries to recall the sensation she was so intent on capturing and comes to the realisation that you cannot recall bliss any more than you can agony.

She whispers, "Music for four hands."

He is silent for a moment and then says, "I'm not sure hands had anything to do with it—more like double concerto for organ and squeeze box."

She digs him in the ribs with her elbow.

CHAPTER 30

....

Dorset and Herford

July 1992

I got up to say my goodbyes to Philip, then returned to the table, gathered my bundle of papers, and wandered next door into the bar, which was now almost empty save for a few locals rooted in their personalised niches. I found an armchair by the brick fireplace, filled not with a roaring blaze, but a vase of plastic flowers.

I was not sure that I needed any more to drink, but equally I did not feel I would be able to sleep, so when the barman approached and asked if I wanted a drink, I enquired about their range of malts.

"You can't call yourself the Ship Inn and not serve Old Pulteney," I said.

"Single or double?" he replied tersely, looking me in the eye with the disdain I deserved.

He brought the whisky to my table with a small jug of water. I lit a cigarette and dribbled a few drops of water in the malt, pondering what I had learnt over the last two hours. At first glance, the diary of the week in August had seemed like an affront, a slap in the face for a sin I did not know I had committed. Although in no way salacious or revealing, the journal with its intimation of *un grand passion* had left me as an intruder, an unwelcome voyeur to a theatre of intimacy. And I had known what it was like to share physical intimacy with this woman; memories of it were something that often found a place in my dreams, sometimes when I was asleep.

My confusion about why I had been chosen to be privy to so many details of her affair had been the source of my hurt and anger, but now I felt different. Although the motivation for my involvement remained elusive, the sadness of her as a lonely widow bringing up her young son without a father touched me. Age, disappointment, and experience had left me a callous old sod in many ways, but her loss had sent a pang through my heart, and rethinking it now brought a tear to my eye. In the face of such a life event, my own unanswered longings seemed pathetic and trivial. In truth, I felt ashamed. That was it: ashamed. Why had it taken so long for me to realise that you cannot make people be what you want them to be?

But that was only the half of it. Then there was the love of the gentle Philip. I had not expected to be taken by him. My first impressions were of a small-minded soul, good on detail but not on breadth, but I had enjoyed talking to him and how could one not be impressed with his tale of persistence and devotion? To him I would say *chapeau*. He had won where I had lost, but I could not have done what he did. Or could I?

I drew on the cigarette and spread the documents over the table, which was still somewhat sticky from the day's beer glasses. I picked out the papers Philip had provided and read the obituaries. It was all here: beauty, charm, friendships, artistic judgement, respect, and even money, although this was incidental. It had been a good life and a worthy one.

I rummaged through the pile and picked out the marriage certificates and the ration book. I thought I had examined them thoroughly before but felt a second look would be worthwhile. I had not seen a ration book since I left England. It was a small, tatty booklet containing ration stamps, the cover printed with MINISTRY OF FOOD and the uninspired logo, then there was the space for the name and address and, at the bottom, the Food Office code number with a red hexagonal stamp. There were various serial numbers stamped vertically up the side and various other digits handwritten in a variety of inks. The paper was cheap machine-made wood pulp paper of poor quality, emphasised by the way the ink had bled into the wove. The name on the front was Audrey Peters, and the address Cambridge Street, both written in ink, but of different colours. Otherwise, it was unremarkable. Judging by its state it had been used but still contained some unused coupons.

The marriage certificates were in better condition, both folded to fit into a standard size envelope. The basic form was printed in green with guilloches of thin wavy horizontal lines, over which the typing or writing was added. Both were identical in form, with the same paper, a better-quality machine-made fine laid, sized to prevent bleed. All the details were handwritten but in different hands. At the top was a space for the registration district to be added and both had been stamped "County Borough of Croydon," then there were spaces for the names of the couple, their residence at the time of the marriage, and their father's name. At the bottom was the registrar's name and his stamp listed as Walter James Prince, followed by his signature. I held them up to the light. Both had the same watermark, "Certified Copy GRO," which I supposed stood for General Record Office. Even on close examination the certificates were identical.

Then I noticed something peculiar: Audrey Peters's address was given as Compton Avenue, Addiscombe, not Cambridge Street as on the ration book. I checked the other certificate. Elisabeth Watson's address was given as Cambridge Street, SW1. Why would Audrey Peters's ration book have a different address from her marriage certificate and, more to the point, why was it the same as Elisabeth's?

I went back to the ration book; I had noticed that the entries of the name and the address were in different inks. I looked more closely, holding the single page up to the feeble, yellow- tinted wall light, to examine the texture of the pulp in more detail. I could see faint changes to the paper in the space where the name was entered. The thickness of the laid was uneven, with subtle changes to the colour and transparency of the paper with evidence of bleaching. The document had been tampered with, and almost certainly the name had been changed.

I looked at the second page, which contained printed information about how to use the book. I scrutinised it under the area on the front page. I could see various indentations, but it was difficult to make anything of them.

It had been a long time since I had done any of this work, but I remembered a technique from Briggens. Getting up I went to the bar and asked the barman if he had a pepper pot. He looked at me quizzically, stepped two paces towards the end of the counter, and grudgingly slid a grubby plastic pepper pot across the bar to me.

Back at my seat I sprinkled the underpage with pepper in the area beneath the entry for the name. I then gently shook away the powder while tilting the paper. At Briggens we didn't use pepper of course, rather a special powder, but the principle was the same, the fine particles collected in the imprint of the writing from the page above.

At first it looked like a jumble of random lines, but then holding the page at an angle and aided by the ghastly light (which it transpires was perfect for my purposes) I could make out "W T SON." Before it there was a clear capital E and then a lower-case b, but no other letters were visible. It was enough; someone had changed the name on the ration book, which had previously been Elisabeth Watson's. There was only one person who could have done it.

I returned the pepper pot to the barman, whose look confirmed his view that my generation was beyond comprehension or redemption. I resumed my seat, sipped my whisky, and looked out into nowhere.

There had to be something else in the marriage certificates.

I placed them side by side next to each other on the table. There was no doubt that they were both genuine; the paper, the watermarks, the printing all looked authentic. But the mystery remained as to why Elisabeth should have the marriage certificate of Audrey Peters. It would, I assumed, have had to be a copy, but I had little idea as to how one would have obtained such a record.

Two young women got married on the same day in the same register office and the section marked "Certified copy of an entry of marriage pursuant to the marriage acts, 1811 to 1939" had wildly different serial numbers.

Sitting in that bar that evening, with only a sniff of Old Pulteney remaining in the bottom of my glass, I felt a wave of exhaustion crawl over me. I suddenly felt all my years and many more.

I felt like an old man.

At the time I wasn't sure on what to blame it; there were lots of possible reasons. I was returning to the old country where I had spent no time for fifty years, I was removed from my normal routine, I had been much busier than usual, I had been battered by a gale of unfamiliar emotions, and I was troubled by a conundrum that I couldn't solve. Surely those were reasons enough.

But now, as I sit and write this some months later, I realise there was something else; it was the relief that I had at least found some hint as to why I was involved at all. I hadn't solved the puzzle, but at least it appeared that there was a puzzle to solve. The reason for the forgery of the ration book was unclear, but at least it related to an area in which I had unique insight. The answer to the mystery remained elusive, but I could construe the reason for Elisabeth's bequest in terms other than punishment, or a poorly thought through gesture made years before.

....

I undressed, washed, got into bed and turned off the bedside light. The curtains were thick rust-coloured cotton and excluded all light, leaving the room as dark as the bottom of the ocean. A two-stroke engine burst into life and then raced through a series of gear changes into the quiet of the night.

Despite the whisky, I did not feel sleepy. I lay semirecumbent, propped up on the pillow staring at the darkness.

What seemed different was the absence of the usual "yes, buts" and justifications that I previously rehearsed to myself when I had thought of Elisabeth, which I had never successfully challenged. Perhaps I had never needed to, or in truth, wanted to. All the nonsense about letters going missing or her having moved as the reason for her not responding to me—that was what it was—nonsense. The twaddle about her one day "coming to her senses," how insulting and demeaning was that?

What felt different lying in that unfamiliar bed, in that impersonal hotel room, was the clarity of how I now saw things. But there was no going back. I would pursue the ideas I had about the mysterious marriage certificates and then head home to face a new reality.

I should have asked Philip as to why one's brain seems to function differently in the middle of the night. Perhaps he would have had some clues as to how one can lie awake with a thousand thoughts churning through a restless consciousness, which by morning have dissipated like the fret on a sea loch.

CHAPTER 31

London

Saturday, August 7, 1948

They sit in the car outside the passenger terminal at RAF Northolt an hour before noon, the hood is raised against a light drizzle. The engine is turned off, but the single Lucas windscreen wiper continues its noisy sweeps across the rain-splattered windscreen.

He has her left hand in his, which he plays with in a possessive way, turning it over, stroking it and then kissing the ringed finger.

The drive to the airport had been horrible. A tense silence had filled the car. Elisabeth was sure they were thinking the same thoughts but somehow couldn't share them.

"The best week of my life," Henry suddenly said as they drove through Kensington. "Let's play a game. Rank in order your favourite memories."

Elisabeth smiled and was immediately distracted as they'd recalled moments, jokes, and events that they shared.

"The walk and the swim with the mysterious dog." They'd both smiled, looking ahead at the rainy road-scape.

"The breakfast with Brahms."

"Lunch in Bournemouth."

"The great bed of Benville."

"Yes, that was jolly nice . . ."

They went on, exchanging the events of the week, all of them coming to life again as they recalled the experiences.

Then, in what seemed a moment, they were driving through the airport's motley collection of hangers and Nissen huts.

"I have a confession," he says.

"You have a wife and five children in Innsbruck."

He chuckles. "God no." He pauses. "They are in Salzburg."

She tries to pinch his thigh, but he pulls her away and gets the upper hand. "I told a bit of a fib; they didn't cancel my flight last week. I invented a sorry tale of an urgent family crisis which I had to attend to. The story about engine problems was an invention. I just had to see you again. Will I ever be forgiven?"

"By whom? Now you're being daft. Go and get your flight and write to me tomorrow with details of when I can come and see you. And don't forget your promise of tickets for the opera." She leans over and kisses him. "Come on, I hate goodbyes—let's get it over with."

She opens the door and steps out, tightening the Hermes scarf under her chin. He does the same, tilting the seat forward to extricate Ludwig and his bag. They step onto the pavement and embrace, standing completely still for a long minute.

"Goodbye, my love."

"Godspeed."

And with that, she turns, gets into the car, pulls the starting wire, and drives away without looking back.

CHAPTER 32

....

Dorset and Hereford

July 1992

I sat at breakfast not feeling at my best, tired and listless. But then there was a voice across the room calling my name.

"Good morning, Peter, I hoped I would catch you."

It was the effervescent Smallwood, smart as a pin in his neat suit and tie. I stood up and shook his hand. "Steven, good morning. Have a chair. Would you like a coffee? There is a clean cup here and they have given me a large pot."

"Thank you, perhaps a quick one."

He sat down, took the coffee cup I passed him, and leant to his side to click open a black briefcase.

"Apropos my promise to examine the archival Knowle files, you are in luck. I found all sorts of papers in the folder and have copied two or three that I thought might interest you. Ordinarily there may have been confidentiality issues, but I feel they can be waived in view of the circumstances." He passed over a manilla foolscap envelope.

"It is not particularly enlightening, more moving than informative, but it sets the scene after Henry's death and Elisabeth's return to Knowle. Mother and Father were very supportive to her at that time. It is extraordinary how she coped at all. Many lesser souls would have run in the other direction."

"Yes, Philip told me how helpful your parents had been to her after

Henry's death. I have learnt a lot over the last two days. A life I knew nothing about fleshed out in a manner I could never have imagined."

"I am so pleased you met up with Philip. He is an admirable man; very wise but also charming. He was the perfect foil for Elisabeth's drive and inspiration."

I nodded.

He continued. "So Peter, what are your conclusions? Do you think there was a particular reason why Elisabeth left you the bundle or was it just that she thought you should have the Briggens material and the other documents were in the same folder? Was there a puzzle for you to solve?"

"The short answer is I am not sure. There are certainly still mysteries, but I am not sure there is a solution." In saying this I was being just a little economical with the truth, as I was keeping quiet about the possibilities that had occurred to me during my restless night.

"When are you heading back to France?"

"By the end of the week, I hope. I am going to make a visit to Hereford and then there is something I must do in London before I leave."

He sipped his coffee and asked me a few more questions about my French life, and then in his perfunctory businesslike way brought things to a conclusion.

"Very good. I have to say that it has been a pleasure to meet you Peter, and I am gratified that Smallwood's has been able to discharge our duties to Elisabeth and bring the matter to a satisfactory conclusion." He stood up and once again assumed his lawyerlike, major-domo role, heels together, slightly bowed at the waist, hands interlocked in front of him. "Please do get in touch if I can be of any further assistance."

"Actually, there is one thing I wanted to ask your advice about; is there a good travel agent in town?"

He looked puzzled but the expression was wiped clean in a second. "Yes of course. We use Barchester Travel, just round the corner in Trinity Street. We find them very efficient."

"Thank you. That's most helpful."

I got up, shook his hand, bade him farewell, and then he was gone.

The envelope only contained six or seven items, and I suppose I was a little disappointed, although I was not sure why. As I had jokingly suggested, two of them were fee notes, but did itemise very thoroughly the work undertaken in organising the wedding; "Communicating with Mr. Updike, assistant registrar Croydon Register Office, 15 minutes." Then there were carbon copies of various letters written to Elisabeth. One was dated August 16, 1948, from Percy which, after a gap where he would have handwritten the salutation, started: "This is a difficult letter to write because there are no words that can express the sadness and loss that you must be experiencing at this awful time."

Then there was a second similar letter about a memorial service. I skimmed them both, knowing I would have to look at them in more detail later.

I finished my breakfast and made my way to the reception area. Mrs. McMurray was at her station behind the counter.

"Good morning, Mrs. McMurray. I will be on my way later this morning but wonder if I could ask you a favour or two."

"I will do my best, Mr. Mackay."

"I am heading for Herefordshire and wonder if you might be able to help me find a hotel or inn to stay in? I thought you might have a guidebook or some such. It could be in Hereford or maybe Presteigne, which I recall people speak well of. I don't have to be in a town."

"Dorchester given you enough of town life, has it?" she said with a subtle smile.

"On the contrary, Dorchester is delightful, Mrs. McMurray, but a country pub might offer other charms."

"Let me see what I can find."

"The second question is: can you tell me if there is a register office in Dorchester?"

"Why, yes, there certainly is. It is very near, next to the museum, along with the other civic buildings."

"I thank you most kindly, ma'am." I said, inadvertently picking up some of her Scottish mannerisms.

It only took me a few minutes to pack my bag, which I placed on the bed while I sat at the dressing table and picked up the phone. The card from the windscreen was still on the stained veneer surface. I rang the number, which was answered almost immediately.

"Hullo." The voice was what I would have described as Cockney, with a strange intonation, the tone rising at the end of the clipped word.

"Is that Mr. Harrison?"

"Speakin'."

"My name is Mackay. I have a Bristol 404. You left a card on the vehicle earlier in the week."

"The red one, on French plates?"

"That is correct."

"Nice motor."

"That, too, is correct. You intimated that you might be interested in the car. I would be pleased to hear what you thought she might be worth."

His tone changed. "Sorry, what did you say your name was again?"

"Mackay, Peter Mackay."

"It would be my pleasure, Peter. You don't mind if I call you Peter, do you?" His tone changed from mild irritation to an unctuous effort at charm and sincerity.

Within the next five minutes we had arranged that I would take the car to his showroom, where we could discuss a possible transaction.

Why did I need a forty-year-old classic car? I had nowhere to go, I hardly did any mileage, and it was expensive to run. Who was I trying to impress? Vanity, that was the largest part of it. Vanity.

I thought back to when I'd bought the car. It must have been in the '60s, with money in the bank from the film. I was in London and came across the Bristol showroom in Kensington. I had never been much of a car afficionado, but I was captivated by the idiosyncratic styling of the early Bristols, and just as with older boats, appreciated their hand-built quality. There was this great beast of a thing, with its prominent snout like a primitive fish, its dark maroon paint oozing class and quality. I was very taken with the looks of it, but it was the test drive along the A4 that sealed the deal. The toff of a salesman had to do very little; it was the car that spoke to me.

And in some ways, it still spoke to me. I had enjoyed the drive from France, certainly more than most of the driving in England, but who was I going to visit next? I loved the style and the build quality. I revered the engineering and the patina of age, but I really didn't need a car nowadays, certainly not an aged, thirsty classic. I hadn't been on a long trip for years and there was nobody to put in the passenger seat. It had to be for me, and I was no longer enchanted. I had sold *Undine* with much sadness. Now I was selling the Bristol with much less heartache.

Why now?

I knew why.

My outlook had changed. Who would I be keeping the car for? There was a vacancy in the space reserved for dreaming.

I descended the squeaky stairs, bag in hand, and made my way to the front desk. Mrs. McMurray had my bill ready, along with a recommendation. I settled up and we said our cheery goodbyes with her promise that she would book me into the Radnorshire Arms in Presteigne.

"Peter?"

I looked around to see Philip.

"I am so glad to catch you. I had to come into town for a few things and thought I would pop in and say thank you for last night."

"It was my pleasure, and it is me who should be doing the thanking."

"Are you rushing off? Do you have time for a coffee? There is a nice little place around the corner."

I didn't want any more coffee but was glad to accept his offer. We walked into a small café and found a table.

"There are a few things that I didn't mention last night that I thought might interest you. I have never before had the opportunity to examine in a methodical way that time after Henry's death and there are a few more details that came to mind as I mulled over things late last night . . ."

And he talked and talked. He told me about Elisabeth's early days at Knowle and more about Henry and the details of their meeting, embellishing the diary entries. He was more voluble than the previous evening, almost as if he was glad to have the opportunity to disburden himself. What he said was of little relevance to my quest, just poignant insights about the remarkable way in which Elisabeth turned her loss into a positive opportunity.

Ninety minutes later we got up and said our final goodbyes. I put my bag in the car and set off to find Barchester Travel. I was the only person in the shop and was warmly welcomed by two pleasant assistants.

I proffered a good morning and set out my requirements. "I need a flight from London to Nice on Thursday. Is that something you could help me with?"

It was all terribly simple. I had too much choice—I just had to name the date and time and hand over my credit card. I thought four days would be ample, and I could always stay at the RORC. I left with an Air France ticket in my hand, not looking forward to making my reacquaintance with a Boeing tin box but gratified that I had achieved an outcome with so little effort.

Then it was a visit to the register office.

Less than an hour later I was on the forecourt of a motor showroom on the Blandford Road with Reg Harrison clambering through my car trying to find things wrong with it. He was a thickset man of a shortness of stature that was the probably the cause of the inferiority complex that led him to dislike his fellow man, albeit this was clothed in a smarmy sycophancy. I stood looking into the showroom, chock-full of desirable shiny automobiles, while he delved into the boot and bonnet spaces and dived under wings to check for rust or other mischief. Eventually he had to agree that its long life garaged in the South of France had protected the car well, and with the limited mileage and smart interior, the car was very saleable. He suggested a price more than three times what I had paid and after some haggling, we agreed to a deal. I did not have all the paperwork with me, as this was in my flat, but reassured by my promise to send the documents to him on my return to France, we shook hands on the deal. He even accepted my condition that we meet to do the final transfer at Heathrow Airport on the morning of my flight.

....

Herefordshire was at its best in September.

Elisabeth often used to talk about her time there. In many ways I think she had had a better relationship with her grandmother than with her mother, and she would often spend parts of her holidays staying with Nanny Mills, as she was known, in addition to the exeats from school when her parents couldn't get up to the Marches.

I had never visited and had little idea what to expect but was charmed by the bucolic intimacy of the soft landscape. How different was this from the baked, arid earth, pink rocks, and majestic pines of the Estoril. Here I was driving through hedged lanes, the vegetation now dying back after the summer, fields of stubble or orchards with boughs laden with reddening apples. This wasn't a grand landscape, although the bluffs of the Black Mountains cut a rugged blue silhouette to the south, more of a quiet domestic affair, less trumpeted and vaunted perhaps, but as a result less spoilt and populous. As I swept through the curves and inclines, I saw the first signpost for Presteigne.

The changing vistas unfolded with each bend and gradient. The buildings were good too. The old vernacular brickwork was sound and unpretentious, charming farm buildings, built with care and sufficient detailing to make them worthy of the setting. And then, every now and again, a set of stone gateposts or a lodge would signal a grander home, gables glimpsed through dense swathes of rhododendron and manicured lawns leading to parkland with fine specimens of beech, chestnut, and wellingtonia. Surely this was the best of English pastoral. If it wasn't so damned far from the ocean it would have been a fine place to live. Or even to die.

My reason for making the detour to the Marches was to visit the churches that Elisabeth had attended exactly, as I now realised, forty-five years before. In particular, I wanted to look at the marriage registers.

My trip to the register office in Dorchester had been most informative. Mr. Holmes, the assistant registrar, had initially been standoffish but had warmed when I produced the copy of Elisabeth's marriage certificate. In fact, I think he rather enjoyed holding forth on a topic that he knew a great deal more about than me. It is easy to be superior in such circumstances and this suited his opinion of his own import. He pointed out minor changes to the current certificates, most notably the change of the Act in 1949, but accepted the certificate at face value, remarking with interest on the postage stamp affixed at the bottom, payment of the one penny stamp duty in addition to the two and sixpence fee. Of course, I didn't mention any concerns about authenticity, but it was gratifying to find that the document caused him no concerns.

What I was really interested in was the process of registration and how the certificates were issued after a marriage.

After a wedding the couple, along with their witnesses, sign the two registers, which are large books kept in the parish church or register office. They get given a copy of the certificate which they also sign, which, as it says at the top, is "a certified copy of an entry of marriage" and is completed by the celebrant. These are printed in a bound book, like a large cheque book, with a stub also completed by the vicar or registrar but retained by the wedding venue, the certificate itself being torn off and given to the couple.

Quarterly, the official, be they vicar or registrar, sends "returns," a full list of all the weddings that have taken place, to head office, the General Register Office, where they are then transcribed into the permanent record. I also learnt that these are accessible to the general public at St. Catherine's House, on Chancery Lane in London. The only way Elisabeth could have obtained the marriage certificate of Audrey Peters was to have visited St. Catherine's house and ordered a copy, which she could have done on payment of the two shillings and sixpence fee. My observations about the serial numbers meant nothing. Of course they would have different numbers, because Audrey's was a copy of the copy.

But what I wanted to see were the registers and paperwork available in the churches of rural Hereford, to confirm my hunch that there had been weddings on the Saturdays marked in her diary. I am not an expert in medieval church architecture and am not, for that matter, particularly interested in it. But I can admire a pretty kirk. My plan was to make a tour of the parishes on the morrow, as might a retired academic, to take time from my troubled musings to ponder upon misericords and vaulting, and perhaps flesh out my ideas about the marriage certificates.

....

I had stopped in Hereford to buy an ordnance survey map, from where it was but a hop to Presteigne, and now I was nosing the Bristol into the car park of the Radnorshire Arms. It had been easy to find sitting aside the main street of the quaint town, a Tudor building of genuine antiquity, the date 1616 etched above the front door. I was becoming something of an expert in rural English hostelries and the Radnorshire Arms sat well in my lexicon. Here it was not the owner who greeted me at the reception desk but a pretty mid-European who couldn't have been older than twenty but had been taught to smile kindly.

There was plenty of time before dinner and I felt a breath of fresh air would do me good, so I set off down the high street to explore the charming town.

I was back within the hour, mindful of two tasks: I wanted to have a closer look at the new material Philip had provided me, and I needed to put a call through to Therese. The best time to catch her was early afternoon, when the whole of Mediterranean Europe pulls down the shutters and takes a siesta.

I have not said much about Therese, but these writings are not about me; it is Elisabeth's story.

Therese. Dear Therese—that is how I think of her.

It has not been a conventional relationship. She has been good to me, possibly too good given that she has not had much back in return. It must be twenty-five years ago that she started to help me with the flat. I still had *Undine* then, was away a lot of the time, and needed someone to keep an eye on the place—a sort of housekeeper and manager really. A concierge in fact. In those days she was very pretty and alluring in the way that French women can muster with seemingly minimal effort. Her husband had disappeared, and she was bringing up a son alone. She had various other jobs, but looking after *La Carriere* suited her, as I was often absent and did not check up on her. I suppose I was also a bit more of a catch then—fitter, leaner, and a lot less grey, although I am not accusing her of trying to make a catch.

We had always enjoyed an easy relationship. She never took herself too seriously, expressing herself with an opinionated honesty that the English often mistake for arrogance in the French. If you are brought up unable to say what you feel and are taught to apologise for things you didn't do in kindergarten, it is not surprising that you can find people who say what they mean and speak honestly to be impolite, or arrogant. I was used to it, and besides, we spoke French together, which reduced the opportunities for the brusqueness that poor English can provoke. She smoked, of course, and we would sit and have a coffee on the terrace and moan—she about the world, men, and the idiocy of the Prefecture, me about the gross behaviour of the type of people who charter boats.

It was an unplanned siesta that enmeshed us to a greater extent. It was early summer, perhaps May or June. One afternoon I came home unexpectedly, let myself into the apartment, and saw her bag on the table, but no Therese. I poked my nose through the open doors to the terrace, but that too was empty. I assumed that she must have gone out for something but then went into the bedroom, where she was fast asleep on the bed. She had kicked off her shoes and her thin, tanned thighs were all too visible under her short skirt. Just for a joke I thought I would surprise her by lying down next to her. I crept in and lay down as softly as possible, but of course, she woke up in a trice and sat up embarrassed and apologetic, pulling her skirt down and smoothing her hair, which in those days she wore very short. I calmed her and insisted she lie back down, not with any intent, rather because I hadn't meant to embarrass her. And then she put her hand on my arm to express her regret, and I put my hand on hers to express my regret at her regret. And a few minutes later we were again both apologising to each other, but for something rather different.

Not much changed. She still did her work as I did mine, the relationship was mostly that: between employer and employee. We smiled more and were more tender, and if I was around at siesta time (which I tried to ensure happened more frequently) we would end up sharing a greater intimacy. She never stayed the night; we never socialised together; we were never a couple. We talked more about our lives and loves, and I suppose I must have told her about Elisabeth, although I can't remember the details.

Thinking about Therese I wondered why I hadn't mentioned her to Philip. What would he have said about our relationship? But then I wasn't sure what I would have said about it either. Was I somehow ashamed? Did I feel our intimacy was something to keep quiet about, fraternising with the staff and all that? Now I needed to call her, tell her what I was doing, and that she could expect me back in France in two days' time. And strangely, I was looking forward to it.

On the phone she was voluble and concerned. I told her briefly of where I had been and my plans for homecoming.

I put the phone down and sat immobile for a minute or two. It had been nice to talk to her. Her Frenchness mostly amuses me, albeit occasionally she can be pigheaded and crass. I like the way she rolls her own cigarettes and shrugs and says "Boof," which means anything you want it to. But on this occasion, she was mostly thoughtful and affectionate. I wasn't used to that, but then I had never put myself in a position to be a recipient of such sentiments.

The envelope that Philip had delivered at breakfast contained little of relevance save for two carbon copies of letters written by Percy to Elisabeth. The first was a letter of condolence written in August addressed to her mother's house in Reigate. The second, a month later, contained details of the memorial service for Henry to be held in Dorchester on November 2. The letter pleaded with Elisabeth to attend, affirming that she was the future of Knowle, suggesting she stay at the Smallwoods' house rather than the big house, and provided a telephone number to call should she want to discuss details. It was a tender letter, as I would have expected from Percy. There is no doubt that he was worried about Elisabeth and concerned that she might be too upset or anxious to come to the service, so he went out of his way to allay her fears and make her feel central to what was happening at Knowle.

But they didn't help me much.

I was putting them back in the envelope when I realised there was something else at the bottom which I had not pulled out with the bundle. It was the order of service for the Memorial Service of Henry Benville. It was a poignant document, somewhat dog-eared and yellowed, but it told me little. There was an address by a brigadier, Sir Timms-Wilson KCVO, and another by one Jamie Bridgenorth. The hymns were "Oh God Our Help in Ages Past" and "Let Us Now Praise Famous Men," sung by the choir. There was other music too, which meant little to me, an organ work by Buxtehude and a Bach cantata "Ich Habe Genug," sung by Terence Chilford. I assumed that the document had been filed in the folder and Steven had thought I might be interested. I was interested, but it didn't take me any further. Then I saw the date of Henry's death. At a stroke things became much clearer, and the sadness and tragedy of their world stuck me properly for the first time.

I put on a tie and my blazer and headed for the bar.

....

I had the whole day to explore the fabric of the Anglican estate within the benefice of Kington. For many this could have been a day of rare joy; the contemplation of the rural tradition of ecclesiastical architecture and an opportunity for calm and contemplation. Is not this the type of thing retired gentlefolk do—visit country churches? Certainly, I could not fault the setting nor the buildings. I started with a stroll through Presteigne to St. Andrews; triangulated windows cut into buff sandstone, a noble site proudly lording over a well-tended graveyard. A perfectly fine parish church. It was early as I pushed on the creaking oak door and stepped into the airy interior. I sensed ceremony and pretention, even in the bulk of its echoic emptiness.

I moved on, walking back to the car and setting off with a map on the passenger seat.

At Kinsham, the simplicity of the rendered building church and spartan interior had much more to recommend it, the taint of damp adding to the sense of earthy honesty. Once again, I was alone and could step behind the curtained apse at the west end. There was a locked door that suggested a vestry or robing room. My suspicion was that at a wedding the paperwork would have been completed adjacent to the altar. It was annoying that I couldn't access the records.

At Titley, the setting was appealing, with an unostentatious squat stone tower, an Early English porch, and a cool interior smelling of mould and polish.

I drove on to Kington. Here the sturdy fortified base to the tower has an external stairway. Inside I met a frail, grey stick of a woman arranging flowers for the forthcoming Sunday service, who was only too happy to engage me in conversation. I watched her skilfully manipulate the blooms, a deal brighter than those on her faded apron, as she told me that the peripatetic curate sadly now only visited monthly.

I envied her purpose and commitment, as well as her skill, as she trimmed and tweaked the sprays of her vibrant floral tribute. Once again, I felt the sense of detachment that I had noted too often on this trip; that I was an observer, not a participant. I felt distant—*pas engagé.* I was a visitor. Worse than that, perhaps even a trespasser. Ancient communities had built and preserved something sacred; I was an interloper who had chosen to reject these opportunities for communion. My isolation, because that was how it felt, was of my making and therefore I couldn't ask for redemption. I had walked away, turning my back on Middle England's social niceties, including organised religion. It seemed unfair to expect succour from the comforts of forgiveness, even if offered apparently without condition.

My last stop was the Church of St. Thomas à Becket in the hamlet of Huntington, and here at last I felt something closer to the divine. The simplicity of the building was key, a rectangle of almost white rubble stone, with a simple gabled roof and an oak porch. Inside the heavy rustic pews spoke of utility not sophistication, hewn from pine as thick as your arm, with a simple trefoil top, smoothed and polished by the calloused agrarian hands of centuries of supplicants. Behind the altar two slender lancet windows with stained glass images of the virgin, and I presumed, St. Thomas, looked over the choir and nave with naive honesty. As I had come to expect, I was on my own, but here I did sit awhile and ponder, at the very back in the corner. If Elisabeth had visited this serene space this is where she may have sat—and what?—wept quietly through the tears of her grief while witnessing a country wedding, the tender bride on the arm of a man she loved? Or somehow extracted some solace from the hallowed austerity of the setting in a timeless ceremony of continuance? Or something else more practical?

Perhaps it had been a triumph of optimism over common sense that I would be able to view the registers or the record books, but nowhere did I meet a vicar or verger who could have let me into the vestries where the volumes were locked away. Perhaps I could have found the telephone numbers and arranged appointments, but I had neither the time nor the mindset. I was not going to achieve anything more in Hereford, however charming many would have found a prolonged stay.

By early afternoon, in a brisk downpour, I turned the Bristol back towards Hereford and then London, aware that it would be my last significant journey in the car. I drove fast through the empty roads of Golden Valley and then onto bigger roads and then the motorway. By early evening I was ensconced in the bar at RORC in much more familiar territory, talking boats and seas and weather with people who thought much as I did.

....

The following morning, I walked into the drab public entrance to St. Catherine's House and took my place in an informal queue at a wooden-framed glass window above a Formica counter. I had some sympathy for the efficient but sad-mouthed attendant who greeted me with a perfunctory "Yes?" when my turn arrived. She did at least manage to remain polite, which I could not have managed in similar circumstances.

I had made a note of what I wanted copied from the certificates and was able to hand over the page on RORC-headed paper to her with the names of the two couples married the same day in July 1948 at Croydon Register Office.

She took my paper and disappeared, keeping me waiting for no more than five minutes. She explained her findings and then said, "There will be a fee to pay."

"Of course," I said, "I was expecting as much."

....

I retrieved the Bristol from an expensive garage in St. James and settled my account with RORC, unclear as to whether I would ever be back again, wondering if I should cancel my membership.

My meeting with Reg Harrison went without a hitch. He was, as promised, waiting at the drop-off area of Terminal Two, which I found without difficulty. He presented me details of a bank transfer of most of the monies and then handed over ten thousand pounds in cash. He had wanted to retain some funds awaiting receipt of the registration documents but backed down in the face of my indignation. I stepped out of the car, loaded a trolley with the few items I wanted to retain, shook hands and turned towards the terminal building.

Within an hour I was being asked to fasten my seat belt on an Air France Airbus as crowded and cramped as I had feared. Happily, I had been able to medicate myself with a large Horse's Neck, surely the best prophylactic against travel sickness. In a matter of minutes, we were taxiing across Heathrow's cluttered tarmac, and then with an extraordinary sense of acceleration, I was thrust back into my seat as we hurtled towards perdition or France, for several moments being unsure which.

We settled into the flight, and I pondered my homecoming. I was not sure if I was leaving something behind or starting out on something new. I reminded myself of the disquiet I had felt when I had set out only a week before. Then I was burdened with a sense of loss and sadness relating to Elisabeth, confusion, and uncertainty as to why she had left me the items she'd chosen to. And then there were all the activities of the week and all the new information I had learnt. A window into a life I had known nothing about, a world unknown to me, and with it a change of perspective and a re-evaluation of my own selfdom and perhaps a revaluation of my own priorities. Regret? Yes, and loss too, but also an awareness of my own folly and pathos. But I was at least leaving with some clarity, and a better idea of why the woman I thought I had loved had done what she had done.

The visit to St. Catherines House had been helpful, confirming my suspicions. I was sure I knew why Elisabeth had left the papers for me. What I was much less clear about was what I should do with the information.

....

Within what seemed a few minutes we were dipping down over the ocean in a steep curve and making our approach to land, the plane buffeted by a stiff breeze. I could see from the palm trees alongside the terminal building that there was a mistral blowing.

There was nobody to meet me. There was, in fact, nobody who could have met me—Therese doesn't drive and doesn't have a car, not that I would have asked her in any event—so I took a taxi.

Even with the mistral there was a warmth and power to the sun nowhere in evidence in Herefordshire or Dorset. I insisted we took the Basse Corniche, and although the traffic was bad and progress was sluggish, I was comforted by the familiar—the Velos and the corrugated Citroen vans, the sunny clothing, short skirts, and the bustle of the tourists.

The frontage of *La Carrière* was unchanged, sultry in the pines and the baked soil of the generous plot. I climbed the stairs and let myself into the flat, which was dark and cool, the blinds lowered, with only the tiny slots in the metalwork letting in specs of light. I wound up the larger shutter onto the terrace, the dazzle of the late afternoon sun still oppressive.

I lit a cigarette and sat in one of the metal chairs looking at the Cape. There were a few boats out but not many sails; in this wind you would need to keep a tight reef. There was a tidy motor yacht heading into Villefranche, and a brace of powerboats closer inshore, bouncing silently from wave peak to wave peak. When you are at sea, the movement is accompanied by other senses—the noise, the breeze, often the smell of the ocean. But when you look at the sea from the land it is monodimensional, just the image devoid of those other crucial elements. But today I had the breeze at least, and the ocean was a deep lapis, as it is with the mistral.

And it was mine, this view. I owned it. It had come to mean much to me—more than a patch of Hampshire or Dorset.

I looked around for the Hotel Negresco ashtray, but it was not in its usual place on the table. I got up and walked into the kitchen. There on the side was a note from Therese and the pieces of the broken ashtray.

"Pom—je suis vraiment désolé, je sais que c'était important pour toi. J'ai acheté des choses que j'ai laissée dans le frigo. Rendez-vous demain. T."

....

The wind abated in the night, and as always, the best, clearest days are to be had in the aftermath of a storm. I was up early, the air still cool, the horizon crystalline, the low sun dancing on the waters to the east. Therese knew my preferences: strong coffee, citrus fruit, and Pain Anglais, which I found in the fridge. I carried a tray to the terrace and ate my breakfast. She burst in, animated and pleased to see me. She looked well, better than well, in truth. She was wearing navy cotton slacks with a white blouse with short sleeves, her natural features enhanced by her eagerness to hear about my trip.

We had lots to talk about. I suggested she get a cup and make a fresh pot of coffee. She got up and went into the kitchen, returning immediately with the three pieces of the ashtray, proffering effuse apologies.

"Ce n'est pas important," I said, as I waved away her "desolation" with a foreigner's attempt at a Gallic shrug.

"But it was important," she said. "It had special memories, no?"

"N'importe quoi," I said, using that great French expression that can mean almost anything you want it to.

She sat and filled our coffee cups. Her English was not good enough to read the material that Elisabeth had left me, so I explained the details while showing her the papers and the diaries, but I kept having to backtrack to explain more of the setting and relevance of my past, the experiences at Briggens and my relationship with Elisabeth.

We chatted, or I should say I chatted, because as we went on, I realised that I had a lot to say, much more than I had thought. Save for the conversation with Philip, I had never talked to anybody about Elisabeth, but now there were many additional layers to the story, not only what I now knew about her life, but also my trip back to Blighty. I also found that in the rehearsal the emphasis shifted; the process of talking allowed me to see the larger picture more clearly, but more than that, I became the storyteller, not a bit-part player in the distant recesses of the saga.

I suggested more coffee and she got up to make it, returning with the replenished pot and a packet of the biscotti that she likes, sitting down again at the side of the table as the sun nudged over the edge of the building onto the corner of the terrace by the hibiscus. She pulled a pouch of Drum tobacco from her bag and began rolling a cigarette. She has small hands and short fingers but rolled beautiful, slender cigarettes with the skill of a watchmaker, and then hardly smoked them at all, taking occasional puffs, inevitably having to relight the stub prior to each gasp, while for the remainder they dangled from between her fingers.

After an hour there was still a lot left unsaid, but she said she must get on, although making no sign of movement. She sat, her elbows on the table, the ashtray now nearly full of our butts, and then finally summoned a sense of purpose and swiftly got up. There really can't have been much to do—I hadn't been in the place for ten days, and it was hardly a palace—but she was good at looking busy.

At midday she was ready to leave and appeared expectant, uncertain if we would resume our old routine of walking down the hill together. It was certainly what I had in mind. I was keen to see the old soaks in the Yacht club and reassure Roberto that I was alive. I put on a tie and blazer and picked up the faded Panama. She was ready and waiting, grasping my arm in time-practised fashion as we set off down the path.

"I sold the car."

"The Breestol?" she replied, the surprise showing in her voice. "Non! Ce n'est pas possible."

"I don't need a big expensive car now. Where do I go? Nowhere. Besides, I got a good price for it, more than I paid."

"But it was your pride and joy," she said. "Fierté et joie."

"Times change," I replied.

"N'importe quoi." Perhaps it was her who I had learnt it from.

We walked on, the heat a familiar comforter on my back after the freshness of Herefordshire. We reached the bottom of the path, where we traditionally parted.

I tell you what," I said, "why don't you join me for lunch at the club?"

She guffawed. "Don't be ridiculous. What would they all think? It is not for me. You go and see your amis."

"All right—we could go somewhere else—where would you go?"

"Moi?" Her tone was unclear as to whether I was being serious.

"Oui, toi."

"Peut-être le petit Pied Noir près de Carrefour pour couscous."

I stood silent for a few seconds.

"Okay a demain." She stood back for a second with a quizzical look and then gave me the usual peck on both cheeks, before turning and heading off down the path.

....

In fact, it wasn't the following day, rather the day after, that I found myself in a bright bistro in a commercial area behind the supermarket, leaning over an orange Formica table and prodding a fatty piece of lamb on a mound of couscous. Therese had insisted that I would need neither jacket nor tie and sat opposite me, energised and humorous in surroundings where she felt comfortable and at ease. The smell of frying was offset by pleasant aromatics and a hint of orange water. It was a far cry from the yacht club, but I was perfectly content. Around us were various documents and papers. Toni, the Berber chef and patron who had greeted Therese with a trio of kisses, was attentive and happy to find a bottle of rosé from under the counter, despite a notice regretting that no alcohol was served.

Therese was captivated by the enigma of the bequest and insisted that I translate lots of the papers and entries. It was the first time that I had ever told her about my work at Briggens, and that added the need for yet more explanations to help her gain an insight into the mystery of the challenge. She was impressed, perhaps almost disbelieving, but I found that added to my enjoyment. It was unusual to have someone listen to something I had to say with what seemed to be genuine interest. Perhaps I was discovering a pedagogic streak that I never knew I had. But it wasn't sombre; there was laughter in the mix, and Therese could swallow rosé like a true Provençalois.

I shouldn't be too judgemental about the couscous; it was tasty, with an edge of pimento and the vegetables weren't overcooked. After, we pushed the plates to one side and Toni came to sit with us for a few minutes, bringing a syrupy confection akin to a doughnut in glue, which was apparently Therese's favourite, but it wasn't for me. Then thick coffee and the inevitable cigarettes.

I needed to move, my legs stiff from sitting too long, and the bottle of rosé was long finished. I called for the bill. We got up and left, starting up the incline into town, the tang of fish and the sea in the air. I walked slowly lest I appear short of breath.

"What are you going to do now?" she asked.

"That is what I was wondering."

"It is a beautiful story," she said. "Une belle histoire. You should write it all down. You are a good storyteller. You did it before with your book, you can do it again."

"For who?"

"Boof!" She waved her arm. "For you, perhaps. As I said, it is a good story, but that's not the point; the point is to set it down. Even if no one read it, it would be there—what really happened."

"Perhaps. It is hard work—writing—and very dull and lonely."

"But you did it before."

"But then I was alone for a winter in Sicily."

"So, what's different? Now you are alone for a winter in France, and I will bring you coffee and empty the ashtray," she said and then added, "and try not to break it."

....

That evening, I went out onto the terrace before I turned in. It was a miraculous night, the moon a tiny slice of cheese way over to the west, the lights from the Cape shimmering in their colourful hues. Cicadas encircled me in an enclave of sound. There was a balm too, the air laden with the perfume of the nicotiana and jasmine. A laser beam from a disco projected slender green sabres that danced into the infinite night, first this way then that, now quickly, then a reverse and a bit slower, now a pulse, now a swirl. The ocean was black, scattered boats invisible save for their way lights peppering the vista, far on the horizon the terrifying glitz of a cruise ship.

I did love this all in my funny old way. Age blunts the sharpness of emotion; the razor's edge becomes an aching bruise. The poignance of longing replaced by a barely noticeable emptiness. The vivid tattoo of devotion fades into a smudge of uncertainty.

Could I write another book? Could I sit every day for three or four hours at my desk and make words flow? I doubted it. The self-discipline that for years I wore with pride and was such a crucial part of my sailing seemed to have been washed away by introspection and more sybaritic pursuits. And indolence.

But I had nothing else to do; no major projects, no family to speak of, no work or responsibilities, and I did now know some things that should not die with me.

Perhaps.

....

The following day Therese arrived as usual, bright and breezy, with a package under her arm.

"Bonjour Pom, j'ai quelque chose pour toi, je t'ai apporté un petit cadeau . . ."

She held out the bundle with a grin.

It was only wrapped in a paper bag, so did not require unwrapping as such. Inside was a ream of typing paper.

It sat on my desk for a few days next to the typewriter, the first letter from Smallwood and Lees sitting next to it. Then, on a cool day of drizzle and cloud, I sat down and started writing; I would tell the story. I would tell the story of a person I knew and loved and how I found she wasn't the person I thought she was, nor perhaps was I the person I thought I was. Perhaps I hadn't really loved her in the way I thought I had. I had her journal to guide me through the week with Henry, I also had a good idea of the things that happened that she did not put in the diary.

But as I got started it became more than that; I was able to bring her back to life. By writing about her I relived my time with her. I allowed myself to fall in love with her again but then see that love for what it really was and put it where it needed to be: just a part of life's journey. Perhaps, writing the story would bring about closure. Complete the circle.

CHAPTER 33

They set out from Mummy's house in Reigate with Elisabeth driving. They journey the ten yards to the end of the front drive.

"Left, or right?" she says, knowing he will have no idea.

"Oh Lord, I am not sure. Do we need a map?" he says, suddenly anxious.

She bursts out laughing, "No, Henry, I think I know the way—well at least I know how to get to Croydon. What we do when we get there is another matter. Good job I wasn't relying on you for directions."

"You tease. You know you can rely on me for lots of things. All the important things in fact."

"Just not geography."

"Just not geography. So how far is it?"

"Half an hour."

"Cripes, we don't have much time, do we?"

"So, what do you think?" she asks a moment later.

"About what?"

"You know—about Mummy."

"I don't need to think, Elisabeth, she is your mother. I can't have an opinion about her. I just have to respect and love her because she is your mother. She's very lovable, actually."

"Really? Do you think so? I find her maddening—just so . . . I don't know . . . empty. I was wondering Henry, do you think she could come and stay for a bit, at Knowle I mean? Would you mind awfully? It might help her; she could chat to Mrs. B and pick roses and lilacs and maybe walk out a bit."

"That's a wonderful idea. We could send her out with Anneliese. Now that would be a winning combination."

They both smile. Henry has his right hand across his body holding the top of the door, his long legs barely fitting under the dashboard. Elisabeth focusses on the road as Evey slows as they climb the escarpment of the north downs out of Reigate.

"I am worried about witnesses, Henry. I know Percy thought it would be all right, but what if we can't find anyone? It is such a pity our friends can't come."

"I know, but I did try—I rang several friends, but it was such short notice. Jamie was going away sailing, Dick is in Cambridge and had tutorials that he couldn't cancel. The only person who might have been available was Pinky Trevelyan, but he's such a prat I couldn't bear to have his name on our marriage certificate."

"But he's a friend! How can you say he's a prat?"

"Not mutually exclusive, darling. Two different things. The great thing about having friends is you don't have to like them. Pinky is the most devoted kindly pal you could wish for, but he's a complete prat."

"You are peculiar. I love my friends. I would never say they were prats."

"Ah but would you ever think they were prats?"

"Well, I may not always think they make good decisions . . ."

"There you are then."

"So, who is this Pinky chap? I haven't heard you mention him before."

"Friend from Oxford. Parents own a pile in Cornwall. Now works in the Home Office. Will end up running the Civil Service or some such."

"Sounds dull."

"Exactly! Actually, you would like him because you would feel sorry for him. He would pin you in a corner and regale you with his inadequacies and self-doubt. He's the kind of man who girls all say needs a nice girlfriend but can't imagine any of their friends wanting to go out with him."

"Oh dear. I will look forward to meeting him. I probably won't be able to keep a straight face now, as I will be thinking of your description."

They are heading towards Coulsdon along a country road across open heathland when the car stutters, misfires, and then stops.

"Oh no," she says, pulling the starting wire. The engine turns over but doesn't fire. "This happened this morning, but Malcolm fiddled with something and fixed it."

She tries again with the same result. Henry looks at his watch.

"Did you see what he did?" he asks.

"No. He said it was something to do with a lead."

"I can have a look, but I really don't have the foggiest idea about mechanical things. The vagaries of the internal combustion engine were not a key part of the ancient Greek curriculum." He speaks flippantly but not smiling.

They both get out of the car, Elisabeth reaches for the bonnet catches, but Henry takes over and opens it. They both peer inside.

"It was down there somewhere," she says, pointing to a collection of dirty wires. "He thought it was a loose connection."

Henry seems reluctant to sully his pallid classicist hands by rummaging in the grimy interstices of the engine compartment but reaches in and wiggles the various wires he can see, emerging with his oily hands held in front of him like Lady Macbeth.

"I'll try it again," she says, getting back into the driver's seat. Once again, the engine turns but doesn't fire. She gets out, her face etched with worry. "What are we going to do?"

"We better flag someone down; there must be a garage nearby."

They haven't seen a car pass since they stopped. They stand side by side looking back along the route. A little Austin appears but in spite of their waving, the elderly woman driver continues on, her gaze fixed unwaveringly on the road ahead.

But then a van appears, "Bradshaw Better Builders" painted on the side, and slows to a halt. The young driver, clad in overalls with a cigarette hanging from his lower lip, steps out of the cab and asks what the problem is.

"She just stopped. The same thing happened yesterday but it seemed to be all right after my gardener fiddled with something under the bonnet. He said something about a lead."

The man opens the car door and sits down on the seat with his legs hanging out in the road. He pulls the starter and once again the engine turns over, but now it labours, groaning with the effort.

"Ain't much juice left in the bat-ry," he says, stepping out and looking under the bonnet. He flicks his cigarette into the road and leans into the engine compartment, reaching down to pull on various wires. He tries the starter one more time, with the engine barely turning over.

"Dunno. Think you need a garage. I ain't got a tow rope but I can give one of you a lift to Wilson's in Coulsdon."

Elisabeth and Henry look at each other sharing a fearful helplessness.

"Oh Lord, you see we are in a terrible hurry. We have to be in Croydon for three," Henry says.

"Take it or leave it, mate. Can't do no better than offer. It ain't be more than a couple of miles," the man says, returning to his van.

"I'll go," says Henry. "You stay here with the car. I can be quite persuasive if need be." He is suddenly sensible and businesslike.

The builder opens the passenger door of the van to reveal a seat strewn with various items of old clothing, tools, and building materials. He clears an area large enough to sit, beckons to Henry, and then walks round to the driver's side and clambers in.

Elisabeth watches them putter off down the road and is left alone with a terrible fear in the pit of her stomach. She has barely been out of Henry's sight for a week, and now when she needs him most, he is being driven away in a builder's van. She is seized with a convulsing, irrational fear that she will never see him again. Those flitting worries about the craziness of the escapade that have visited her throughout the last few days swoop down to crush her with a tragic foreboding.

It will never happen. I knew something this wonderful had to be an illusion. Damn fool for believing in it. How crazy to think it might be possible to find love and happiness with someone as special as Henry. What an idiot I was to think it could be otherwise.

She opens Evey's door, climbs in, and with her hands on the steering wheel, bursts into tears. She sits, shaken by heaving sobs as the tears roll down her cheeks and onto the steering wheel.

"You orright, lady?"

She turns her head and sees the concerned face of an older man peering into the car.

She must pull herself together. She snuffles while reaching for her handbag on the back seat and finds a small hankie with a bluebell on it.

It is a minute before she can talk.

"Thank you, I am fine. We have broken down. My husband has gone to find someone to help us." She had said it. Involuntarily it had just slipped out. He had become her husband. But how could she now explain that the reason she was in pieces was because she was going to be late for her wedding? She musters an effort at a smile. "He shouldn't be too long. I am fine."

The man looks no less confused. "You sure? You don't look fine."

She nods. "I don't suppose he will be long. The man said he was going to Wilson's. That's not far, is it?" She prays for the answer to be positive.

"No, not far. Just down Coulsdon Hill. Shouldn't be more than ten minutes, I'd say. Righty-ho. If you're all fair, I'll bid you good day." He doffs his hat and walks back to his car parked behind hers. Elisabeth hears an engine start and then the car drives past, the man giving a wave as passes.

She regains some of her composure, at least outwardly. No more tears. Focus on the now. She wishes she had a watch. Perhaps not. Knowing the time might make it worse. Guessing means she can will it not to be too late. She can't bear to sit in the car any longer, so she opens the door to get out and paces the road.

It has been an age since she has felt as tense as this. Waiting for a piano grade exam perhaps, or her interview for the FANYs. Her tummy is in a knot and her mouth is dry. Two more cars slow at the sight of the pretty girl in the yellow dress, but she waves them on with a forced smile.

At last, she sees a larger truck approaching with two people in the cab. It slows and stops, Henry and a mechanic in grimy overalls emerge. Henry immediately walks towards her, puts his arms around her, and gives her a peck on the cheek.

"This is Mr. Wilson, who will have us going again in a flash."

The sullen mechanic gets into Evey and pulls the starter. The engine barely turns over. He gets out, steps towards the truck and extricates a battery, which he connects to the car with jump leads. He tries the engine again, which turns over quickly but still doesn't fire. He moves towards the bonnet and starts fumbling in the interstices.

The couple moves towards him, peering at the dark engine. He bends further under the bonnet, manipulating something while looking to the side. Every second is a minute, every minute ten. They will him to be the magician who will produce a white rabbit from the pit of their disappointment. He finally pulls out a grubby part, which he examines and cleans with a rag.

Elisabeth can't bear the silent theatre. She needs a commentary to reassure her increasing desperation.

"What do you think it could be?" she asks helplessly. "Did Henry tell you we are in a desperate hurry." She glances at Henry. "We have to be in Croydon for three o'clock."

"Yes, lady, he told me." He pauses, as if imparting even this much information was outside of his comfort zone. "No spark."

"So, can you fix it?"

"Probably the coil, but it's six-volt, ain't it. Don't have one on the truck."

Henry steps in "What are the options? Time is of the essence, but I know you appreciate that."

Elisabeth recognises the shallowness of his smile but suspects the man doesn't.

"I can tow you back to the garage or I can go and get the part and bring it back."

"Which is quicker?" Elisabeth dives in.

"I 'spose givin' you a tow."

"Right." Henry is all action, "Let's get moving. I will drive. Elisabeth, you go in the cab with Mr. Wilson."

Elisabeth clambers up to the cab and is horrified at the torn dirty seat. She steps down and fetches her jacket from Evey, which she places on the seat. Wilson turns the vehicle around and affixes the tow rope before cautiously setting off. He shouts back to Henry to be careful on the hill, and they grind towards Coulsdon.

In ten minutes they are pulling up onto the forecourt of a roadside garage, Wilson leaning out of the window indicating to Henry where to leave the car.

Henry and Elisabeth get out of their respective vehicles and embrace. Elisabeth's face is riven with worry, her mouth pinched as she chews on her cheek. If Henry knows the time he doesn't let on.

"Don't worry, my love," he says. "It will be fine. Surely it can't matter if we are a couple of minutes late. I can't believe the registrars of Croydon are overly busy on a Friday afternoon."

She forces a thin, unconvincing smile but says nothing.

Wilson is back under the bonnet, with a selection of spanners, assisted by a spotty youth carrying a small cardboard box, from which he takes a tubular part the size of a jam jar and inserts it somewhere under the bonnet. Within three minutes he is back in the car trying the starter. The little engine stutters and then bursts into life.

Elisabeth beams and squeezes Henry's hand, making towards the car.

"Hold on, lady. Got a few things to finish off before you go gallivantin."

The minutes drag on as the man continues to fiddle with the engine, his ponderousness leaving her wondering if he is being deliberately obstructive, but eventually the bonnet is closed, and Henry extracts his wallet to settle up. The total is three pounds three and eight pence but Henry hands over three pounds and a ten-bob note, stating that he doesn't expect any change.

"Who will drive the fastest?" Henry asks, hinting that it is him.

"Me," she says, a proper smile at last. I know her better than you."

"You are probably right, but being perennially late has given me lots of practice at rushing."

"Do we know where it is?" she says.

"Croydon?"

"No, nitwit, the registry office."

"Haven't a clue," he says.

"We might have to ask someone."

"Heaven forfend. Won't there be a sign?"

"I doubt it; it's hardly a tourist attraction."

She drives urgently, sitting forward in the seat, hands gripping the wheel. They fly through Coulsdon's suburban roads well over the speed limit, and then parallel the railway line towards Croydon. Henry spots a milestone telling them they have three miles to go. He glances at his watch and grimaces.

"Don't tell me," she says.

They drive into Old Town, the bomb damage still evident, with nothing obviously looking like a municipal building. Elisabeth slows to the side of the bustling shopping street and leans across Henry to ask a passerby, who tells them where to go.

The register office is an imposing Victorian building adjacent to a small green. They can park almost outside the Gothic portico, which is being used as the backdrop for a photograph of a couple who have clearly just tied the knot. Parents and bridesmaids jostle to keep on the steps as a photographer offers cheery instructions.

Elisabeth and Henry have to pause for a moment before feeling able to push their way past into the marbled hall. There are several people milling around, most looking more like guests than officials. On the wall opposite the door is a large clock. Now the extent of their lateness cannot be concealed any longer; it is twenty past three.

Henry drags Elisabeth towards a door marked RECEPTION, he with long-legged, purposeful strides, she skipping along beside him, handbag swinging from her arm.

He addresses the uniformed officer sitting behind a sliding glass window. Elisabeth can see the schedule of ceremonies pinned to the notice board adjacent to the window. There they are, Mr. Henry Benville and Miss Elisabeth Watson at three o'clock, sandwiched between Audrey Peters at two and Emelia Davies at four. But the day had been full, with three more marriages in the morning.

Henry starts his pitch in a voice persuasive and calm. "Benville is the name. I am so terribly sorry that we are rather late. Unfortunately, our car broke down and we had to get towed into a garage to get it repaired. I do hope you will be able to still fit us in."

"What was the name?"

"Benville, Henry Benville, and this is my fiancée, Elisabeth Watson."

She looks at a ledger on the desk. "Three o'clock."

"Yes, that's right."

"Sorry, but you're too late. Five minutes allowed, ten at a push, but not twenty-five. You'll have to rebook."

"Oh lord, but it is rather important, you see, as I am going to Austria tomorrow and it is imperative that we get married before I leave. Could you possibly make an exception, just this once?"

"I'm sorry sir, no exceptions. Especially when we have a ceremony booked at four and it is Friday afternoon."

Elisabeth steps forward to say her piece, the distress evident on her strained face. "Is there really nothing you can do to help us? It really is a unique situation. Henry does terribly important work rehousing refugees in Austria, and we just must get married today."

Her charms and anguish are wasted on the icy clerk, who avoids eye contact, seemingly continuing to focus on the paperwork on the desk in front of her.

Elisabeth turns away, her eyes filled with tears.

Henry changes his stance, becoming much more severe. "I refuse to accept that you cannot make an exception. We are late through no fault of our own. I would like to speak to the registrar in person. What would be his name?"

"You can't speak to the registrar; it is not in order."

"Madam, I do not appear to have made myself clear. I demand to speak to the registrar."

The woman gets up and walks towards a door at the back of the room. She knocks and walks in without waiting for a response.

Henry turns to the crumpled Elisabeth, putting his arm around her shoulder. "Bloody clerks. They are all the same. Don't worry, darling. It will be fine."

She nods her head, dabbing her eyes with a handkerchief retrieved from her handbag. "No. It's not going to work. They won't budge, Henry. I can tell. She won't lose face now." She heaves silently in his arms.

The woman reappears with a moustachioed spiv of a man with black oiled hair and a waistcoat. In his hand are a bundle of papers held together with a paper clip. Rather than speaking through the window, he emerges through a door and approaches the couple. He doesn't shake hands, lifting his chin and trying to look down on Henry, who is a good four inches taller.

"Benville is it?" he says, the condescension evident in his timbre.

"Henry Benville," Henry says, attempting to take control of the dialogue. "Unfortunately, we suffered a breakdown on the way here this afternoon and were unavoidably delayed—"

"Let me stop you there Mr. Benville. Miss Harland has informed me of the details. Unfortunately, we have a rule that we are unable to proceed with a ceremony if the couple arrives later than five minutes after the designated time. Besides which, I have made a note here," he refers to the pages he is holding. "I specifically told Mr. Smallwood that you should arrive early, as paperwork needed to be completed due to the short notice given. You will be aware that it was in breach of the regulations that we were able to assign you the appointment at such short notice in any event."

Now even Henry looks deflated but persists, "The problem is Mr . . . I'm sorry but I didn't catch your name?"

"White."

"Mr. White, I am seconded to a refugee agency in Austria and on a flight there tomorrow morning. It is imperative for various reasons that our marriage is completed before my departure. I appreciate that we are asking a lot from you and your staff, but it really is vital that we exchange our vows today. I am asking you to make an exception on this one occasion. If there are additional costs, then of course we will cover them."

"The rules exist for a purpose, Mr. Benville, and I am unable to bend them to take account of happenstance or misadventure. Besides which, as I informed Mr. Smallwood, it is against statutory requirements and most irregular to even schedule a ceremony at less than a week's notice. I was prepared to make an exception, given your special circumstances, but that required concessions on your part with which you have failed to comply. I am afraid that our gesture of goodwill has now expired. We will not be able to conduct your marriage here today. I am sorry if that is not the outcome you desire, but that is how it is. We can, of course, assist you to make another booking." He turns, chin aloft and returns through the door from whence he came.

"Bugger. Damn and blast. Narrow-minded little twit. I am so sorry, my darling. I take the blame—should have been more organised and thought more about the arrangements. Perhaps I expected the whole world to be sharing my own optimism and joy. I didn't think that trivial bureaucrats could stand in the way of our happiness."

"No, don't blame yourself, Henry. That's not fair. Maybe it was slightly crazy, but it was worth the try." Now she is trying to console him, not being able to bear his discomfort. "If anyone is to blame it's Evey, and yet she's always been so reliable." She finds his hand and embraces him, sliding her arms under his jacket, feeling his firm warmth and inhaling his comforting smell.

For an age they stand silent and still in the empty lobby, now with no need or any wish to move. There is nowhere to go; no deadline or appointment to keep. And what passes between their enfolded limbs is the weight of their disappointment, the emptiness of a plan unfulfilled. This thing they were about to do, was all that she had in her power to give to him as an irrefutable confirmation of her love, and now it wasn't to be. Although she had first thought the idea of marrying so quickly was dotty, once the idea had moved from impossible craziness to feasible reality, she had become a committed partner in the endeavour, and its loss was painful. It was as if the world outside had made a judgement on them and said: "No, we won't let you do this. It can't be allowed."

She wondered what he was thinking as he gently moved his hand over her head and through her hair. Was he hatching some new magical plot that would resolve things and make it all better?

That is what she had always wanted from her father when she was a little girl and something had gone wrong or a toy had broken; Daddy would mend it. Or was he going to lose interest and fly back to Austria, immerse himself in his work and, in true Henry fashion, get distracted and procrastinate?

But as they stand, oblivious to the sneering look of Miss Harland, who exits the office and clatters across the terrazzo in hard-soled shoes, the comfort of his arms works a change in her thoughts. It is magic, but it is a different sort of magic; it doesn't matter. Here in his arms inhaling his alluring musk, the ceremony doesn't matter. It is only a piece of paper. It is only the approval of others, the validation and approbation of society. There will be time for that. What really matters is this embrace, this sanctuary, something unsayable and timeless. The overpowering wonder and magic that is being in love.

She looks up at him. "It's all right. It doesn't matter. We'll do it properly at Knowle with all our friends and family and it will be wonderful and marvellous, and we won't have to deal with petty-minded officials."

He doesn't say anything for a minute.

"Are you sure you don't mind?"

"I mind, but I can cope. It doesn't matter, Henry; it can't matter."

"You are a wonder. I was still trying to work out ways around the pettifogging bureaucracy."

She smiles. "I thought you might be! Leave it. It will all be fine. Take me out to a smashing restaurant, buy me dinner, and everything will be perfect."

They drift back to the car, pensive and deflated. As they walk, she remains connected to him solely by a finger linked with his. She automatically gets in the driving seat. Evey starts on the pull of the wire. She sits, holding the steering wheel looking straight ahead.

"Where to, maestro?" she says.

"What would you like to eat? Italian? Would you prefer lively and fun or quiet and romantic?"

"I think we could both do with fun and lively, don't you think?"

"Agreed. Top hole. What about Frascatis? We could have oysters."

"I've never had oysters, but Frascatis would be smashing. I have never been."

"Well, I am not sure it is as good as it was, but let's find out. Come to think of it, probably not oysters in August, but there might be a Dover sole."

"So, Oxford Street, correct?"

"Absolutely. Spot on."

Elisabeth steers the little car through the streets of South London, thronged with Friday afternoon traffic. There is little appeal here. She can find nothing to celebrate in the uninspired roads of soot-blackened houses and unkempt shop fronts, with little on display in their uninspiring windows. The scars caused by blitz are still evident, with gaps and gashes in facades and occasional low piles of rubble where a building should have been.

"It's pretty grim, isn't it?" Henry says as if reading her thoughts. "Might have been better to flatten the lot and start again from scratch."

"Ghastly," she murmurs.

But it gets better by Clapham Common and then they cross the river in filtered sunlight.

"Tell you what," he says, "it's frightfully early, how about a drink at my club? I could do with a stiff drink."

Elisabeth stays silent, looking straight ahead as they cross Vauxhall bridge.

"I think I would rather go to a pub, Henry. You don't mind, do you?"

"Oh, all right. If that's what you prefer." Now he sounds a bit miffed.

"It is just that I don't really want to meet clubby formal people right now, not after the frustration of this afternoon. I would feel on the back foot and having to own up to regret and disappointment. I can't cope with sympathy. Not just now."

"Chances are there would not have been anyone I knew, but I know what you mean. Pub then."

"I know just the place, a surprise for you. I bet you won't have been there before." She smiles to herself, looking forward to being able to delight him with the unexpected.

She turns into Eaton Square and then into a side street, where she pulls up, jabbing on the handbrake with a jolt.

Henry enjoins the game. "So, a surprise then . . . I know, The Surprise?"

She chuckles. "No, not that Surprise, but that would have been nice, mind. This way." She drags him into a narrow lane of mews houses.

"Where are you taking me? Some lurid club with no sign on the door, knock three times and ask for Mitzi."

"No, you'll see."

They turn a gentle bend into a small mews, revealing a small pub, understated and incongruous amid the white stucco grandeur of its surrounds. The street is cobbled and empty.

"Well, I never," he says. "The Grenadier; how ever do you know this place?"

"A single girl has to have somewhere intimate where she can meet admirers."

They climb the steep steps and enter between the two bars. The outside calm of the early evening is instantly transformed into a hubbub of chat and laughter. The air is thick and the interior is gloomy compared with the brightness outside, the corners of the yellowed ceiling invisible in the shadows. Both bars are crammed, mostly with men standing holding pint glasses, some leaning on a ledge or the bar corner. Everyone is smoking, mostly cigarettes, but there are a few pipes. It is animated, alive, vibrant. The yellow dress and the exuberant hair turn heads as Elisabeth squeezes into the saloon bar, where there are two women standing in a foursome, but all the tables are occupied by men.

Immediately a younger man with a military haircut stands up and offers her his chair, taking vicarious pride in being able to win a smile from a girl of such loveliness. His friend follows suit, the pair draining their glasses and moving towards the bar, arguing as to whose round it is.

"What can I get you?" Henry asks.

"Gin and it," please.

Henry dives through the throng to the bar, his height enabling him to attract the barmaid's attention and shouting his order before reaching the mahogany surface.

Elisabeth sits, observing the world at play, immediately suffused with the bonhomie of her surroundings. She loves the jollity and chat of a busy pub. She doesn't have to be engaged in conversation herself to be touched by the laughter of others. Even before the gin arrives, she has forgotten about the disappointment of the afternoon, brought down to earth by the lives of others. In fact, she has only visited twice before: the first time on a date with a man from work, the second with Wendy, walking over from Victoria on a warm evening. Normally it is much quieter, the gloomy landlord serving his clientele with a permanent look of regret, but she doesn't mind that it is crowded now. It's what she needs after the week of such intimacy: people. What a pity none of her friends are here to share in the fun and meet Henry.

And then the gin arrives, the diluted ruby liquid served in a cocktail glass, embellished with a cherry on a stick. Henry takes a swig of his pint of bitter and edges into the chair beside her. He fixes her in his gaze and raises his glass smiling broadly.

"Cheers, darling."

She raises her glass to his and takes a sip before putting it back on the table and moving her hand discreetly to his knee.

"You look happy," he says.

"I am happy," she says. "I am with you."

"Not too disappointed about this afternoon?"

"I can cope. I've told you before, I'm a big girl now."

He puts his hand on hers and then takes it in both of his, kissing it briefly and then looking at the pale skin, touching the engagement ring. "It should have had a companion by now." He reaches into his jacket pocket and takes out the jeweller's box containing the wedding ring, which he puts on the table. He opens it meticulously with a care and precision which Elisabeth has come to realise is such a part of his makeup. He takes out the ring, reaches for her hand, and slides it onto the finger. "There, much more the part; in an instant honest and respectable." He chuckles, "Were it always so easy to make an honest woman of someone!"

"Oh Henry, I'm not sure—it feels as if we're fibbing—anyway not sure I want to be that respectable."

She holds her left hand up in front of her admiring the two rings side by side, twisting her wrist as the light catches the stones and precious metal.

"I tell you what," she says. "We can pretend." She takes his hand in hers and says, "I do."

Henry looks confused. "You do what?"

"Take you to be my wedded husband, you ninny."

"It's not I do, it's not the present, darling, it's the future; I will."

"Are you sure?" she says with a puzzled look.

"Absolutely."

She remains quiet for a second.

"The question is will you take this man to be your wedded husband, and then all the other stuff about having and holding and sickness and death." He pauses expectantly. "Well, will you?"

"I will, I will, I will," she says, now grinning.

"In that case, it is settled. So will I."

....

They arrive at Frascati's, their joie de vivre enhanced by the drinks and the normalcy and thrum of the Grenadier. But entering the galleried dining hall the atmosphere is stuffy and sedate, the painted walls faded, and it is half empty. Henry slows his normal brisk pace and looks around, the diners, mostly frail and grey-haired, chomp silently on colourless food.

He whispers an aside into Elisabeth's ear, "This isn't how it is supposed to be. This isn't what we need... What do you think, darling? I think we go elsewhere," and he swings her around, reverting to his usual hurried step, and pulls her back through the foyer. They take stock on the pavement, "Do you mind awfully, darling? I remember it as being très chic and the place to be seen. I just couldn't be doing with it—not on our wedding night. I couldn't bear to sit among those fossils with their judgemental silent scrutiny."

"Quite, darling," she says mockingly. "Especially on our not-wedding night."

"Where else is near? I am starving."

"Jazz? The Café de Paris?"

"Topping idea. Lead on."

"We could go dancing," she says.

"Not sure about dancing. My legs get in the way."

....

It is after eleven-o-clock. Elisabeth and Henry climb the stairs, enter the flat and flop onto the lumpy grey sofa. The streetlights cast a yellow glow into the sitting room through the open-curtained window. She is still wearing the yellow frock, at the end of her slender legs the elegant silk shoes, which she kicks off to the side. They had eaten at Chez Victor, and had indeed found some jazz, the French food being served to a background of a crooning vocalist accompanied by a piano. She had loved it, despite Henry's occasional questioning as to whether it was what she had really wanted.

As usual the flat was empty. Elisabeth was glad they had the place to themselves, while at the same time longing to update her friend on her adventures.

Now they were both full, tired and a little tipsy. He has her hand in his as a strange silence falls between them. They don't look at each other, staring ahead emptily at nothing, as if struggling with something of which they cannot speak.

Elisabeth gets up and turns on the wireless.

CHAPTER 34

....

S he doesn't remember the drive back from the airport. She supposes she must have made logical decisions about where to go, when to stop, turn left here and right there, but she can't recall any of it. She floats aloft in a sea of happiness, uncertainty, and heartache. She has never felt such a strange mixture of emotions. The wondrous tug in her heart remains, a thrilling bursting joy that is physical, here inside her, in fact through every part of her. It makes her smile. Suddenly all those sonnets and love poems that seemed a bit over the top when she read them at school, now they get nowhere near to what she feels. How can one do anything feeling like this? She is in a dither, completely useless.

But then there is the ache of want. She needs him, wants him, longs for his touch and laughter, for his smell and his skin next to hers. This is a bodily thing, deep in her person somewhere, although God knows where. It is not in her mind; it is more real than that.

So, this is what it is like to be apart from someone you love. It is horrible. Impossible. I wont cope for an hour let alone weeks or even months I will go bonkers.

And with this comes a fear for him. She can't remember ever having had this terror before; that someone matters more than you yourself. What if something were to happen to him? She wouldn't cope. It is unimaginable, so black she can't even contemplate it, so she pushes it from her thoughts, where it lies restless like a medieval beast whose terrifying presence you can never escape from. She never worried about Daddy because he was unassailable, invincible. That's why his death was so terrible—because she had never believed it could happen. But with Henry it is different. The invincible father was a product of her mindset, not his armour, but she has changed since then. That's what the war taught her: that we are all vincible, all susceptible, and Henry, for all his magnificent strengths, also has these vulnerabilities, these boyish enthusiasms that defy risk.

She arrives back at the flat, which is empty and soulless. The memories of the previous late evening echo from the walls and furniture. It is unbearably glum. Henry fills a space; his presence distracts from the ordinary and dominates her senses. When he is with her, she does not notice the mundane or the shabbiness of her milieu; she can remove herself to another world. She has no idea what she will do for the rest of the weekend. She knows she won't see Wendy until Monday morning at work, but it is still only Saturday. She wonders if she can call any of her other friends but is sure they will be doing things and besides it is such short notice. She feels as if she has been out of circulation forever, although it has only been a week. Still, everything has changed. How will she explain it to her chums? It is a novella in two parts: the dashing prince carries her off with the promise of forever, but then it all goes wrong at the last hurdle.

No, it doesn't.

She won't believe that. She knows that it will all be fine, but how to explain it to her crowd, who will inevitably smirk, even if not to her face. Jealousy maybe, or justifiable scepticism perhaps, but they will smirk.

She knows she needs to do things and keep busy, so she starts with some washing, which she hangs out to dry over the bath. Then she needs to go shopping, but has hardly any money, and the banks are not open because it is Saturday. She is in limbo, betwixt and between. Everything has changed, utterly changed. She is not the person she was before, but she can't yet step into the new life that beckons. So close, but so far. The pieces of the vision are set out ready to be assembled, but just not quite yet.

His plane will have landed by now, he will be in a car or a meeting or the Gasthaus or somewhere. She can't quite envisage the setting nor the atmosphere. Will he be thinking of her this minute, just as she thinks of him? Could there be a strand of connectivity somehow linking them? It does feel like that. That's the thing with Henry, he is contrary and unpredictable. He might be thinking of her, and pining even, but then he might be thinking about Greek poetry or, she supposes, his work. She imagines that he gets completely immersed in that too, to the exclusion of a girl sitting at home pining for him.

No, not pining, she must try to push that to one side. Then she notices her piano sitting empty and unloved, beckoning her with comfort and reassurance. There is Bartok bidding to take her back to her school days and Mrs. Varga. How often had her time in the music room assuaged the unhappiness and homesickness she had experienced while locked away in the Marches?

She plays some of the easier pieces that she knows so well and is surprised at how the music flows from her fingers with a life of its own. She is drawn in, focused and distracted. Making this music has so many resonances for her, they take her to another time, not a happy time necessarily, but a mechanism for coping with difficulties. They put her back in control, push the unwelcome intrusions of worry and loneliness to a corner of her cognisance.

Then she feels ready for something a little more challenging and gets off the piano stool to rummage through the music that it contains. Chopin, that will do. But the études are more challenging for her because she can never get anywhere near the perfection and finesse of Rubinstein, who was Nanny Mills's favourite.

She plays for two hours and feels much better, but then gets claustrophobic and needs to get outside. The day is pleasant enough but not as warm as it should be, and the clouds look as if they might do their worst.

She leaves the flat heading north and finds herself at Hyde Park Corner, so she wanders into the park. She sits by the Serpentine watching a couple of girls in a boat laughing as they incompetently row round in circles.

As she sits with her hands in her lap, her right hand finds the rings on her left. She is still wearing the wedding ring. Finding it shocks her. She had forgotten all about it. Although it feels right, a signal of belonging, a part of her feels guilty at the deceit. She will take it off before going to work on Monday and revert to being just engaged. That is acceptable. Better than acceptable. Wonderful.

Now she feels good, there are more distractions outside and the physical act of walking is comforting. She decides that it is time to head home and turns south when she sees the Albert Hall.

A prom!

She isn't sure of the time but imagines it is not yet six o'clock. She could queue and get a ticket to the promenade. That would be a perfect distraction for the long evening ahead. But she is starving and so walks quickly to Kensington High Street, where she finds a Lyons Corner House and buys a cup of tea and a bun, which is all she can afford. The Prom will be a shilling, and she has to have some money for her bus fare in the morning.

She has no idea what or who will be playing, but that is the lovely thing about the proms; it doesn't matter much. It's like going to dinner with a really good cook. You don't mind what you get served up because you know it will be nice. Then she realises that it was exactly a week ago that she attended the Prom with Henry. A pang of regret pricks the bubble of her contentment. How she wishes he was here now with her, at her side, pondering scotch eggs. She smiles. *Lovable, lovable man.*

She finds herself in a long queue and wonders if she will get in, but the couple ahead reassure her and tell her it is the London

Symphony Orchestra with a very popular programme. There is a Bach double piano concerto, Tchaikovsky's "Romeo and Juliet" and then the "Carnival of the Animals," along with some other pieces.

The queue edges towards the hall, and then she is in the arena and swept up in the throng. The atmosphere is light-hearted and expectant, the excitement and crush the perfect distraction. The red velvet, the magnificent organ with its huge pipes set off by the gilt ornamentation, are the perfect backdrop to the crisp black-and-white decorum of the orchestra. They tune up, the lights dim, and Basil Cameron enters to warm applause. He raises his baton, and the orchestra starts the gallop through the overture to der Freischutz. At first, she finds herself testing the piece for Henry's approval, but the music sweeps her up in its power, carries her to a different place and she forgets about everything save for the sounds and rhythms that envelope her.

The programme finishes with Ravel's "Bolero," which she has never heard. It is extraordinary; the mesmeric rhythm on the side drum incessant and enticing, seducing the crowd into a gentle, swaying expectancy, the intensity and passion reaching a crescendo that finally bursts into a scream of discordant brass. The Promenaders erupt with whooping cheers and applause. She feels exultant, though drained, but as the crowd disperses and she steps out into the cool evening air, her pain returns.

A week ago, she was walking the same steps with the man she loves. She can't bear to retrace the steps alone on foot, so she gets a bus.

She is dreading the next twenty-four hours, with no clues as to how she will occupy herself on the morrow, and then after that not at all sure what she is going to tell her boss. Should she hand in her notice now or wait to hear from Henry?

CHAPTER 35

....

London

Monday August 11, 1948

T he alarm rings at seven o'clock Monday morning, but she does not feel rested. She had felt tired the previous evening but couldn't sleep due to the knots of thoughts and ideas rushing through her head. Sunday had dragged as she had feared. She longed for the company of friends but was still paralysed by uncertainty as to what to say and how to tell her story. In addition, she had virtually no money and the only thing to eat in the flat was a tin of baked beans, which she warmed without enthusiasm on the gas ring. In the afternoon she wrote a letter to Henry telling him about the concert and the Ravel piece. On the way out she had overheard someone saying that Ravel himself had thought it ironic that the piece he was most famous for wasn't "musical," but she had loved it.

She had found it comforting to sit at the table in the lounge with pen and paper, describing the pieces she had heard and the atmosphere in the hall. Writing brought him closer. But then she got a bit soppy and, with tears in her eyes, proclaimed her love for him and how she couldn't wait until they were together again.

But now she is leaving the flat and walking to the tube to go back to work, wishing she could talk to Henry.

Outside the tube station is a newsstand stacked with newspapers. Her eye is drawn to the front of the *Daily Sketch*, which holds an image which she somehow recognises. The picture shows the broken wreckage of an aeroplane amongst pine trees on a rock-strewn hillside, an angular peak looming over the grainy background. Her mind is both frozen and racing. She cannot process the image, but a part of her knows that it is terrible. What she feels is a paralysing fear. The image is a hazy memory buried in her subconscious. It gradually comes to the fore.

The image is from her dream the first night she met Henry, waking up in panic and seeing the shapes of twisted metal, fire, and mountains. Her vision is drawn to the headline, which reads: "Eight Britons Killed in Plane Crash in Austria."

....

A commuter walking the same pavement would have seen a well-dressed young woman, with a head of auburn hair tied back in a blue ribbon, staring blankly at a copy of the paper that she holds in front of her.

"No, no, no . . . There must be a mistake. No, it can't be. Not Henry. He would have been more careful." She clutches the paper in clenched hands. "No, no, no." She sinks to her knees on the pavement, clutching the paper to her bosom. She has a distance to her gaze, staring nowhere, seeing nothing, as a blind person might. Her lips are tremulous; she is transfixed as might be the image of a twelfth-century martyr or someone suffering a seizure.

"Eer lady, do you want to buy the paper or not?" the vendor says.

The busy commuters step around her, glancing avoidantly at her display, torn between pathos and embarrassment. But then she seems to gather herself together and, still clutching the paper, walks slowly away, her makeup smudged by tears, still with the distant look etched onto her broken face.

As she wanders away from the attendant he raises his voice; "Oi, lady. Is you going to pay for the paper?" Unwilling to leave his stand

and the steady stream of customers he resorts to shouting, "Bloody cheek. 'Ere, you can't just walk off like that."

But the lady is now ambling away from the scene, heading nowhere, a terrible distance in her eyes.

Years later, when finally provoked by Philip to recall that day and the ones immediately following, she realised that she could recall virtually nothing. That is how it was; just an empty oblivion in which she was aware of nothing save the emptiness of the end of life.

....

Later that morning a Morris 8 arrives at RAF Northolt airfield and stops at the barrier. A uniformed guard approaches the car. A woman leans out from under the hood and explains that she must get to Innsbruck urgently as her husband needs her. He notices the pretty face, the blotched makeup, the mascara smeared by tears, and the agitated manner, but "rules are rules" and tells her simply that she can't enter without a pass.

She is insistent. "My husband is doing very important work. I dropped him here only two days ago to fly to Austria." Her voice is urgent and insistent but tremulous and on the point of breaking.

He tries once more to tell her that she really must move along but is already uncertain that she will obey. She seems not to hear what he says.

She is unrelenting; she must be allowed to see her husband, who she is sure is here. "He is very strong and can look after himself, but I need to see him. You have to help me get to him."

"Sorry lady, who do you say he is? Is he based here?"

"He might be. He might not have got on the plane. He loves me."

"Who?"

"Henry. I dropped him here on Saturday. He is very strong. But I have to get to him. He will need help."

The airman is confused by the mix of a sensible woman who at times is rational with a logical story, and at other times makes no sense at all, is hysterical, and is almost delusional. He is uncertain what to do other than refuse entry.

A large truck appears behind the car wanting to access the station and, in an effort to resolve his dilemma, he instructs her to pull to the side while he waves the lorry through.

She gets out of the car clutching the copy of the *Daily Sketch*.

"I must find him. I am sure he needs help," she says, waving the folded newspaper.

The guard looks at the newspaper and catches a glimpse of the headline. He now understands that she must be a next of kin of one of the casualties of the fatal crash which formed the core of the conversation in the mess at breakfast. He suggests that the woman waits in her car while he phones through to his sergeant.

An hour later she is sitting in the guardroom while the sergeant is in the next room in a telephone conversation with the duty medical officer, trying to work out what to do with the increasingly distressed woman. An attempt at a calm conversation about the tragedy does little to shake her conviction that Henry needs her help, and that she must find him.

"If he really isn't here," she asserts, "then I must get to Austria."

The balding, grey-moustached sergeant instructs one of the guards to make a cup of tea, and although moved by her pitiful crumpled state, is better at the practicalities of providing tea than being sympathetic. Elisabeth accepts the drink but remains adamant that she must get to Austria.

The RMO can't be found but an orderly arrives, although he is of little help. He acknowledges that the woman is hysterical and suggests she needs mental help but can make no recommendations. The only suggestion is that the padre is approached.

All agree that she is in no fit state to drive, and they can't just pack her off back to whence she came. On the telephone the acting station commander is heard to mutter, "Well she can't bloody-well stay here."

The sergeant is instructed to find Elisabeth's next of kin and reappears with the mother's telephone number and a call is put through. This doesn't help; the mother herself appears either distraught or senile and has neither a car nor a driving licence. Perhaps one of the service crew could drive her to Reigate? But how would the driver get back?

Privately the officer is cursing the intrusion into his routine, but eventually agrees that the most expedient way to resolve the issue is for two men to escort her home, one to drive her car and the other following with the woman.

Two hours later it is the corporal who knocks on the door of the house in Reigate. He stands aside as the two crumpled women meet in a stiff embrace. He passes to Mrs. Watson the message given to him by his senior, that the woman might benefit from a visit from her doctor and perhaps from a sedative, and then takes his leave.

....

Elisabeth sits in the sitting room while Mummy brings in tea on a tray. Her hair has long since freed itself from the blue ribbon and is now a wild hood of unkempt amber. Her face is taught, the usual loveliness trampled by uncertainty and fear, and the still evident smudges of makeup. She still clutches the *Daily Sketch*.

Mummy is almost silent, having said little other than "You poor dear" several times. She has no repertoire of consolation. Her fragile world, one that can barely cope with the demands of her own routine, struggles with the news of Elisabeth's tragedy.

Elisabeth shakes her head repeatedly.

"Why won't they let me go? I knew I shouldn't have let him out of my sight. Henry can't look after himself. He could hardly find the way to the airport. He needs me. I know I could help. He will be all right; don't you think Mummy?"

"I think you are better off with me here, dear."

"Perhaps I could get an aeroplane from Croydon. They must have flights; Henry said there are flights to Prague." She speaks vehemently, with a distant look.

Even Mummy can detect a disturbing irrational absence in her daughter and reminds herself of the message from the driver about calling the doctor.

"Perhaps it might be helpful if Dr. Wilkinson came and saw you, dear. He could give you something to calm you down."

"I don't need calming down—I need to be on a plane to help. They must need help, surely." She turns her face up with a terrifying look of anguish that Mrs. Watson can't ignore. She gets up, leans over and kisses the top of Elisabeth's hair and then walks out of the room to call the doctor.

It is not until after six that there is a knock on the door. Mummy gets up, leaving Elisabeth to her reverie, opens the door to the GP and explains the situation in her inadequate way. The doctor enters the sitting room, a tall, weary, thoughtful-looking man with bags under his eyes and leather pads on the elbows of his worn tweed jacket. He carries a rectangular black doctor's case. He knows Mrs. Watson is not well and has never met Elisabeth. Initially he says little, awaiting an exposition from the patient, but soon realises that this won't be forthcoming.

Elisabeth answers his questions, seeming entirely logical and rational save for the complete lack of acceptance that Henry has been harmed, stuck in her reiteration that he needs her help. As she talks, she anxiously twirls the wedding ring on her left hand.

"I don't think it will be possible for you to go to Austria, Elisabeth," he says after a long silence, "and besides, I don't think it would be helpful. This is shocking news you have had—truly shocking—it is not surprising that you are feeling upset."

She says nothing, her face taught and strained, her bottom lip tremulous, her right hand no longer fiddling with her wedding ring but now still, with fingers intertwined, tightly resting on her knees. The room is silent for a moment, then from outside a blackbird noisily warns of the settling gloom.

He leans forward to lay a hand on her shoulder and then straightens, opening his medical bag to reveal several small drawers. He opens one and removes a small bottle labelled "Chloral," which he passes to Mummy.

"Take a couple of teaspoons now and then get ready for bed. I am sure you will be feeling a bit more yourself in the morning. I will drop in to see how you are then."

He smiles with more pity and hopelessness than encouragement or optimism, as if he knows there is worse to come. He says nothing else, heads for the door and is ushered out by Mummy.

Over the next two days the surety of her conviction that she must go to Austria is gradually replaced by something much worse; an acceptance that she can do nothing. With it comes blackness so dark that she cannot speak of it or describe it, but equally she has no wish to talk of it to anybody, or anything, the latter relevant because her world involutes to a pit where there is little to distinguish between the animate and the inanimate. The days seem to have no beginning or end, she may be dressed, she may not be, she may be in bed or on the sofa. She eats nothing save for when her increasingly perturbed mother's protestations overwhelm her beleaguered resistance. Her face is tattooed with pain and hurt but there are no tears. Although she sits in the garden for hours, she sees nothing, she notices not the thrushes scurrying through the leaves in the borders or the neighbour's cat silently stalking them. There is no joy in the roses that are the only plants that her mother tends with any care. She doesn't feel the chill wind or the splashes of a summer shower that causes Mummy to steer her back indoors.

The following day sister Claire appears at midday having been driven over by Ian, her policeman husband. Elisabeth is buried in a morass of bed clothes, a silent spectre of misery.

"Oh, my darling Bethy. I am so sorry . . ." Claire moves across the room to sit on the bed and finds one of her sister's hands that she cradles and strokes against her obviously expectant tummy. "You poor,

poor darling . . . I just can't believe it. No one deserves that much rotten luck." She leans across to move the mass of hair that obscures Elisabeth's face. She is shocked by the anguish on the usually soft features of her sister. This is her big sister, the pretty one, the confident, assertive one, always in control, never lost for words or cowered by emotion. Ever calm, with her feelings buttoned up and neatly compartmentalised.

Claire now looks on a face so distraught she cannot believe that she is not physically ill. Claire is usually one who finds chatter easy, who loves to prattle with her friends, who can muster a commentary on all the everyday trivia that besets her friends and neighbours, but now she is wordless.

Elisabeth lies still, saying nothing, unacknowledging of her sister's presence. They stay silent for minutes before Elisabeth says, "Thank you for coming to see me."

"That's all right, pet. Of course I would come to see you, you poor darling."

But then the silence returns, a silence that grates for Claire, eaten up by her impotence and sense of helplessness. But Elisabeth doesn't notice.

"How is the bump?" Elisabeth says.

And Claire is suddenly freed from her discomfort. She thinks of her baby and starts talking about the crib and the antenatal classes and the pram that Ian's mother has bought and her ankles that are swollen and the back pain and that she has to get up twice at night to spend a penny, and Elisabeth hears it all without listening to a word.

And then it's time for her to go and she hugs her sister but can really find nothing to say except that she will feel better soon, and she must come to see her when the baby arrives.

....

Things change later in the week with the arrival of Nanny Mills. Mummy had telephoned her soon after Elisabeth's arrival, and in her logical and businesslike manner, Nan had said she would return the call in two days to see how things were. When it emerged that Elisabeth was still submerged in an avalanche of grief, she booked a ticket to London and arrived the following afternoon just before five, having walked up the hill from Reigate station.

Seeing Nan startles Elisabeth, who is thrilled to see the most beloved member of her family. She gets up and hugs the shrunken old woman. And then, with her arms around the dumpy cardiganed bundle, the person she now most loves in the world, the tears come.

"Oh Nan, he was so wonderful. I loved him so much. I loved him so much . . . I should never have let him go. It's all my fault . . ." her voice tails off into a sea of sobs.

"There, there, dear. It was nobody's fault. Certainly not yours."

Nan persuades Elisabeth to get dressed and sit at table for supper, but there is no conversation to speak of, Elisabeth saying nothing spontaneously and only answering questions in monosyllabic answers. She eats a bird's portion of shepherd's pie.

At breakfast the following morning, with a crumpled Elisabeth in her dressing gown sipping tea and playing with a piece of toast, Nan pronounces, "I think it would be a good idea if you came to stay with me for a few days. We can walk and play some music. Get you away from London and all the painful memories."

Elisabeth says nothing.

"You can drive me back to Hereford tomorrow or the day after— just when you are ready. It will do you good to get out of the house and focus on a task."

Elisabeth cannot imagine anything outside of the terrible dark space in which she is imprisoned, let alone anything as practical or tangible as driving a car, but Nan's pronouncement registers with her in a way that nothing else has for the previous five days.

Later Nan sits with her on the sofa and insists she speak about Henry.

"I want to hear all about this man you fell for," she says, "and then we can have a wee cry together."

Elisabeth can focus on nothing save the mantra that it was her fault and that she should have stopped Henry from leaving.

"I could have stopped him, Nan . . . Why did I let him go? It was all my fault." The tears come again. And then again and again.

But Nan is more insistent, probing in her questions: where did you go then, tell me more about the house, explain about the stepmother, what music did he like, what did you play together? And while Elisabeth is talking, she is at least not crying, and when she recalls the breakfast in the music room, she even becomes quite animated, only to dissolve again when she glimpses the rings on her finger.

"What is the point of a bloody ring now? I will never be married to anyone now . . ."

Nan again suggests again that they should go to Hereford, a notion that Elisabeth has no will to fight, but like every suggestion, falls on a mind incapable of appraisal and emotion, and so she doesn't object.

On the following Sunday morning, helped by her mother and grandmother, she puts a few clothes in a soft bag borrowed from her mother, packs it and Nan's little valise into the back of Evey, and climbs in. Then clutching the black steering wheel, she reassures her mother that she is capable of driving, and they set off towards London on the way to Hereford.

They speak little. There is nothing to say. The usual chat they enjoy with a repertoire of happy memories is not accessible. The future is out of reach. The present is unbearable, but driving is doable, and as Nan had suspected, a useful distraction.

They pull up outside the flat in Victoria and park. Nan offers to buy some food for lunch while Elisabeth enters the flat, which is cool and unwelcoming. It seems hostile and complicit, and she shivers. The fusty smell seems stale and tainted.

On the table in the hall is a typed envelope addressed to Lady Elisabeth Benville (née Watson) with a Dorchester postmark. For a moment she is confused before realising that it is addressed to her.

She opens it and recognises the headed notepaper of Smallwood Solicitors and Commissioners for Oaths. The letter is typewritten with the salutation and valediction handwritten.

My Dear Elizabeth,

This is a difficult letter to write because there are no words that can express the sadness and loss that you must be experiencing at this awful time. I want to write to offer you the condolences of everyone at Knowle, but also to assure you that you are not alone; there is nobody here who is not devastated by the tragic and untimely passing of a wonderful man.

Henry was a truly remarkable person. One of the best. His loss has cast a shadow over Knowle that will be long in resolution. He was of course, kind, charming, and wise, but his warmth and genuine "common touch" threw a comforting cloak over all he met. What fewer are aware of is his bravery, unwavering moral compass, and sense of duty, for which this country has every reason to be grateful.

But most of this you know. What you do not know is that none of those of us who saw him with you had ever seen him as happy and liberated as he became when you were together. You brought a light and a joy to his being, which we have never witnessed before.

There is nothing that can diminish the tragedy of this loss. Even the most devout struggle with explanations or comforts to assuage the overwhelming waste of a premature

death such as this. There is no logic, no
sense, no rationale, just beastly sadness
and injustice. But you must never forget the
happiness that you brought to the last week
of his life. That was your gift to him and
could just perhaps offer some solace within
the desolation of your grief.

There will be a memorial service in due
course, and I will write to you again with
details of this.

Miriam and I send you our heartfelt
condolences at this difficult time.

Our kindest wishes to you.

Yours sincerely,

Percy Smallwood

She reads the letter calmly and doesn't cry. For the first time since his death, she feels that she is sharing her loss with people who knew Henry, friends and colleagues, and that brings more to her than the well-meaning efforts of her family. But more than that, she is taken with Percy's comment about what she brought to Henry's life.

Was that true?

She had never doubted that they had shared the joys of their week together, but had it really been unique? Could that be correct? Had that been her gift to him? For a few moments the impossible burden of her guilt and loss is nudged aside by the thoughts that she had made him especially happy.

And although functioning better than she had been during the previous week, she is an automaton, involuntarily distanced from the context of the world she sees. Today the tears are dry, replaced by blank emptiness. She wanders through the flat, which is dusty and soulless. She roughly bundles a few clothes into her case, peers into the sitting room, and awaits the return of Nan, who rings the bell minutes later with a loaf of bread and a tin of sardines. They make toast for the fish and brew a pot of tea, which they consume in the kitchen before washing up and setting off for the Marches. She had managed the first part of the drive satisfactorily, now she had to do it again, on the much longer leg to Hereford.

....

Arriving at the cottage four hours later Elisabeth feels relieved that she has brought Nan safely home, but the nostalgic joy she usually felt when at a site so warmly etched into her makeup is absent. She opens the low slatted gate and walks down the brick-paved path to the front door carrying the bags. Ahead of her Nan has opened the oak front door, leaving it ajar behind her. The beds either side of the path are still vivid with colour. On one side, bright globes of staked dahlias hold sway above more muted asters. On the other, statuesque gladioli clash with vermillion crocosmia. It is a pretty scene, and a part of her can recognise that, but absent is the joy that normally accompanies it. It is as if she is seeing things through a veil that dulls the colours and mutes her voice.

She clambers up the old cottage staircase to her room. She knows it so well—it is unchanged since she was thirteen—the bookcase with the bound edition of Dickens is where it always was. The copies of *Black Beauty* and *Little Women*, the latter with its cover torn, the quilted bedspread, the long-legged rabbit with the missing ear. But as she stands in the low doorway and surveys the scene, there is no warm glow. Instead, she flops onto the bed, burying her head in the pillow and sobbing.

Nan insists on a routine and Elisabeth is incapable of putting up a fight. The old independent wilfulness has been replaced with a placid apathy. She gets up, has a piece of toast for breakfast, helps Nan with domestic chores, and attempts to read. Nan suggests she try playing the piano, but she waves the idea away without consideration. In the afternoons they go for walks. The late summer countryside is at its best, with the orchards burgeoning with ripe apples and cohorts of youthful pickers laughing and joking on the back of trailers and carts. The beauty is not lost on her. She can recognise the tones and textures as being lovely and would say as much if asked, but just doesn't feel anything when describing them.

She feels nothing about anything—save the terrible hollow emptiness that haunts her every night and most of the days. She knows that she will never laugh again. There will never be a return of fun or levity.

So much of the week with Henry had seemed like a dream to her. It was a fairy tale—she had felt that on many occasions and even said it to Henry, who in his typically down-to-earth way had insisted she kiss him to prove that he wouldn't turn into a frog. She had never been the dreamy one; that had been Claire. She was the one always imagining lovers and handsome film stars whisking her off to fantasy castles. She hadn't willed the meeting with Henry, nor even dreamt it. It had really happened in all its blissful wonder. And then been so cruelly taken away. *What kind of fairy-tale ending was that? What have I done to deserve this?* It was hard not to fall back on that basic tenet of punishment and retribution, and that so quickly spiralled into guilt. Could she have prevented him from getting on that plane? What was it he had said in the car at Northolt? "I won't go if you insist on me staying."

Why hadn't she insisted?

She had never insisted on anything—that was her pathetic weakness, and now she would pay for it for the rest of her life.

In the evening, they listen to the wireless and sometimes play the gramophone. Nan talks and continues to ask questions to get Elisabeth to share her story, which she thinks will help her process her jumble of thoughts and feelings, but Elisabeth seems reluctant.

Nan goes to the cupboard under the stairs and after a few minutes of rummaging emerges with an unused school exercise book which she hands to Elisabeth, who sits with her face blank and pained, her shoulders gaunt, her mane unkempt, her clothes unfilled and shapeless on her stringy frame.

"You must write," she says. "Write it all down. I know you don't find it easy talking to your old grannie. You might find it easier to put it on paper. I am sure it will help."

The following morning Nan sits her down at the dining room table with the notebook and a fountain pen and leaves her to get the bus into town to do some shopping.

Elisabeth sits looking at the blank lined page, its white emptiness swimming before her, vast and unwelcoming. That is what she is right now—a blank page, pale and empty—lined by misery. She had always preferred reading to writing in school. Her essays got good marks because she could spell and punctuate but the content wasn't inspired. She didn't have the imagination to write creatively, that was for Claire. But now she doesn't have to write creatively, just write what happened.

Where should she start? The evening when he barged into her life apologising for being him but hoping for a bed . . . or the falling asleep? But before that, leaving the cello in the road. Ludwig! And she starts reassembling the evening in her mind and can't help smiling. She picks up the pen and writes at the top of the page: "Friday, July 30, 1948."

Now homework is added to her routine. Every day she writes something in the book. Sometimes it is too painful and she is subsumed by loss and apathy, but other days it feels nice. The problem is that she keeps remembering things and so goes back over the previous pages and adds details in pencil or different coloured pen.

In the daytime Nan is surprisingly busy. Elisabeth can't help but contrast the vitality of her late seventies with her mother's apathy. Nan's days are filled with cooking, housework, and washing, with every spare minute spent bottling, pickling, jam making, and what she describes as "putting the garden to bed." Then there is the

Women's Institute and visiting "the old folk," some of whom are younger than Nan. Elisabeth remembered it from her schooldays, but then she was working as well.

In the evening, they sit and read while listening to the wireless. Nan sits in her favourite wooden armchair knitting, making a jumper for the baby of a friend in the village. Elisabeth sits to her side in a little armchair draped with a crocheted blanket.

Nan sees Elisabeth looking at her hands, effortlessly moving with instinctive industry.

"I still don't know how you do that," Elisabeth says. "Tie a piece of string into something you can wear."

"I thought I taught you. Or was it your mother?"

"I remember you trying to teach me, but I don't think I ever got the hang of it."

"Well, do you want to learn now?"

No, I don't think I could concentrate just now."

"But that's the point. You don't really have to concentrate once you can do it; it is a distraction and quite relaxing, you know. And at the end you have something useful."

She doesn't answer immediately. The room is silent save for the tick of the mantel clock and the clack of the knitting needles.

Suddenly Elisabeth says, "How did you cope when Bert died. I mean how did . . . what did you do?" And at the end she gives a sort of controlled sob.

Nan puts her knitting down on the floor and slides the chair a little nearer so she can reach across to grasp Elisabeth's hand.

"I cried a lot—I remember that."

"Did you? I don't think I have ever seen you cry."

"Well, that's perhaps just as well. I don't like crying when others can see me. I mostly did it alone."

"But I am doing it all the time. I hate it. I am so feeble. I thought I was strong, but I am not; I am pathetic," Elisabeth says, her face screwing up with misery like a little child denied an ice cream.

And Nan is taken back to exactly that; the distraught look on her five-year-old strong-willed granddaughter when things didn't go her way.

"Come here, love. Come here, you poor dear," says Nan.

Elisabeth moves to the floor and rests her head on her granny's lap, accepting the hand on her head gently stroking the mass of hair.

"When you are where you are, you can't see the light, but that doesn't mean it isn't there. It is, and gradually it comes back. It is healing. Just the same, really. When I was nursing in your grandfather's war you couldn't believe the injuries we saw. Shattered bones and limbs and faces. And gradually, very slowly, they got better. That's what it taught me—the body's ability to heal itself. It wasn't the doctors—it came from inside."

"But that was different. They were physical injuries. I have nothing to show for my hurt."

"No dear. They are not different; both can heal. They are all part of the same; we are just us, one part the body, the other the mind."

....

They have been in Hereford for two weeks. It is early September, and rain and squally gales disrupt the end of the fruit harvest. They sit in the tiny kitchen slicing runner beans listening to the "Third Programme." It is a recording of Artur Rubenstein playing Chopin. They both sit listening to the master. Elisabeth is captivated and transported to a place of wonder.

"Oh, to be able to play like that," she says, but then immediately thinks of what Henry would think and tries to cover up the tear that sneaks down her cheek.

"My favourite," Nan says with a distant look in her eye. "I think we have some Chopin."

Elisabeth dabs her eye with the hankie she now keeps tucked into her sleeve.

"Do you?"

"Let's look," Nan says.

They get up and go through to the little dining room, where an upright piano stands against the lime-washed plaster. Elisabeth is taken back to her childhood. This was where she would sit, often with Nan by her side, practising her scales and learning pieces for her exams, sometimes happily and willingly and at other times fighting and furious. She opens the lid and plays a simple left-handed scale. It is a little out of tune.

The music is kept in a low walnut stand, a tattered collection of yellowing papers. Nan pulls out a bundle and starts leafing through.

"Oh, look what I've found!" she says, smiling while handing over Bartok's "For Children." "You used to love this. Do you remember Mrs. Varga?"

"Of course I remember Mrs. Varga. She made school just about bearable," Elisabeth says, taking the book and thumbing through the pieces. She sits down on the piano stool, adjusts the music on the holder, and starts to play. Nan continues to rummage through the music cupboard.

"Here we are, Chopin's 'Fantasia in D Major for Four Hands,' well I never. I don't think I have ever played it, but we could try."

They can't both fit on the piano stool, but Nan finds another low chair which, with an added cushion is the same height, and they start to play together. After taking turns in some introductory arpeggios the melody emerges which is elaborated and becomes more taxing. They alternate in their apologies, and one lower C note is way out of tune, which causes them to smile whenever it is required. Then it becomes much more difficult, and Nan stops.

"More practice," Nan says.

"Much more," Elisabeth agrees. "But that was fun."

Nan smiles, more inwardly than outwardly, but says nothing.

Over the next week Elisabeth spends more and more time at the keyboard. Nan finds some more Chopin and a book of Mazurkas.

She has a friend from church who she is sure will have some more, and sources a book of nocturnes.

Elisabeth finds that when she is playing, she is distracted and focussed. The pieces are challenging to get through, and she gets cross with herself because they sound a thousand miles from Rubenstein's miraculous aplomb, but they suit her mood because they can allow her to be introspective and melancholic within the focus and demands of the notation. She finds that they can say things that she can't put into words, and the sudden thumps of grief that hit her at any time don't appear when she is playing.

Why didn't I realise that playing would be helpful? she asks herself. *Playing saved me when I was at school and when daddy died, music was hugely helpful. Why not now?*

"Did I tell you that Henry wants to build an opera house at Knowle?" Elisabeth says to Nan. They are again sitting in the kitchen listening to *The Marriage of Figaro* on the wireless.

"I don't think so," Nan replies.

"There is a huge tythe barn, which is where he wants to hold concerts, and he has made a model of an auditorium to be built on the grounds. He is dotty about opera, says it is the highest form of art."

Nan says nothing about the use of the present tense. She notices that Elisabeth still tends to do it—refer to him in the present—but doesn't correct her. "I have never been to a proper opera," Nan says. "Well not in a grand opera house. Gilbert and Sullivan at the Corn Hall." She smiles. "But that doesn't quite match up, does it?"

"Well, perhaps we should go sometime?" says Elisabeth.

Has she dared to think about making a plan? Most of the things that she knows she should think about, like her job and the flat, she has just put them out of her mind. Not consciously, rather her mind just isn't capable of properly thinking about complicated things.

....

In the first week of October a letter arrives for her. It has been forwarded from the flat in Victoria to Reigate and then onward. She recognises the envelope as being from Smallwood's. She is startled again to see it is addressed to Lady Elizabeth Benville.

She opens it standing in the sitting room by the front door. Once again it is typed but with the salutation handwritten. It is dated ten days before.

My Dearest Elisabeth,

I sincerely hope that you have been well supported over the last few weeks. It cannot have been easy, as all at Knowle will testify. Grief is a terrible thing, from which there can seem to be no escape. But somewhere there is a path through.

In spite of the continued sadness you must be experiencing, there are some administrative aspects which must be dealt with alongside the details of the memorial service which we are planning, and for which we must obviously have your input. There is some urgency about this, and it would have been nice to talk on the telephone, but we do not have a number for you.

Henry's memorial service will be held at St. George's church in Dorchester on November 18. In a more normal situation, it would be of paramount importance to take into account the widow's views when organising such an event. In fact, it should rightly have been largely within the purview of the next of kin, however I am sure you will forgive us for not involving you in these early arrangements. However, it is now a prime concern of the executors that you be part of the ongoing planning. My suggestion is that you telephone me so we can arrange to meet at your earliest convenience.

The second, and arguably more important point, is a legal one and one that involves some jargon. The Knowle estate is "held in fee" and not entailed. What this means is that the estate does not pass with the baronetcy, as is often the case with lords and their heirs but will pass to his next of kin. As Henry's widow, even in the absence of a recent will, you are the heir to the estate. There are various trusts and other arrangements in place, but for all practical purposes, Knowle House and most of the estate is now yours.

I have discussed this with the other executors and have various proposals to put to you to enable support and advices to be provided to you for the foreseeable future to assist you in your role as owner of Knowle. We are confident that your abilities and mindset are ideally suited to discharging the not inconsiderable responsibilities involved in this role.

I would like to talk as soon as possible with a view to setting up a meeting before the end of the month. Please contact me on the above number at your earliest convenience.

For completeness, I would be grateful if you could bring a copy of your marriage certificate at this time.

With kindest regards,

Percy Smallwood

Elisabeth opens the front door and walks down the path to the side of the cottage with its views over the rolling hills of Golden Valley. The sky is ocean blue, with stuffy flat-bottomed cumulus queuing up to sail by in the brisk westerly breeze.

Tears once again roll down her face.

But they have it all wrong; they have made a terrible mistake. She sobs as she lets the letter drop down to her side as she looks unseeing across the timeless landscape.

I must phone Percy tomorrow and tell him that he's made an awful error.

And then she realises.

They don't know.

Nobody knows, except me and a wonderful, wonderful man who will forever keep the secret.

And maybe, just possibly . . .

CHAPTER 36

Cap d'Ail, Var, France
November 1992

I t is another clear morning—and warm—hot even.

The days are often like this in late fall. The perturbations of the equinox past, the land and sea still warm, the air clear. The stifling baked heat of the summer has subsided and although not fresh like an English autumn, the land breathes again. It is good for the soul and offsets the gloom of shortening days. The hibiscus is still in flower, every new day presenting a pageant of crimson trumpets which, when spent a day later, roll themselves into cigars and drop onto the stone to be explored by legions of tiny ants. I am grateful in the way a dog owner might be, pleasure given and received unconditionally, endless beauty demanding nothing in return.

In the early evening, when the sun sinks behind the building, the nicotiana breathes its sweet perfume into the still air, attracting a squadron of hovering moths in search of their nightly sugar fix. It is quieter now. The traffic has diminished, and the discotheque booms are confined to weekends.

I am fortunate to be here; I know that. I will always be here now.

My days have changed, though. I have always been a creature of routine, but surprisingly that routine has altered somewhat. Every morning I write for two hours, not in the cool gloom of my study, but in the crystal bright of the terrace. Therese has transplanted me from the inward-looking dusty grey to the brazen Mediterranean glare. I sit under an umbrella emblazoned with "Estrella," that Therese has "borrowed" from Toni, the restaurateur. I have a wooden folding table and a metal chair padded with a chintz cushion. The coffee cup sits in its saucer, congealed grounds visible in the bottom; the mandatory ashtray—now an abalone shell since the demise of the Negresco—is full of crumpled stubs. When I look up, the ocean dances.

I am just about finished. I have found it easy to transport myself back into Elisabeth's life; I can see her playing the piano in Nan's front room or quietly reading, an inescapable look of sorrow across her soft features.

Now I can see her standing looking out over the early evening tranquillity of the golden valley. In her hand she holds the letter from Percy, but it is by her side. She looks blankly at the scene before her but registers neither the charm nor the beauty. The air is dense, barely a breeze stirs the autumnal hues of the distant trees. In the distance a motor churns, probably a tractor with a trailer of fodder or manure. A cloud of midges circle an invisible planet.

She is cloven by an insoluble dilemma. The biggest choice she will make in her life.

She faces two options: revert to the person she had been for twenty-six years, return to London, find another job and perhaps a husband, and settle down somewhere into suburban anonymity while always remembering the blinding joy of that week with that golden man, with his vibrant love of life and crazy aspirations.

Or become someone she isn't. Become Mrs Benville.

Create his memorial, pursue his ideals, make his dreams a reality, honour him, and maybe prove something to herself—that she was worthy of him. That she was the one.

And this was the lie. Forever after she would be living a lie.

A thought returns that has often visited her in the worst moments of her gloom; how ridiculous that were it not for the faulty coil in Evey, she would indeed be Mrs. Henry Benville. That tiny quirk of fate has denied her what would have been hers by right. Why should saying words in front of a pompous little man in Croydon mean anything different from the words she exchanged with Henry in the Grenadier? The commitment to honour and obey was the same, and the loving and cherishing was unquestionable, so why did that not count? And she looks at the ring still on her finger and knows that as far as she is concerned, she is married. She feels married. She will stay married. She will never marry anyone else.

The only way she could justify her action is to lie only once and do it on a piece of paper. She had done that for her country and had been proud of it. Then it had been allowed. She had created beautiful falsehoods that had kept good men and women alive and perhaps, just perhaps, had helped her country win a war. Not only had she been paid to deceive and to tell untruths, but she had then been sworn to tell nobody of it. She had even signed a document committing her to forever lying about what she'd actually done.

She had done it once; she would do it again.

The man she loved had been, for a time, Pieter Mueller, doing crucial work for the benefit of king and country and nobody knew he really was. And that was allowed, lauded even. She could be Lady Elisabeth Knowle and nobody would know that she wasn't. And she could also do something worthwhile.

But there is something else that she feels but has not admitted to herself, let alone anyone else. She has not had a period for two months, not in fact since before she went to France. And she has noticed some other things which she has pushed away from her cognisance: her body just feels different, a changed awareness, sleep, and appetite. If she was to have a baby, the disparity between the two futures was stark indeed.

She would create this falsehood on this one occasion. She would never speak of Henry as her husband, nor would she speak of being married or her marriage, she would never mislead others by suggesting she had rights to Henry's heritage, she would see herself as a chatelaine of Knowle, and always try to be guided by him even in his absence. As at Briggens she would do the job that was required of her, and do it as well as she could, because that was the way she could keep alive the memory of the man she loved.

For the second time in her life, she would tell nobody. Not a soul, ever.

....

The next day the practicalities confound her; could it be done?

Might it be that Mackay's would have the right sort of paper? She assumes that Graham is still running the business, but that means a trip to the East End. There is no way of avoiding a journey to London and Reigate.

But the more difficult challenge is how to get a certificate to copy?

She finds the number of the Hereford Register Office and talks to a helpful man who informs her that duplicate marriage certificates are available from St. Catherine's House in Chancery Lane. But whose certificate? If she could get a duplicate certificate from a marriage at the Croydon Register Office, most of the details would be the same: the venue, the date, the registrar. That would make it much easier.

She thinks back to the horrid encounter in Croydon and racks her brain to remember the names of the other couples on the list. Peters. She is sure there was a Peters, but what was the Christian name? Was it Deborah, or perhaps Audrey? She can't remember. A telephone call to the Croydon office would solve the problem but what reason could she have for seeking the information?

Unless she is honest.

Could I say that I was at the office on August 6 and ended up talking to the family of this nice woman who was getting married that day and wanted to get in touch? Not perfect but it might work.

She plans to drive to London on the Thursday, explaining to Nan that she needs to go and see Mummy and check if there is any post for her. It is a long trip, and she is tense and worried. In fact, if she stops to think about it, she is terrified, but also aware that the acute hurt of her grief has been subsumed by her new focus.

She presumes that she will need some sort of identification to secure a copy of the marriage certificate. She has a second ration book which she thinks she can alter to read Audrey Peters, but she needs her forgery kit, so the work will have to wait until she has visited Mummy.

Two days later, after a gloomy meal of a pork chop and two veg with Mummy, she is sitting alone in her old bedroom in the house in Reigate. In front of her on the dressing table is the donkey pencil case and various papers, illuminated by the glow of the bedside light placed by her side. An array of pencils and implements are spread over the surface. She wears a look of intense concentration as she peers through a magnifying lens hanging around her neck. Using diluted bleach and her finest brush she applies a tiny amount of the mixture to one of the inked letters. The print dissolves before her eyes but the paper is very absorbent and a yellow stain spreads beyond the letter. She must use even less on the brush and work very precisely, keeping just to the individual letter, but it is successful and within forty minutes she has removed her name from the document. The paper has slightly ruffled and lies uneven where she has worked. She takes a piece of blotting paper, which she moistens and places this over the page, covering it with writing paper. Then she sandwiches it in the largest book she can find, *Ransome's Children's Treasury* and places several other books on top. In the morning she will be able to write in the new name.

By nine-thirty the next day she is standing at a sliding window above a counter in St. Catherine's house requesting a copy of "her" marriage certificate. She proffers the ration book as proof of identity.

"Don't need that." The chirpy clerk responds, smiling at the pretty face on the other side of the glass. "Just name, date, and place of marriage."

Fifteen minutes later and two shillings worse off, she leaves the building holding a copy of Audrey Peters's marriage certificate.

She can't help but smile. *How simple was that!*

She curses that she went to the trouble of forging the ration book. How stupid. She walks up Chancery Lane to Theobalds Road and finds a café, where she orders a cup of tea. She unfolds the certificate and scrutinises it. She doesn't know much about paper, to her it seems like an ordinary machine-made laid typically used for official forms and documents. What worries her is the water mark and the guilloches in green; she realises she will never be able to make an acceptable copy of the document. She feels guilty and helpless, as if the other occupants of the café are suddenly aware of her complicity. She flushes with terror and embarrassment and hurriedly folds away the paper.

It will never work. In a trice her sadness returns and rushes over her in a great wave. She heaves with sobs that she is powerless to control. The loss and pain that she had put to one side since getting the letter from Percy were now swept forward in a torrent of pathos and grief.

The waitress comes over to ask if she is all right, and in her embarrassment, she manages to regain a semblance of composure, dabbing her eyes with her hankie. There is really no point in visiting Graham Mackay, but she feels bad about missing the appointment.

Although her mother had tried to persuade her to stay, Elisabeth was adamant, at least in her own mind, that she was better off with Nan and made various excuses. The problem was that mother treated her as if she had a headache or a grazed knee. She kept calling her "dear" and suggesting it would be better in the morning or if she had a cup of tea. She wanted to fix the problem and most of what she said just made Elisabeth cross. Strange, this as Mummy was the one whose life had been transected by the loss of her man.

Nanny was different, as if she understood that she could offer consolation but not resolution. They would sit in their respective chairs in the tiny sitting room of Nan's cottage, and Nan would see her looking distant and wistful and reach across, taking her hand in hers, interlocking the fingers, knowing the comfort of physical nearness.

"The darkness does lighten, Elisabeth," she would say, "and we get better at not looking into it."

But now she is struggling through the twilight on the A40, facing another kind of blackness, trying to see the road signs in the feeble glow of the headlights.

The drive is ghastly. She can't remember feeling as alone and helpless as she does now. She can barely breathe for fear of dissolving into sobs.

Nan has made leek and potato soup, but she can hardly finish it before tiredness overwhelms her and she makes excuses to climb the stairs to the consolation of her solitary room. Again, she is alone with her emptiness, her doubts, and her loneliness. She is barely able to drag off her dress before collapsing into sleep.

When she wakes, too early yet for the sun, there is a tiny moment of calm, a split second when she is just awake in Nan's house, with no tasks, husband, or deceit to trouble her, but then all her terrors and sadness flood back. She lies staring blankly at the ceiling, an occupation that she has become fearsomely accustomed to.

As the daylight strengthens, she reaches for her handbag and retrieves the certificate, staring at it without a clue as to what to do next. She thinks for a moment what it would be like to have the real one, the one with Elisabeth Watson and Henry Benville written on it. She would have danced down the steps of the register office in the yellow dress, with official proof of a legal union, not this idiotic idea she has of falsehood and lies.

It's been ages since she went to a wedding, but she can recall that there is always that time when the choir sings or the organist plays a piece, and the couple sign the register. Even in a register office—after any marriage—you go away with a certificate.

Where do they come from?

Churches must have a supply of certificates.

If she could get hold of a blank certificate, the rest she could do; it would be easy to fill in the details and make it look official. For someone with her skills it would be simplicity itself.

She gets up with renewed purpose and pushes her melancholy aside. At breakfast she tells Nan that she might go to church on Sunday, a comment which is greeted by a momentary raise of eyebrows, followed by a chat about the local parishes.

Later in the morning she sets off in Evey with a list of the nearby villages to visit.

First on the list is St. Andrew's in Presteigne. It is a large well-tended church in the middle of the town. She lifts the iron latch and pushes against the heavy door, which groans in complaint. On the table inside, next to a stack of prayer books and hymnals, she finds a pile of *Parish* magazines. She picks up a copy and thumbs through it. On the second page she finds a list of banns of marriage with the dates of forthcoming weddings. What is more, it also includes the banns for Kinsham and Knill. She allows herself a slender smile.

She drives on towards Kington, stopping in Titley on the way.

She finds sleepy parish churches, all empty save for a plumber fixing a leaking radiator in Kington. They are cool, sacred, and reverential in their damp English way, but she is too focussed to be moved and feels no tug of faith. Somehow, whatever she feels about Henry and her loss, it has bypassed God.

By the end of the afternoon, she has a list of dates of weddings in the assorted villages that she puts into her diary. She isn't sure what to expect or how to achieve her end but has a date the following afternoon in Kington, where the plumber assured her that he would have cured the leak well before the three o'clock wedding.

She doesn't know what to wear, not wishing to draw attention to herself either because she is too smart or too scruffy but settles on a skirt and cardigan. She arrives early and finds a pew in the side aisle tucked against the marble tomb of Thomas Vaughan and his serene looking wife. Nobody pays her any attention, which is just as well, as she struggles to keep her composure amongst the excitement of the arriving throng. It is all too tender. Too pertinent.

But with the arrival of the groom and then the bride, who looks at least forty and appears to be marrying a pensioner, she gets engrossed in the service itself, and even sings the hymns. Then it is done; they are husband and wife and move to sign the register. She can't get a clear view of what happens in the vestry, which is off the nave away from her.

The choir sings and then there is a pause while the organist improvises. She recognises a hymn tune and perhaps a bit of Bach, and then they all reappear, the single bridesmaid proudly clutching her posey, as they make their way out back down the aisle and out into the churchyard to the warm smiles of the congregation.

Elisabeth holds her ground until the last guest has left, but instead of leaving the church, she walks towards the vestry, arriving at the same time as a sidesman who bustles in, tidying the room. On the table is a large book which contains the certificates, the top one of which has been signed by the couple. He tears this off and folds it into an envelope. He looks up with a pleasant but quizzical look on his face.

"Hello," he says.

"Hello," she replies, followed by a pause when she realises he expects her to say something. "I am going to be married next month . . . just keen to see how it all works . . . with the certificate and all that." She smiles, trying to convey naive ignorance, which she manages well. "So that's what the bride and groom sign, is it?"

"That's it. Bride, groom, and the witnesses sign here. The vicar enters all the details in here before the ceremony. Not supposed to, mind, but everyone does it. My job is to put the books back in the safe and make sure the groom gets the certificate." He smiles as he collects up the paperwork and the pen, which he returns to a wooden box. Various members of the choir bustle around.

"Thank you," she says. "Very interesting." She turns and slowly walks back through the pew to the door.

She sits in Evey, contemplating what she has learnt.

Her supposition is right. If only she could get one of the blank pages of the book of certificates, she could do the rest. But there would have been no chance that she could have done that in Kington; it was too busy, what with the verger in attendance. The book and papers would never be away from prying eyes.

She will have to wait at least a week and see if other venues provide better opportunities.

In fact, she has to wait three weeks. Three terrible weeks when she barely sleeps and is flayed by uncertainty and guilt. On several occasions she vows she will abandon the scheme. Nan picks up on the distraction and tension, and tries to help in her gentle supportive way, simply comfort and cooking.

And throughout, Elisabeth never tells Nan what she is up to. In fact, she never tells anyone, but then she is good at keeping secrets.

Then on a grey day in Titley, when the bride has to dash from the beribboned Vauxhall to the porch to avoid a soaking and the little church is full of weathered villagers wearing their Sunday best and the singing is off key and a baby cries, it works. She is sitting in the side aisle; the vestry is in front of her completely open. The couple move just in front of her to sign the register, where they stand with their witnesses and complete the paperwork. Then after the fussy attentions of the bride's mother adjusting the veil and train, the self-conscious couple make their way back to the nave and exit the church, followed by the congregation, the vicar, and the verger. The organist embellishes the final hymn theme, and Elisabeth is just yards from her prize.

She strides with intent up to the table where the signed certificate sits. She glances around her, opens the book and turns to the back page. She tears out the final certificate, even in this petrifying moment doing it with the utmost care. She turns the book back to the top page, folds her trophy neatly and slips it into her handbag.

It is done.

CHAPTER 37

....

Cap d'Ail, Var, France
November 1992

A lthough I sit in the warm air of Provence, my mind is elsewhere. I am a bystander watching Elisabeth sitting at the table in the basement of Briggens, her flowing mane tied with a crimson ribbon. She wears her magnifying necklace and works intently. There is nothing that distracts her focus or concentration. In front of her is the donkey pencil case with its contents spilling onto the desk. In the background are the sounds of the world around her: chat, barked orders from the Poles doing calisthenics on the lawn, the grind of the printing press, a motorcycle, the clatter of a typewriter, but she hears none of it. She has been there for an hour and will be there for another.

I transpose my vision to the little bedroom in Nan's cottage.

She has decided to fill in the marriage certificate by hand, as she had seen done in Presteigne. She frequently had to handwrite entries into documents at Briggens and had been instructed by the inestimable Arthur Gatward. He had been seconded from the Metropolitan Police on account of his expertise in all aspects of handwriting. He was a taciturn soul, a loner, distant and unknowable, but had taken to Elisabeth, perhaps for dubious reasons. I am not sure in what he instructed her or how he approached the tasks required, but the results were impressive. Gatward knew how handwriting became characteristic of the person, or even the country, and, especially in someone as young as Elisabeth, enabled her to develop what could be called a generic handwriting style that she could use when required. French script is very rounded and upright, with prominent looping of the descenders and tall letters. German writing is more slanted, with a more italic look and greater embellishment. These are often the giveaways that enable us to identify the hand of foreign national, or of a friend or relative. At Briggens, what was crucial was that any handwritten documents had to look anonymous, to blend in and not draw attention.

She looks at the certificate she got from St. Catherine's House and starts to practise the entries she must make on sheets of writing paper. It gets easier and more fluid as she rehearses. She feels positive, the anguish of the decision-making is over—now she must do. And she finds she is drawn back to the intensity of her time at Briggens and the responsibility of completing a crucial task. It makes her feel good. She senses inklings of the pride of that past world, a pride of which she cannot speak.

Then she is ready, and smoothly fills in the form, concentrating on every word to maintain the style and form, constantly referring to the template she has made. She smiles at the thought that she is taking much more trouble than would a common-or-garden Herefordshire vicar. She is pleased with the result; the skills she learnt haven't vanished. She can still do it.

On the copy she has, all the entries are in the hand of the copyist, even the signatures, which makes it very simple, as she doesn't have to forge them, just replicate the names from the form. But when it comes to her own name she pauses; logically she should just use the same style, but a part of her wants to sign properly. After all, it is her marriage certificate. Every married woman signs their own marriage certificate, why can't she?

She compromises. It is not her usual signature but a modified version. A graphologist would note the change, but she is sure that Percy Smallwood won't—if he even bothers to look at the document.

She is sure that all he would do was acknowledge its presence and scan the names.

How strange, that as she completes the certificate, so she comes to believe in it. It has become real to her. Like an imposter who becomes the person they claim to be, so she feels the forgery validates the lie.

But now she has the difficult part, she has to make two stamps saying, COUNTY BOROUGH OF CROYDON and the registrar WILLIAM GEORGE DAVIS. She has bought some long rubber erasers, which she has to carve to create a stamp in reverse that she can use to complete the form. The first task is to use a surgical scalpel to cut the rubber into strips exactly the height of the word. Then she must write in reverse the wording, which she does using a fine pencil using one strip for each word. Next she must carve out the gaps between the letters. This is exacting work, made more difficult because of the seraph style of the font. She needs her magnifying glasses, which hang around her neck. She starts with the word WILLIAM, which is easier because it is all straight lines. When she has finished the letters, she tests it using an ink pad. She makes a series of impressions after one single application to the ink. and finds that the third one is much better than the first, but she also needs to make some adjustments, the letters being too chunky. She works for another hour before taking a break.

She finishes the task the following afternoon, having worked all day. She inks the stamps, makes two impressions on rough paper and then, using a ruler to ensure they are perfectly aligned, makes the final imprint onto the certificate. She sits and looks at the result. She is satisfied but not pleased. Roberts would have made her do it again, but she is comforted by the thought that it won't be a suspicious Nazi border guard scrutinising the result.

The last thing the document requires is a one penny stamp, which she has purchased, and which goes in a square at the bottom right of the page.

She holds the completed form up to the light. There is the

watermark CERTIFIED COPY G.R.O. She moves it back down to the desk. It is complete.

She has become Mrs. Henry Benville.

CHAPTER 38

....

Cap d'Ail, Var, France
December 1992

T hat was then. Tonight, my world is different.

I thought the last several months had taken me to a place that would finish with the completion of my writing, but now the events coalesce into something different.

Therese appeared in the afternoon. It was a grey day, and I was inside with the Briggens papers and Elisabeth's diaries spread across the table before finally putting them to bed.

She came in and stood beside me, looking at the various documents, picking things up without properly reading them. She came to the envelope that contained Elisabeth's son's picture and pulled out the photo. Immediately her demeanour changed.

"Qui est-ce? Je n'ai jamais vu ça auparavant."

"Robert, Elisabeth's son."

"Mais c'est toi, non ? C'est exactement toi." It is you, exactly you.

I looked at the picture, studying the features in a little more detail. The vague familiarity that I had noted remained just that, a sort of amnesic recollection of something faintly recognisable.

Therese got up and went into the study. She emerged two minutes later carrying *Undine*'s log for 1948.

"C'est ici quelque part, j'en suis sûr. Eh Viola !"

She found it, a picture of me taken as we sailed through Biscay, standing at the wheel looking focussed but happy, with my eyes on the horizon. I would have been twenty-eight.

She placed the pictures next to each other and turned to look at me.

"C'est toi. Sans aucun doute."

Why is it women can see these things? I looked at the two pictures together and could see the similarities: the nose was my father's, and one which I had been disappointed to inherit, also the eyes and the brow, they were the same and the hairline was identical.

"Quand est-il ne?"

"I don't know, but it would have to be nine months after Henry's death." Could she have been pregnant when she fled back home from Marseilles?

We stood looking at each other. She found my hand and then put her arms around me.

"Oh Pom."

Later, much later, I lay thinking it all through. Could it be that Robert was my son? What did it change for me? But more importantly what would it change for him? I would need time to think it through.

What was it Maurice Shilton had on his door—"The Confabulatorium of Ipseity"? In a way Elisabeth had never left Briggens. She created new identities there, and then a new one for herself and lived that life. But now there was Robert to think about. What about his ipseity, was he the person the world thought he was? Should he know the answer to a question he didn't even know was a question?

I gave up on the idea of sleep and, picking up my cigarettes, stumbled out onto the terrace. There was no moon and the glitter of the lights of the cape failed to illuminate my steps, but I knew my way and sat at the small table looking out at a black invisible sea. This was as close as the Cape ever got to silence. The flare of my lighter illuminated the scene for a moment before it reverted to secrecy.

Did I ever know Elisabeth? I thought I did and spent my life living with the vision of my creation. But was it her?

I found I was thinking about something Philip said.

"Well, of course Henry and Elisabeth didn't really know each other at all. One week of lust and love. That's not knowing a person. That is not sharing."

I have never craved children. In fact, I have never really thought about parenthood. My life was too peripatetic to feel envious of stable couples with kids and close families. But what would have happened if I had received a letter from Elisabeth saying that I was the father of her unborn child? The dilemma became more tortuous, not simpler. The love that I craved and thought I had wanted I now found terrifying. I could no more imagine giving up *Undine* and running a paper business in Essex as flying to the moon. Perhaps I was in love with a dream, a poorly formulated imagining of an unattainable perfection. But was that not what Elisabeth also did? She lived her dream, but she also never had to destroy the vision of perfection of passionate love with the disappointments of reality.

....

I look at the bundle of papers on my desk. Should I have written it down?

I am not sure, but I have an idea about what I should do with it.

Something has become clearer—if Elisabeth left me the papers with the desire that I was to solve a riddle, what would she have expected me to do next? She had absolved her deceit but transferred it to me.

Was it to be entrusted to me alone? Or did she want it to be shared? With whom? What about Robert? Should he also live a lie? But perhaps it wasn't a lie. Maybe he was Henry's son in any event.

Later I sit at my typewriter for the last time and insert a clean piece of paper.

Dear Mr. Smallwood,

May I firstly say how grateful I am for the friendly and efficient service your firm provided in discharging your duties concerning the bequest by the late Elisabeth Benville.

Since I have been domiciled in France, my legal affairs have been managed by a local practice run by a sailing friend, Pierre Dumant, whose contact details I include. However, I would like to commission your firm to undertake one request set out in my will, a copy of which I enclose.

You will see that upon my death I wish the enclosed computer disc to be forwarded to Robert Benville. The disc contains some information that I feel might interest him, but which I would prefer not to be disclosed until after my demise.

I have instructed Dumant et cie to contact you after my death, when the time comes to enact the letter of the will.

I also enclose the documents that you have previously had seen; namely the diaries and documents left to me by Elisabeth. It would be more appropriate for these to be contained within the Knowle archive.

I ask this of your company in the sound belief that you will discharge my requests with the utmost discretion and professionalism.

Yours sincerely,

Peter Oliphant Mackay

NICE MATIN

March 10, 2009

Obituary

Peter "Pom" Mackay, sailor and author, died on March 4 in Sunnybank Nursing Home in Cannes. He was 89.

Peter Oliphant Mackay was best known for his 1957 book *Convoy North*, based on his experience on the Arctic Convoy PQ13 when his ship, the SS *Induna*, was sunk by a German torpedo and he and several other crewmen spent five days in an open boat. The book was made into a successful film of the same name.

After the war he bought a yacht and spent many years sailing in the Mediterranean before settling in the South of France.

He is survived by Therese, his wife, who he married at the age of 75.

AUTHOR'S NOTE

On a fine late summer day in 2016, I drove to Hunsden, in East Hertfordshire to find Briggens House. Since the war it had been a school and a hotel, but more recently had been empty.

The gate lodge was easy to find, a dilapidated folly behind a padlocked wrought iron gate, but the entrance was more elusive. After a detour of two miles, I found myself on a tree-lined drive approaching a large house, grand but run-down and unloved. I parked the car in the golf club car park and walked up to the house. It was empty and I was alone as I clambered over the weed-strewn stonework of the gardens.

I peered through empty windows and made my way to the rear where there was a more recent extension. At the back, the lowermost windows were at semibasement level, with wells intruding into the ground. I jumped down into the largest of these and tried the sash window. It rattled but didn't move, locked by a conventional catch. I searched the ground for a suitable tool and located a thin strip of metal. Inserting this between the frames, I was able to slide the catch across and lift the sash. A minute later I was in an empty basement room with a low ceiling, low sunlight slanting in through the angled window alcoves. I walked out of it into a long corridor running the length of the building with several rooms off either side, the outer lit by natural light, the inner smaller rooms dark and uninviting, with no electricity.

And here I was alone, walking through the very same spaces where Morton Bisset and his brilliant team had done their miraculous work. I stood silently imagining the noisy Poles and the clank of machinery, quiet people craning over desks under enamel lamp shades. I could imagine Elisabeth sitting here, her quiet poise and her intense concentration, her wild hair tamed by a velvet ribbon.

Dennis Collins sitting doing one of his caricatures during a break sitting in the gardens, a motorcycle arriving at the front of the house to pick up a vital package.

I left the basement by a small stone staircase and found myself in a large wood-panelled hall. I took two steps further when an alarm suddenly started hooting. I scampered back down to the basement, clambered back out of the window, which I closed behind me, and walked nonchalantly back to the car. Seventy years later, an intruder had been spotted on the premises . . .

For those interested in the best history of Briggens, a volume was published by the National Archive by Des Turner, and is now available as a paperback, who remarkably obtained interviews with some key people before they died along with various photographs and examples of Briggens forgeries.

Although Elisabeth, Peter, and Henry are characters from my own imagination, many of the names mentioned as populating Briggens are not, (for example Morton Bisset, Ellic Howe, Charles Roberts) and for details of these I am most grateful to Des Turner, the archives of the Imperial War Museum, and in particular, the archive deposited by the brilliant Dennis Collins.

Dennis became the cartoonist responsible for the artwork of the "Perishers" strip published for many years by the *Daily Mail*. His archive contains copies of *Snoop,* the Section IVX magazine, and the amazing Lord's Prayer written in a square measuring 5mm x 6mm

Many other of the characters from Briggens I have inserted into the narrative are real souls whose names deserve to be remembered, including Morton Bisset, Charles Roberts, Arthur Gatward, and the Poles, Antoni Pospieszalski and Jerzy Maciejewski. The latter two are clearly key figures in the history of the SOE and the efforts of section XIV. Jerzy died at the age of ninety-nine in 2004, Pospieszalski at the age of ninety-five in 2008. Both lived full and interesting lives after the war.

Peter's experience on convoy PQ13 is based around the

extraordinary oral testimony of Thomas Byrne in the Imperial War Museum archives. It is he who witnessed the destruction of the *Induna* and spent three days freezing in an open boat watching colleagues dying of cold before being picked up by a Russian vessel and taken to Murmansk.

ACKNOWLEDGMENTS

Writing a novel is a lonely business—mostly it is just you and the blank screen—but I have had great support from fellow aspirant novelists and writer's groups, including the enduring Richmond Writers Circle. The industry is not helpful, with most literary agents I approached not even bothering to reply. Such arrogance in the face of their bleating about understanding how difficult it is for new authors is inexcusable.

My biggest thanks are due to those friends who read my early drafts and were always supportive and helpful: Emma Galloway, Claire Williams, Gareth Tudor-Williams, Jonathan Morrish, Sarah Ingham, Georgina Petty, David Crwys-Williams, Colin Fergusson, Diana Farr Louis, and Steven Lunn.

Thanks are also due to the expert skills of the team at Köehler Books, including the assiduous Becky Hilliker and visionary Lauren Sheldon.

Milton Keynes UK
Ingram Content Group UK Ltd.
UKHW030340071224
452074UK00003B/73